ALSO BY ALI HAZELWOOD

The Love Hypothesis
Love on the Brain
Love, Theoretically
Bride

ANTHOLOGIES
Loathe to Love You

NOVELLAS
Under One Roof
Stuck with You
Below Zero

YOUNG ADULT NOVELS
Check & Mate

NOT IN LOVE

ALI HAZELWOOD

BERKLEY

NEW YORK

BERKLEY
An imprint of Penguin Random House LLC
penguinrandomhouse.com

Copyright © 2024 by Ali Hazelwood

Penguin Random House supports copyright. Copyright fuels creativity, encourages diverse voices, promotes free speech, and creates a vibrant culture. Thank you for buying an authorized edition of this book and for complying with copyright laws by not reproducing, scanning, or distributing any part of it in any form without permission. You are supporting writers and allowing Penguin Random House to continue to publish books for every reader.

BERKLEY and the BERKLEY & B colophon are registered trademarks
of Penguin Random House LLC.

Berkley hardcover ISBN: 9780593641040

The Library of Congress has cataloged the Berkley Romance
trade paperback edition of this book as follows:

Names: Hazelwood, Ali, author.
Title: Not in love / Ali Hazelwood.
Description: First edition. | New York: Berkley Romance, 2024.
Identifiers: LCCN 2023051452 (print) | LCCN 2023051453 (ebook) |
ISBN 9780593550427 (paperback) | ISBN 9780593550434 (ebook)
Subjects: LCGFT: Romance fiction. | Novels.
Classification: LCC PS3608.A98845 N68 2024 (print) |
LCC PS3608.A98845 (ebook) | DDC 813/.6—dc23/eng/20241102
LC record available at https://lccn.loc.gov/2023051452
LC ebook record available at https://lccn.loc.gov/2023051453

Printed in the United States of America
1st Printing

Book design by Daniel Brount

To Jen. Sometimes I wonder what I would do without you, and I get super scared.

PS: White chocolate is good, actually.

PPS: When you read this, give Stella a cookie from Aunt Ali.

Dear Reader,

I just wanted to drop a quick note to let you know that *Not in Love* is, tonally, a little different from the works I've published in the past. Rue and Eli have dealt with—and still deal with—the fallout from issues such as grief, food insecurity, and child neglect. They are eager to make a connection but are not sure how to go about it except through a physical relationship. The result is, I think, less of a rom-com and more of an erotic romance.

Rue and Eli's story has, of course, a happily ever after! But it also contains some serious themes, and I wanted to give you a heads-up so you know what to expect.

Love,
Ali

NOT IN LOVE

1

SIMPLE ENOUGH

RUE

Ladies, this is a genuine, nonrhetorical question: How do the two of you survive in the real world?"

I stared at Nyota's contemptuous expression, reflecting on the unique brand of humiliation that came with having one's best friend's little sister (who'd been repeatedly rebuffed when attempting to enter the backyard tree house; who'd publicly feasted on a booger at Christmas 2009; who'd been caught French-kissing a clementine in the linen closet a few short months later) question one's ability to carry out a productive existence.

Then again, back in the day, Tisha and I had been three whole years older than her, and we'd harbored a clearly misplaced superiority complex. We knew better now that little Nyota was twenty-four, a law school prodigy, and a newly minted bankruptcy lawyer whose billable hours were worth more than my tragically high car insurance premium. To add insult to injury, I followed her on

Instagram, which was how I knew she could bench-press more than her weight, looked incredible in a monokini, and regularly baked onion rosemary focaccia from scratch.

In a powerful flex whose brilliance kept me awake at night, Nyota had never followed me back.

"You know us," I said, choosing honesty over pride. Tisha and I were holed up inside my closet-sized office at Kline, FaceTiming someone who'd probably never even saved our phone numbers. Dignity was the least of our worries. "We are barely hanging on."

"Can you just answer the question?" Tisha bristled. As humbling as this was for me, it had to be much worse for her. Nyota was *her* sister, after all.

"Really? You call me in the middle of the workday to ask what a *loan assignment* is? You couldn't google it?"

"We did," I said, omitting that we'd added *for dummies* to the search. And yet. "We got the gist of it, we think."

"Great, then you're golden. I'm hanging up, see you both at Thanksgiving—"

"However," I interrupted. It was late May. "The reactions of other Kline employees seem to suggest that we might not be fully grasping the implications of this *loan assignment*." My threshold for odd was high, and I'd been able to brush off the HR rep brazenly browsing monster.com at his standing desk, the chemists who'd bumped into me face-first and run away with nary an oops, the vacant stare of my usually dictatorial boss, Matt, when I'd informed him that the report he was waiting on would take at least three more hours. Then, while I was emptying my water bottle into a potted plant that had lived in the break room longer than I'd been in the workforce, a technician had burst into tears and suggested,

You should take Christofern home, Dr. Siebert. It shouldn't die just because of what's about to happen to Kline.

I had *no clue* what was going on. All I knew was that I loved my current job at Kline, the most important project of my life was at a pivotal point, and I was too socially challenged to easily transition to another workplace. Today's event did not bode well. "There's going to be an assembly in fifteen minutes," I explained, "and we'd love to walk in with a better idea of what—"

"Ny, stop bitching and just regurgitate it for us like we're five," Tisha ordered.

"You guys are *doctors,*" Nyota pointed out—*not* as a compliment.

"Okay, listen carefully, Ny, 'cause this will blow your mind and we might have to report it to the UN and have a trial at The Hague: the topic of private equity firms and loan assignments did *not* come up in *any* class during our chemical engineering PhDs. A *shocking* oversight, I know, and I'm sure NATO will want to take military action—"

"Zip it, Tish. You don't get to snark when *you* need something from *me.* Rue, how did you find out about the loan assignment?"

"Florence sent out a company-wide email," I said. "This morning."

"Florence is Kline's CEO?"

"Yes." It seemed reductive, so I added, "And founder." Still not exhaustive, but there was a time and place for fangirling, and this wasn't it.

"Did it say anything about which private equity bought your loan?"

I skimmed the body of the email. "The Harkness Group."

"Hmm. Rings a bell." Nyota typed away in silence, the New

3

York City skyline gleaming behind her. Her office was in a high-rise—thousands of miles and an entire universe from North Austin. Like Tisha and me, she'd been eager to get out of Texas. Unlike us, she'd never moved back. "Ah, yeah. *Those* guys," she said eventually, squinting at her computer screen.

"Do you know them?" Tisha asked. "Are they, like, famous?"

"It's a private equity firm, not a K-pop band. But they *are* well known in tech circles." She bit her lip. Suddenly her expression was the opposite of reassuring, and I felt Tisha tense beside me.

"This is not the first time something like this has happened," I said, refusing to give in to panic. I had graduated from UT Austin a year earlier, but I'd been working for Florence Kline since before finishing my PhD. None of this felt new. "There are management shake-ups and investor issues all the time. It always settles down."

"Not sure about this time, Rue." Nyota's brow creased into a scowl. "Listen, Harkness is a private equity firm."

"Still don't know what that means," Tisha bristled.

"*As I was going to explain*, private equities are . . . groups of people with lots and lots of money and spare time. And instead of frolicking in their hard-earned cash Scrooge McDuck–style, or leaving it in savings accounts like the two of you—"

"Bold of you to assume I have savings," Tisha muttered.

"—they use it to buy other companies."

"And they bought Kline?" I asked.

"Nope. Kline hasn't gone public—you can't buy Kline's stocks. But back when it was founded, it needed money to develop . . . ravioli? Is that what you guys do?"

"Food nanotechnology."

"Sure. Let's pretend that means something. Anyway, when

Florence founded Kline, she got a big loan. But now, whoever gave her the money decided to sell that loan to Harkness."

"Which means that now Kline owes the money to Harkness?"

"Correct. See, Rue, I knew you weren't *totally* useless. My sister, on the other hand, never ceases to . . ." Nyota's voice drifted as she frowned at her computer.

"What?" Tisha asked, alarmed. Nyota wasn't the type to stop mid-insult. "What happened?"

"Nothing. I'm just reading up on Harkness. They're well respected. Focused on midsize tech startups. I think they have a couple of science guys on the inside? They acquire promising companies, provide capital and support to grow them, sell them for a profit. Buying a loan seems a little out of their MO."

Tisha's fingers closed around my thigh, and I covered her hand with my palm. Physical comfort was rarely in my repertoire, but making exceptions for Tisha was no trouble. "So all Florence needs to do is pay back the loan to Harkness, and Harkness will be out of the picture?" I asked. Seemed simple enough. No need to involve monster.com.

"Uh . . . in the rainbow world you live in, maybe. Have fun frolicking with the unicorns, Rue. There's no way Florence has the money."

Tisha's grip tightened. "Ny, what does it mean, in practice? Does it mean that they take control of the company?"

"Maybe. It'll depend on the loan contract."

I shook my head. "Florence would never let them do that."

"Florence might not have a choice." Nyota's voice softened abruptly, and that—out of everything, *that* made the first tinges of fear hook into my stomach. "Depending on the terms of the agreement, Harkness might have the right to install a new CTO and seriously interfere in day-to-day operations."

Asking what a CTO was wasn't going to get me any closer to an Instagram follow, so I just said, "Okay. What's the bottom line?"

"Harkness might end up being a nonissue. Or it might be the reason you need to find new jobs. Right now, it's impossible to tell."

Tisha's "fuck" was a soft muttering. *Florence,* I thought, and my mouth felt dry. *Where is Florence right now? How is Florence right now?* "Thank you, Nyota," I said. "This was very helpful."

"Call me after today's assembly—we'll have a better idea by then." It was nice of her, that *we*. "But it wouldn't hurt to start sprucing up your CV, just in case. Austin is a great place for tech startups. Look around online, ask your nerd friends if they have leads. Do you guys have any friends, aside from each other?"

"I have Bruce."

"Bruce is *a cat*, Tish."

"And your point?"

They started bickering, and I tuned them out, trying to calculate the likelihood of Tisha and me finding another job together. One that would pay well and afford us the scientific freedom we currently had. Florence had even allowed me to—

A horrifying thought stabbed at me. "What about our personal projects? Employees' patents?"

"Mm?" Nyota cocked her head. "Employees' patents? For what?"

"In my case, a bio-nanocomposite that—"

"Uh-huh, hold the TED Talk."

"It's something that makes produce stay fresher. Longer."

"Ah. I see." She nodded in understanding, her eyes suddenly

warmer, and I wondered what she knew. Tisha would never mention my history, but Nyota was observant and could very well have noticed on her own. After all, for years I'd spent every spare moment at their house, just to avoid returning to my own. "This is *your* project? *Your* patent? And you have an agreement that guarantees *you* ownership of this tech?"

"Yes. But if Kline changes hands—"

"As long as the agreement is in writing, you're good."

I remembered an email from Florence. Long words, small fonts, electronic signatures. Relief punched through me. *Thank you, Florence.*

"Guys, try not to sweat this too much, okay? Go to the assembly you're probably already late for. Find out all you can and report back. And for the love of Justice Brown Jackson, update your damn CVs. You haven't been a pet groomer since undergrad, Tish."

"Get off my LinkedIn," Tisha muttered, but she was flipping off an already blank screen. So she leaned back in her chair and settled for another subdued "fuck."

I stared ahead and nodded. "Indeed."

"Neither of us has the emotional constitution for job insecurity."

"Nope."

"I mean, we'll be all right. We're in tech. It's just . . ."

I nodded once more. We were happy at Kline. Together. With Florence.

Florence. "Last night, Florence texted me," I told Tisha. "Asked if I wanted to go over to her place."

She turned. "Did she say why?"

I shook my head, feeling half-embarrassed, half-guilty. *Way to show up for your friends, Rue.* "I told her I had plans."

"What were you—oh, right. Your quarterly sex-up. Rue After Dark. Oh my god, how have we not talked about *the guy*."

"What guy?"

"Really? You send me a picture of some dude's driver's license and then ask *what guy*? Nice try."

"It was a valiant attempt." I stood, trying to avoid remembering deep-set blue eyes. That Grecian urn profile that had forced me to stare. The short brown curls, just this side of too messy. He'd kept his eyes straight ahead as he drove me home, as if adamant not to look in my direction.

"Have you heard from him? Assuming you did the unthinkable and"—she gasped, clutching her sternum—"gave him your *number*."

"I haven't checked my phone." It now lived at the very bottom of my backpack, pressed under an extra hoodie, and my water bottle, and a stack of books that were due back at the library in two days. It was going to stay there, at least as long as I caught myself wondering every ten minutes whether he had texted.

I liked to force myself to keep a certain detachment when it came to *he*s.

"I should have gone to Florence's," I said, remorse prickling at the bottom of my stomach.

"Nah. Having to choose between you getting laid and having a heads-up on this here clusterfuck, I'd probably choose orgasms for you. I'm a generous soul like that." Tisha lowered her voice as we walked side by side, treading down Kline's sea-blue, ultramodern hallways that teemed with employees, all heading toward the open space on the first floor. They all smiled at Tisha—and nodded at *me*, polite but much more somber.

Kline had started out as a small tech startup, then quickly ballooned to several hundred employees, and I'd stopped keeping track of new hires. Plus, the solitary nature of my project made me a bit of an unknown quantity. The tall, serious, distant girl—who always hung out with the *other* tall girl, the funny and delightful one everybody loved. At Kline, Tisha's and my popularity levels were as mismatched as they'd been since elementary school. Luckily, I'd learned not to mind.

"Sadly," I murmured, "no orgasms were had."

"*What?* He did *not* look like he'd be bad at sex!"

"I wouldn't know."

She scowled. "Isn't that what you met him for?"

"Originally."

"And?"

"Vincent showed up."

"Oh, *fuck* Vincent. How did he—I don't even wanna know. Next time, then?"

Since you never do repeats, he'd said, and my body had heated at the wistfulness in his tone.

"I don't know," I whispered truthfully, feeling some of that wistfulness myself as Tisha and I took a seat on a couch at the back of the room. "I think that—"

"Never a dull fucking moment," said a musical voice, and the cushion dipped on my left side. Jay was our favorite lab technician. Or, more accurately, Tisha's favorite, whom she'd swiftly befriended. By virtue of always being around her, I'd been folded into that relationship. It was the unabridged story of my social life. "I swear to god," he said, "if they fire all of us and my visa falls through and I have to go back to Portugal and Sana breaks up with me—"

"Love the optimism, babe." From the other side of me, Tisha leaned forward with a grin. "We researched this whole mess, by the way. We can tell you what a loan assignment is."

Jay's eyebrow arched, and the piercings speared through it flickered. "You didn't know *before*?"

Tisha shrank back, disappearing behind me. "There, there." I patted her leg comfortingly. "At least we've never pretended to be anything but what we are."

"Dumbasses?"

"Apparently."

A waterfall of red curls appeared in the crowd, and the knot of panic in my chest instantly loosened. *Florence.* Brilliant, resourceful Florence. She *was* Kline. She'd fought tooth and nail for it, and wasn't going to allow anyone to take it from her. Certainly not some—

"Who are those four?" Tisha whispered in the sudden hush of the room. Her gaze had drifted past Florence, to the figures standing beside her.

"Someone from Harkness?" Jay guessed.

I had expected slicked-back hair, and suits, and that uniquely off-putting finance bro flair. The Harkness people, however, looked like they might have belonged at Kline in a different timeline. Maybe dressing down was just a power move on their part, but they seemed . . . normal. Approachable. The long-haired woman was at ease in her jeans and seemed pleased with the turnout, and so did the broad-shouldered man who stood just a little too close to her. The tall figure in the well-groomed beard surveyed the room a touch haughtily, but who was *I* to judge? I'd been told several times I didn't exactly inspire fuzzy warmth. And the fourth man, the one who joined the group last, gait unhurried and smile confident, he seemed . . .

The blood congealed in my veins.

"I already hate them," Jay mumbled, making Tisha laugh.

"You hate *everybody*."

"No, I don't."

"Yes, you do. Doesn't he, Rue?"

I nodded absently, eyes stuck on the fourth Harkness man like a bird caught in an oil spill. My head spun and the room ran out of air, because unlike the others', his face was familiar.

Unlike the others, I knew exactly who he was.

2

VERY WILLING TO LET HER CONTINUE

ELI

THE PREVIOUS NIGHT

She looked even more beautiful than in her picture.

And she'd looked pretty fucking stunning in that, too, standing in front of a painfully familiar UT Austin sign. Not a selfie—a regular old-school photo, cropped to cut out her companion. All that was left was a slender, dark-skinned arm slung lazily around a shoulder. And, of course, *her*. Smiling, but only faintly. There, but remote.

Beautiful.

Not that it mattered much. Eli had hooked up with enough people to know that a person's looks had a little less impact on the quality of casual sex than what that person was looking for. Still, when he arrived at the hotel lobby and spotted her at the bar, sitting straight on the tall stool, he stopped in his tracks. Hesitated, even though his meeting with Hark and the others had run behind, and dropping home to check on Tiny had put him a few minutes late.

She was drinking Sanpellegrino—a relief, since given their plans for the night, anything else would have given him pause. Her jeans and sweater were simple, and her posture was a thing of beauty. Relaxed, yet regal. Spine unbent, but not on edge. She didn't look nervous, and had the easy air of someone who did this often enough to know exactly what to expect.

Eli remembered her pertinent questions and straight-to-the-point answers. She'd messaged him the day before, and when he'd asked, **Where would you like to meet?** her response had been,

Not my apartment.

> **My place doesn't work either. I can book a hotel and cover the cost.**

I'm okay with splitting.

> **No need.**

Works for me, then. FYI, I'll share my location with a friend who has my login info to the app.

> **Please do. Would you like my phone number?**

We can keep messaging here.

Sounds good. Whatever made her feel safest. The dating app game could be dangerous. Then again, the app they were using wasn't for dating, not by any correct meaning of the word.

Eli glanced at the woman one last time, and something

resembling the anticipation he used to be capable of rose inside him. *Good,* he told himself. *This is going to be good.* He started walking again but stopped a few feet away.

When another man approached.

Some poor asshole hitting on her, Eli originally figured, but it quickly became apparent that she already knew him. Her eyes widened, then narrowed in a one-two punch. Her spine locked. She shifted back, seeking more distance.

An ex of some kind, Eli thought as the man spoke urgently. A hushed conversation began, and while the elevator music was too loud for Eli to pick up the words, the tension in her shoulder blades wasn't a good sign. She shook her head, then ran a hand through her dark, glossy curls, and when they swept to the side, he caught the line of her nape: stiff. Stiffer as the man started talking faster. Inching closer. Gesticulating harder.

Then his hand closed around her upper arm, and Eli intervened.

He was at the bar in seconds, but the woman was already trying to pry herself free. He stopped behind her stool and ordered, "Let her go."

The man glanced up, glassy-eyed. Drunk, maybe. "This is none of your business, bro."

Eli stepped closer, bicep brushing against the woman's back. "Let. Her. Go."

The man looked, *really* looked. Had a brief moment of common sense, in which he estimated, correctly, that he had no chance against Eli. Reluctantly, slowly, he unhanded the woman and raised his arms in a peacekeeping gesture, knocking over her glass in the process. "There's a misunderstanding—"

"Is there?" He glanced at the woman, who was rescuing her phone from a puddle of Sanpellegrino. Her silence was answer

enough. "Nope. Get out," he ordered, at once amiable and menacing. Eli's entire professional life relied on his ability to find something that would motivate people to successfully do their jobs, and
in his expert opinion, this shithead needed to be scared a little.

It worked: shithead glared, ground his jaw, glanced around as
though searching for witnesses to join him in denouncing the in-
justice he was being subjected to. When no one stepped forward,
he scuttled angrily toward the entrance of the hotel, and Eli turned
toward the woman.

Electricity jolted through him. Her eyes were large and liquid,
a dark blue he wasn't sure he'd encountered before. Eli stared into
them and briefly lost track of his question.

Ah. Right. It was something very complex, something along
the lines of "Are you okay?"

Instead of replying, she asked, "Do you often engage in vigi-
lante bullshit to compensate for whatever your issues are?" Her
voice was tame, but her glare blazed. Eli noticed that her upper lip
was slightly fuller than the lower. Both were dark pink. "Because
maybe you could just buy an infantry tank."

His eyebrow rose. "And maybe you could choose better men to
spend your time with."

"That's for sure, since I came here to spend time with *you*."

Ah. She'd recognized him, then. And she wasn't a fan.

Eli didn't blame her for thinking him a brash, hotheaded jerk,
but the last thing he wanted was to make her uncomfortable. She
clearly didn't want him around, and *that* had him feeling a small
tinge of disappointment. It swelled larger as he looked at her lips
one last time, but he shrugged it off.

Too bad, but not *that* bad. He gave her one last nod, turned
around, and—

A hand closed around his wrist.

He looked at her over his shoulder.

"I'm sorry." She screwed her eyes shut tight. Then took a deep breath and smiled the faintest smile he'd ever seen, which sent a new, heated wave of interest vibrating through him.

Eli was no aesthete. He had no idea whether this woman was objectively, *scientifically* beautiful, or whether her face simply came together in a way that seemed to work perfectly for him. Either way, the result was the same.

A big fucking turn-on.

"Eli, right?" she asked.

He nodded. Fully turned to her.

"I'm sorry. I was still in fight-or-flight mode. I'm usually way less defensive about . . ." She gestured vaguely. Her nails were red. Her hands graceful, but trembling. "Being helped. Thank you for what you did." Her hand dropped from his wrist to curl into her lap, and he followed every inch of that journey, mesmerized.

"You didn't mention your name," he said, instead of *you're welcome*. On the app, she'd just used one initial: *R*.

"No, I didn't." She didn't elaborate, and her uncompromising tone was a thrill all by itself.

Rachel? Rose. Ruby turned to watch the entrance, where the man still loitered, giving them resentful glances. When her throat bobbed, Eli offered casually, "I could go scare him off." His brawling days were over—had been since high school, when his life had been hockey practices and detentions and lots of rage. Still, he knew how to deal with assholes.

"It's okay." She shook her head.

"Or call the police."

Another shake. Then, after a moment of reluctance, she added, "But maybe you could . . ."

"I'll stay," he said, and her posture softened in relief. With the way the shithead was acting, Eli had planned to keep an eye on her anyway—which was probably a whole other degree of creepy, but here he was. Making this random girl whose name he didn't even know his business. He leaned back against the counter, arms crossed on his chest. A large group approached the bar and took a seat next to them, forcing him to shift a little closer to her.

R.

Rebecca.

Rowan.

"I know we're supposed to . . ." She gestured vaguely upward, and a million things flashed in his brain at the flick of her index finger.

The pragmatic tone of her first message to him: **Are you still in the Austin area? Interested in meeting up?**

The *only casual—no relationships or repeat meetings* in her bio.

Her answer to the *Kinks?* question on the open survey.

The list of what she was *not* willing to do. Of what she *was.*

At this point he doubted anything would happen between them tonight, but he was still going to mull over the latter. A lot.

"I don't want to anymore," she continued, voice steady. He liked that she didn't say *can't,* but *don't want.* The lack of apology in her tone. Her serious, quiet expression.

"You mean, you don't want to go upstairs and fuck a man you don't know minutes after a man you *do* know assaulted you?" He gave her a look of mock surprise, and she nodded thoughtfully.

"That's a good recap. I bet it's too late to get a refund on the hotel room, so if you need to make plans with someone else for tonight, feel free."

He felt the corner of his mouth quirk up. "I'll survive," he said dryly.

"As you prefer," she told him, indifferent. She clearly couldn't care less whether he took his phone out and booty-called half the city or swore his undying loyalty to her, and Eli bit back a smile. Her head cocked. "Do you do this a lot?" she asked.

"Do what? Fuck?"

"Save damsels in distress."

"No."

"Because you don't encounter many, or because you leave them in distress?" Her voice was soft, and on anyone else's lips the words would have sounded like flirting. Not hers, though. "Either way, I'm flattered," she added.

"You should be." He glanced at the man, who was still outside, glaring. "Do you live alone?"

Her eyebrows rose, and he noticed a faint scar bisecting the right. His index finger tapped once against the counter, itching to trace it. "Are you trying to find out if I'm single?"

"I'm trying to figure out what the chances are that the dipshit will be waiting for you where you live, who could help you if he is, or whether your pet could protect you."

"Ah." She didn't look flustered to have misunderstood him. Fascinating. "I do live alone. And he shouldn't know where."

"Shouldn't?"

"I'm not sure how he tracked me here. I can only imagine that he found out where I lived, wasn't allowed inside by my doorman, and followed my Uber when it picked me up." She'd been shaken until a minute earlier, but now she sounded disarmingly utilitarian. *Just like in her texts,* Eli thought. She'd messaged him with no emojis. No LOL or LMAO. Correctly placed punctuation and proper capitalization. He'd guessed it was a localized quirk, but her demeanor seemed like the embodiment of her writing.

Serious. A little impenetrable. Complicated.

And Eli had never been a fan of easy.

"How are you getting home?" he asked.

"Uber. Or Lyft. Whatever's quicker." She picked up her phone, but when she tapped on it, it refused to light up. Eli remembered the spilled water. "Well, this is a new development." She sighed. "I'll hail a cab."

No fucking way, he almost said, but stopped with his mouth half-open. This woman was not his friend, sister, colleague. She was someone with whom he'd been planning to have a sexual relationship that would last part of the night, then never see again. He had no right to tell her what to do.

Though he *could* try to convince her.

"He's still out there," Eli said evenly, pointing at the man with his chin. He paced outside the revolving door, skin glistening with sweat. "Waiting for you to step out of the bar."

"Right." She scratched her long neck. Eli stared far longer than he should have. "Could you walk outside with me?"

"I will. But what if he *does* know where you live, and waits for you there? What if he follows you?" He watched her ponder the situation. "Do you have a neighbor you trust? A friend? A brother?"

She laughed once, silently, in a wistful way that Eli didn't understand. "Not quite."

"Okay." He nodded, experiencing the opposite of annoyance at the thought of what would have to happen. "I'll drive you home, then."

Her look was long and even. Eli wondered why her wide, limpid eyes felt like a punch to the stomach. "You're suggesting I get in the car of a man I do not know to avoid being harassed by a man I do know?"

He shrugged. "Pretty much."

She bit her lower lip. Suddenly, Eli was more physically aware of another human being than he remembered being in a long, *long* while. "Thank you, but I'll have to pass. The potential for situational irony is a bit too high, even for me."

"I don't think this qualifies as situational irony."

"It would if you turned out to be a serial killer."

Smiling wasn't going to win him any points, but he couldn't help himself. "You were going to go upstairs to a hotel room booked under my name and spend hours alone with me."

"Hours?"

The way he was feeling at the moment, more than that. "Hours," he repeated. She held his gaze for every letter. "Seems late in the game to worry about whether I'll murder you."

"A friend knew where I'd be and how to check on me," she countered. "A second location is a whole different beast."

"Is it?" He had no business being this pleased by her self-preservation.

"Vincent's a dick. But for all I know, you're the Unabomber."

Vincent. She knew the dickhead's name—and Eli still didn't know *hers.* Fucking irritating. "Unabomber's dead."

"That's what the Unabomber would say to throw me off," she deadpanned, unknowable. He couldn't tell whether she was flirting, making fun of him, or dead serious.

It was exhilarating.

"He made bombs and solved math theorems. He didn't kidnap young women."

"You know a lot about the Unabomber for someone who supposedly isn't him."

Eli looked up at the ceiling to hide his amusement, exhaling slowly. Then he straightened. Took his wallet out of the back pocket of his jeans and the driver's license out of his wallet. Dropped it on the counter, right by her hand.

"What's this?"

He leaned back against the counter without replying, and she nimbly picked it up. Her eyes shifted between him and the picture on the card, as though solving a Find the Difference puzzle. "Eli Killgore," she read. "This is not a reassuring name, Eli."

He frowned. "It's Scottish."

"It sounds like the name of someone who trims girls' pubes and sews them into dolls. You look younger than thirty-four. And are you really *that* tall?" He sighed heavily, and she returned his license, straight faced. "So we've established that your last name is closely related to the term 'blood splatter.' But I still don't know that this isn't a fake ID you made to lure women into your moth-decorated lair."

"I bet you think you're so funny."

"Actually, I *know* I'm not. I was born without a sense of humor."

He huffed out his amusement. She was fucking with him, had to be. And Eli was apparently very willing to let her continue, because he pushed his entire wallet toward her. "Knock yourself out." He watched eagerly as her slim fingers opened it, wondering why her elegant movements seemed to be unlocking some kind of long-hidden fetish part of his brain. She brought it to her nose to smell the leather (an odd, inexplicably appealing move), pulled out a random credit card, then another.

"Eli Massmurderer," she said.

"Not my name."

"You have a library card." She sounded bemused, and he clucked his tongue.

"Here I am, trying to help you out in a difficult situation, and you repay me by being surprised that I can read."

She smiled, something small and mysterious that shouldn't have sent a thrill up his spine. "I thought you'd be more of a Planet Fitness cardholder."

"Not at all condescending." He tried not to grin and failed. But it was okay, because she kept methodically rifling through his life via the wallet, stopping to peruse the more interesting pieces, once humming audibly. Eli felt it like a physical thing, a thrum through air and flesh. Like her slender fingers were peeling out the layers of him, slowly, inexorably.

"Well, you do have health insurance, which hopefully covers the necessary amount of murder-prevention therapy," she said dispassionately before folding the wallet and handing it back to him with a solemn nod. She gave one last look at the doors, where Vincent was nervously smoking a cigarette. Still in wait.

"This is one consistent wallet. Despite the fact that your name is literally Carnagemonger."

"Not literally. Not figuratively, either."

"Regardless." Her lips curved in the shadow of a smile. Eli felt it in his marrow, wrapped around his balls. "Mr. Killgore, you may drive me home."

3

IT WOULD HAVE BEEN FUN

ELI

His heart skipped a beat, then thudded hard. He felt oddly, foolishly like running a victory lap around the bar. He curbed the impulse and said, as dryly as he could muster: "What an honor."

"You're welcome." Another unsmiling nod. There was something astonishingly effortless about this woman. Like she had no interest in being anything but herself.

"Am I allowed to know your name now?"

"No."

"Figures." Eli sighed and handed her his unlocked phone. "Take a picture of my driver's license, text it or email it to a friend, and then let's go. Share my location with them, too."

"Is this an order?"

Yes, and an out-of-place one at that, but she didn't seem too put off. Whoever her friend was, they were close enough that she had their number memorized. She sent a picture of his license, typed a short explanation that Eli forced himself not to peer at, and returned the phone. Then she gracefully hopped off her stool.

Fuck, she was tall. Even in flats, her eyes were only a handful of inches below Eli's—and, no use in denying it at this point, right on the verge of spectacular. He forced himself to look away.

"You're sober enough to drive, right?" she asked.

"Yeah. My plans fit better with sobriety."

"Very well." Her words were somewhat queenly, and his grin widened.

"You know you're not doing *me* a favor, right?" he asked, even though she was. With Vincent around, he couldn't have let her return home alone without losing whatever peace of mind he had left, which was very little.

She blinked at him serenely, and he was briefly certain that she could read his mind. The filthy thoughts he couldn't rein in. The way her sweet scent seemed to settle inside his brain.

No. She couldn't, because she was obviously relaxed with him. Trusting enough to send him on a bit of a power trip. Still difficult to decipher, but his gut told him that she didn't mind prolonging their time together any more than he did. "Come on. My car's in the parking garage."

They avoided the main entrance, where Vincent waited, and called the elevator, a comfortable silence between them. A middle-aged man joined them inside the cabin, and Eli did *not* like the long, clinging look he gave to . . .

He still didn't know her damn name. Which meant that he had no right to scowl at some creep just because he was looking at her tits. He did anyway, and the man must have felt the aggression coming off Eli in waves, because he abashedly lowered his gaze.

Eli felt like a primate, half-locked in some ridiculous dominance battle, like the last twenty minutes had regressed him some fifty thousand years of evolution and—

Jesus. He needed to . . . get the fuck laid, probably. Or sleep. A vacation. Time, that's what he needed. The past six months had been nothing but exhaustion and work, with no chance to think about any of this. Then, yesterday, she'd messaged him on an app he hadn't opened in nearly a year, and it had felt like a cosmic gift.

A celebration for what he, Hark, and Minami had achieved. A prelude to what would come. Tomorrow.

He was deluded. A fucking break, that's what he needed.

"Where do you live?" he asked, steering her toward his car with a flick of his hand. He tried to touch her as little as possible, but it was hard when she was the one drifting closer. Her shoulder brushed his arm, and the spot felt electric, itchy even through his clothes. The cool air of the underground lot was a welcome distraction.

"I can put the address in your GPS—"

"Can you please listen to me for *one minute?*" someone called, and when they turned back, Vincent was running toward them across the empty parking lot. "You can't make this decision for the both of us, and I just need you to—"

"Go home, Vince," she said.

Vince stopped. Then started again in their direction, his gait more menacing. "No, not until you listen to me—"

"I *have* listened. And I've asked you for a few days so I can think it through."

"You're being a bitch, as always—"

Eli had heard enough, and stepped in front of the woman. "Hey. Apologize and get lost."

"Oh, for fuck's sake." Vince glowered. "This has nothing to do with you."

Eli wasn't so sure. He unlocked his car remotely, tossing the woman his keys. She caught them without hesitation. "Get in the passenger seat. I'll be with you in a second."

She didn't move, instead staring at Eli with an expression that he could only define as crestfallen. After a long moment, her lips parted. *Don't hurt him,* she mouthed.

Eli ground his teeth, wondering how this loser could have this much power over her. How he'd gotten someone like *her* in the first place. But he nodded, watched her disappear inside his car, and turned to Vincent.

He was tall, too, and wide shouldered, even if not as much as Eli. Still, he must have seen something in Eli's eyes, because his first reaction was to take a step back. Then, once his spine met a pilaster, to flatten himself against it.

"You need to stop bothering women who ask you to fuck off, Vincent," Eli said. Amiably, he thought. He was being a damn gentleman about this.

"You have no idea what she—"

He stepped close enough for Vincent's boozy smell to hit him. "It doesn't matter," he said calmly. *Don't hurt him*, she'd asked, but god, Eli was tempted. "You can walk away now on your own, or I can make you. Your choice."

Vincent didn't take long to deliberate. With a couple of curse words, he scurried away, jumpily turning every few steps, always finding Eli staring at him. Once he'd disappeared, Eli found the woman was in the passenger seat of his car, hands in her lap.

Rosie, maybe. Rosamund would fit her, too.

"Where did you say you live?"

She lifted her eyes but didn't reply. "I'm surprised." She looked around, and he could smell her so intensely, he had to get a grip. Skin and flowers and fabric softener. It was well past *good*, straight into dangerous territory. "I didn't peg you for a hybrid kind of guy."

He snorted and started the engine. "Don't say what you *did* peg me for."

"A Mustang, maybe."

"Jesus." He wiped a hand over his face.

"Or a Tesla."

"Get the fuck out. You're walking home."

She laughed once, low in her throat, and the sound made him feel dizzy and powerful and accomplished. She was safe in his car, making jokes. Not on high alert as she'd been earlier. She was letting him take care of her.

He just needed to stop noticing how close she was.

"Here." He handed her his phone. "Put your address in."

"It's locked. I'll need your password."

He turned to tell her and forgot to speak. Her haircut, he realized, was more elaborate than he'd originally thought. It was cropped close to the skull for a couple of inches around her left ear. *Pretty.* He'd have to ask Minami what the style was called.

"Are you embarrassed because it's a string of sixty-nines?"

His mind took a brusque, inappropriate, sexual turn. Unavoidable, too. He'd been on the edge of it for a while, and it was getting harder to leash it back. "Two seven one eight two eight."

"Your password is Euler's number?"

They exchanged a surprised, plane-tilting look. Like they were only just now meeting.

"Are you a scientist?" she asked, suddenly curious, and it was the first time he could perceive this kind of interest in him on her part. She'd asked to use his body and volunteered hers in exchange, she'd gone through his documents with the efficiency of a DMV clerk, but she had *not* considered him beyond the here and now.

Until this moment.

"If I say yes, will you take it as proof that I'm the Unabomber?"

She smiled. A little wider than before.

"I'm not a scientist," he admitted, loath to disappoint her. But it was the honest, if painful, answer. "I just studied science for a bit."

"A minor in college?"

"Something like that." No point in bringing up the rest.

"What do you do, then?"

"Boring money stuff."

"I see." She didn't seem disappointed. She was still looking at him, searching. It was intoxicating, having her eyes on him. Her attention felt more precious than gold, stocks, market crash predictions.

"Are *you* a scientist?"

She nodded.

"What kind?"

"Engineer." He pulled out of the lot, then turned to her when the soft weight of her hand settled on his forearm, a sudden shock of warmth in the blow of the AC.

Fuck. Just—*fuck*.

"Thank you," she said simply. She sounded serious, as usual. Sincere.

"For not being a Tesla owner?"

She shook her head. "For being kind."

He wasn't *kind*. No one *kind* would wake up tomorrow and do what Eli was going to, relishing every moment of it. But it felt nice to have her think so.

"And for caring, I guess."

There was something lost in her tone. Something that made Eli's voice rough as he told her, "You should call the authorities, tell them what happened tonight. Take out a restraining order."

She closed her eyes, leaning back against the headrest—a sign of deep trust if he'd ever seen one. Eli studied her slender throat, imagined burying his face in it, then reminded himself that he was about to merge into traffic.

Eyes. On. The. Road.

"It's for your safety," he added.

"It's complicated."

"I don't doubt it. But even if you two have kids together, or you're married, it doesn't change that he could be very dangerous—"

"He's my brother," she said.

Eli winced. "Shit."

"Yeah." She turned toward the passing streetlights. "Shit."

The resemblance was there, now that he knew to look for it. The height. The near-black hair. The eye color was different, but not the shape. "Shit," he repeated.

"He's not always like this. But when he drinks . . . well. You saw."

"I did."

"I don't think he would actually hurt me."

"You don't *think*? Not good enough."

"No." She bit the inside of her cheek. "My . . . our father, our *estranged* father, died a few months ago. He left us a small cabin in Indiana, of all places—we didn't even know he lived there. We disagree on what to do with it." Her head rolled toward Eli. They were all alone, and it was disarming, how at ease she seemed. "Are you bored yet?"

"No."

Her smile was dim. "It's not easy to say no to someone who shares fifty percent of your genes."

"I know."

"You do?"

He nodded once.

"Brother?"

"Sister. No public harassment, but she's always found highly creative ways to drive me nuts."

"Such as?"

Eli thought about teenage Maya, screaming at him that he was ruining her life and she wished *he*'d been the one to die. Grabbing fistfuls of his shirt and soaking the cotton after being stood up for homecoming. Poking her nose through his things because she was "looking for batteries," then following him around the kitchen to criticize his choice of condoms *and* lube. Bitching at him on the phone that he always left her alone, that he might as well have let her go into foster care—and then lashing out whenever he'd tried to spend time with her. "Siblings can be hard."

"I'm sure Vincent would agree."

"*I'm* not sure Vincent has any right to agree."

She was silent for a long beat. But when Eli thought that was the end of the conversation, she said dully, "One day, when we were still kids, he was late coming home from a friend's place. I waited for him, worried out of my mind, for one, two, three hours. Wondered if he'd been run over, or something. Eventually he *did* return home, but instead of being relieved, when I saw him in the entryway, I thought, 'My life would be so much easier if he'd just disappeared.'"

He turned to meet her eyes. Found a bemused expression in them, as though she'd surprised herself by divulging something that was clearly a source of deep shame. And he surprised *himself* by saying, "When my sister was born, my parents kept saying how perfect she was, and I was so resentful, I refused to even *look* at her for weeks."

There were no platitudes, no raised eyebrows, no attempts to soften what he'd just said. She just studied him with the same lack of judgment he'd reserved for her, as though he hadn't just shared the most fucked up of stories, until he glanced away. He didn't even know her name, and he'd spilled about something he'd never acknowledged before, not even to his closest friends.

Probably *because* he didn't know her name.

"How do you think your brother found out your address?" he asked, mostly to shut down whatever that exchange had been. An anomaly. Had to be.

"Online?"

"Well, fuck." He turned right, heading for North Austin—the same road he'd take tomorrow morning. He was going to drive it thinking about her instead of the day ahead, he just knew it. This girl, she was going to stick around, even if only in his head.

"Right. Fuck." She did it again—leaned back against the seat, closed her eyes—and this time he took advantage and let his gaze roam over her. Her long, long legs. Her full chest. The beautiful, rounded curve of her ear. There was something jagged, sharp-edged about her personality, but her body was soft. His type, really, if he even had one.

If it hadn't been for her brother, he could have known for sure. What a fucking pity.

"How old are you?" he asked to distract himself.

"Six years, two months, and five days younger than you," she said without missing a beat.

"Nice. Did you also memorize my social security number?"

"You should invest in some identity theft protection before you find out."

"I will, if you take out a restraining order against your brother." There he was again. Glaringly overstepping. "If you believe he won't hurt you to get what he wants, you are too trusting."

"I think *you* are too trusting."

"Me?"

"Yes. Has it occurred to you that *I* could be the serial killer? Right here, in your car."

Eli looked at her again. Her smile was faint, her eyes still closed. He wanted to run his knuckles against her cheekbones. "I'll take my chances."

"With some girl who's luring you to a second location and never even told you her name."

Robin? No, didn't suit her. And Eli was starting to wonder if ignorance was best. The less he knew, the vaguer and fuzzier she remained in his imagination, the quicker he'd stop thinking about her. And yet: "Tell me, then."

"It's the third time you asked."

"It's the third time you didn't answer. Do you think the two things might be connected?"

She pressed her lips together—really, he might just have conjured them. They were something out of some extremely lurid dreams he'd had when he was very young and very hormonal. "I think it would have been fun," she said, a little melancholic.

"What?"

"Tonight. You and me."

Eli's blood thudded in his veins—once, loud, violent. When he glanced at the GPS, their destination was three minutes away. He slowed down to well below the limit, suddenly a scrupulous driver. "Yeah?"

"You seem like you'd know what you're doing."

Oh, you have no fucking idea. We still have time. I can be gentle. Or not. I could be lots of things if you—

Jesus. She'd just been manhandled by her brother. He was disgusting. "Maybe you're overestimating me." Even though, no. He'd have made sure she had fun. And had fun himself in the process.

"I think I'm just estimating myself correctly." A small smile. "I'm the one who messaged you, after all."

He was starting to wish she hadn't. It was destabilizing, all of this—at a time when all he needed was his feet firmly on the ground. "Why did you do that, anyway?"

"I appreciated that your photo wasn't a gym selfie, or you doing the peace sign next to a sedated tiger."

"I see the bar is underground." He tried to remember what his picture was. Something from Minami, probably. She was always taking candids of him and Hark. *For the website. So much better than the smarmy suits-and-ties shit in our current photos.*

"Your profile said you hadn't been active for a while. I figured you'd either settled down and found someone, or you were overdue. Did you?"

"Did I what?"

"Find someone?" She sounded . . . not pruriently curious, but at least interested, and Eli had to remind himself not to squeeze any hope out of it. Hope for *what*, anyway? It wasn't like he was in the market for a girlfriend. He'd failed abysmally at that.

Not everyone has the capacity for love, Eli.

"No. What about you? You wrote 'no repeats' on your profile."

"I did," she confirmed, and damn her for this habit of hers not to offer any explanations. Damn her for not living farther away. There it was, her apartment complex. He gripped the steering wheel, aware that he couldn't go any slower without getting pulled over.

"Is it a rule of yours?"

She nodded, unperturbed.

"Seems arbitrary," he said casually while parking. *Seems like what's standing between me and you having a fucking spectacular time.*

"All rules exist for a reason."

He killed the engine and ordered himself to let it go. It wasn't good for either of them, talking about something that wasn't going to happen. "Come on. I'll walk you inside, just in case your brother's waiting around."

But Vincent had given up on her, at least for the night. No car had followed them.

It was late May and it was Texas, which meant instant, oppressive heat, even at night. Eli was pleased to see a doorman in the lobby, one who didn't look just burly and alert, but also highly suspicious of Eli. *That's the attitude,* he thought, nodding at him, making a mental note to let him know the situation on his way back.

"You know I'm not going to invite you inside, right?" she asked when they stopped in front of her apartment.

Eli had had a myriad of highly inappropriate thoughts in the past twenty minutes, but this specific one hadn't even grazed his brain. "I'll leave once you're inside and I hear you lock your door. And you should put your phone in rice," he added, wondering what the fuck had come over him. Among his friends, he was famous for being the easygoing one. Laid back. Never like *this*, intrusive, commanding—not even with his sister. Probably because Maya would have guillotined him.

But this woman only seemed faintly amused. She regarded him with that placid, sphinxlike expression that Eli was already getting used to, and took a step closer—one that had his heart pumping louder and faster for no reason, since all she said was "Thank you. I really appreciate what you did for me tonight."

"It was the bare minimum." Not a good time to tell her he was considering sleeping outside in his car just to intercept her idiot brother.

Fucking nuts. Was he developing a *crush*? He hadn't even known he was capable of it.

"It was not." Her key chains jingled in her palm. A sparkly ice skate shoe, one of those flashlight and pen combinations, a supermarket loyalty card with H-E-B printed on the back. He had the very same one. "You are kind. And I find you very attractive."

Eli's brain blanked for a split second. He wasn't shy, not by any means, but he couldn't remember the last time someone had complimented him that matter-of-factly. She had that somber look in her eyes and no guile whatsoever, and he was half-smitten.

He needed to get the hell home.

"That seems beside the point," he said, not liking the gravel of his voice.

"Does it?"

"Since you never do repeats. Isn't that your rule?"

She was pensive for a moment. "You're right. Then, it's farewell."

It was. Unavoidably. But before Eli could remind her once more to be safe, she did something as simple as it was unexpected: she took another step in to him, rose on tiptoes, and placed a soft kiss on his cheek.

Of its own volition, Eli's hand rose to hold her waist, and that near imperceptible touch blossomed into something exponential.

Possibilities.

Current.

Warmth.

Her scent enveloped him. The world shrank to *them* and nothing else. Eli turned his head, curious to see what he'd find on her face in response to all this electricity. She briefly held his eyes, then closed the distance between their mouths.

It barely constituted a kiss. Her lips pressed against his in the slightest of contacts, but his body was aflame. A surge of heat coursed through him, violent and sudden. Eli tried to remember the last time he'd felt anything approaching this, and came up empty handed. But it didn't matter, because her fingers found his, and he was dizzy, lightheaded with all the things he was imagining.

He could *take* her. Abscond with her. Press her back against the door of her home, tucked under his bigger body. He could *show* her how beautiful she was to him and—

"Although, it occurs to me," she murmured against his mouth, breaking the spiral of his thoughts, "that rules exist for a reason."

She took a step back. Eli was entranced. Her servant. Spellbound. He considered begging her to let him touch her. To let him go down on her here in the hallway. He would go grocery shopping and make her dinner off a YouTube recipe of her choice. He'd wash her car, read her a book, sit here outside her door and just make sure she was safe and protected. They could hold hands all night. They could play Scrabble. He was very close to imploring for something, everything, *anything*, when she added, "And sometimes the reason is that they should be broken."

Her fingers were still around his, thumb stroking his palm, but Eli could not tear his eyes from hers. That warm, sinking blue. Her hands, cool against his. *Her damn skin,* he thought. It was soft. He could do a lot to her skin. Her skin could do a lot *for* him. He wanted to see it flush and redden and bruise for a million different reasons. He wanted to *defile* it.

"Good night, Eli." Her full, beautiful, obscene lips curved into one last smile, and before any amount of oxygenated blood could return to his brain, she was gone. The dull gray of her door closed in Eli's face, and all that was left in the dimly lit hallway was her clean scent, the heat of her lips on his flesh, and his raging hard-on.

He heard the click of the lock and took a vacillating step back, disoriented, wondering what the fuck this woman had done to him. Then the cool air of the night hit his hand, and he finally lowered his eyes.

While he'd been drowning in her, busy unspooling the filthiest of thoughts, she must have been at work, because there were ten digits written on his palm—just enough for a phone number.

And underneath, three letters that knocked the breath out of his chest.

Rue.

4

NOT ENEMIES

RUE

"There are two main reasons I called this meeting," Florence Kline said, and if she was in the grip of even a tenth of the panic her employees seemed to be experiencing, no one would have been able to guess.

Then again, Florence was like that. Steel nerved. Yes-can-do. Indomitable. A rising tide. I'd never seen her doubt herself, and no private equity firm could force her to start.

"The first is to reassure all of you that your jobs *are* safe."

Murmurs of relief scrambled around the room like ants in sugar, but many remained unconvinced.

"There are no plans of reshuffling. I am still the CEO of this company, the board remains unchanged, and so does your employment situation. If you're not pocketing printer ink, you can expect your professional life to remain constant."

That had most people laughing. And it was, in a nutshell, the reason Florence Kline had built a successful company in just a few years. Being the inventor of a promising biofuel made her an outstanding scientist, but Florence was more than that. Florence was a *leader*.

As well as one of my closest friends. Which meant that I knew her tells well enough to doubt most of the words currently flowing out of her mouth.

"Second: the representatives from Harkness, our new lender, are *not* enemies. Harkness has a long history of uplifting tech and healthcare startups, and that's why they're here. Their objective is, of course, to conduct due diligence and make sure that their financial interests are met, but our work—*your* work—has always been impeccable. They'll be setting up meetings with some of you, and you should make them your priority. And I want to make sure that you recognize them if you see them around: Dr. Minami Oka, Dr. Sullivan Jensen, Mr. Eli Killgore, and Mr. Conor . . ."

"Rue?" Tisha asked in a low whisper.

I didn't reply, but she continued anyway.

"That driver's license you sent last night?"

I nodded. The floor beneath my feet was gone, dropped to the core of the earth. I was sliding right through it, and nothing was going to break my fall.

"The pic of that guy . . . his face."

I nodded again. It was, undeniably, a memorable face. Striking. *Attractive*, I'd told him, meaning it. Short, wavy—no, *curly* hair, just this side of too wild. Square jaw. Strong, aquiline nose that sat somewhere between the Roman and Greek civilizations, deep in the Adriatic. Long vowels and the occasional dropped consonant.

"And his name. Killgore."

I'd teased him about that, and it had felt like a first. Joking around with people required a degree of ease that usually took me decades to reach, but with Eli it had been simple, for no reason that I could discern.

He was just some ordinary man, and last night he'd exuded the same energy he did now: nice guy, radically unafraid, fundamentally comfortable with himself and others. He'd kept it well into our car ride, that unsettling calm. Meanwhile, I'd been barely able to tear my eyes from him, my hands shaking as I stepped into the circle of his warm, woodsy scent to write my number on his palm.

"That man on the stage. It's him, right?"

I nodded one last time, unable to speak.

"Okay. Yeah. Wow." Tisha made to massage her eyes, then remembered her elaborate makeup. "That's quite a . . . I believe the scientific word for it is 'coinkydink.'"

Is it? Could it be? Acid rose in my throat, because I wasn't sure coincidences of this magnitude existed. Had Eli known who I was? Where I worked? I stared, hoping an answer would appear on his face. He was wearing glasses today. Dark rimmed. The most ridiculous of Clark Kent's disguises.

"I can't believe they sent *four* lender representatives," Jay said, breaking through the fog in my brain.

I turned to him, dazed. "Is that weird?"

"They don't even *own* us yet, do they? It seems like a lot of resources to expend on a company they haven't even acquired, but"—he shrugged—"what do I know? I'm just a humble country lab technician."

"You were born in Lisbon and have a master's degree from NYU," Tisha pointed out. "Maybe they just like to travel together, entourage-style. Share an omelet chef and a CVS card."

"Are the four . . . are they all employed by the private equity?"
I asked.

"I just looked up the Harkness website—they are the *founding
partners*. I understand that they want to send someone to check
on whether the covenants are being met—"

"The *what* now?" Tisha sounded done with this fucking day. I
could vigorously relate.

"You know, those promises you make when you sign a contract? They give us the money; in exchange we deliver a partridge
in a pear tree? Why are the *partners* here, though? Why not send
a VP? Is Kline that big a deal for them? It just sounds a bit sus."

Tisha and I exchanged a long, heavy glance.

"We need to talk to Florence," I whispered. "In private."

"Do you still have the keys to her office? From her birthday,
when we stuffed it with those 'you're old as shit' balloons?"

I stood. "I do."

"Great. Jay, see you later."

"*If* I don't get fired, and lose my visa, and end up deported out
of the country."

"Yeah." Tisha waved him goodbye. "Try not to walk into the
sea, okay?"

We left the room just as Florence invited everyone to keep
calm and return to their workplaces.

———

It had all started with fermentation. Which, admittedly, was a less-
than-enthralling topic—even for someone like me, with a relentless passion for chemical engineering and an unwieldy interest
in the production of ethanol. Still, a couple of boring chemical

reactions had changed the trajectory of food microbiology, and Florence Kline was the person who got credit for that.

Less than a decade earlier, Florence had been a professor at UT Austin with a really, *really* good idea for how to perfect a process that could cheaply convert food waste into biofuels on a mass scale. Because she was a faculty member, UT's labs had been at her disposal, but Florence had known that any sort of discovery made on campus grounds, using campus resources, would end in the university owning the resulting patent. And Florence was *not* about that.

So she'd rented lab space at a nearby facility. She'd done her own work. She'd filed her own patent, and founded her own company. Others had trickled in later: private grants, angel investors, venture capitalists, a handful, then dozens, then hundreds of employees. The company had expanded, perfected Florence's revolutionary tech, and brought it to market.

Then, about four years ago, I'd jumped on board.

Florence and I both lived in Austin at the time, but by a fluke of fate we first met in Chicago, at the annual conference of the Society for Food Technology. I was dutifully standing by my poster, wearing a frumpy cardigan and a pair of Tisha's slacks that dug too tightly into my waist, and was bored out of my mind.

Alone.

The academic networking game required a healthy number of interpersonal graces, of which I had none. In fact, by the time I reached grad school, I'd been set in my ways for over a decade— ways that entailed concealing my shyness, self-consciousness, and general inability to offer rewarding social interactions to another human being, mostly behind a standoffish facade. But people were *hard*—to read, to understand, to please. At some point in my youth, without quite meaning to do so, I'd gone from being incapable of carrying out a conversation to coming across as though I did not *want* to be approached for conversation, not ever, not by anyone and not under any circumstances. I still remembered the day in middle school when the realization dawned on me: If people perceived me as aloof and detached, then they would want to keep their distance. And if they kept their distance, then they wouldn't notice how nervous and blundering and inadequate I was.

A net win, in my humble opinion. A form of masking, in my therapist's professional one. She thought I was hiding my real self and squashing down my feelings like jumbo marshmallows, but it had been so damn long, I wasn't so sure there was anything to hide inside me. The disconnect I constantly felt toward the rest of the world was unlikely to go anywhere, and whether it was *real* or not, it shrouded me with a comforting sense of security.

It did, however, have some downsides. For instance, people weren't exactly lining up to hang out with me, which in Chicago had made for a fairly solitary, tedious conference. It didn't help that I'd firmly refused to change my presentation title ("A Gas Chromatography and Mass Spectrometry Investigation of the Effect of Three Polysaccharide-Based Coatings on the Minimization of Postharvest Loss of Horticultural Crops") to my adviser's preferred "Three Microbes in a Trench Coat: Using Polysaccharides to Keep Your Produce Fresher, Longer," or my coauthor's suggestion, "Take a Coat, It'll Last Longer," or Tisha's appalling "If You Liked It, Then You Should Have Put a Coat on It."

I knew that science communication was an important job, crucial to building public trust and informing a wide array of policies, but it wasn't *my* job. I had no talent for enticing people to care about my work: either they saw its value, or they were wrong.

Unfortunately, the overwhelming majority appeared to be wrong. I'd been dozing off from boredom and considering ducking out early when a woman stopped by my poster. She was much shorter, and yet imposing. Because of her assertive air, or maybe just the sheer mass of her red curls.

"Tell me more about this microbial coating," she said. Her voice was deep, older than her looks. She asked many pertinent questions, was impressed at all the right parts, and once I was done with my spiel she said, "This is a brilliant study."

I already knew that, so I wasn't particularly flattered, but I thanked her anyway.

"You're welcome. My name is—"

"Florence Kline."

Florence smiled. "Right. I keep forgetting that we're wearing name tags, and . . ." She looked down at herself, where there was no lanyard. No tag. No name. Then back up to me. "How did you know?"

"I've read up on you. Well, on your patent saga."

"My patent saga."

I had no idea whether Florence's case had been legitimately high profile or just felt so because of the circles in which I moved, but the facts were simple: Despite the incontrovertible proof that she had independently developed the biofuel tech, UT still claimed ownership of her (very lucrative) patent. Lawyers had gotten involved, which would have heavily tilted the scale in favor of the university, but Florence had been able to turn things around by bringing the matter to the media.

I was no PR strategist, but it was obvious that the framing had been brilliant: a woman, a *female scientist*, was being stripped of her life's work and intellectual property by some greedy Texas bureaucrats. The news had picked up steam, and UT had back-tracked faster than a yo-yo.

"You were able to maintain ownership of what you created," I told Florence, truthful. "I thought it was very impressive."

"Right. Well, that's nice." She seemed to be wondering whether she was being patronized by a grad student nobody who was clearly wearing someone else's too-small pants, so I didn't mention that I would have known about Florence even sans patent scandal, because her name was brought up often in UT's chemical engineering department, usually in the hushed tones reserved for those who were deeply resented for managing to free themselves from the ruthless academic clutches of teaching Biophysics 101 every third semester.

"You seem like a great scientist," Florence said. "If you apply for jobs, do consider Kline."

I thought about it for a handful of seconds, but dismissed the idea. "Biofuel is not really my area of interest."

"What *is* your area of interest?"

"Shelf life extension."

"Well, it's pretty closely related."

"Not as much as I'd like." I sounded inflexible and stubborn, and I knew that. But I also knew what my endgame was, and could see no value in pretending that nonnegotiable things were up for debate.

Compromise was never my forte.

"I see. Want to stay in academia?"

"No. I'd like to do something that's actually useful," I said solemnly, with a self-importance I'd manage to shake off in the second half of my twenties, but whose memory will make me cringe well into my eighties.

Florence, however, laughed and handed me a card. "If you're ever looking for an internship, a *paid* internship, shoot me an email. I'd be open to hearing about your project ideas."

I had grown up poor, poor in a way that meant duct tape on skinned knees and the flavor of ketchup on toast and prayers that I'd soon stop getting so tall, because I'd reached the end of my hand-me-downs. Thanks to scholarships and my PhD stipend, I'd recently graduated from poor to broke, which was downright inebriating, but I still wasn't the type to turn down money.

That summer, I did shoot Florence an email. And I did begin an internship at Kline, and then another, and a few more. I worked in research and development, manufacturing, quality assurance, even logistics. Above all, I worked with Florence, which turned out to be life altering in the best possible way.

Before her, all of my mentors had been men—some of them great, supportive, brilliant men who'd made me into the scientist I'd become. But Florence was different. Something closer to a friend, or a brilliant older sister who could answer my reaction kinetics questions, pat my back when my experiments didn't work out, and later, once I'd graduated, provide me with the means to do the kind of work I wanted. I didn't fuck with emotions, not if I could avoid it, but it didn't take a therapist and months of navel-gazing to tease out what I felt for Florence: gratitude, admiration, love, and quite a bit of protectiveness.

Which was why I absolutely loathed the deep lines that halved her forehead when she walked into her office.

"Shit on a tit!" Florence clutched her chest, startled. After a calming breath, she eyed us with an indulgent expression: the way I'd helped myself to her orthopedic chair, and Tisha's enthusiastic mouth shoveling of the peanut butter pretzels on her desk. "Why, don't be shy. Make yourselves at home. Break your bread."

"They're not even good," Tisha said, scarfing down two more.

Florence closed the door and smiled wryly. "Thank you for your sacrifice, then."

"Anything for you, my liege."

"In that case, could I bother you to key a couple of people's cars?" She dropped her tablet on the desk and massaged her bloodshot eyes. She was young for the size of her success, barely in her forties, and tended to look even younger. Not today, though. "To what do I owe the pleasure?" It was clear that she was pleased to see us.

"Seemed like you might be having a shit day, so we let ourselves in." Tisha's blinding smile displayed no shame.

"I do love a pity visit."

"What about recon visits?" Tisha laid her chin on her hands. "Also a fan of those?"

Florence sighed. "What do you guys want to know?"

"So much. For instance, who the hell are those Harkness people, and what the hell do they want?"

Florence glanced back to make sure the door was closed. Then exhaled slowly. "Fuck me if I know."

"Anticlimactic. And a bit less informative than I expected. Wait, I know that look. Fuck you if you know, *but* . . . ?"

"What I say doesn't leave this room."

"Of course."

"I'm serious. If anyone hears of this, they'll panic—"

"Florence," I interrupted, "who would we even tell?"

She seemed to briefly consider our lack of meaningful relationships and then nodded reluctantly. "As you know, they bought our loan. Neither the board nor I had any say in the sale, and Harkness only ever interacted with the lender. We only communicate through lawyers." She sighed. "According to legal, the most likely case is that Harkness bought the loan because they want full control of the fermentation tech."

"The tech is yours, though." I scowled. "They could take the company, but not the patent, right?"

"Unfortunately, Rue, the tech *is* the company. More accurately, the patent is part of the collateral for the loan." She grabbed one of the chairs and took a seat. "The problem is, whenever we borrow funds to expand our operations, we have to make certain promises."

"Of course. The *covenants*," Tisha said with the tone of someone who'd appeared on god's green earth with a genetic knowledge of the myriad facets of bankruptcy law and had *not* learned the word five minutes earlier, courtesy of a twenty-three-year-old lab technician. Florence gave her an approving nod, and Tisha made a show of dusting herself off.

I shook my head at her.

"Some of these covenants are straightforward—provide financial statements, noncompete, that kind of stuff. But others are . . . harder to interpret."

I scratched my temple, already suspecting where this was going despite the heights of my managerial ignorance. If both parties approached a contract in good faith, muddy covenants could be resolved with a simple conversation. But if one party had ulterior motives . . .

"Now that Harkness owns the loan, they still don't own the company, but they have the right to enforce those covenants. Which gives them the right to come in, snoop around, and find something to complain about. If you ask them, they'll say they're just making sure we're using their capital in the best way, like good little borrowers." Florence sank back in her chair. Her posture was exasperated, but not defeated. "This has been in the making for weeks."

"Weeks?" Tisha's jaw dropped. "Florence, you should have told us. We could have—"

"Done nothing, and that's why I didn't tell you. Legal has been fighting, but . . ." She shrugged.

"They are trying to take the tech away from you." I leaned forward, a frisson of some intense emotions I couldn't immediately name stirring inside me.

I was concerned. Or angry. Or indignant. Or all of the above.

"That seems to be the case, yes."

"Why? Why *your* tech and not a million others?"

Florence widened her hands. "I'd love to spin an elaborate tale in which I once abducted Conor Harkness's dog to traffic him to pelisse makers, and his sudden interest in Kline is just a tassel in his revenge master plan. But I think it simply has to do with the earning potential of the biofuel."

Tisha turned to me. "Rue, did Eli mention anything about Kline when you two met last night?"

"Hang on—Eli?" Florence's eyes widened. "You met *Eli Killgore* last night?"

If I'd been the fidgeting type, this would have been my time to squirm. Luckily, I'd long trained myself out of that kind of stuff. *Robotic,* I'd once heard another grad student whisper after I was cold-called in bio-nanotech class and neglected to display whatever the appropriate amount of distress was. *Stone-cold bitch,* my fellow ice skaters had said, because I was the only one not to burst into tears when our team missed the podium by a fraction of a point. "I did."

"How?" Florence scowled. "Was it a date?"

"Ha. A *date*." Tish waved her hand and ignored the narrow look I gave her. "That would imply a degree of emotional availability homegirl could only aspire to after a heart transplant."

It was true enough. I wasn't sure I'd ever been on a date—in fact, I was sure I had *not*. "We matched on an app, made plans to meet last night. Nothing physical happened." *Even if it feels like it did.*

My hookups were pleasurable but ultimately insignificant parts of my life, and with the exception of Tisha, who was my built-in safe call—*If you ever get abducted, I'm going to cheese grate the guy's dick and rescue you in no time*—I never discussed them. Everything Florence knew of my sex life came from Tisha's occasional jokes, but it must have still been a pretty thorough overview, because she seemed befuddled by the idea of me going out with some guy and *not* getting laid. "Why not?"

"Long story. Vince is involved."

"I see." Unlike other men, Vince was a frequent topic of conversation among us.

"What a dick," Tisha muttered. "I've let years of him parentifying you and holding you responsible for the utter fuckup your mother was slide, but now he's cockblocking you? Not on my watch."

"I guess a line has to be drawn," I murmured.

"Damn right."

"Did he say anything about me?" Florence asked, alarmed.

"Who?" I cocked my head. "Vince?"

"No, Eli. Did he say anything about Kline?"

"No. He . . . I don't think he knew I worked here." *Or did he?*

Florence's eyes narrowed. She parted her lips to add something, but Tisha was faster. "Listen, Rue, when you next see him—"

"I won't." I remembered the blossoming heat in my chest this morning, when I found myself wondering if a man would call for what felt like the first time in decades—maybe ever. The way he'd studied me last night, as if amused by his own inability to untangle me. His warm skin when I'd kissed him on the cheek, freshly shaven and yet already stubbly. "Not now that I know what he does."

"It might be for the best," Florence said slowly. "But not as easy as you think."

"Why?"

"Harkness is going to be here for a while. Contractually, they can ask to be briefed by the head of every research and development project. And they did." Florence picked up her tablet, tapped at it several times, and then held it out to me. On it, there was a list. And on the list, there was my name.

When I looked up, Florence's mouth was a thin line. I could read nothing in her voice as she said, "Eli Killgore will be doing some of the interviews."

5

A BIG ACCUSATION

RUE

I arrived just in time to see Arjun, the man I desperately wished would take Matt's place as my supervisor, step out of the conference room. He approached me with a smile, and bent his head to my ear to say in low tones, "I was nervous as shit to go in there, but they're decent."

"Who's *they*?"

"I forgot their names, honestly. Two of the dudes?"

A sixty-six percent chance of Eli, then.

"They're approachable," Arjun continued. "I was sure they'd be looking for reasons to say that everyone's position is redundant, but they seem genuinely interested in the science. Asked lots of questions."

"About what?"

"The scale-up stuff I've been working on. I got to complain

about the whole pH saga we had last quarter. The initial hydrolysis step. They got my pain."

"They understand hydrolysis?" I knew how arrogant the question sounded, but I couldn't picture a normie having a working knowledge of it. Then again, I barely spoke with non-Tisha humans, so what did I know?

"Oh yeah. I started giving them the crayon version, but they nipped that real fast. They must have some kind of chemistry background, because they know their shit. Maybe—"

"Are you Dr. Siebert?"

I glanced past Arjun's shoulder, at the person idling stiffly by the conference room. "Yes, I am."

"I'm Sul Jensen. Come on in." He was a square, stocky man who looked like he'd last smiled in the early 2000s. Not quite rude, but stone faced and glaringly uninterested in exchanging pleasantries. My first impression of him was probably highly similar to others' first impressions of *me*—with the caveat that serious, unsmiling men tended to be considered consummate professionals, while serious, unsmiling women were often written off as haughty shrews.

Oh well.

Sul Jensen's frostiness suited my inability to perform extraversion just fine. He gestured me toward the room, his movements jerky, with a slight animatronic quality, and I followed, bracing myself for impact.

Finding Eli Killgore inside didn't surprise me, not as much as the jolt of heat in my stomach. He wore black jeans and a button-down shirt, the sleeves rolled up to the tops of his strong forearms, and now that I saw him up close, I just couldn't reconcile it—the way he could be, at once, the man I'd met last night and someone completely divorced from that; the air of disheveled elegance as he riffled through a stack of papers, when a few hours earlier I'd thought him rough enough around the edges to cut deep and draw blood.

The glasses were certainly interesting. His face was already complex, a dissonant combination of rugged and refined, and with their frames added to the mix, there was suddenly one too many elements to parse. But there was something undisputably magnetic about him, something that could catch and trap. The fact that his attention was too focused on the papers for him to look at me felt like a small, temporary mercy.

"Sit?" Sul closed the door and pointed at the closest chair, like this was *his* house, instead of the conference room where Tisha and I held journal club and drank beer once a month. Resentment twitched in my belly.

"No, thank you," I said, and Eli . . . he must have recognized my voice. His neck straightened and his eyes rocketed to mine, widening behind the glasses.

I was ready for him. I met his gaze, watched the shock play on his features, savored the disorientation in his parted lips.

Yup. That's exactly what it felt like, seeing you up there.

Unhurriedly, I turned to Sul. "Florence mentioned that you wanted to see all team leaders, but I probably shouldn't be included. My position is nontraditional. I spend twenty percent of my time—one full day per week—working for Matt Sanders on regulatory compliance."

"Rue?" Eli said. Sul glanced at him in confusion, but I powered through.

"The rest of the time I lead my own project, unrelated to the biofuel tech."

"Rue."

"I do have a couple of lab technicians helping me, but aside from that I'm a team leader in name only—"

"*Rue.*" Eli's voice cut through the room, snapping the thread of my speech, forcing me to turn. He was staring at me, equal parts disbelief and a million other things.

"Yes?" I asked. It came out almost sweetly, and Eli seemed just as taken aback as I felt. He didn't spare a single glance for Sul. Instead he slowly took off his glasses, as though they might be the means through which he was conjuring me. The dull sound of them clicking against the conference table reverberated inside my bones, and so did Eli's soft words. "Leave us, Sul."

Sul looked between us, seemingly tempted to protest, but after a few beats, he left as rigidly as he'd come in—conspicuously leaving the door open behind him.

The room plunged into a long, unpleasant silence that ended only when Eli said, once again, "Rue." Not *What are you doing here?* Not *Why didn't you tell me?* Not *Did you know about this?* It was nice, since they would have been stupid questions, and I doubted either of us was a fan of those. "You seem less surprised to see me than I am to see you," he said.

"I had the advantage of standing in a crowd," I conceded.

He nodded slowly. Regrouping, or maybe just buying time to stare with hungry, eager, calculating eyes. Take in the shape of me in the light of this new day.

I doubted it flattered me.

"Rue Siebert," he said, seemingly more in control. Then repeated, "Dr. Rue Siebert," with the tone of someone who'd found the answer to a crossword cue.

Somewhere in his head, or at the very least on his phone, this man had a list of my sex preferences. He knew that I didn't enjoy penetrative sex, but didn't mind being held down. That I wasn't interested in threesomes or humiliating language, but I was open to incorporating toys.

I refused to be ashamed of what I enjoyed, but it still felt discomfiting. Like being ripped open.

"Did you know who I was when you contacted me on the app?" he asked, and I wished I could have scoffed or dismissed it as deranged paranoia on his part, but my mind had initially gone there, too.

This cannot be a coincidence.

Except, it could be. It had to be, because *I* had been the one to message him. *I* had chosen not to reveal my real name. *I* had given him my phone number. It put a real damper on all the conspiracy theories my mind wanted to craft.

"No. I didn't know Harkness existed until this morning. And I didn't . . ." I hesitated. "I didn't look up your full name. Not even last night, after." It had felt wrong, when he hadn't known mine. Plus, I wasn't used to this. Wanting to know *things*, about a man.

"Okay," he muttered, running one hand through his hair and leaving it no more mussed. Some kind of ceiling effect, clearly. "I didn't know, either," he said, clearly aware that I'd contemplated the possibility, as ridiculous as it was. If Eli had been inclined toward corporate espionage, I'd have been a terrible choice. I was utterly, fantastically irrelevant in the grand scheme of Kline.

And yet, here he was. Looking at me like nothing else existed in the world.

"It's okay. It doesn't matter." He made a gesture with his hand, and I noticed the number I'd scribbled last night on his palm. Just the faint, illegible shadow of it, like he'd washed his hands several times in the interim, purposefully avoiding scrubbing hard enough to erase all traces. "It changes nothing," he added.

"Nothing?"

"Between us." He smiled. That knockout, nice-guy, grown-up-surrounded-by-love-and-confidence-and-the-certainty-of-his-worth smile. "I'll talk to HR, but I don't think this causes any conflict of interest. We . . ."

He paused, so I cocked my head and took a curious step toward him, entering a new gravitational field. His body was not the reason I'd chosen to message him, but I couldn't deny that it was beautiful. Big frame. Full biceps. More what I'd expect from a pro athlete than from someone who sat behind a desk for a living. "We?" I asked.

He looked down at me, eyelashes fluttering. "You seemed interested in *we*, last night."

"I was." I bit the side of my cheek. "But last night I had no idea you were trying to steal the company I work for."

Abruptly, the temperature in the room dropped. Tension pulled, instantly hostile.

Eli's jaw twitched, and he took a step forward. His expression was outwardly amused, but his muscles were taut. "Steal the company." He nodded, making a show of considering my words. "That's a big accusation."

"If the shoe fits."

"Remarkably poor fit for a shoe." He held my eyes. "Did Harkness barge in wearing ski masks? Because *that* is what thieves do."

I didn't reply.

"Did we take the property of someone else without offering compensation? Did we obtain something through subterfuge?" He shrugged. With ease. "I don't think so. But if you suspect foul play, by all means. There are several authorities to which you can report us."

I thought of myself as a rational person, and rationally I knew that he was right. And yet, Eli being part of Harkness felt like a personal betrayal. Even though we'd barely spent an hour together. Maybe the problem was that I'd shared about Vince with Eli, shared more than I should because . . . because I'd liked him. I'd *liked* Eli, and that was the crux of it. Now that I'd finally admitted it to myself, I could let go of it. Of *him*.

How liberating.

"We didn't steal anything, Rue," he told me, voice low. "What we did was buy a loan. And what we're doing is making sure that our investment pays off. That's it."

"I see. And tell me, is it normal for the highest-ranking members of a private equity firm to be on-site interviewing employees?"

His mouth twitched. "Are you an expert on financial law, Dr. Siebert?"

"It seems like you already know the answer to that."

"As do you."

We regarded each other in silence. When I couldn't bear it any longer, I nodded once, silent, and turned around so that—

His hand closed around my wrist, and I hated, *hated* the scorch of electricity that traveled up my nerve endings at the contact. Even more, I hated how he instantly let go, as if he, too, had been burned.

What I felt was bad enough. The thought of Eli experiencing the same was a recipe for disaster.

"Rue. We should talk," he said earnestly, any pretense or hostility dropped. His fingers returned to my wrist. "Not here."

"Talk about what?"

"About what happened last night."

"We didn't even hold hands. Not much to discuss."

"Come on, Rue, you know that we—"

"Eli?"

We both turned. Conor Harkness was leaning in, palms against the doorframe, watching us with the air of a shark who could smell blood from miles away. His gaze focused on our closeness, on the way Eli's eyes seemed unable to let go of me, on his hand, still circling my wrist.

"A moment," Eli said.

"I need you in the—"

"A *moment*," he repeated, impatient, and after another raised eyebrow and infinitesimal hesitation, Conor Harkness was gone, and I remembered myself.

I stepped back from Eli, taking in the strong set of his brow, his beautiful blue eyes, the tension in his jaw. Someone had to put an end to this. Me—*I* had to put an end to this, because he clearly would not. "Goodbye, Eli."

"Rue, wait. Can we—"

"My number." At the door, I spun on my heels. "Do you still have it?"

He nodded. Eagerly. Hopeful.

"It might be better if you got rid of it."

Eli dipped his head and let out a silent exhaled laugh. I left the room, not quite sure where his disappointment ended and mine began.

6

A SHORTCUT HIS BRAIN DID NOT NEED

ELI

After the scene Hark had witnessed earlier today, it was no surprise that the first thing he asked when Eli let himself inside
Hark's Old Enfield home was: "What the fuck is up with the girl?"

"Woman," Minami corrected him distractedly. She was on
Hark's couch, feet in Sul's lap, frantically pressing buttons on the
PlayStation controller. Eli checked the screen, wondering whom
she was shooting dead.

Bafflingly, the game appeared to be about cake decorating.

"Right. Sure." Hark rolled his eyes. "What the fuck is up with
the *woman*?"

Eli ducked into the kitchen, which was spotless in a way only
never-been-used steel surfaces could manage. He helped himself
to a bottle of Hark's imported beer and returned to the living room.
"Just checking: If my answer were to be 'What woman?' then . . ."

"I would lose all my respect for you."

"I think I can handle that." He sat next to Hark with a grin. This was their routine when they all happened to be in Austin—increasingly less common as Harkness expanded. Minami and Sul on one half of the sectional, being disgustingly in love, and Eli and Hark on the other, being . . . *Disgustingly in love in your own manly, grunting way,* Minami had once said. She was probably right.

"Her name is Dr. Rue Siebert," Sul volunteered.

Eli lifted an eyebrow. "Dude, you have a budget of fifty words per day, and you use six of them to give me shit?"

Sul smiled, pleased with a job well done, and went back to massaging Minami's feet like the whipped traitor he was.

"What's up with Rue Siebert, Eli?" Hark asked, with the tone of someone who wanted an answer ten minutes ago. Eli saw no particular reason not to give him one.

"We matched online. An app. And met up last night."

Minami paused her game so forcefully, her thumb might need X-rays. "To . . . ?"

"Fuck."

"Actually, I knew that. I just wanted to hear you say it."

"Jesus, Eli. You rode her?" Hark asked, and Minami laughed.

"Good to see that after fifteen years in the US, Hark is still a living, breathing Irishism."

"Shut your bake, Minami."

Eli bit back a smile. "No one *rode* anyone, because she was having a rough night. But."

I wanted to.

I've been thinking about her nonstop for the past twenty-four hours.

I've been distracted, irritable, and horny, and I wanted to text her first thing in the morning. I decided it was best to wait since her phone looked busted and she might need to get another, and fuck, I shouldn't have hesitated.

Eli couldn't remember ever overthinking an interaction with a woman this much. And he'd been engaged.

"But?"

"No buts, actually. She's pissed because she thinks we're trying to take over Kline."

Minami gasped and clutched her throat. "Us? No *way*."

This time Eli couldn't hide his smile. Until Hark asked pointedly, "Is she going to be a distraction?"

"I don't know." Eli leaned forward, elbows on his knees, and stared at Hark with a hint of a challenge. "Do I *ever* get distracted, Hark?"

Hark's gaze narrowed. Thick, fat tension rose between the two of them—and then everyone burst into laughter. Even Sul's shoulders shook silently.

"I *just* remembered!" Minami clapped her hands. "That one time Eli fell asleep while *riding his bike*?"

"And the Semper deal?" Hark spoke as if Eli wasn't there. "He got so sucked up in it that he forgot to pick up Maya from overnight camp—way to traumatize her, asshole."

"The bike thing was at three a.m., after a forty-eight-hour experiment, and we all know that ninety percent of Maya's trauma was already there." He took another swig of his beer. Then, zeroing in on Minami, he drawled, "Also, if we want to talk about unfortunate driving mishaps, let's discuss that Missouri fair where you got a DUI on the bumper car rink."

"It was thrown out in court!"

"Or"—he pointed his finger at Hark—"that time someone sent

the entire Harkness mailing list a message about *pubic* liability insurance."

"Embarrassing," Hark acknowledged, "but not driving related."

"Or"—Eli circled to Sul—"the guy who forgot his vows in the middle of his wedding ceremony."

"I would like to be excluded from this narrative," Sul requested.

"Rein in your wife, then. If the marriage is even *legal*."

"Oh, it is." Minami beamed, tapping Sul's cheek with her socked toe. Some might have felt self-conscious about this level of PDA in their ex's house, but Minami had been reassured, over and over, that Hark didn't mind. Only Eli knew how much of a lie that was.

Silence dropped, comfortable, familiar, the product of years of being together in the same room, tireless and stubborn, always after the same goal. "Today went well," Hark said eventually. "Not like I'd imagined."

"How so?" Eli asked.

He shrugged a single shoulder, which meant that he *did* know, but wasn't ready to put it into words.

He would soon enough. He was the angriest out of all of them, and the one most likely to let his rage coalesce into something sharp and focused. Nine years ago, Eli had been drowning in student debt while epically failing at taking care of a tween, and Minami had been drowning in something else, something that made her struggle to get out of bed to brush her teeth in the morning. Hark had been the one to drag them out of their wallow, to go to the father he despised and ask—*beg*—for the firm's starting capital. "This is how we get even," he'd insisted, and he'd been right.

"We should name the firm Harkness," Eli had suggested a week before signing the paperwork, sitting at a table lined with his sister's homework sheets, wondering why she could solve college-level math but not spell *spaghetti* for her fucking life, wondering what the hell he should be doing about it.

"It's a shit name," Hark had grunted.

"It's not. It's just your father's name," Minami had said, not without compassion. "I think it has the sophisticated supervillain flair we're going for. Plus, what's the alternative? *Killgore?* Too on the nose."

Eli had given her the finger. Nearly a decade later, and look at them: still giving each other the finger on a daily basis.

"Dr. Florence Kline," Hark said now, like the words tasted bad in his mouth. "Have any of you talked to her yet? In private?"

"Sul did, for some minor logistical stuff. And the lawyers, of course," Minami added.

"Not you or Eli?"

She shook her head. And then, after a beat, "She reached out to me via email."

"And?"

"Just asked if we could talk. Alone. Outside of Kline." She rolled her lips. "I bet she thinks I'm the weak link."

"She clearly hasn't seen you open a jar of pickles," Eli muttered, and she smiled.

"Right? Kind of amusing, given that I'm the one most likely to push someone under a lawn mower."

"Did you reply?" Hark asked.

"Nope. I'd rather drink battery acid, thank you very much. Why? Do you think I should?"

Hark glanced at Eli. "Any benefits you can think of in Minami having a one-on-one with her?"

Eli mulled it over. "Maybe in the future. For now, let Florence sweat it a bit."

Minami nodded. "She's properly freaked out, I can tell. Despite her bullshit speech today, she must be hiding something."

"I, for one, really appreciate the collaborative environment she's trying to foster," Eli said dryly, which had Minami sniggering and Sul snorting.

"You know what it means, right?" Hark asked. "If she's hiding shit, it's not just from us, but also from the board. And she's dead certain that we won't find out."

"That's fine." Eli drained what was left of his beer. "I don't mind proving her wrong." The biofuel tech was as good as theirs. That was all that mattered.

"Tomorrow I'll meet with the core research and development team," Hark said. "Reassure them that they're not going to get caught in the cross fire."

"Yeah. They're not the ones who should be worried." Eli stood to leave. "I gotta get to Tiny. I'll see you—"

"Wait," Minami interrupted, eyes on her phone. "About Rue Siebert."

Eli halted.

It was a problem, knowing her name. It made conjuring her image that much easier—a shortcut his brain did not need. "We're still talking about her, aren't we?"

"Well, I googled her. Just to know what your type looks like these days."

Eli sighed.

"Apparently she was a student athlete just like you, which is interesting. But even more interesting is this fluff article that came up, from the *Austin Chronicle*." She held out her phone, and he read the title aloud.

"'Industry Mentor Offers Exciting New Opportunities for Women in STEM Who—' Is this about Florence?"

"Yup. She has become a champion of the underclass, clearly." Minami snorted. "Rue Siebert and Tisha Fuli were hired by her a year ago. Your girlfriend has no social media that I could find, so I looked up Tisha—who, by the way, is a *rock star*. Summa cum laude at Harvard, scholarships, awards. She's hot shit, and judging by her unlocked Instagram account, she and Rue might be besties. Look at this #tbt pic of them. They can't have been older than ten."

Eli did look. Rue was angular and gangly, eyes and mouth too big for her face, holding hands with her friend as they skated side by side in the middle of an ice rink. The contrast with the adult she had grown to be, tall and strong and *lush*, made Eli lean in for closer inspection, but Minami had already turned the phone away.

"Love Tisha's bio, by the way. 'No im not looking for a sugar daddy and ur not Keanu reeves stop DMing me.' Might steal it. Anyway, *this* is the biggie." This time she handed him her phone. It was a picture of three women hugging in front of a rainbow-colored brick wall. The redhead in the center was much shorter, a little older, and very familiar.

Since my little sister @nyotafuli STILL won't follow me back, I'm officially swapping her for Florence Kline. Best friend, best boss, and now best sister ever. Ilu, happy birthday!

He glanced back at the picture. Florence's and Tisha's grins were ray-of-sunshine wide. Rue's was more subdued, closemouthed, like she felt the need to hold back. Eli had to pry his eyes from her face.

"I see." He did. There was clearly a personal relationship here. Rue's words today, her hostility, suddenly made much more sense.

What *did* she know? What had Florence Kline told her about Harkness? About *Eli*?

"There's more. Guess where your future wife got her PhD?" Minami asked.

"Don't say UT engineering, please."

"Okay. I won't."

"Well, shit." Eli turned to Hark. They exchanged an uneasy look.

"Tisha and Rue, they might have better access to Florence than most other people at Kline," Minami continued. "We might want to keep an eye on them. See if they know anything."

Eli pinched the bridge of his nose. "Let me guess. 'We' means 'me'?"

"You know her already. Just saying."

"Going by what I walked into earlier today, I'm not sure it's an advantage," Hark pointed out.

Minami only smiled in a curious, secretive way. "Why don't you go to her lab tomorrow, Eli? See what she's working on. Snoop."

Eli's "*fuck*" was soft. "Is this some abortive attempt at match-making?"

"Who? Me?" She slapped her chest. "Never."

"Minami. Her work is not even related to biofuels. She's beyond irrelevant."

"What do we have to lose?"

Eli opened his mouth to protest—then closed it when he realized how unhinged his response would sound. He couldn't say it out loud, that he felt like he'd *already* lost something, or at least the possibility of it. That he needed distance from Rue. It was bullshit, since they *were* distant, miles apart on parallel streets, and inserting himself in her life was not going to bring them any closer. "You're *so* generous with my time."

"Give it two days, and she'll have you sleep with her for info," Hark muttered. Eli's hand, which had been patting his pockets in search of car keys, briefly stuttered.

"Poor Eli." Minami smiled, sly. "He's so put off by the idea. What hardship."

Eli flipped them all off half-heartedly and headed home, resigned. Minami always thought she knew best. Unfortunately, she tended to be right.

When he stepped into his kitchen, Maya was sitting at the counter, frowning into her tablet at something that could have been a physics article or Wattpad fan fiction. She was *that* eclectic.

"I made dinner," she said distractedly. "You hungry?"

He dropped his keys on the counter and tilted his head skeptically. "You *made* dinner."

She looked up. "I ordered Chinese on Grubhub—with your money—and I put it on one of the paper plates I bought—also with your money—because I'm sick of loading and unloading the dishwasher. Would you like some?"

He nodded, smiling faintly while she spooned rice and chicken out of the containers for him. His gaze wandered to the table, where she'd made a move in their ongoing chess game. He made a mental note to study it later and accepted his plate.

The home where they'd been raised had been foreclosed a decade earlier, but Eli had bought this one about six years ago, after Harkness had taken off, after he'd paid off his sizable debt, after he'd become financially stable enough to cover Maya's undergrad tuition wherever she chose to go. At the time, he'd figured Allandale would be a nice neighborhood to settle down in, with its well-kept parks and quiet atmosphere and good food. He and McKenzie had been talking about marriage, maybe not enthusiastically, but often enough that he'd taken for granted they'd eventually get around to it. They'd live here, and . . . hire a photographer for bucolic family photos, argue over the thermostat, grill every night. Whatever the fuck it was that happy, well-adjusted people did. They'd soak in the peace of the place, since their relationship was all about calm and harmony and restraint.

But here he was, living with his sister. His sister, who used to accuse him of crimes against humanity and couldn't get away from him soon enough at eighteen, had decided to "come back home" for her master's, her magnetic poetry stuck on his fridge and the syrupy scent of her candles cozy in the too-hot evening. As for McKenzie . . . Before today, Eli couldn't remember the last time he'd thought about her.

That was telling enough.

"Where's Tiny?" he asked.

"Not sure. *Tiny?*" Summoned, Tiny barged in through the garden doggy door and threw all of his one hundred and eighty pounds of mutt delight at Eli, who was just as happy to see him. Maya rolled her eyes. "He was busy pining for his one true love to return from the war. I just walked him, by the way. The ingrate. How was work?"

Eli just grunted, vigorously scratching the backs of Tiny's ears to his exact specifications. The reward was as close to a smile as a canine could physically achieve. "How was school?"

She grunted just the same, and they exchanged an amused look.

Look at us. Related, after all.

"Did you see Hark today?" Maya's tone was the personification of casual disinterest. Eli swallowed a snort and sat on the stool next to hers. "How is he?"

"Still not age appropriate for you."

"I think he's into me."

"I think it's a felony."

"Hasn't been for a while, since I am almost twenty-two years old." Tiny whimpered softly at Eli's feet, as though in agreement. Traitor.

"Yes. Fair point. Until you remember that when *Hark* was twenty-two years old, you had yet to achieve full control of your bowels."

She shot him a baffled look. "Do you think nine-year-olds use diapers?"

Yes. No? What the fuck did *he* know? He'd barely paid attention to her before she'd been shoved into his life. "This feels like a trick question, and I don't plan to engage with it."

"Seems kind of puritanical of *you*, someone whose entire download history is hiking trail maps, solitaire, and sex-forward dating apps."

His eyebrow rose. "Hark doesn't do relationships, either."

"That's fine. I don't want to marry him. I just want to—"

"Do not say it."

"—use his beautiful, former rower's body."

"She fucking said it," he mumbled. "Can you please not put in my head images that a therapist will have me reenact with dolls five years down the line?"

"But it's so *fun*."

"Listen, you are legally free to engage in orgies with people four times your age, but—"

"'But don't expect me to facilitate any of that,' I know, I know." She sighed. "How was the date last night?"

"It was . . ." God, it was so messed up that the only thing he could think of saying was, "Good."

Because it was true. Being with Rue, even just to talk, had been good. Wasn't that incredibly fucking pitiful?

"Will you see her again?"

He thought about the following day. "Maybe." He bent his head to focus on his food, then on Maya's recounting of her computational physics class, then on Tiny's soft snores rising up from his feet. And told himself that if he couldn't avoid Rue Siebert, he should at least try to think about her a little less.

7

NOT A CONDITION FOR ANYTHING

RUE

Meals were always tricky business for me, but none more than breakfast on days in which I planned to be in the lab for several hours. I couldn't skip eating, not if I wanted to avoid feeling like I'd pass out around midday. And yet, those days also tended to start very early in the morning, which meant a significant risk of oversleeping. Which meant no time for a sit-down meal.

Which meant a lot of fucking misery.

A normal person would have bought a snack at the vending machine or packed a sandwich. But I wasn't normal, not when it came to food: eating quickly, eating standing up, eating on the go, it all triggered some of my most cavernous anxieties. And I would have taken the hunger over *those* any day.

To eat I needed time and quiet. I needed to stare at my meal and know, *feel*, that more food would be waiting for me after the bite I'd just swallowed was gone. My issues were deep-rooted, multilayered, and impossible to explain to someone who hadn't grown up hiding expired Twinkies in secret spots, who hadn't discovered fresh produce only well into her teens, who hadn't fought with a sibling over the last stale cracker.

Not that I'd ever really tried. Tisha already knew, my therapist had pried out my history piecemeal over years, and I couldn't imagine anyone else caring about me enough to want to listen. After all, I hadn't been food insecure in over ten years, and I should have been over this shit.

Though clearly I was not.

That morning, I fucked up on a staggering number of levels: woke up late after a fitful night of sleep, let the hot shower boil my skin for far too long, went downstairs without my car keys, and finally met Samantha from quality assurance in the parking lot, who wanted to know if, in my opinion as "Florence's favorite," we were all soon going to be living in a tent below the underpass, like a big happy family. Eating was the last thing on my mind, and when I stepped into the lab I'd booked, I was twelve minutes late.

And *he* was there.

Parked on a stool.

Loose jointed and relaxed as he waited for me.

We regarded each other with equally masked expressions. Neither of us bothered to say hi or, god forbid, *How are you?* We just stared and stared and *stared* in the deathly early morning quiet, until his eyes began roaming over me, and his pupils got larger, and my skin began to tingle.

I wasn't proud of the way I'd acted the day before—not because he hadn't deserved to be called out on whatever Harkness was up to, but because I hated losing control. The world was a constant, full-on maelstrom, and my emotions were the one thing

I could govern. Eli Killgore looked like the kind of person who'd love to take that away from me.

"Why?" I asked plainly. Diplomacy was past us.

"I'd like to hear about the work you do." His voice was deep, more gravelly than yesterday. Not a morning person, either.

"Did you clear this meeting with Florence?"

His jaw tightened. "*I* did not."

"In that case—"

"Your general counsel did, though."

It was my turn to tense. "I'm about to start an experiment that will need constant monitoring. Your timing is not ideal."

"What's the experiment?"

I bit into my lower lip, and immediately regretted it when his eyes darkened. It felt dangerous, the two of us alone in the same room. *Again.*

"I've created a new type of protective layer for fruit and vegetables. It's an invisible substance that I put around produce. Then I measure whether it extends the shelf life of that produce in different types of situations."

"Such as?"

"Today, humidity. So I'm not sure I can—"

"What's the layer made of?"

This was pointless. I swallowed a sigh. "Its main ingredient comes from shells, but it's combined with lactic acid."

Eli's eyes shone with amusement; he was clearly laughing at me. Suddenly I was the Rue I'd always been: awkward, lost, unable to decipher the nuances of social interactions or to grasp *what the hell* people found so funny about what I'd said. Filled with the certainty that the world was in on the joke, and I'd once again failed to keep up. A beat too late. Out of sync.

Yet another unabridged summary of my life.

Except that the Eli I'd met the other night hadn't made me feel this way, not a single time. Which was the reason this hurt so sharply.

"Anything else you'd like to know?" I asked coolly.

"Yeah. How will you test the efficacy of this chitosan-and-lactobacillus-based microbial coating, Rue?"

I stiffened in surprise. How the hell did he even—

"Will you be using salt solutions?" he continued when I didn't reply. "Spraying?"

"I . . . we have a humidity chamber."

He glanced around with the air of someone who knew what a humidity chamber looked like and found none in his surroundings.

"In the adjacent room." I pointed at the door, half-hidden past the filing cabinet.

"Ah. How many hours?"

"Six."

"And how will you—"

"I'm here—I'm fucking here, sorry." Jay slammed the door open and burst into the lab. His green Mohawk flopped onto the left side of his head, nearly brushing his ear. "Sorry, it's that fucking piece of *shit*. Matt decided in the middle of the night that it would be so fun to kill me and fuck my corpse, so he asked for that allergen report before nine today. I was trying to finish it, didn't manage to, and now that *whoreson* is going to—"

Jay noticed Eli and shut his mouth so energetically, his teeth clinked. The entire spectrum of human emotions passed on his face—surprise, shame, resignation, guilt, anger, and, eventually, defiance. "He is a whoreson. I stand by what I said."

Eli nodded, as if expecting no less, and held out his hand. "I'm Eli Killgore. From Harkness."

"Jay Sousa." His tongue darted out to play with the ring on his lip. "Nice to, um, meet you?"

"Jay is assisting me today," I said. "The humidity chamber room is quite small, so if you want to stick around, space might be a little tight." *Go away. Leave me alone. It's for the best and* you *know it, too.*

Eli looked between Jay and me, sharp-eyed. "How much would you like to not have your corpse defiled, Jay?"

"Um. A normal amount?"

"I assume you were going to help log the data?"

"Yeah?"

"I can do that. Why don't you finish your report?"

Jay shifted on his feet. "Are you even capable of doing that?"

"Capable of using a click pen, you mean?"

Jay pondered the matter. "I guess you'll manage," he conceded. "Rue? Okay with you?" he asked, with something that felt a lot like hope.

I considered my options. Say no, let Matt unjustly use Jay as his whipping boy—probably to take out on an innocent bystander the fact that his HOA wouldn't let him install a garden gnome or similar shit—deal with Eli later. Say yes, let Jay turn in the report, finish my business with Eli once and for all.

"Okay with me," I said. Pain now, freedom later. Delayed gratification. "Come back when you're done. No rush."

Jay looked up to the ceiling, did the sign of the cross, and scurried out as quickly as he'd arrived, leaving me to wonder why god deserved gratitude when his salvation was clearly Eli's doing. Once we were alone again, I stepped closer to him and folded my arms on my chest.

I couldn't remember why I'd chosen to message *him* of all people. To avoid dick pics, name-calling, and requests to smell my used panties in lieu of hello, I only used apps that required women to make the first move—as at ease as I felt in sex-forward spaces, I liked to consent before seeing someone's junk. But my selection criteria were sparse: men who were local, who'd been marked as safe by other users, who were willing to accept my limits. Their looks had always been little more than an afterthought, and I'd had perfectly satisfying sex with guys who were objectively not handsome *and* with guys whose particular brand of attractiveness did little for me.

Eli, however. He defied categorization. There was something all-encompassing about his presence, something physical and vis-ceral and simmering that had a near chemical effect on me. He crossed his arms, too, and the bands of muscles under his thin shirt made me picture reaching out. Tracing. Touching.

"That was heavy handed," I said without inflection.

"It was," he agreed. Then something occurred to him. "Do you feel unsafe? Being alone with me?"

I thought about it. Considered lying and dismissed the idea. "No."

"Then I won't call him back." His shoulders relaxed. "At what intervals do you measure?"

I cocked my head to study him, reassessing his role here at Kline. Remembering Euler's number. *You know this man's phone's passcode, his opinions on anal sex, and his interest in negotiated kinks, but you have no idea where his knowledge of food engineering comes from. Nice work, Rue.* "Why don't you guess?"

His mouth twitched, indulgent. "I'm not your dancing bear, Rue. I don't perform on command."

"No. You like the element of surprise." His silence read like assent. He stared at my mouth until I asked, "What's your educational background?"

"Is it relevant to what we're doing here?"

I licked the backs of my teeth. Was it? Did I *need* to know? Or was I simply unjustifiably, uncharacteristically curious about this man I should be ejecting out of my life and mind? "I'm harvesting microbial growth every thirty minutes, and logging chamber conditions every fifteen, just to be safe." I tore my eyes from his complicated face and put on my lab coat, facing away from him. When I turned around, he was staring with hungry eyes, as though I were something to be eaten, as though I were peeling off layers instead of the opposite.

Jay's lab coat was larger than mine but turned out not to be big enough for Eli. He put on rubber gloves with the ease that only someone who visited a lab every day—or a serial killer—should have. I stared at his hands stretching the latex and thought, *This is dangerous. We shouldn't be together, he and I.*

"When I was eighteen or nineteen," he said, "I was working in a lab as an undergraduate RA, and I accidentally messed with the settings of the liquid nitrogen tank. My lab lost several important cell lines that were stored in it. It was a dumb mistake that set their research back by weeks." He bit the inside of his cheek. "Everyone assumed that it was machine malfunction, and even though I felt guilty as shit, I never corrected them. The following semester, I moved to another lab."

I blinked at him. "Why are you telling me this?"

His mouth quirked. "Just confessing something terrible to you. I thought it might be our thing."

I remembered the car. My admission that I'd wished Vincent would just disappear. How jealous of his sister he'd been. Then, inexplicably, I heard myself say, "I once accidentally crushed a mouse's skull while putting him in ear bars." I swallowed. "The postdoc who was supervising me said that it wasn't a big deal, and I pretended I didn't care, but I couldn't handle it. I haven't worked with lab animals since."

He didn't say anything, like he hadn't in the car, nor did he react in any other way. We just stared at each other with no disappointment and no recrimination, two terrible people with horrible stories, two terrible people who maybe were more interested in judging themselves than each other, until I couldn't bear it anymore. I quickly grabbed an apple, and didn't protest when he followed me to the humidity chamber. "Hot in here," he commented. "Is the seal broken? I can take a look."

"It's just a small space. And a constantly running motor. You ready?" I started my timer before he could respond.

Admittedly, he was a good assistant. He knew how, and where, and what to log, did not ask me to repeat myself, and never once looked bored while I took my measurements. He asked questions about my research, about the company culture, about the work I'd done before coming to Kline, but he seemed to know instinctively not to bother me when I was harvesting samples or diluting them with buffers.

For the most part, I answered. I was certain that his intentions were sketchy, but couldn't figure how sharing any of this information was going to harm Florence. The work we did was important.

Florence was a fantastic leader. Maybe it was perverse of me, but I wanted Eli to know how much Kline had accomplished. Whatever Harkness was trying to achieve may have been legal, but it wasn't *moral*, and I wanted him to feel like a villain for it.

But he didn't seem upset, only happy to listen and ask questions. Above all, he seemed fully in his element. Like a lab was where he belonged.

"How long has it been?" I asked, grabbing a fresh pipette tip.

"Less than five minutes—"

"I mean, since you were last in a lab."

He looked up from the clipboard, his face so blank, it had to be deliberate. "I haven't kept track."

"No?" He had. To the day. I was certain. "Why did you stop?"

"Don't remember." There were only two or three feet between us. His eyes were a light, predatory blue. Close enough that I could *touch* the lie.

"You don't remember why you decided that you'd rather be a hedge fund manager than a scientist?"

"You really don't know much about private equities, do you?"

My hand tightened on the pipette. "*You* know a lot about food engineering, though."

"And where does that leave us?"

"I don't think there is an us." My hand tightened even more—so hard, I accidentally pressed my thumb against the pipette's ejector, dropping the tip. "Shit." I knelt to the floor, bending my head in the cramped space.

"Here," Eli said. When I lifted my eyes, the tip was in the center of his open palm. When I lifted them higher, he was crouching in front of me.

Close.

Closer than he'd been since the other night.

"Thank you," I said, without reaching for the tip. Not sure whether I could trust myself.

Eli stared as though my skull were made of glass, and he could see the exact mess passing through my head. He took my free hand, gently pried it open, and deposited the tip on my palm.

Then, just as gently, a lot more slowly, he closed his fingers around mine.

There were two layers of gloves between our skin. I could barely feel his heat, but his grip was possessive, at once taking and making an offer. My heart beat in my throat, and heat rushed to my cheeks.

"Have you been thinking about this as much as I have?" Eli's voice was low and husky, scratchy with something I didn't dare to name, but could have easily picked out in a lineup.

"I don't know. How much have *you* been thinking about this?"

He let out a soft laugh. "A lot."

"Then, yes." I licked my lips, then almost begged him not to look at my mouth *that way.* "I wish there was a way to stop it."

"Rue." His Adam's apple moved. "I think there is."

"What's that?"

"You know."

I did. It was unfinished between us. What we'd started the other night was there, suspended, oscillating wildly. I could feel it in my teeth. "It's not a good idea."

"Is it not?"

"You're with Harkness. I'm with Kline."

"Yeah, well." He sounded self-deprecating, as though he wasn't a fan of his own feelings. "Right now, I don't give a fuck about Harkness. Or Kline. Or anything else except for . . ."

You. This. Us. My brain wanted him to say the words, and I hated that about myself. "I don't think I like you as a person. I certainly don't like what you're doing, nor do I respect it."

If he was hurt, he didn't show it. "Thankfully, that's not a condition for anything."

He was right, and I closed my eyes. Imagined saying yes. Imagined the process of working this *thing* out of myself, the act of sweating him out. How good it would feel, and the peace and satisfaction I'd feel later. I imagined hearing his name, seeing his face, and not having an instant, uncontrollable, incendiary gut reaction.

I could do it. If I had him, I could stop wanting him. It's what always happened. No repeats.

But. "Florence wouldn't like it."

For the first time, Eli seemed genuinely upset. "And that's what matters most to you? Florence's approval?"

"Not her approval. Her well-being."

He inched back his head. "Okay." This time he looked disappointed, maybe in me. But his tone was casual, the discrepancy jarring even as his fingers tightened lightly around mine one last time. "Then maybe you should know that—"

He didn't finish the sentence. Because the door opened without warning, and when we glanced up, Florence and Jay were staring down at us.

LIKE STARTING A NEW BOOK
BEFORE FINISHING THE ONE ALREADY
CHECKED OUT FROM THE LIBRARY

RUE

It wasn't what you think," I said later that night, spearing a green bean and dropping it onto the edge of the plate so abruptly, the clink echoed throughout the living room. My monthly dinners with Florence and Tisha were something I usually looked forward to, and fun, and pleasantly compatible with my onslaught of dysfunctions surrounding food and social situations.

Except that tonight I wasn't having much fun.

"It wasn't anything at all." I made my tone even, to avoid sounding like a five-year-old who'd wet the mattress after assuring her mom that no, she did not need to go potty before bed.

"What I heard is"—Tisha wagged a crab rangoon at me—"that you and Eli Killgore were engaged in a passionate, child-making embrace on the floor of the humidity chamber lab."

Jay. And his nosy, gossipy mouth. Even the guy who came to

refill the vending machines once a week had undoubtedly been apprised of today's events. The Kline WhatsApp group that I'd never bothered joining had probably already commissioned the fan art.

"There were no embraces."

"Child-making *without* embraces." Tisha stroked her chin. "The plot thickens."

"No child-making, either. We were looking for a pipette tip."

She deflated. "Sadly, the plot thins."

"You're a fully grown adult, Rue." Florence's voice was warm with understanding, but I could hear an edge of displeasure that she wasn't quite able to hide. "You don't have to justify yourself."

"Aside from the fact it took place in a lab and therefore consisted of highly unprofessional behavior that would prompt HR to put you through years of additional sexual harassment training." Tisha took a relishing bite, and I pointed my fork at her.

"Last year you dated that guy from legal, and had sex with him in at least three conference rooms."

"Man, this is *good*," she said around a mouthful of tofu.

"It would be best for me not to know about the abundance of fornication that goes on in my labs." Florence sounded pained. "Really, Rue, I wouldn't dream to tell you who to . . . You can do whatever you like." It was still there, that tinge of hurt and worry in her tone. "But."

"It could be your Mata Hari moment, Rue," Tisha added.

"My what?"

"That hot spy in World War One? Or Two? Or the Sack of Rome—I don't know *history*. What I mean is, you could sleep with Eli in exchange for information."

"*Deeply* unethical." Florence shook her head, amused. I was ready to let the matter drop, but she added, "You should be careful, Rue. Because of the kind of person he is."

"What do you mean?"

"Well." She took a sip of her bubble tea, collecting her thoughts. "Eli and his friends are Harkness, and you know what Harkness is doing to Kline. I simply think that anyone who feels free to take what's others' without consent in one context might just be willing to do the same in another."

My eyes widened at the implications. Would Eli really—

"Why did he seek you out? Did he want to know anything in particular?" Florence asked.

"Just an overview of my project. Generic info on Kline that he could have found online, or by asking literally anyone else." But he'd come to me. And hours later I still felt him buzzing in my skull, as if my brain wanted to hold on to precious fragments of him.

The way he pulled at the hem of his shirt to wipe his glasses clean.

His large hand around mine.

The acquisitiveness in his eyes.

And then Florence's interruption. She'd looked so surprised and hurt to see us together, and Eli had made things worse by staring defiantly at her until she'd averted her eyes. Retreating was such an un-Florence-like behavior, I couldn't make sense of it, nor could I understand why Harkness seemed to be treating Kline like their own personal playground.

And earlier today I'd decided to find out.

After work I'd opened the dating app and scrolled through men's profiles in search of someone who wasn't Eli—and then I'd given up without messaging anyone. It had felt wrong on some base, instinctive level, like a nagging prickle that I was forgetting something, like starting a new book before finishing the one already checked out from the library—something truncated that wouldn't allow me to move on yet.

So I'd moved on to do what I *really* wanted: to figure out Eli Killgore's deal. And the research had proven fruitful.

"Did you guys know that Minami Oka has a doctorate in chemical engineering from Cornell?" I asked. "She was at UT at some point, too."

Tisha gasped. "No shit."

"Did Eli tell you?" Florence asked, sounding a little alarmed. Maybe at the thought of us exchanging small talk. Or perhaps at the prospect of being invited, three months down the line, to a barefoot, lakeside ceremony in which I'd wed the guy who'd pilfered her life's work.

She might even be asked to officiate.

"No. I looked it all up online."

"Was Minami there when *we* were there?" Tisha asked.

"I'm not sure. UT is listed as a past institution on her profile, but it doesn't give years." I glanced at Florence. "Did she overlap with your faculty time there?"

She gave it a good think. "I can't remember. But it's a large department, and it's been years. If she was an undergrad . . . there are so *many* of them."

"Too many," Tisha muttered darkly, clearly flashing back to her TA years.

"Eli seems to know his way around a lab," I added. Despite having majored in finance at St. Cloud State University. He didn't list an MBA, which I thought odd. Then again, what did I know about the credentials necessary to start a *Pac-Man* company whose only purpose was to eat other, yellow-pebbled companies?

"For real?" Tisha was curious.

"More than some of the engineering undergrads I dealt with at UT, for sure."

"Well. Bars and lows and all that."

"Rue," Florence interjected, changing the topic, "anything new on the coating patent front?"

"Still on track to file the application next week." I gave Florence a small smile. "The agent suggested that I collect a couple new humidity data points. Other than that, we're doing great."

Florence's smile was much brighter. "Let me know if there's anything you need from me."

"What about what *I* need from you?" Tisha asked.

Florence's eyes widened in concern. "If there's anything—"

"Nutter Butter in the vending machines. It's been ages and I'm still *waiting*."

I nibbled on my green bean, and while Tish and Florence bickered over the worthiness of various types of snacks, I forced myself to enjoy the rest of the evening.

9

YOU SIMP

ELI

He'd lost his mind earlier that morning, and the results had been a bit of a fuckup.

Or a lot.

When he'd gotten in his car to meet Rue at Kline, he'd *not* meant to come on to her. But her physical presence in his space was heady, a little hypnotic. The room had been small, and she'd smelled amazing, like the shower she'd just had, and buffer solutions, and something sweet and personal and *her* underneath it all.

Not Eli's best moment.

But it was contained now. Her refusal had cooled things enough to knock some sense into him, and he was very relieved not to be tempted to drive to her house just for the privilege of doing something appalling, like . . . staring at her dark balcony windows and ordering himself to *not* masturbate furiously, probably.

Distance. He needed spatial, temporal, *physical* distance from her, and he was determined to carve it out.

"Good boy," he told Tiny when he brought back a stick Eli had never thrown. He tossed it, then smiled fondly as Tiny ran in the wrong direction to fetch it.

My best friend in the whole world, ladies and gentlemen.

As if aware of his dethronement by a dog who needed expensive drugs just to get his nails trimmed, Hark chose that moment to return Eli's earlier call. "What's up?" he asked.

The sun was about to set, but the sweltering heat still pressed down every cell of his body, and the dog park was infested with gnats. Tiny abandoned not quite fetching and began following trails left by other dogs with gusto. Pee-mails, Maya called them, and that's how Eli had started to think of them, too.

Maybe there *was* such a thing as hanging out too much with his sister.

"Eli?" Hark prodded.

"Sorry." He wiped sweat off his forehead. "I have news. What do you want first, the good or the bad?" Eli asked.

"I *hate* it when you do that," a voice screamed through the phone, fainter than Hark's.

Eli smiled. "Hi, Minami." He heard an approaching shuffle, and when she next spoke, she sounded much closer.

"If I know bad news is coming, I'm never going to be able to enjoy the good one. Best approach is: Tell me the good, allow me five minutes of happiness, and then break the bad. How many times have I explained this to you?"

The dry "feels like hundreds" in the background was quintessentially Sul's.

"In my defense," Eli said, "I didn't know you were there. Or that I'd been put on speakerphone without my permission. I could have opened with a murder confession."

"Is that the good news?"

"Nope." He sighed. "Kline did come through and gave me access to the documents we asked for. Financial, taxes, inventory, accounts, you name it."

A pause. "Color me surprised," Hark said.

"Me, too. Until—and we're entering bad news territory—I started going through them. They're all physical copies, approximately twelve forklifts' worth of paper. If an intern bought a Cobb salad six years ago, I guarantee you there's a twelve-page report on the aftertaste of the blue cheese. I asked accounting if they had digital files, and they politely implied that I could go fuck myself. Legal's reaching out to Kline's general counsel, but it's likely Florence just stopped listening to them. We'll need to get arbitrators involved."

"Paperwork burial. A beloved classic," Hark muttered. "Fucking grand."

"It would take ten people *weeks* to go through everything and figure out if any of the contract terms have been breached and we have grounds to take over Kline. I can't say for sure it's obfuscation, but there's no doubt it's a deliberate effort to buy time. If I had to guess . . ."

"What?"

"I have no proof of it. But my hunch is that Florence is busy trying to buy time while she contacts other investors to find the capital to pay back the loan, *before* we can discover that she's in breach. Because she knows that once we catch her in the act, the biofuel tech is ours."

Hark swore softly. Sul grunted. "Do you happen to have more good news?" Minami urged. "Like a good news Oreo?"

"You know I don't, because I told you in advance. Aren't you happy you were adequately prepared?"

"No."

"Well, Rue Siebert's microbial-coating project could be considered a piece of good news. It's at a very advanced stage and great for—"

"You simp," Minami muttered, and he didn't bother denying it. He *liked* Rue. The no-nonsense looks, the plain speaking, the way the air around her always seemed to turn a darker, more serious color, that constant sense of something simmering just beneath her still surface.

Her body.

I don't think I like you as a person.

Eli did not have a people-pleasing complex, nor a humiliation kink. Unlike Hark, he was also *not* a natural-born contrarian. When people—no, when *women* didn't like him, he was happy to leave well enough alone. He really didn't know what to do with this urge to change someone's mind.

Rue Siebert's mind.

Maybe he'd just ignore it. Let it fester inside him. That should be healthy.

"What are the lawyers estimating, time wise?" Minami asked.

"Weeks."

"Shit. Is there any other way to—"

"The board," Hark interrupted. "What about Kline's board? They might agree to force her to turn over the documents. They override the CEO."

"But Florence handpicked the board," Minami pointed out. "Remember I looked into that? They're all very loyal to her."

"Except for one."

"Who?" Eli asked. Tiny was galloping back to him, at last content with his explorations.

"Eric Sommers. I went golfing last weekend—"

Eli winced. On the other end of the line, a deep "ew" rose.

"What?"

"Could you just . . ." Minami sighed.

"Just what?" Hark asked defensively.

"I don't know, attempt to meet the private investment fund executive's stereotype with *slightly* less open arms?"

"I fucking like golf. It's a good sport."

They all made gagging sounds, and there was a muffled crash, as if objects were being thrown around. Eli stared at Tiny's happily wagging tail, pleased with his vastly superior company. Tiny would either *eat* or *shit on* the entirety of Hark's golf equipment.

"You guys can shove your sport prejudices up your asses—"

"Eli, should we bully him a bit?"

"It's the only way."

"—because Sommers invited me to his retirement party."

"Where?"

Silence. "At the country club where we play," Hark admitted begrudgingly.

More gagging sounds. Eli rubbed his eyes, wondering if an intervention was in order.

"Listen, pricks," Hark grunted. "We're going to his party, where we'll attempt to talk him into forcing Florence's hand."

"He's still just *one* person," Minami objected. "Would he even make a difference?"

"He has the ear of other board members. And he's about to have lots of spare time." A pause, in which Eli could imagine him shrugging. "I'm not saying it's foolproof, but he was an early investor, too. He might have a stake in this."

"Sure. Once again, nothing to lose," Minami agreed. "Though Sul and I are leaving for Atlanta tomorrow morning. Health check on Vault. Their Q1 numbers just finalized."

"Eli can be my date."

"Fantastic." Eli sighed and rubbed his eyes. "I do love country clubs and shots in the dark."

"I'll pick you up at seven. Wear something nice."

Eli hung up and bent to scratch the sweet spot on the top of Tiny's head, starting the long and tedious process of coaxing his dog back home. A night spent schmoozing some rich old man who thought plugging holes was a dignified activity was not in his Friday top twenty, but at least it'd take his mind off Rue for a while.

10

WE SETTLE THIS. ONCE AND FOR ALL.

RUE

My idea of a fun Friday night tended to include skating, or Tisha, or sleeping, and while I wasn't delighted to be accompanying Florence to an event that was unlikely to have any of those, the party came with one saving grace: the attire was formal, and I always welcomed a chance to dress up.

Large social gatherings full of people I wasn't familiar with were gas giants yielding infinite supplies of nightmare fuel, but at least I got to dig into my closet and show off my cat-eye routine—trained by the incessant pipetting, my lines were straighter than a bubble level. As in awe as I was of Tish's habit of showing up to the lab with Met Gala–like sophistication, I didn't have it in me to make that kind of effort on a daily basis, and never before 11:00 a.m. When I met up with men from the apps, I rarely bothered with makeup or nice outfits, aware the clothes would come off soon enough, and that nobody wanted my face goop smeared on their skin. It meant that most of my fancy dresses were beloved but unworn, and they'd only get a chance to come out for Tisha's wedding—because she was the kind of person who'd require three engagement parties and a handful of rehearsal dinners, but couldn't be bothered to tell her maid of honor what to wear.

And for parties like tonight's.

"You look beautiful," Florence told me when I slid in the back of the Lyft, fingering the shimmery fabric of my green cocktail dress—which had *pockets*.

"So do you. It feels like there should be some chromatic reason for gingers to look bad in pink, but that's not true at all."

She laughed. "This is why you're a better date than my ex."

"Because I tell you that you defy color theory?"

"That, and you're hopefully not sleeping with my accountant."

When I first met Florence, she'd been married to a guy named Brock who worked some bank-related job, had been her childhood sweetheart, and, according to Tisha, was "a total silver fox thirst trap." Privately, I'd always considered him a giant bag of dicks unworthy of scraping grime off the grout lines in a public restroom. I'd hated his brash, car-salesman humor, how he'd presumed to tell Florence how to run Kline, and the way he looked at my chest and Tisha's legs whenever Florence would have us over, like we were pieces of meat, little more than chicken wings delivered to his doorstep for his pleasure. I'd been relieved when they'd divorced, because Florence deserved better than him.

Then again, I was always a little too protective when it came to my friends, maybe because I had so few of them. Like in eleventh grade, when Cory Hasselblad had cheated on Tisha because she wouldn't sleep with him and I'd sprayed a bottle of Heinz ketchup through the grates of his locker. Or in college, when I'd filled two

Hefty bags with my roommate's ex's belongings after she'd caught him stealing money from her. My very few friends were the best people I knew, and I was ready to cut a bitch. Or, on one memorable occasion, a tire.

"Are you interested in doing that again?" I asked Florence. The AC in the car struggled against the summer heat. The sun would set soon, providing no respite, and yet downtown Austin had been buzzing for hours. I had no idea where we were headed, just that it'd be swanky.

"What? Sleeping with my accountant?"

"Dating. Maybe get married again?"

She laughed. "After all I went through to get rid of Brock? No, thanks. If I get lonely, I'll adopt a cat, like Tisha. Is that who she's with tonight?"

"I believe she's with Diego, the tech bro. But Bruce might be tagging along."

"I'm sure things will get wild." She gave me a sideways look. "What about you? Are you going to start dating again?"

A flash of Eli Killgore flooded my brain, and I swiped it away with the vehemence it deserved. "Technically . . ."

"Technically, it wouldn't be *again*, because you've never actually *dated*?"

"Correct." I shrugged as the car slowed down. Not only was interacting with others a challenge for me, but the feeling was mutual.

Why are you always so quiet?

If you smiled more, people would think you like them, and then they'd actually want to spend time with you.

I wish I was as cold as you. I love that you just don't care about stuff.

I'd been an odd child, then an odd teenager. Then I'd become, maybe as a result, maybe unavoidably, an odd adult. Tisha had been easy—*Want to jump rope with me?* she asked in first grade, and the rest smoothly unfolded—but as grateful as I was for my best friend, she was also a constant reminder of what I could never be. Tisha was smart, outgoing, quirky, imperfect in a way that was universally considered fun. I was *weird*. Cringe. Too awkward or too withdrawn. Off-putting. There had been whispers, snickering, and a conspicuous lack of invites by the same crowds that adored my best friend. Tisha had never chosen others over me, and she never hesitated to tell those who were openly rude to me to piss off. But we both knew the truth: people were inexplicably, never-endingly difficult for me. So while Tisha had boyfriends, friends, high grades, a promising future, I was busy with figure skating and faint hopes of getting the hell out of Texas, soon.

But then I *had* gotten out. And while being with humans hadn't been any easier in college, I'd realized that there was one type of social interaction I could rock. I may struggle to keep the conversation flowing, or fail at exuding the kind of warmth that made others want to be in my orbit, but some people did approach me. Men, for the most part, with something very specific in mind, something I discovered I found highly enjoyable myself. I didn't mind if they wanted to use my body, not if I got to use theirs back.

Only fair, I thought.

As college morphed into grad school and grad school bled into internships, meeting new people organically became harder. On top of that, lots of men my age seemed to be looking for something more. Shortly after joining Kline, I had some fairly mediocre sex with another team leader at the company, and was confused when he emailed the following day, asking me out for dinner.

I must have gotten better at hiding the way I am, I thought. I briefly let myself imagine saying yes, and the scenarios rolled through my head like a movie. Me, frantically trying to keep up the pretense of being an appealing, easygoing person and not just dozens of neuroses in a lab coat. The dismay I'd feel when my ability to fake it finally reached the end of its rope. His disappointment after my mask slipped, showing how socially inept and messed up I was. The potential for hurt was bottomless, and I didn't even *like* the guy.

Sticking to the apps and avoiding repeats seemed like the better course of action.

"Is this the place?" I asked Florence when the Lyft came to a stop outside of a manor-like building.

"Yeah. We won't stay long, just an appearance. But he has an ego and would notice if I didn't show up."

"There's nowhere else I need to be. I'll find a nice corner and wait for you."

Florence squeezed my hand over the leather seats. "You take such good care of me."

"You do the same."

I'd never been to this part of Lake Austin, but I recognized the name of the club from some of the charity drives Mom would take us to as kids, to stock up on hand-me-downs and school supplies. It was the sort of fancy place frequented by people who loved prenups and air-kisses, where folks like me should set foot only on select, philanthropy-themed occasions. I spotted an easel at the entrance, and on top of a picture that could have been the stock photo for an investment banker, the words *Happy Retirement, Eric* in handwritten calligraphy. Florence signed the guest book, but I gave it as wide a berth as I could.

The crowded reception area was full of suits and evening gowns. A small band was preparing to play, and waiters weaved through the crowd, carrying large trays of drinks and appetizers. My stomach clenched at the idea of eating *anything* among these people.

"There is Eric," Florence said, pointing at where the stock photo held court. "I'll introduce you. He'll say, 'You're too young and beautiful to be in a lab all day,' or some shit—sorry in advance."

He didn't say that. But he did tell me that if he'd "known engineers came in this pretty shape," maybe he "would have switched majors." Because I loved Florence, and Kline, I smiled amiably down at him, and didn't mention that I'd have reported him for sexual harassment without hesitating. In my high heels I brushed six feet and relished his obvious discomfort when he had to crane his neck to utter his crap.

While he and Florence chatted, I glanced around, trying to be discreet in my boredom. Then Sommers's tone switched to delighted surprise. "Ah—you came! Look at you!"

I turned to find Conor Harkness, and my heart sank.

"No, sir." His smile was all charm. "Look at *you*."

He had a slight accent—Irish, according to Tisha, who'd spent a summer in Dublin for a research fellowship. My first impression of him had been of someone a few years older than Eli, but now that I studied him up close, I could tell that he was just prematurely graying. He had a magnetic presence, something I could tell even without being a victim of its pull. Men and women around us turned to glance at him, eyes lingering, and he seemed accustomed to having that kind of effect.

He and Sommers hugged like father and son, which they could

easily have been, given the "white man with money who summers in New England" energy they both exuded. "Ladies, this is Conor Harkness, a dear family friend of mine." Sommers grinned as he made introductions. "So glad you made it, Conor. Do you know Florence Kline, and . . ." He stared blankly at me, my name forgotten.

I did *not* come to his aid. *Come on, Eric. I thought we had a thing.*

"Um, was it Rose . . . ?"

"Rue," a deep, familiar voice said from beside Harkness. "Dr. Rue Siebert."

My lungs turned into concrete.

"Ah, perfect." Sommers rubbed his hands. "I see you all know each other."

"You might be the odd man out, sir. Have you met Eli Killgore? He's a partner at Harkness."

He was here. Standing right *here.*

"I have not—nice to meet you, son. Do you happen to play golf?"

"I'm more the hockey type," Eli said affably, southern accent on broad display. In the soft lights, his eyes seemed as dark as my own. I couldn't tear my gaze away.

"Well, you look it." Sommers admiringly took in his shoulders, broad in the three-piece suit. "I grew up in Wisconsin, and used to play, too. Then, of course, I got old."

"I feel you. Used to get in the most vicious fights on the ice and go back to the rink the next day—then I hit thirty, and now my back hurts before I even get out of bed."

Sommers's laugh was genuine. Conor Harkness was smooth and powerful, cutthroat in a sophisticated way that was clearly meant to appeal to Sommers's rich side. Eli, on the other hand, was a man's man. An outwardly simple, nice guy who used power tools and rescued kittens from burning houses and knew statistics about the NFL draft. Appealing for a whole other set of reasons.

I suspected they'd been perfecting the routine for years. In fact, I was ready to bet my patent on it.

"This is going to hurt," Harkness said, suddenly serious, "but Eli played for St. Cloud."

"Huskies." Sommers shook his head. "I'm a Fighting Hawk myself."

Eli nodded thoughtfully. "Sir, I think this conversation is over."

Sommers laughed again, delighted. "Tell you what, son, hockey sticks and golf clubs ain't that different. How about this Sunday I teach you a few moves?"

Eli's tongue roamed the inside of his cheek as he pretended to consider it. "Can't be seen walkin' away from a fight with a Hawk, can I?"

"Damn well you can't."

It was the kind of easy interaction that had me feeling superfluous and out of place, like I'd accidentally wandered into the men's locker room. Same old boys' club, now in Technicolor. Beside me, Florence was forgotten. I'd never even existed.

"Conor, I need to introduce you to my wife. I told you we stayed at your father's resort when we went to Ireland, right? We had dinner with him and his wife a couple of times."

"Oh, if she had *two* dinners with Da, I absolutely need to give her my deepest apologies."

It didn't sound like a joke to me, but Sommers chortled. Florence emanated gory, murderous energy. "Florence, you haven't met my better half, either, have you?"

"Not yet, no," she said sweetly. Ready to snap.

"Come on, then, or I'll be in the doghouse. I was just telling her about Kline the other day . . ."

They drifted away while Sommers rambled on, unaware of the strife in his unlikely trio, and after an everlasting, stretching moment, it was just the two of us.

Eli and me. Alone in a room full of people.

The charcoal three-piece suit fit him aggressively well, and not just because of the tailoring. There was something about the straight line of his nose, the curl in his hair, the slant of his brow, that matched and enhanced this kind of attire. Somehow, he was as comfortable in this environment as he'd been in my lab.

I simply did *not* understand this man.

He stepped closer, eyes looking right into mine. "Well," he said, in his deep, calm voice, and I didn't reply, because—what was there to say?

Well.

Did you go to college on an athletic scholarship?

I wish I'd never messaged you on that damn app.

Dressed this way, you look different. Less like my *Eli, and more like the kind of person who—*

My Eli. What the hell was I thinking?

"What are you doing here?" I asked.

He sighed. A waiter stopped to offer us glasses of . . . something. Eli took one, held it out to me, and then drank it in a single swig when I shook my head. "Same thing you and your boss are doing."

Schmoozing a Kline board member. Fantastic. "Did you know we'd be here?"

His mouth twitched. "Despite your impression of me, I don't

know *everything*." His eyes slid down my body, following the shimmery flares in the green fabric. They seemed to remember themselves halfway through, and abruptly skittered back to my face.

We couldn't just stay here, in the middle of a crowded room. Staring in silence. "Are you really going to play golf with him?" I asked.

"Probably. Unless the Virgin Mary appears to Florence in a fever dream and orders her to turn over the documents we need."

"I believe she's an atheist."

"Golf it is, then. Or do *you* want to talk her into it?"

"Me?"

"Why not, if Kline has nothing to hide?"

I snorted softly. "Why would I?"

"To spare me from the dumbest fucking sport in the universe?"

I smiled. Then my amusement darkened. "He's disgusting."

"Who?"

"Sommers."

"Yeah. Most men who are his age and wield his power are."

"Doesn't give him a pass."

"No," Eli agreed, with the tone of a choir who wasn't sure why they were being preached at. "Believe me, I want to see them crash and burn just as much as you do."

"Sure you're not one of them?"

Emotions passed on his face, all too fast to decipher. Then he started, unhurried: "My mother had a beautiful silver ring, one of those priceless heirloom pieces passed down for more generations than I could count. All the women in my family, that kind of stuff. When Mom died, I took the ring and set it aside, thinking I'd give it to my sister when she was old enough. But then, a little while later, she really, *really* wanted to go on a trip with her friends, and

I—I just didn't have the money to send her, you know? So I told myself, easy fix. I'll pawn the ring, and then repay the loan on time." His smile was mournful. I didn't need him to spell out the ending for me. "A few months later, she brought the ring up. Asked me if I knew where it was. And I pretended to have no idea what she was referring to."

I looked at his open, unflinching eyes, and wished I could ask, *How old were you?* and *How did your mother die?* and *Why do you keep doing this, baring the worst, most vulnerable and squishy parts of yourself to me?* Instead, what I did was bare something of mine. Something dreadful. "When I was eleven, I stole thirty-four dollars and fifty cents from a drawer in my best friend's house." I forced myself to hold Eli's gaze through the shame of it, just like he'd held mine. "They never locked anything when I was around, because they trusted me. They treated me as their own. And I stole from them."

He nodded, and I nodded, a tacit agreement that we were both terrible people. Telling terrible stories. We'd let our masks slip enough times that they now lay shattered on the floor, but it was okay.

We were okay.

Then the band began playing, and the understanding between us snapped. Eli returned to his amiable default setting as the notes purred softly, shaped into something soothing and smooth that perfectly matched the blandness of the gathering. Several couples began swaying.

"We should dance," Eli offered. There were no tells that he was joking.

"Should we? Why?"

He shrugged, and abruptly he seemed lost, as uneven as I always felt in his company. "Because I like your dress," he said, nonsensically. It occurred to me, for the first time since our meeting three nights ago, that maybe he didn't want this, either. Maybe he, too, was desperately fighting off this inexplicable attraction between us. Maybe his success was just as abysmal as mine. "Because *I* like *you*. As a person." His eyes were teasing all of a sudden. Warm. "Even if you don't like me."

"You don't know me," I pointed out.

"No." He offered his hand. *I want to touch you, though,* that outstretched arm seemed to say. When our fingers met, the electricity thrumming between us felt like free fall and relief.

"Okay, then."

He didn't plaster my body to his, and I was glad, not sure whether I'd have been able to take that much contact. My dress was long sleeved and high backed, offering few points of possible skin-on-skin contact. But his hand enfolded mine, and when his big palm ran down my spine, our breaths hitched at the same time.

"I can't remember the last time I danced," I murmured, mostly to myself. Not like *this*, for sure. It was barely related to the music, just an excuse for people to stand closer than appropriate.

"You don't spend your Friday nights on dinner cruises?"

"Do you?"

He tut-tutted. "You know where I spend my Friday nights, Rue."

We fit well. Because of our heights, likely. I could smell the skin of his neck, clean and spice and something a little dark. "Do you really meet a different woman every Friday night?" It was an unexpectedly dismaying idea. What did I care if—

"Excuse me," someone interrupted us, and we instantly took small steps back from each other, recovering the distance that had drifted closer. It was a middle-aged woman, pointing at the camera she was carrying. "May I take a picture of you two? It's for Mr. Sommers's retirement album."

The idea of being in any part of Eric Sommers's life repelled me on a visceral level. Eli, too, apparently. "You don't want our picture," he said amicably. "We both met Mr. Sommers ten minutes ago. It'd be a waste of space."

"Oh." The photographer frowned, then picked herself back up. "You're just such a beautiful couple." She left for more receptive pastures, and Eli gathered me close once again.

"She's right," he murmured softly.

"About what?"

"You do look beautiful." He didn't sound happy about it.

"It's the dress. And the makeup."

"No. It's not." His eyes lingered on me, then shifted away. I couldn't bear the silence.

"Maybe we have displeased the jester god of hookups, and he won't stop throwing us together until we sacrifice a quail at his altar."

"I don't think *that's* what he wants from us," Eli muttered under his breath. "And why is the jester god of hookups a dude?"

"I'm not sure, actually."

We exchanged an amused look. A beat too long, and it was my turn to glance away and change the topic. "You're trying to turn the board against Florence, then?"

"Nope."

"You already admitted to that."

When he shrugged, the ropes of his deltoids shifted under my fingers. *Backache, my ass.* "What do you think the purpose of a board is?"

I'd asked Nyota the very same question that very morning, and received an only mildly disdainful response. Or maybe Nyota just came across as nicer via email. "They oversee. Make strategic decisions."

"You've been reading. Nice."

"Quite patronizing of you."

"No, I . . ." He gave me a surprised look. "I'm sorry. It wasn't my intention. But I did have the impression that you don't concern yourself with anything admin related." I didn't like how correctly he had me pegged. I was in the industry for the science, and the games of thrones were beyond my pay grade. "Regardless of what you think of Harkness," he continued softly, palm flexing on my back, "there's no denying that CEOs need accountability and oversight from people with relevant experience."

"Kline is Florence's company. She knows what's best for it. People like Eric Sommers know nothing about science."

"No. But it's not just about Florence and her petri dishes anymore, is it? Kline has a staff of three hundred and sixty-four."

"And?"

"One bad decision can take away the paychecks of three hundred and sixty-four families."

I couldn't disagree with that. But I also knew Florence, whose actions were rational and well thought out. I wished she could be here to list them for Eli.

As if she'd been summoned, my phone buzzed with a text. "Excuse me," I told him, slipping it out of my pocket.

Florence: **You okay? I'm stuck with Sommers and his wife. Pls tell me Eli Killgore is not harassing you.**

Rue: I'm fine. Eli and I are just making stilted conversation.

Florence: Just excuse yourself and walk away from him. He CAN-
NOT be trusted.

I know, I thought, and suddenly the hall was suffocatingly hot.
"I need some air," I said.

Eli pointed somewhere I couldn't quite see, and when I hesitated, his hand found my lower back and pressed forward, guiding
me firmly through the throng, out to a stone balcony. It gave onto
a small courtyard, and a pool, and what looked like—

"Fuckin' golf courses," Eli muttered. A laugh bubbled out of
me, clearing my head. For once, the temperature was bearable, the
night balmy and cool on my skin. Muffled through the glass doors,
even the music seemed almost palatable. I leaned against the wall,
tilting my head to take in the starry sky. Eli did the same with the
high railing, facing me. He looked idle, but I knew he was not, and
the app's checklist flashed in my mind.

Kinks? a box asked, and he'd answered, *If negotiated.*

I was dying to know more about all of that. But Florence was
right—he couldn't be trusted.

"Has your brother been leaving you alone?" he asked.

I nodded.

"Do you have a contingency plan in case he shows up at your
apartment, or at Kline, or at your gym?" His voice was gruff. Like
he wished he hadn't been asking, but couldn't help himself.

"Can't believe I fooled you into thinking that I'm the gym
type." It was a half-baked attempt at teasing, the kind he'd responded well to during our first meeting, but his expression was
serious. A strict lab supervisor, demanding to know why my bac-
teria culture was suddenly giant-blobbing all over the city. "I've

asked a friend—who's a lawyer—what my options are. I don't have a plan, though."

"Make one," he ordered. And then shook his head, massaged his eyes, and repeated more gently, "Maybe you should make one."

"It's not that simple."

"You need someone to call if—"

"What about I call *you*?" I joked.

"Yes, please. *Please*, fucking do that. Do you want my number now, or . . . ?" He stared, waiting for an answer. And then his eyes softened. The breeze picked up between us, and he kept looking, looking, looking.

Looking.

"It's unsettling when you do that," I said softly.

He turned away, chest heaving. "I'm sorry." His Adam's apple moved. "I forget to look at other things, when you're around."

"I'm sure I do the same." *I feel it, too.*

He huffed out a silent laugh. "Has this happened to you before?"

I shook my head in a first, instinctive reply, then forced myself to slow down and think about it. I'd been attracted to men before, but attraction had seemed like a conscious choice on my part, a feeling to chase and feed. Generic. The product of focus and cultivation, more than this current that seemed to rejoice in sweeping me under. "Not like this. You?"

"Me, neither." His long fingers drummed on the metal rail, the rhythm almost meditative. "You know what's funny? A while ago, I almost got married."

"Oh." I pictured the kind of woman someone like Eli might fall for, but my mind could only conjure vaguely alluring traits. Smart.

Socially adept. A nice wholesome girl, willing to tame that hungry undercurrent of impatience in him. Proud builder of a solid investment portfolio, able to gently but firmly call him out on his passion for brain-injury-inducing sports at dinner parties. "I'm sorry," I said, and when he laughed softly, I added, "No—I wasn't trying to be a smart-ass. But 'almost got married' implies that something went wrong."

"It definitely didn't work out, but it was for the best. I think she'd agree, too. But since I met you, I've been thinking . . ." The sentence fizzled out. Eli glanced toward the city lights. The occasional skyscraper.

"What?"

"I tried to imagine a reality in which she and I had gone through with it. I'm still with her, I love her, we're a family, and . . . and then I meet you by chance. And this thing between you and me, it's there." His eyes roamed the landscape, then landed on me. Contemplative. "I keep thinking about how fucking tragic it would be. For me. For *her*. I've never even been tempted to cheat on a partner, but this pull, it would still be in my head. *You* would still be in my head. Do you have to go through with it, for it to be cheating? How would I deal with . . . what would I do with all of this?"

He pointed at himself when he said *this*, but I knew he was referring to the gravitational energy between us. We were both caught in it.

"I think, the same way we're dealing with it right now," I said, trying to sound dismissive. Falling short. "Nothing is going to happen between us, even if you're not married. You're trying to take over my friend's company. That's not something I'll ever be able to overlook."

"Yeah."

But what if this chemistry between us was a once-in-a-lifetime opportunity? What happened when the person who tore you apart was not the person you'd chosen to cherish? My concept of love was far from idealized, but this still seemed crucifying.

It's all in your head, I told myself, but it was a lie. It was, at the very least, in *both* our heads. And now would have been a *really* good time for some elderly lady wearing an opal brooch to come out and interrupt this conversation, because Eli and I were starting to be absorbed in each other, and a reckless idea was germinating inside me, growing stronger by the second.

"Can I try something?" I asked, barely audible. He heard, though.

"Try what?"

"I'm not sure yet. Can I?"

That half smile again. "Knock yourself out."

I took a step forward, until the toes of our shoes nearly touched. I remembered the powerful shiver that had raked through me the other night, when I'd pushed up and kissed his cheek. The memory had to be magnifying the real thing, and a do-over would prove it and break the spell.

If I lifted my hand to his face, like this.

And traced the high line of his cheekbone with my thumb.

And cupped his freshly shaven cheek in my palm.

If I touched him for seconds, or maybe minutes, and despite his heat, his darkening eyes, the wild, blistering feeling that pumped into me . . . if despite all of it we managed to still walk away from each other, then—

With a guttural sound, he pushed my back into the wall of the balcony, so fast that I found myself instantly dizzy, held upright by two things: the stone and Eli's strong body.

He didn't kiss me. Instead his hand wrapped around my jaw, and his thumb pressed into my lower lip, slow, inexorable. I had all the time in the world to push him away, but found myself urging him on.

Eli.

Anyone could find us.

But whatever you are about to do, do it anyway.

"Your damn mouth," he murmured, "is the most obscenely lovely thing I've ever had the burden of seeing."

The kiss that came after was open mouthed and unbound. We exhaled against each other's lips, and when my hands closed around his nape, Eli groaned low in his throat. I moaned when he broke from me, but he simply found the hollow of my neck, the valley behind my ear. "I just want to make you come. Maybe come in the process, too. It's *all* I fucking think about," he said roughly. He nipped at my clavicle through the thin fabric of my dress. "But we're on different sides of a fucking takeover, and apparently that's too much to ask."

I lost myself in the weight of his body against mine, his grip on my hips. It was a new, different kind of pleasure, at once drugging and screaming. He licked into my mouth, and I did the same to him, trying to remember if anything had ever felt like this.

"It's disconcerting." His breath was hot on my cheek. "But in the past seventy-two hours, I've found myself thinking over and over that we could fuck however you wanted. For however long you wanted. Wherever you wanted. I'd consent to any and all demands, and it'd be so good that you'd probably just ruin me for the rest of my life, and I'd just sit there, grateful." He let out a laugh. "Rue. It's humbling, how bad I want you." His thumb stroked my nipple. It was instantly hard, and we both shuddered into another rich, frustrated kiss. Because *this* wasn't close enough.

"If you think that this is easier for me," I gasped. "If you think that I want it any less—"

"No." His hand trailed up my thigh, gathering my dress in its wake. His fingers were as shaky as my knees felt. "It's not a game. Not for you, and not for me." He reached the elastic of my underwear, lingered, and he could do—whatever. Anything. In that moment, I'd have let him do anything, begged him for something I didn't even know. His thumb slid to the inside of my thigh, brushed against the cotton covering my mound, discovered how wet it was. He hummed his approval in my mouth, and when he found my clit, he drew one single, slow circle over it. He'd done barely anything, but the pleasure was so close, I was hurtling toward it anyway. I wanted this *done*. And Eli did, too, which meant that we—

Suddenly, I was cold. Because Eli had taken a step back and was taking another.

Trembling, I watched my dress drape over my thighs once again, feeling bereft.

"Not here," he said, shaking his head as if shrugging off a haze. My lipstick was smeared on his lips. "And not like this."

Silence settled between us. *Where, then? And how?* I didn't ask out loud, but he answered anyway.

"Tomorrow," he rasped. He moved closer, and I could once again feel his heat. His hand rose to my cheek in an involuntary twitch, then pulled away, as if Eli was scared by what he might do. By his lack of control. "Seven. In the hotel lobby. You know which one."

I swallowed. "I don't—"

"Then *don't*. It's your decision." He was close. I *hoped* he'd kiss me again. I *needed* him to kiss me again. "But, Rue, if you come, we settle this. Once and for all."

He tore his eyes away and stalked back inside.

I was alone on the balcony, chest heaving, hands unsteady in the jasmine-scented night air.

11

WE WORK IT OUT OF OUR SYSTEM, AND NEVER THINK ABOUT IT AGAIN

ELI

He had no idea whether Rue would show up.

All signs pointed to no—chief among them, the fact that she saw him as a villain, bent on robbing her mentor for his own diabolical amusement. And yet, Eli had managed to foolishly hold out hope until ten minutes past seven. At which point, in the very hotel lobby where he'd first laid eyes on her, he had to face the truth: however out of control his attraction to Rue might be, she was coping with hers far better. And damn him if he wasn't fucking envious.

His draft beer was still half-full, and he didn't hurry to finish it. He had nowhere to be, and since Rue was going to be all he thought about anyway, he might as well do so in a place that reminded him of her, where he could nurse his foul mood just as thoroughly as his drink.

The obvious distraction would be to find someone else. There were apps, or the old-fashioned ways: bars, colleagues, friends of friends, who'd help him exorcize the last woman he should be taking up with. But Eli didn't need to try it to know that no one else was going to be *enough*. He would rather go home on his own, catalog everything he knew about Rue Siebert, and jerk off like the pitiful loser he clearly was.

"It's a bad idea," Hark had told him the night before, driving home from the party. "And you know that."

"What is?"

Hark had rolled his eyes. "Come on, Eli. You look at Rue Siebert like her pussy tastes like beer. Stop pining."

"You're the one who sent me to her the other day. And I don't *pine*."

"Then why are you being like this? Jesus, you've been in actual relationships and never lost your mind. What's so different *now*?"

Did you look at her? he'd wanted to ask. *Tonight? Did you hear her voice? Did you see her expression when she first noticed me? Did you see her* mouth?

"I'm not saying she isn't beautiful." Hark. Reading his mind. "And she obviously has that energy you like—"

Eli had laughed. "The *energy* I like?"

"Hyper-competent. Mysterious. 'I scored better than you on the quiz, and I could kill you with a pencil' energy."

"Not *one* of the women I've been with was mysterious. Or murderous."

"Because you used to know better."

"Yeah, fuck off," he'd said mildly. "Nothing's happening with her." A long pause. "I just want to fuck her. We're not going out for milkshakes or planning a coastal town weekend."

Hark had dropped his head to the steering wheel. "Don't do

any of it. We *are* going to take Kline, and she's going to fucking hate you for that. She already does. Plus, she chose to put her trust in Florence Kline, which clearly indicates shit judgment. *Who* would do that?"

They'd exchanged a dry, self-commiserating glance. "Three dumb assholes, that's who," Eli had muttered.

Twenty-four hours later, he could admit that Hark was right. His best bet was to avoid Rue. Get her out of his—

"Eli."

He looked up. She stood less than three feet away.

"Hi," she said.

The green dress and complicated hairdo from the night before had been punch-in-the-gut, spank-bank-directory material. Tonight she was a completely different person: plain white T-shirt tucked into jeans, no makeup, and . . .

Still a punch in the gut. Still spank-bank directory. He wondered if there was a version of her that wouldn't be.

"I'm sorry I'm late. I . . ." She shrugged.

"Couldn't make up your mind?"

"Something like that." She climbed onto the stool next to him, lips curled in her small non-smile. "Then I did. Figured that if you were still here, maybe it was fate."

"You don't believe in fate."

"Never have. You?"

"I think it's all bullshit."

She was quiet, that silence full of stares and pulled strings simmering between them. "Tomorrow. Are you still going to play golf with Eric Sommers? Try to convince him to . . ."

He nodded, and she glanced away, lips thinning.

"It's wrong. What you and your friends are doing is wrong,

and cruel, and—" She stopped, collecting her anger, and he'd never been more tempted to justify himself. *You don't know everything, Rue. In fact, I suspect you know nothing at all. Let me tell you a few things.*

"Listen, we don't have to go upstairs," he told her softly. Because suddenly, even more than he wanted to fuck her, he wanted to *explain*. If Rue understood, maybe the two of them could have a fighting chance at . . . *A fighting chance at* what, *Eli?* "We can just stay here and I can—"

"No. I'm already betraying Florence. If we stay here and *talk*, it's even worse." She bit her lip. "I don't want any misunderstanding: I despise Harkness and what you are doing."

"Right." He tried to keep his tone light and amused. *Are you hurt?* a Hark-sounding voice taunted. *Because this woman you barely know doesn't like you?*

"It's just sex," she continued. "If it's just fucking, there's no need for moral dilemmas."

Oh, Rue. Are you sure?

"We do this *once*," she continued, voice firm, as if laying down important rules. "It'll be as though Vince didn't interrupt us that first night. We . . . pretend. It's still Tuesday, and this is happening before I found out that you work for Harkness. We work it out of our system, and never think about it again."

I hope you're right, Rue, because I'm not sure my self-respect can take much more of you.

Maybe she was right. They needed to expel each other from their heads, quickly. Novelty was a powerful stimulant—take that away, and maybe there would be little left between them.

Eli lifted his hand, hotel key card between index and middle finger. "Ready to go?"

"I have been for a while."

They were silent in the elevator, at first staring ahead at the closing doors, then turning to face each other. Eli considered closing the distance between them, getting an early start, pulling her in to let her feel his eagerness, but he just drank her in. *Delayed gratification*, he thought. There weren't going to be repeats. He had to file away every moment.

When he smiled at her, she didn't smile back, but neither did she avert her wide, studious eyes. The doors swished open, and he gestured for her to go first. His heart, remarkably steady until then, began racing.

He followed her into the hallway. Opened the door for her. Watched her step inside the room and glance around indifferently. Before he could touch her, or kiss her, or even take her hand, she faced the window. Giving him her back, staring at the urban glow of the Austin skyline, she began taking off her clothes, and Eli lost his ability to breathe.

There was nothing sensual, or purposefully titillating about it. It was the most utilitarian striptease he'd ever witnessed. Nevertheless, he had to lean back against a section of bare wall. Take a moment and a steadying breath as her shoes, shirt, pants, bra, and underwear were not quite folded, but neatly set aside on the wooden desk. And as she undressed, still facing away from him, she began talking. "My first time, I was a freshman in college. With some boy whose name I either forgot or never learned. My roommates, they wanted to throw a party before the winter holidays. They invited a bunch of guys, who invited *other* guys, and one of them was the one I had sex with. He was actually not bad at it. He knew what he was doing. Made it good for me. I think I was really lucky. But I fell asleep after, and by the time I woke up, he was gone. Didn't leave a note, didn't ask for my number. My roommates kept saying how much of a dick move it was, how terrible that my first had been such a jerk. Even Tisha, when I told her on the phone, was enraged on my behalf. I performed the disappointment that was expected of me, and never had the courage to tell anyone that I was so *relieved*. That guy and I had gotten what we wanted from each other, and then had a clean break before things could go south. Seemed ideal to me." She removed her earrings, and as her head tilted in Eli's direction, their eyes met again. She turned his way, and he could only stare.

It was her.

Rue.

Naked.

Eli's cock got so hard, so suddenly, he was sure it was all over for him.

He was her servant. Anything she wanted, Eli would do it. He had to slide his hands behind his back, trap them between himself and the wall, just to stop himself from touching and gripping and *taking*.

"What's wrong?" she asked.

He couldn't compute her body. She was full in a way that reminded him of the movies his grandmother used to watch, of the actresses he'd think about when sex was just a hazy notion in his head. *Mediterranean,* he thought. With rounded hips and a rounded stomach and rounded shoulders and some rounded, truly luscious, magnificent tits. Her legs were smooth, nicely shaped, and maybe it was because of the anticipation of the last few days, but he didn't think he'd ever seen anything this lovely in all his years on this damn planet. He'd enjoyed looking at a lot of women, and they were all made different, and they'd all been beautiful, but there was something here, with Rue, that felt almost . . .

Poignant, he thought, and laughed at himself, soft yet loud in the quiet room. A few days of being horny, and he was ready to write a fucking sonnet about her ass. Her lush, spectacular ass. It bounced slightly as she took a side step—a fucking work of art.

"What?" She came toward him, eyebrows lifting inquisitively.

Her body was on full display, unfaltering, and her effortless confidence kicked his arousal up another notch, even when he'd thought it had nowhere else to go. "Nothing. You look . . ." *Amazing. Sweet. Enchanting. Fuckable.* "Good."

"Thank you." Her mouth curled upward, as though she enjoyed the compliment, and he wanted to give her a million more. Scribble them in the fucking burning Library of Alexandria. "On the app you wrote you'd be fine with my limits?"

He nodded, remembering the message he'd been pulling up at embarrassingly frequent intervals in the past few days. He had it memorized, but all those clinical words felt so at odds now with her pink, soft glory. He would die one day, and med students would find the sentences carved in his brain.

FYI, I don't enjoy penetrative sex much. If that's a deal-breaker, then we should both move on.

"You still don't want to have sex?" he checked.

She frowned in confusion. Then her eyes widened. "You mean, penetrative intercourse?"

A gynecologist, that's what she sounded like. And he was dying to touch her. Ready to beg to smell the crease where her abdomen met her thigh. "Yup."

She nodded. "Correct."

He was curious about the reason, but she didn't volunteer an explanation. Narrowing his options might be a good idea, anyway. He had things in mind, enough to fill the next week with, that didn't require putting his dick inside her. He could probably just look at her for a while, and things would happen.

"Okay," he said, finding himself split. He wanted Rue to enjoy this, *a lot*, but he was also absolutely, single-mindedly focused on his own desires and needs. It had been a long time coming. It had been . . .

Shit. *Four* days. They'd met four days ago. He felt like he'd been trudging upstream for the last year.

"Come here," he murmured, and he was half in love with how quickly she complied, how close to him she stopped, how straight her posture. She was within reach. He could touch her wherever he wanted. His fingers twitched with impatience.

And yet, Eli found himself lifting his thumb and pressing it into her lips. His true north. "There is something about your mouth," he mused.

"You mentioned." She shrugged. The way her tits bounced would likely count as a formative moment in his sexual history. "It's weirdly asymmetrical. The top and bottom, I mean." She sounded calm, but her voice was eager. "Would you like me to go down on you?" she offered plainly.

His muscles, his nerve endings, the entire bone structure of his body tensed and stretched and reached toward her. "Would *you* like to?" he asked.

She nodded without hesitation. Eli could barely process it.

"I don't think it's a good idea," he said eventually. "Not this time."

"There won't be another time," she reminded him.

The edges of his arousal sharpened. Eli clenched the back of his teeth before forcing a smile. "If this is my only chance, then yeah. I'd love for you to suck my cock." They were being so *goddamn* polite, from his pragmatic tone to her minute nod. Her hands made quick, sensible work of unbuckling his belt, undoing the top button on his pants. Her knees bent to—

"Wait," he stopped her. She gave him a wide-eyed look, and the impulse to carry her to his home and keep her there for months or until this mess with Kline was over, whichever came first, was so overwhelming, he had to consciously get a grip. Hand on her upper arm, he dragged her back up. "I owe you a story. One of ours."

Something terrible, he meant. Shameful and hitherto untold. Rue's lips parted. She nodded, expectant.

"My first time was with my high school girlfriend. I was crazy about her, Rue. We were together for two years, and I swear to god, I was ready to marry her. Then one day, when her parents were gone, I walked into her house for a surprise visit and found her having sex with someone else." He swallowed. "He was one of my teammates, and it had been going for months. They ended up getting married. Last I heard, they had kids. I think they're happy."

There was no pity in Rue's blue eyes, just a silent acknowledgment that she'd heard him—just like he had heard her. Exactly what they needed. He pressed her against himself, combed his fingers through the hair at her nape, and kissed her as deeply as the night before. Except, this time she wore nothing at all, and he was fully dressed. His brain wasn't at its most functional, his memory was foggy at best, but this could have easily been the most erotic moment of his adult life.

Beyond belief, he thought, pulling back, looking at her breasts wedged against the light cotton of his shirt. He was already out of breath. His cock punched through the fly of his jeans. "*Now* you can suck me off," he said.

Rue gracefully went on her knees. Unbuttoned his pants and took him out of his boxers with hands at once soft and calloused. Her breath was hot against his skin.

"Stop," he ordered, a hint of panic in his voice, and Rue drew back with a puzzled frown.

"You've done this before, right?"

He laughed. God, he was *gone* for her. "I forgot to ask if you want to use a condom."

She grimaced. "I hate the taste, and you sent your STI results through the app. But if you prefer—"

"No. Very much no."

Then her mouth was on him, and Eli was dying. It was warm and wet and slow in a way that was at once familiar and completely new, and he was convinced that someone had slipped a high dose of a potent drug in his beer, because only *that* would explain his buckling knees and the expanding tingle at the base of his spine.

He shut his eyes and tilted his head to the ceiling, just *feeling*. Her fingers around the base of his cock. Her tongue swirling around the head. Then, when she pulled back, just the cold air in the room. "You're not even watching." She pressed a light kiss down his length, followed with a tender graze of her teeth. Her knuckles brushed against his testicles and oh, *shit*. "After all that talk about my mouth."

"I can't quite—"

He grounded himself. Searched for the part of him that knew better than to come in a woman's mouth twenty seconds into a blow job. Dug into it, heels deep. Stubbornly pulled back from that very humiliating cliff.

"Give me a second."

"Sure."

She waited, and it was what he needed. A moment later he could hang his head and open his eyes without embarrassing himself. "Okay," he said, vaguely amused by his own short fuse. "Okay."

"Back to work?"

He nodded and this time he watched, her plump mouth and everything else: the dark curls blanketing her shoulders, the rosy tips of her nipples as they got hard and puffy, the warm blue of her eyes whenever they held his. Her slightly arched spine. Her position at once subservient and defiant, and in the blurry edges of the pleasure, he thought about having her at his mercy. A universe in which she gave him control. The power to hold her down and do with her what he wanted.

He exhaled a laugh and cupped her cheek, trying to remember the last time someone had given him head. At the start of the year in Seattle, maybe. Or Chicago? Not *that* long ago. Had it felt this obscenely good? Had *anything*, ever? He wanted it to last forever. He wanted to touch her some more. He wanted to fuck her tits, but it would have required her to stop what she was doing.

"Fuck me, but you look so fucking good with my dick in your mouth. You're as good at this as you are at everything else," he murmured, and the humming sound she made before slowly licking his balls told him she took it for the compliment it was. She couldn't take all of him but gamely did her best, and *that* was the hottest thing about this. No fancy tricks, just enthusiasm and the fact that it was *her*. He liked—no, he fucking *loved* that the knuckles of her free hand were moving between her own thighs.

"You like this?" he asked, genuinely curious.

Rue pulled back with a filthy popping sound that was going to echo in Eli's head on his deathbed. "You mean, do I like sucking dick in general?" Her tongue pressed against the underside, and he grunted. "Or do I like to suck yours?" If there was an award for this, he'd nominate her. Fuck, *no*, he'd keep her a secret. He'd abscond, covetous, greedy with his own little treasure.

"I don't love thinking about you doing this with anyone else," he said, thumb tracing her right cheek, the impression of him. He was once again inappropriate and out of bounds, as though he had a right to her, but instead of chastising him, she buried her head at the base of his cock, and pressed a kiss on his hip that had him wondering if it had become an erogenous zone.

Rue Siebert. Changing his cellular makeup, one solemn look at a time.

"Usually, I don't mind it. But . . ." Two parallel lines between her eyes, and maybe it was wishful thinking on his part, but—no. She actually said, "This is more of a turn-on than I can remember it being."

Eli had heard his fair share of dirty talk, and he unabashedly enjoyed having women ask him to spank them, to fuck them in different orifices, to do with them what *he* wanted. And yet, he couldn't recall getting as worked up as he was right now, just from Rue's soft-spoken, bemused admission. "I think this is enough," he said, tightening his grip on her hair and gently prying her head away. She sucked on him one last time, a lurid sound that made his knees tremble.

"But you haven't come yet," she said.

He gripped his cock, as if that would restrain it. Shit. *Shit.* "Should I?" *I could, easily. I could make a mess of you.*

"Isn't that the point?"

Precisely, every vertebra in his spine roared. Except. "When is

126

this over, Rue?" She gave him a blank look, and he continued. "To-morrow morning? When you get bored? When we both come?"

She thought about it with that serious expression that made him want to do unspeakable things to her beautiful face. "When we both come."

"Then we move to something else," he told her, and she let him tug her up, kiss her again, and roam his hands over her, palming the soft globes of her ass, molding his fingers into pliant flesh. "This is just . . ." He groped her crudely. But Jesus, he could have done much worse. "I might like your ass as much as your mouth."

She looked him in the eye. Smiled faintly. "I should have guessed it."

"Guessed what?"

He could feel her amusement. "That you'd talk so much during sex."

Did he? He had no idea. Had never thought of himself as par-ticularly verbal. "I think," he said with a kiss to her throat, "I like to remind myself that it's *you* I'm doing this with." As though he could ever forget. "What do you want? How should I get you off?"

Her smile widened. "Aw. You're not sure what to do."

"Correct," he deadpanned. "I've never once made a woman come. Teach me, please."

She pulled him away from the wall and took off his shirt, her cool fingers brushing against his torso. He tried to recall anyone else undressing him, but couldn't, not even women he'd lived with. He toed his shoes off, but then her hands began exploring, linger-ing in unexpected places. The side of his midriff. The line between his pecs. The inner part of his upper arm. He wanted to feel her naked skin against his own, but she seemed lost in her own world. "I didn't think," she started. Stopped.

"What?"

"That I'd be much into men made like you." Her palm curled around his shoulder. A red fingernail traced his bicep, and the polish was starting to chip. "Is this from college hockey?"

"This?"

She shrugged. "The muscle, I guess."

"For the most part." He pushed her until she lay on her back, hips on the edge of the bed, and bent over her, licking the side of one breast while cupping the other in his palm. Her tits were big, and sensitive, and fit into his hands in a beautiful, overflowing manner that was intensely pornographic. Her breathing sped up as he stroked her nipples with his thumb, sucked them into his mouth and between his teeth, nibbled at the undersides. He pinched a hard pebble, just north of delicate, and her whole beautiful, soft body arched off the bed and into his mouth. Perfect. She was fucking *perfect*.

And he was going to be so *good* to her. "How would you prefer I make you come?" he asked. "Fingers? Mouth? Cock?"

Her chest heaved. "I said no—"

"Come on, Rue. You know I can make you come with my cock *without* putting it inside you."

Her eyes fluttered closed, and when they opened again, they were glossier. "Why don't you surprise me?"

"Because you clearly have limits and preferences, and I don't want to fuck up my one chance." They held each other's eyes for a long, swelling moment. He waited and waited, but she never replied. "Okay," he murmured, kneeling in front of the bed. When he yanked her hips closer, she gasped in shock, but her heels remained on his shoulders, exactly where he'd placed them.

She liked it—a bit of roughness. A hint of violence. Yielding control. Just as much as he liked to clutch it. If this had been the beginning of something, they could have explored it. Negotiated. She'd let him take charge, he was sure, maybe a little more than that. But this was more like an end, so he parted her with his thumb—her beautiful, plump, shining cunt. "Very nice." He kissed her just above her clit. Felt her tremble. "I like women who get really wet."

"D-do I?"

"Fuck yeah," he said before swiping the length of her with his tongue.

He loved doing this. It was something he'd unabashedly, enthusiastically enjoyed since he was in his teens—the flavors, the scents, the sounds. And with Rue . . . maybe it felt special because she was usually so guarded. Now she was still quiet, no loud moans or over-the-top whimpers, nothing purposefully meant to broadcast pleasure, but her breath hitched, her thighs tightened around his ears, her pelvis tilted to rub against his mouth. Eli felt each little tell right in his cock.

I would do this a million more times, he thought. *I would spend a million more hours like this. With you.*

He hoped he'd feel differently after an orgasm. And since Rue was likely to agree, when she began cresting closer to her peak, when her abdomen started contracting under his palm and she shuddered against him, he pulled back.

She let out a small, plaintive breath. Eli wanted to go back and finish her off—or keep her here forever, with him, on this edge. "Not yet." He looked down at her flushed, trembling body. She was so *close*. So *beautiful*. "Can I put my fingers inside you?" he asked.

She nodded eagerly.

He showed her his hand. "How many?"

A pause. "No more than two."

He lay down next to her, and being inside her was a slick, tight fit that made the prospect of never fucking this woman absolutely devastating. When her face showed nothing but pleasure, he added another finger, and that was a game changer.

"Oh my god," she whispered, canting her hips against him.

"Yeah? You like it?" He crooked his fingers, and her thighs began trembling. "I think you like it," he said against her shoulder. He found the hood of her clit with this thumb, tapped it gently, and it was like lighting a match.

This was supposed to be a brief stop. Just a slight detour before Eli got to do all the other things he wanted. Bite into her ass, eat her out some more, maybe fuck her tits for real this time, and *then* get her off. But Rue contracted around his fingers abruptly, with a breathless, shocked gasp, and all of a sudden every single thing within the hotel room was pushed miles beyond his ability to control. "Fuck. *Fuck*, you're so close."

She turned her head, gazing blindly at him. "I—" She gasped against his mouth. "Yes. I'm going to."

He grazed her clit, and that was it. She arched in a curve of pure pleasure, eyes open and unseeing, lips parted in a soundless scream, and she looked so—beautiful and fuckable and lovely, Eli was completely ruined. His orgasm thundered through him with no warning. He ground his cock against the tender flesh of her hip and came like a freight train, the pleasure pulled from him in large, pulsing gusts.

He started kissing her instinctively, before fully coming down. And then he kept on kissing her, and kissing her, and kissing her, through the tail end of her orgasm and through the crest of his own. She didn't always kiss him back, overwhelmed by the shudders running through her, but her mouth stayed underneath his, even as the pleasure slowly subsided. Sweat cooled on their bodies, the tempo of their hearts quieted, and once it was time to pull away from her, Eli found that he couldn't. His fingers remained between her thighs, and he began to trace soft, aftershock-inducing circles around her clit, dragging his fingers through the damp mess at her opening, and . . .

It wasn't over yet. It *couldn't* be over. They'd just gotten started, and the things he could do for her, the things they could do for each other were beyond this world, and—

Rue turned away from him. "Eli." Her fingers slid down to grip his wrist. "I have to go."

"What?"

"Please."

He moved away, giving her space. But said, "Rue. Come on." Body still twitching with pleasure, she slid out of bed. The moment she stood, her legs almost gave out. Eli reached forward, steadying her before she collapsed. "Rue? What the hell?"

"I'm fine." She took a deep breath and held out a halting hand. She sounded weak. Not like herself. "Just a . . . a cramp, I think." She turned to him, and she was *undone*. Destroyed. As ruined as he felt, and Eli wanted to pull her back. Have her underneath him. He wanted to clean her up and do everything all over again, a thousand times over.

"Rue."

She ignored him, silent in a busy, industrious way that involved cleaning herself of his semen with her underwear, pulling on her T-shirt with trembling hands, retrieving her pants. *Not* meeting his eyes.

He exhaled a laugh. "Are you really . . . you're done," he half said, half asked.

"Yeah." She shrugged. Her breathlessness belied her indifference. "You aren't?"

Fuck no, he thought. Said nothing.

"I'm going. I . . . thank you. It was fun. Maybe I'll see you again. If not, have a good life and all that." She was gone before he could think of a response. He watched the door close behind her, and when he glanced away, his eyes fell on her panties, forgotten in a heap of dark blue cotton on top of the sheets.

Eli covered his eyes, wondering how he'd ever thought that once was going to be enough.

12

BECHDEL TEST: FAILED

RUE

Early on Sunday I dragged myself out of bed after an unsettled night of tossing and turning. I showered, had a long, quiet, luxurious breakfast of oatmeal and berries, and went to work.

Going in on weekends wasn't part of my normal routine. I'd done enough free labor during grad school and my pre-Florence internships, and liked to keep a semblance of work-life balance, even if my weekends tended to be spent underwhelmingly, doing very little either at home or at Tisha's.

But Tisha was somewhere south of Austin at some grandaunt's birthday party, and even though I had a standing invitation to all Fuli family things, I skipped the ones involving relatives I'd never met. So I went into work, staying until the sky turned dark and my stomach growled. In those nine hours, my phone buzzed with exactly two texts, but I was busy running flow cytometry on my samples. I only bothered to read them as I headed back to my car, and it was almost an accident—a misplaced tap when I pulled up the flashlight app, because the sensor lights outside of Kline were busted, and maintenance hadn't yet gotten around to switching them out.

The texts were from an unknown Austin number. The first: **Are you okay?** And, approximately one hour later: **Rue, I need to know if you're okay.**

Eli had *not* deleted my number when I'd asked him to. Or maybe he'd found it in the Kline employee directory—who knew? And really, who cared? The sheer triviality of it all could have swept me away like a leaf in a storm. I tossed my phone in the passenger seat, not intending to reply. After starting the engine, I changed my mind.

So, we'd had sex, and it had been . . .

It had been all that.

We'd agreed that mutually satisfying sexual activity would be the period terminating the sentence of our acquaintance. Not re-plying would just worry Eli, and tack on subordinate clauses we could both do without. And since he'd probably spent the day trying to convince one of Kline's board members to hand him the tech that was the product of Florence's blood, sweat, and tears, I did *not* want that. I did *not* want him in my life.

> **I'm fine. Been working all day. Have a great weekend.**

It was Sunday night—little weekend left to be had greatly. I drove home, had dinner, and then tossed and turned until it was finally time to go back to Kline.

Eli did not text again.

Monday I was on duty with Matt, a chore that had me wist-fully wishing that giving wedgies didn't constitute an HR viola-tion. Tuesday I spent holed up in the lab. Wednesday it was my office. For the first time in my life, my paperwork was complete well before its deadline. When Tisha visited, I had to get up and let her in.

"Did you *lock* yourself in your office? Were you like, mastur-bating over spandex porn?"

"I'm just sick of people dropping by."

"Do that many people drop by? I thought your nicely frosty personality was enough of a deterrent."

"I must be slipping."

"Don't worry, I still get 'would not save ninety-nine percent of humanity in case of apocalypse' vibes from you."

"Phew."

Tisha asked me to go for a walk at the nearby park, to accom-pany her to the vending machine, to visit Florence. "I'm drowning in reports," I said, and maybe Tisha knew it was a half lie, but she was the kind of friend who gave me not only unconditional love, but also the space I needed.

Florence stopped by to check on the progress on my patent, and the guilt and shame I felt at seeing her smiling face nearly par-alyzed me. "Any updates on Harkness?" I asked, without bothering to sound casual.

Florence rolled her eyes. "All that asshole licking they've been doing on Eric Sommers's taint must have worked, because a board meeting was called. At least the Teenage Mutant Ninja Turtles of hostile takeovers haven't been around." I should have been disap-pointed that the person I'd gone to great lengths to avoid for the last three days hadn't even been at Kline, but relief drowned all other emotions. Florence's expression switched to concern. "Eli Killgore hasn't been bothering you, has he?"

My stomach sank. I was unable to reply, and Florence could tell.

"Rue, if he's done anything to you, I swear to god—"

"No, he hasn't. He . . . I haven't seen him."

Liar. Liar. Ungrateful, blatant liar.

"Okay, good." She seemed relieved. "I can tell you're worrying about me and Kline, Rue, but don't, okay? Not worth your time. Just focus on the science."

Her compassion and protectiveness intensified my guilt. I tried to imagine how I would feel if Florence slept with some guy who was trying to steal my patent, and the magnitude of the betrayal was staggering. I'd fucked up, knowingly. Selfishly. And I was going to have to deal with the shame of it, and the knowledge that being with Eli had been so . . .

It didn't matter.

By Thursday I'd managed a decent night of sleep, and on Friday I was back on track. Kline's blue hallways felt less like the open sea, full of ambushing, flesh-mangling sharks, and more like a tranquil pond in which the height of excitement was figuring out who'd started a fire in Lab D.

Then a heron dove in.

"Are you fucking kidding me?" Tisha asked at lunch, after I told her about the letter. "Your brother does *not* have his shit together enough to have a *lawyer.*"

"Apparently he does."

"Is he suing you?"

"No. It's a letter of demand."

"What does it say?"

I moved my penne around the plate. "That under Indiana law, if two parties are in disagreement, the court can order the sale of the property."

"Is it true?"

"According to my lawyer, yes."

"Who's your lawyer?"

"Google."

"Bullshit. Nyota's your lawyer. My bitchy sister will take care of your shitty brother. It's like poetry, it rhymes."

I smiled. "I don't even know why I'm being so stubborn about this cabin."

"I do." Tisha leaned forward. "I don't need a psych minor to know that now that your relationships with your mom and your brother have irreparably broken down, you want to connect with *some* part of your family, and the cabin is all that's left of your dad."

"I'm not usually this sentimental, though." I tilted my head. "And you minored in computer science and French."

"Exactly my point."

Later in the afternoon, I was returning from a quality assurance meeting when I saw them.

Saw *him*.

Eli stood at the end of the hallway, wearing glasses once again, head hung low as he focused on what Minami Oka was saying, something private and exclusive about the way they bent toward each other. He raised one eyebrow in that manner that was imprinted in my brain, and Dr. Oka laughed and pretended to punch him on the arm, and—

I walked away, heat rising up my throat.

He was there, again. On Harkness business. Laughing, as though the terrible things they were doing to Kline, to *us*, were just a joke. I sat at my desk for several minutes as every moment, every second, every touch and hitched breath and heated look from last Saturday raked through me like nails down my back. I'd had him. Why did I *still* want him? What was I supposed to—

A knock on the doorframe. "Dr. Siebert? Hi."

Shit. "Hi."

"I'm Minami. With Harkness. It's so nice to meet you."

"Rue." I stood and we shook hands over my desk, my mountains of Post-its, the weekly calendar Tisha had given me as a Christmas present. Each page had a different selfie.

Of Tisha.

"Do you have a minute to talk?"

I wondered if it was going to be about Eli. Then whether I was losing my damn mind: we were two engineers in a professional setting—surely we could pass the Bechdel test. "Please, sit. How can I help you?"

"I was looking at your project, actually. A colleague told me about your microbial coating, because it aligns with the work I did during my PhD."

Bechdel test: failed. "You worked on food conservation?"

"For a bit. I ended up writing my dissertation on biofuels."

"I see." It explained why Harkness had been targeting Kline. If Minami was an expert, she must know the value of Florence's research.

A curl of anger unfolded inside my stomach.

"I have some time before a meeting." Minami sounded genuine. Nice. "I'd love to hear more about your work."

"I turn in biweekly reports that are available for everyone to read. Do you have access to our science directory?"

"I do. But I'd love to hear from you—"

"No," I said softly. "I'm sorry."

Minami's eyes widened, but her smile was steady. "If you're busy, we could—"

"That's not it. I'm not trying to be rude, but I don't want to waste your time. Florence Kline is one of my closest friends."

Minami's smile didn't dim, but her eyes lost some brightness. "Well, this is disappointing, but I understand." She pressed her lips together. "Listen, Rue, it might not be my place, but I think fair warnings are everyone's right, and—"

Another soft knock interrupted her. "You ready? The board is here."

It was Eli's voice. My heart thudded so loud, I was sure he could hear it. His hands gripped each side of the door, and I focused on his long fingers to avoid meeting his eyes. It was only when Minami stood that I realized that he wasn't there for *me*.

"I'll make a restroom stop and meet you there, Eli."

"Sounds good."

She waved her goodbyes at me, ducked under Eli's arm, and left us.

Alone.

I stared at the place where she'd disappeared, feeling out of sorts.

"Rue," Eli said. I couldn't do anything except tense all my muscles. Hope that it'd keep me from shattering into tiny pieces.

"Rue," he repeated, this time sounding entertained. Like he was laughing at me.

You have to answer him. You cannot ignore him. You have no reason to.

I glanced up. "Sorry. I was distracted. Hi, Eli."

Our eyes met, and all of a sudden I felt as though he were touching me. He was spooling grateful, filthy praises in my ear as I came uncontrollably. He was gripping the hair at the back of my neck and showing me what he liked.

Then the floodgates opened, for real this time, in hot, near painful flashes. His open mouth trailing down my rib cage. His obvious arousal against my hip. The way his eyes had rolled back when I'd first taken him in my mouth. And then, the absolute befuddlement of coming apart around his fingers.

I'd had sex before, good sex. But with him it had been just—

"Rue."

"Yes?"

His throat worked through a swallow. For a second he seemed—angry, maybe, or something else. For *more* than a second. But he quickly cycled through the emotion and emerged on the other side with one of his self-assured smiles. "Have a good day," he said, maybe amused and maybe not. He pushed away from the door-frame and left, his determined steps ricocheting against the walls of the empty hallway, and it wasn't until I couldn't hear them anymore that I bent my head and managed to whisper, "You, too."

13

THE AWFUL, SECRET ONES

RUE

It took about two hours for Eli's words to stop echoing inside my head. After two more, Florence stopped by to see me.

"What happened at the board meeting?" I asked.

"Not much. Eric bought some of their lies, and they got some concessions, but nothing to worry about. I'll need to send them some documents in their *preferred format*." She rolled her eyes. "They'll review and find nothing suspicious, because there's nothing to be found, and everyone's precious time will be happily wasted." She shrugged. "At least Harkness promised not to have an on-site presence anymore. Hey, did I see Eli Killgore and Minami Oka loitering around your office earlier?"

"I . . . wasn't here. I wouldn't know."

She left with a wave of her hand and a satisfied smile, and I wondered when the last time was that I'd lied so deliberately to a friend.

Never, I thought, the shame of it sour in my throat. At least, not that I could recall.

If one good thing could be said of Harkness, it was that it kept its promise, because I didn't see Eli during the following week. His absence from my life—and the absence of the havoc he wreaked in it—felt like a reward for being, if not a *good* person, someone who returned grocery items to their original places when she changed her mind mid-shopping, even if it was several aisles away.

I went over to Florence's for Tisha's birthday dinner, and found her mostly annoyed. "They keep asking for more and more documents, beyond anything that's reasonable or that has been agreed upon," Florence said, cutting a slice of cheesecake. The dark circles were back around her eyes. "I'm starting to wonder if they're using the copies we send them for their kids' papier-mâché projects."

I paused with my glass midair, remembering Eli's words at the retirement party. "Can't we just give them access to everything? We have nothing to hide, after all."

"We could, *if* we believed that they're acting in good faith. But we know better. Plus, it's not so simple. A lot of these documents have to be prepared by the accountants. Like I said, a huge time and money pit."

See, Eli? I knew that Florence had an answer.

"But it doesn't matter, because I have a plan to get out of this mess." Her smile was suddenly broad and infectious.

"A plan—I love plans!" Tisha clapped her hands. "Do tell?"

Florence stuck a single candle in Tisha's slice and handed her a plate. "I've been talking to some potential investors. Ideally, they'll decide to back us and give us the capital to pay off our loan to Harkness."

"Would Harkness agree to take the money and leave?" I asked, skeptical. Wasn't their endgame the biofuel?

"They wouldn't have a choice."

I imagined a future in which Harkness was out of the picture. What it would do for the constant, low-level buzz of guilt I'd been dealing with, knowing that I hadn't slept with the guy who might take Florence's company away from her—I'd slept with the guy who'd *failed* at it.

I wanted that future so, *so* bad.

It wasn't until later that night, while I was adding nutrients to my hydroponic garden, that the implications fully hit me: If Florence succeeded, I might never see Eli Killgore again. The relief was so strong, it felt like something else altogether.

⁂

"Do you have any idea how much one of my billable hours costs?" Nyota asked me the next time we FaceTimed. Her phone was propped on her treadmill, and she appeared to be running an easy six-minute mile with barely a puff. I'd been an athlete for half my life, but *holy shit.*

"Hundreds of dollars, I'd guess."

"You'd be right. Remind me, why am I consulting for you for free?"

"Because I've been holding on to that picture of your goth phase for the last decade?"

She muttered a word that sounded like *twitch*. "For the record, this is extortion and blackmail. Both felonies. And I hate you." A sigh. "I got the contract you emailed. The one that supposedly says that the ravioli patent is yours, no matter what."

"It's a microbial coating—"

"Yes, you're a nerd first and a human being second. We're all aware. Anyway, I haven't gotten a chance to look at that contract yet. But I *did* check your brother's letter."

"And?"

"Honestly, I'm not a real estate lawyer, but your best bet is to buy him out. Can you afford it?"

Could I? The tech industry paid well, and I did have savings. Enough to buy Vince's half of the cabin, though? "Probably not right now."

"You could get a loan."

I could. Except that my credit score was still convalescing after the abuse I'd put it through during my PhD. "With my luck, the loan would end up being owned by a pack of hyenas. Or by Harkness—same difference."

Nyota chuckled, which made me feel oddly proud. *Booger eater*, I reminded myself. *You don't need to impress her.*

"Tish tells me things are looking up," she said, still breathing easily. "With Harkness, I mean."

"Hopefully. If Florence finds a better lender. Or *any* lender, since I'm not sure there are worse ones."

"Don't be so sure. Harkness is not that bad." She noticed my surprised eyebrow and continued, "Don't get me wrong, there are no ethics in capitalism and all that. But these guys are on the less gross end of the spectrum of it. Guess how many companies they've bankrupted?"

I had no idea what a plausible number was. Three? Seventeen hundred? "Twelve."

"That's disturbingly specific, and no. Zero."

"What does that mean?"

"I wouldn't go as far as saying that they're putting social responsibility before profit, but at least they try. Or maybe I'm just mildly fascinated because I work in finance—doesn't exactly crawl with people with a strong moral compass. Or weak. Or any." She shrugged mid-stride. Impressive. "At least they're not saddling the companies they acquire with debt, or cutting jobs. They're long-term. Their MO seems to be to invest in companies they believe in and use their capital to grow them. And they seem to be very intuitive when it comes to figuring out what tech has good market potential."

I thought about Minami and her degree. "What about what they're trying to do to Florence? Have they ever targeted a company to obtain control of their tech?"

"Not that I know of. But don't worry, Rue. They're still making money out of money and all that gross shit." She grinned. "You *are* allowed to hate them, if that's what sparks joy."

Tisha and I hadn't been the ones to start Kline's monthly journal club, but Florence had forced us to take over when our predecessor moved to a cushy job at the CDC and a dearth of volunteers became apparent. And yet, while we may not have been the club's *first*, we were undoubtedly the club's *best*.

No one wanted to read scientific papers in their spare time, let alone have roundtable discussions about them. So, after the first monthly meeting had an attendance of three (Tisha, me, and a strong-armed Jay, who did not read the paper and threatened to call HR), we decided that some changes were overdue. Among them:

moving the club to Thursday afternoons, snacks, and, most importantly, a keg budget—which Florence had agreed to, "in order to incentivize continuing education."

Attendance had skyrocketed. "Journal club" had become a synonym for "company-wide nonmandatory party." Even I, no social butterfly, enjoyed it for several reasons: nine times out of ten I got to choose the paper (no one else remembered to submit ideas in time); it was much easier for me to interact with people within the structure of a guided discussion; and beer was a powerful social lubricant. *You give out way less of a "talk to me, and I'll fuck up your human rights" vibe when you're drunk,* Nyota had told me years before, watching Tisha and me stumble home sloshed, mistake the bathtub for a bed, and use Mrs. Fuli's loofahs for pillows.

I had elected to take it as a compliment.

That Thursday, amid some bisphenol A soapboxing, modeling techniques slander, burps, and someone pointing out over and over that they'd been in grad school with the third author on the paper, I was several beers in.

"... without even considering the ethical ..."

"... always such a know-it-all ..."

"... is this my glass or yours?"

"... they *completely* misattributed the catalytic activity."

The last one was Matt. Tragically, I agreed with him, but I wasn't about to admit it under threat of anything less than radical annihilation. So I stood, gave Tisha a pointed *should we maybe wrap this shit up and go home?* look, and headed for the closest restroom.

I was lightheaded, definitely buzzed—but not wasted enough to warrant the apparition coming toward me in the hallway. Eli couldn't be here, could he? He wasn't allowed at Kline anymore.

His slacks and button-down looked like they'd been a full suit and tie about eight hours ago. His hair had been cut since the last time I'd run my fingers through it. Still messy, a little shorter. The glasses were there, too. They didn't make him look smarter, or softer, or more distinguished, but they did transform him into Private Equity Eli.

Even worse, they suited him, which was just unforgivable.

"Are you okay?" he asked. His voice sounded too real to be something pulled from my memories. And yet, it must be.

"Why do you ask?"

"You've been staring at me for thirty seconds." He looked happy to see me, and the thought was infuriating, whether he was *actually* happy or I'd conjured him that way. He had no right. My brain had no right. That happiness was unearned.

"Rue," he said, amused.

"Eli," I said, trying for the same tone. I reached out, poking the closest part of him. An unfathomably solid, very unimagined bicep.

Fantastic. I *loved* coming across like an idiot. "You know," I told him prosaically, "once upon a time, back before I'd ever heard the word Harkness, this startup used to be really nice."

"Uh-huh. Is that why you're so clearly drunk at your workplace at six p.m.?"

"It's journal club."

He seemed intrigued. "You get drunk at journal club."

"Maybe." I shrugged. My head swam. "The first rule of journal club is, don't talk about journal club."

"Whoa." He pretended to recoil. "Drunk Rue makes *jokes*?"

I considered giving him the finger, but he'd enjoy it way too much. "Why are you here?" My eyes fell on the manila folder in his hand. "Stealing company property. Should I call security?" I thought about adorable, elderly Chuck, with his beer belly and quick smile and cheerful *good mornings*. Pictured him trying to escort a resisting Eli outside. My fantasy did not end well for Chuck, and since he was approaching retirement, I decided to abandon it.

"Everything that's in this folder belongs to me," he said, a little harshly. I wasn't in the best state of mind to spot a lie, so I didn't question him. Not even when a prolonged, vaguely uncomfortable silence fell between us.

"How are you, Rue?" he asked quietly, once a century or two had passed.

"Drunk, as you pointed out."

"Aside from that?"

I shrugged—as accurate a description of my feelings as I could muster.

"It'd be nice to have an answer, since you've ignored me for weeks," he said amiably.

"Have I? Or did our acquaintance come to its natural and predetermined end?"

"Maybe it did." His jaw tensed and his eyes cooled, like he was no longer in the mood to feign nonchalance. "And maybe you don't have any obligation to value my peace of mind. I'd still love to know if when you and I were together I did anything to upset you. Or hurt you."

"No." Had he been carrying this around for the past two weeks? I studied him, and the vaguely inebriated thought hit me that he was absolutely the type to do that. There was something white knight-y about him. Observant. *He cares, he really does care about doing the right thing. Why is he with Harkness, then?* "Everything was fine."

He scanned my face for lies. His lips twisted into a slow smile. "Fine, huh?"

"Good. It was very good." Though not as good as I remembered, I was certain of it. I must have inflated the night in my head. Glorified it past reality.

Nothing was *that* good.

"Yeah." His eyes darkened. When he spoke again, his voice was rougher. "I thought the same. Too bad for no repeats."

Tragic, really, I thought. With the beer sloshing through my veins, that rule seemed flimsier than ever. And maybe Eli could read my mind, because he said, "Go out on a date with me." The words seemed to explode out of him, unpremeditated. He appeared just as surprised by them as I was, but didn't backtrack. "Dinner," he continued, decisive, as if happy that he'd managed to ask. "Let me take you to dinner."

It was all I could do not to laugh in his face. "Why?"

"Because. I haven't seen you in two weeks and—I actually *do* like this. Being with you." That self-effacing, teasing smile of his— I wanted to touch it. "You can tell me more stories. The awful, secret ones. I'll listen and tell you mine."

It occurred to me that if there was a person in the world who could come to dinner with me and not be disappointed by how awkward, boring, inadequate I was, it was probably this man. We'd been nothing but brutally honest with each other, after all. No pretenses between us. But if having sex with him felt like a betrayal of Florence, *talking* with him would be pure treason. "Stories? Like of how you ended up trying to steal my friend's work?"

His expression hardened. "Yes, actually. I *could* tell you about—" Abruptly, he stopped. His strong neck tensed as he turned over his shoulder, and a moment later he was pushing me through the closest doorway and into a lab. He pressed me into a workstation that couldn't be seen through the glass walls.

My sluggish brain couldn't keep up. "What are you doing?" I asked, and then fell silent. A handful of voices were getting closer.

"You know who that is?"

I shook my head.

"Kline's CEO and its general counsel." His eyes held mine in what felt like a challenge. "I have no problem with your *friend* seeing us together, but I figured you might?"

I did. So I fell silent, letting the bite of the workbench dig into my lower back, listening as Florence's voice grew fainter. Eli remained close, his hands caging me to the table, and it soaked the air between us, the shame of what I'd done. What I *still* wanted to do.

"What are you thinking?" he asked.

I blurted out the truth. "You said 'negotiated.'"

A confused look. "What?"

"On the app. The checklist part of it, it asks about kinks. You wrote 'if negotiated' but didn't elaborate."

His gaze sharpened to something so intense, I couldn't conceive it. It was heady. A little unhinged.

"You want to know what I'm into?"

I nodded.

"Why?" His head tilted. "Are you hoping I'll take control? That if I'm the one calling the shots, it'll make you feel less guilty about being with me?"

Uncomfortable, how spot-on he was. "I just think we should fuck again," I heard myself say. The alcohol dulled the bluntness of my words, but Eli's pupils still widened.

"As far as I can recall, we never did that."

"Semantics."

"How much have you had to drink, Rue?"

"I don't know." I did. "A few beers." Three. A few sips of a fourth.

"Yeah. Okay." He took a step back. Turned away to stare at an embossed Kline logo on the wall, tendons tense on the side of his neck, as if under great strain. Then he looked back at me, once again tightly leashed. "We can revisit the matter when you've metabolized the alcohol out of your system."

"Just like I metabolized you?" I said under my breath. His nostrils flared. "We could leave together. Tonight."

"Rue."

"Unless you're busy."

"Rue."

"You can say no, if you—"

"Rue." His interest was a palpable presence, as concrete as the floor between us. *He's going to say yes,* I thought, elated. But: "Tomorrow." His knuckles whitened around the edge of the bench. "We revisit this tomorrow, if you still want to. Call me, and I'll tell you what I like." He had the final look of someone who hadn't budged in years.

"Sure. In the meantime, feel free to touch me. Or kiss me."

He exhaled. "Rue."

"What? It's a kiss. Are you scared of me now?"

He stepped closer, slowly leaning into me. My heart hammered in my chest, then exploded when he let his hand slide upward under my sweatshirt.

My brain stumbled. The AC blew across the exposed skin of my torso, turning it into gooseflesh. Then his large palm wiped the chill away, and a powerful shiver shook my spine.

"Rue." Eli clucked his tongue, patient, inching even closer. His lips pressed against me—corner of mouth, cheek, ear. He spoke in a low whisper. "Fair warning: if you don't stop pushing me, I'm going to bend you over this bench and show you *exactly* what I'm into."

14

THE CURRENT VILLAIN OF HER STORY

ELI

The flush on Rue's cheeks reminded him of the hotel room—heated, pale skin, the rush of red on her chest as she arched against his hand, the half-moon of her teeth biting into his shoulder. He'd never doubted that she'd enjoyed what happened between them. But enjoyment and consent were very different things, and once she'd disappeared off the face of the earth, his worries had lain on more unsettling grounds: Had he crossed a boundary? Had he scared her?

Was she really done with him, even after *that*?

"That wasn't a kiss," she said. Eli wished her voice was as shaky as his hand, but the dark pink dusting her cheekbones was the only hint that she was affected. "It wasn't anything at all."

"Ask me again when you're sober."

"And you'll say yes."

It was a question without a question mark, and two weeks

earlier he'd have said that he was a sure thing for her. But after hours of waiting for her to reply to a simple text, after the way she'd run out, leaving him in a mess of sweat and tangled sheets, he wasn't so certain. She had a power over him that he couldn't explain. Yielding more would be incredibly stupid.

But maybe Eli *was* stupid. He'd gotten more of a charge from one very tame hour with her than with anyone else before. He'd come like he was a fucking teenager, and his knees had shaken for twenty minutes after she'd left. He couldn't think straight around her, and had no clue how to fix his dazed brain. This shit didn't come about very often.

He took a step back, letting her sweatshirt fall back down. She was still obscenely beautiful to him. He should be inured by now, but the shape of her eyes, the bow of her lips, they struck him anew every time. Populated these new fantasies of his in ways that ranged from absolutely filthy to almost architectonically banal.

What if he took her out for drinks to discuss the merits of high-pressure processing versus thermal techniques, and his fingers brushed against hers across the table?

What if he did her laundry to silently thank her for some of the best sex of his life?

What if he tied her up, fucked her ass, and made her like it?

"Dude, I thought you were going to the bathroom." They both turned. Tisha Fuli was standing at the door.

"I was." Rue put some distance between herself and Eli. "I forgot."

"You *forgot* that you needed to . . . ah." Tisha began the curious process of looking back and forth between them. It lasted for many seconds and culminated in a dumbfounded "Oh. My. God."

Rue's shoulder slumped—a rare break in her perfect posture.

Eli's eyebrow rose. "What?"

"You two hooked up, didn't you?" Tisha asked. He glanced at Rue, who remained stoically silent. "First of all, I can't believe you didn't tell me. Secondly, he's literally the reason I had to figure out my LinkedIn password, how is *this* a good idea? Thirdly, how was it?"

Rue sighed, shook her head, and walked out of the lab, leaving Eli and Tisha alone.

She was tall, maybe even taller than Rue. Smooth dark skin, classically beautiful. Far more put together than anyone had the right to be at the end of a workday. They'd never talked before, but they obviously knew who the other was, so he decided to spare them both the gimmick of introducing himself. "Do you two need a ride home?"

"Nah. I'm the designated driver tonight." She smiled at him like they weren't on opposite sides of a hostile takeover. "Anyway, it's nice to finally make your acquaintance, Eli Killgore, Texas resident, born on June twenty-first—"

"I wondered who she'd sent that pic to."

"It was *moi*. Tisha." She pointed at herself with a flourish. "T-I-S-H-A, if you want to add my contact to your phone. I added yours, just in case someone finds Rue's body in a ditch."

"They're more likely to find mine."

"Nah. She's a bit frosty, but she wouldn't. She'll just ghost you." She scowled. "Not like, literally."

"Right."

"She won't *turn you* into a ghost—"

"I got that."

"Boy, if Florence finds out, she's *not* gonna like this." Tisha ran a hand down her straight hair. "How long ago was it? The consummation of your lust, I mean."

"Two and a half weeks." Not that he'd been counting.

"Sounds like the title of an erotic thriller. Wait—that's long enough that Rue should have forgotten you ever existed. Why are you two still—ooh." She grinned. "I see."

"What?"

"You want *more*."

He huffed. Nearly said, *She wants more, too*, like a fucking petulant child. But did she, or was it a handful of beers? "I'm not going to get more."

"It's very unlikely," Tisha agreed sagely. "Rue doesn't doubledip, and you *are* the current villain of her story. Although, we both know that Florence is going to win. Your douchebaggery will mostly be irrelevant then."

He wondered what Florence had been telling her employees. Whether Tisha would have still been so sure of Florence's victory if she knew why Eli was here and what he'd been doing for the past few hours.

The thought was a good reminder that he was here to get shit done—not to stare open-mouthed at Rue and moon over how good she smelled. "It was nice to meet you in person, Tisha, but I'd better go."

"'Kay. And, like, no hard feelings, but feel free to never come back," she said cheerfully.

"I'll do my best."

He couldn't help his smile as he headed for the exit. When he heard the bathroom door open and shut, he was proud of himself for not turning around.

15

WHAT THE HELL ARE YOU DOING?

RUE

When I stepped out of the bathroom stall, Tisha was there, nonchalantly leaning against one of the sinks, studying her perfectly lacquered nails. She didn't bother looking up before asking, "Rue, what the hell are you doing?"

I said nothing and went to wash my hands, wondering if I was too drunk for this conversation.

"Listen, I love you, Rue. I'm not here to judge you, or to make you feel bad—because it's clear that you already feel like shit. Otherwise you'd have told me what you were up to."

My chest hurt. I tried to think of a response, and found none.

"Are you in love with him?"

"What?" My eyes met Tisha's through the mirror. I tried to let out a derisive laugh, but the sound that came out of me was choked. "No."

"Do you think you could be? If this continues?"

"I—*no*."

She sighed. "I know it's a ridiculous question. But this is so *ridiculously* out of character for you, I had to ask."

"No. No, I'm not *in love* with him. I've met him a handful of times." I turned around to face her directly. "It was once. The sex was good. And he's . . . I don't know. Easier for me to be around than most people. But it's not—there's nothing."

Tisha examined me, a vertical line forming between her brows. "Listen, if you . . . if there's something between you guys, something real, I'm going to be first in line to support that. My loyalty is to you before Florence, or Kline, or even my own damn sister. Not Bruce, though." Her lips twitched. I exhaled a small laugh, too. "But if you're seeing Eli just because he's a good fuck, then you need to stop right now and find someone who's going to be less of a problem. Because he and his buddies could still take away Florence's lifework. And even if they don't manage that, who knows how many people they've stolen from. *Will* steal from. Florence deserves better than this, but the most important thing is, *you* deserve better than this. Okay?"

I didn't know what to say. So I just nodded, and when Tisha came closer and wrapped her arms around me, I hugged her right back.

16

HIS HEAD BETWEEN
ANOTHER WOMAN'S LEGS

ELI

Just as Eli had expected, he didn't hear from sober Rue—not the following day, nor the following week. It was one thing to be drunk and horny, another to follow through in the harsh daylight. Rue clearly ran her life like a tight ship, and Eli couldn't imagine there being room for him in it—not past the chemical help alcohol could provide.

By a stroke of luck, time didn't allow him to be too mournful. One of Harkness's agri-tech startups was in dire need of a sudden influx of cash, and someone was required on-site to figure out the best strategy. Hark was in California, so Eli volunteered, thinking that some distance from Austin would be ideal. Then a two-day trip to Iowa turned into five days of meetings and inspections, and on the return flight he fell stone-cold asleep in his seat, his head a jumbled exhaustion of aerial imaging, crop health, and asymmetrical lips. The amused look the flight attendant gave him told him he'd drooled all over himself.

Once he was back, Minami got sick, and Sul took time off to take care of her, which meant that most day-to-day shit fell to Eli and Hark, but he didn't mind too much. Because Eli *liked* his job.

The realization had sunk into him not too long ago, a gradual acknowledgment more than a thundering moment of self-awareness. His conscientious choice of an expendable major aside, finance had never been part of his dreams. And yet, he was good at it. Nearly ten years ago they'd started Harkness with a singular, specific destination, but the journey had surprised him more than once, and he couldn't help wondering what would happen once they reached their port of call. Whether they'd come far enough.

Had *he* come far enough?

A week after his trip, he stumbled home past midnight, exhausted by the back-to-back meetings, and found a note scribbled in Maya's handwriting on the kitchen counter.

I know you're busy making several shitloads of monies, but will Tiny and I ever see you again?

To the side there was a chicken potpie covered in cellophane wrap. He smiled, recalling the whys and the hows of his past choices.

Maybe it wasn't far enough, but it was certainly far.

———

Minami and Sul returned to work looking rested and more joined at the hip than usual, so much so that Eli wondered if they'd faked being sick and gone on a sex cruise. There was a newlywed energy between them that was about three years late, and if Eli had picked up on it, it was being drilled into Hark's skull with the force of a swarm of termites.

That night Hark said, "Need to blow off some steam," and Eli drove them to the gym without any comments. But the racquetball court they'd reserved was already occupied by two women. "Fucking brilliant," Hark muttered under his breath.

"Did you two book the room?" one asked.

Eli smiled. "No worries. We'll ask for another."

"There are none. Someone else was using the one *we* booked, so we came in here."

Eli glanced at Hark, whose mood was rapidly deteriorating. "That's fine. We'll just wait till you're done."

"Or, want to join us for doubles?" the other player asked with a grin.

Eli looked at Hark again, who shrugged an indifferent *why not.* They split up one man and one woman per team, and if Eli thought that it was because he and Hark would otherwise have an advantage, that notion was instantly, humblingly dispelled.

"You two play a lot?" he asked his teammate half an hour later, during a much-needed water break. He used the hem of his shirt to wipe his sweat. It was already drenched.

"Almost every day when we were in college. Increasingly less so for the past five years," she told him. "I'm Piper, by the way."

"Eli." He shook her hand. She was older than he'd originally thought, then. Tall, with long dark hair. Blue eyes. Beautiful, objectively so, but in a way that was completely different from Rue, who had the uncanny ability to soak up all the light in a room, like a prism that refused to spit out rainbows. Piper was bright and luminous and smiled a lot. *Because she doesn't despise you,* a sardonic voice in his head suggested.

It was right.

They chatted for a while, and Eli thought that Piper was skirting the thin line between friendly and flirty, a familiar dance. He listened to her stories about being a pharmacist, wondering if he was interested. He should be. How refreshing, the idea of spending time with a beautiful, intelligent, funny woman who didn't loathe the idea of being attracted to him.

It would be good for him—a hard reset. Rue had messed up his parameters, but someone else might bring him back to factory default. Someone with whom a simple conversation wouldn't be a land mine. Someone who wouldn't look at him like he'd turned into a balloon animal when he asked for a date, who saw him as more than a quick fuck. At the very least, racquetball was on the table.

Did Rue play any sports? Basketball or volleyball, maybe, given her height. She'd be good at it, he was sure. She seemed coordinated, and her body was strong. He'd felt the muscles tense under the pliant flesh of her thighs, and just that little moment had been more of a turn-on than some of the seriously dirty stuff he'd been up to in the past decade.

"You guys ready?" Hark asked from his side of the court, and Eli had his answer. He was *not* interested in Piper. Not if while she told him about her last Pacific Northwest road trip, all he could do was think wistfully about having his head between another woman's legs.

"That was unexpected," Hark told him in the parking lot after more racquetball, after Eli pleaded a previous commitment when invited out for dinner, after a shower spent contemplating the severe idiocy of being hung up on Rue Siebert.

"Yeah. Really good players."

"I meant, the part where you debuted your monastic endeavors."

"Just tired is all." Historically, Eli had been the one who got

around. Girlfriends, friends, people he barely knew. Dates, relationships, hookups. Hark . . . even before Minami, his sex life had
been more circumspect. They hadn't discussed it much after, because there was little to talk about.

"Right. Nothing to do with Dr. Rue Siebert, then?"

Sometimes Hark was insufferable. "Nothing at all," Eli lied.
"Did you like . . . ?"

"Emily."

"Did you like Emily?"

"She's pretty fantastic. Gave me her number," Hark said quietly.

A beat. "Are you going to use it?"

He didn't reply, but they both knew the answer.

The last transcript of a three-part witness deposition was dropped
on Eli's desk that Friday night. "In case you're in search of some
light bedtime reading," Minami told him.

When he looked up, her smile was mischievous.

"Is it . . . ?"

She nodded. "The lawyers are still combing through it. They
refuse to commit on whether the depo gives us reason enough to
send a notice of default and acceleration, but they have no doubt
that something weird is going on. At the very least, we'll be able to
go to court and ask for more discovery."

"Thank fuck."

"I *know*. Let's get dinner. To celebrate," Minami offered. "Just
the two of us, no Sul or Hark. I'm tired of my stupid husband and
your stupid husband getting in the way of our affair."

Eli checked his watch and got to his feet. "Can't. Meeting
Dave."

"Right, I forgot. We're still on for tomorrow, though? All four of us."

"Sure." He gathered his stuff, and couldn't help chuckling when she began chanting, *"He was a skater boy, he said, 'See you later, boy.'"*

"C'mon."

"His friends weren't good enough for him."

"It's for a noble cause."

"Now he's a hockey star, driving off in his car."

"You're the worst," he told her lovingly as he slipped out of the room.

The face of Dave Lenchantin was smile-wrinkled and sun-weathered—somewhat surprising, for a man who'd lived two-thirds of his life inside an ice rink. He immediately spotted Eli, and quickly wrapped up a conversation to weave through the crowd and greet him.

The yearly fundraiser was an informal occasion, not unlike the carnival Eli's middle school had organized when the district refused to allocate funds for graphing calculators. There were bake sales, crafts stations, portrait artists, temporary tattoos, ring tossing, and even a dunk tank—in which, Eli was amused to see, sat a terrified Alec, Dave's partner. The event was a great moneymaker for the charity initiatives sponsored by the rink. "Dr. Killgore," Dave said, reaching up to hug Eli. They'd first met when Eli was in his early teens, but the man had never been less than half a foot shorter than him.

"I never did get that doctorate, Coach." Being reminded of that part of his life never got easier. "I'll take mister, though."

"I ain't calling you mister, Killgore. Not after that time you bent down to pick up a cracker, threw out your back, and sat out three games."

"Lies."

"Hell no."

"It was an Oreo."

"Well, I hope it was worth your dignity." Dave smiled, genuinely happy. "Thank you for the generous donation, Killgore."

Eli shook his head. "Thank you for . . ." *Training me for years, even when I was a dumbass teenager who thought he was hot shit and knew better than anyone around him. For believing in me. For calling over talent scouts. For providing me the structure I needed and didn't even know it. For being there when Maya and I were alone. For my entire fucking life, really.* "Making me do bare-knuckle push-ups on the ice that time I showed up wasted to practice, even though it was Rivera's fault for spiking the Gatorade."

"It was my pleasure, son."

"I just bet." Eli wasn't sure why he'd responded so well to Dave's brand of discipline, especially when the relationship with his own parents had always been so strained. He'd been a rebellious, defiant child. One of Eli's teachers suggested that a physically demanding extracurricular activity might soak up the hostility coursing through him, and he'd been forcibly enrolled in every team sport the greater Austin area had to offer. Only hockey—and Dave—had stuck.

"How's Maya doing?" Dave asked. "I think I saw her around a couple weeks ago?"

"Visiting Alec, probably. She's staying with a friend, or she'd be here with me." When Eli had become the sole caretaker of his eleven-year-old sister, his financial situation had been disastrous.

He'd had several minimum-wage jobs on top of debt and a mort-gage, which meant long hours and no money left for childcare. Leaving a clearly bereaved, obviously confused, extremely angry child home alone had been out of the question, but Dave had of-fered Maya a spot on Alec's figure skating training team—which, to Eli's surprise, she'd accepted. Access to a rink, let alone a trainer, would have been cost prohibitive, but Dave had covered most expenses—thanks to fundraisers like this one. Maya had never been more than an amateur skater. Nonetheless, the sport had grounded her.

"You two should come over for dinner soon."

"Just name the night." Eli smiled. "But let's order out."

"You damn princess. It was *one* time. And how is ketchup on mac and cheese not a good idea? I was just tellin' Rue that Alec and I have been taking these couples cooking classes—"

"I'm sorry," Eli interrupted. The hairs at the back of his neck lifted. "Telling who?"

"You don't remember her? Ah, I bet you were gone when she started training with Alec. But she might know Maya. There she is! Rue!" Dave waved at someone, a wide gesture, impossible to ignore. Blue eyes flashed in Eli's head.

A small key chain, shaped like a skating shoe.

Minami's voice: *Apparently she was a student athlete.*

"Rue, could you come here for a moment?"

She was wearing a Lenchantin Rink T-shirt. Handing a slice of pizza to a child in an ice-skating dress. Focused, a little remote. Out of place in the loud, bustling crowd.

As usual, Eli was irreparably lost at the sight of her.

She didn't hear Dave calling, but the older woman next to her tapped her twice on the shoulder and pointed in Dave's direction. Rue's eyes lifted, met Eli's, and he thought, *Fuck. Me.*

He'd managed not to think of her obsessively for the past week—except when he hadn't. Which was an embarrassing amount of time. Most of the time. All the fucking time.

He didn't need this. He didn't need to be reminded of how *physical* she was, of the way she soaked up the air in his lungs. He didn't need to witness her full lips parting in surprise, or the moment she went very, *very* still.

And he certainly didn't need Dave hollering, "Rue, c'mere. There's someone I wanna introduce you to."

17

HER EXISTENCE, APPARENTLY, DID A LOT FOR HIM

ELI

Rue's mouth shaped a muted *excuse me*, and she walked toward them, wiping her already-clean palms on the sides of her jean shorts. Eli was suddenly, intensely, pleasurably aware of the warmth of his own blood. He was alive, very much so. Because Rue Siebert was walking toward him with the air of someone who'd rather be anywhere else.

Her existence, apparently, did a lot for him. More than an elaborately staged erotic show.

"Rue, this is Eli. Used to be on my hockey team before you began skating with Alec."

Rue and Eli regarded each other, the usual current lighting the space between them. Wordlessly, they reached the same decision.

Fake it.

"Nice to meet you, Rue." He sounded too intimate to fool anyone.

She, too sultry. "Likewise."

They shook hands, and a spark traveled through him, positively pornographic. He wanted to take her home and spread her out on his sheets. He wanted to tie her to his bed. He wanted to exhaust her until she could no longer fight this unyielding pull between them. His hand engulfed hers, and he imagined drawing her closer. Pressing an open-mouthed kiss into her palm. Taking her away, someplace that could only be classified as *elsewhere*.

He was unstable. She made him so.

"When you were training with Alec, you might have met Eli's sister. Maya Killgore?"

She looked away from Eli, with some difficulty. "Younger?"

"Early twenties now."

"I doubt it, then."

They stared at each other with a touch of resignation. Some excitement. Relief. And when Dave spotted someone else and excused himself, they remained there, unmoving, the chatter in the hall receding past this moment in time.

Eli tried to imagine a reality in which he didn't know Rue Siebert existed. The empty misery of it. The sheer relief. "Hi, Rue," he said softly.

Her braided hair hung past her shoulder, as thick as his wrist. She nodded her head. A somewhat awkward response that somehow made perfect sense. "Why is it that we keep meeting like this?"

"Like this?"

"By chance."

He huffed a laugh. "Maybe we just have lots in common."

Her marvelous lips pressed together. "That seems unlikely," she said, obviously unwilling to admit that they belonged to the same places. Loved the same things. What a mindfuck this woman was to him.

"Alec trained you?" He'd seen a lot of skaters in his life, and Rue didn't look the part too much, but she nodded. "When did you stop?"

"Final year of college."

"Injuries?"

"Some minor ones, but that wasn't the reason."

He'd just bet she'd been like him: not good enough to go pro, but good enough to get a full ride. "You're tall for a figure skater."

"That had more to do with it."

Her long, strong legs. The muscles in her core, tightening as she shuddered and arched into him. He tried to picture what it would take to dance on the ice with a center of gravity as high as hers. With the length of her limbs, the kind of control she'd have mastered to achieve the elevation, precision, speed during jumps. He savored the mental image, the anticipation it created. He'd never given figure skaters a second thought, but her strength did something for him. Rue, sweating and doing beautiful things. Rue, powerful and quietly fierce. She would match him. In fact, she already had.

"Did you want to go pro?" he asked.

"I was done with the whole thing about two weeks into college. It was actually a tightrope to walk, being just decent enough to have my tuition waived."

"I can imagine."

"Insisting on choreographing my routines to 'Pump Up the Jam' helped."

He felt himself smile. "I still can't tell when you're joking." *And I fucking adore it.*

"I told you, I was born without a sense of humor. It's congenital."

Bullshit. "Yeah?"

"You've met my brother. Do you think he's the type to giggle over puns?"

He assessed her. Tried to solve her. Failed. "It's okay, if you prefer to play it this way."

"Rue," the woman from the pizza stand called, "we're out of water bottles. Could you get some more from the back?" Her eyes slid to Eli, suspicious. "Maybe that brawny gentleman can help?"

He smiled. "It'd be my pleasure, ma'am."

He followed Rue to one of the many storage rooms. Uniforms, old helmets, and the occasional stick piled on all surfaces, and he had to sidestep several boxes of pucks just to find the light switch. His brain hiccuped, disoriented in time: he hadn't been in here in over a decade, but the logo on the green jerseys was as familiar to him as the weight of the head on his shoulders.

"Have you kept in touch with Alec since graduating?" he asked. If he couldn't have her, he at least wanted to *know* things about her. Tiles for the Rue mosaic that had taken up residence in his brain.

"Yeah." She unearthed a cart from under a box of shin guards. In the harsh ceiling lights, she was paler than usual, her curves meeting dramatic shadows and narrow angles. "Did your sister?"

"Yup. Alec has done a lot for our family."

"For me, too."

"Yeah?"

"When I was a teenager, he'd bring food to the rink, just for me. Sandwiches, veggies and hummus. Healthy snacks with protein." She stopped unloading the cart, eyes unfocused in the middle distance. "I never even said I was hungry."

He observed her, recalling the slight frame of teenage Rue. Wasn't her project on shelf life extension of produce? "And *were* you hungry?"

She shook off the memory of it, and he realized that this one hadn't been one of the ugly stories they'd gotten into the habit of exchanging. She'd shared it with him without quite wanting to. "Do you see the water?" she asked.

He pointed at the cart he'd just loaded with eighty bottles.

"Ah. Right." She scratched the back of her neck, uncharacteristically flustered. A fucking sight to behold. He wanted to pull her apart, watch the atoms of her squirm in pleasure, and take his own sweet time putting them back together. He wanted her to feel the way *he* did.

"My ex-fiancée was a chef," he said.

Her look was blank. "And?"

"She was—is—damn good. And she thought everyone should have at least three signature dishes they could prepare without needing a recipe."

"To impress at dinner parties?"

He laughed. McKenzie would, too, at the idea of wanting to impress. "To be able to eat good food. By yourself or with others."

"I'm not sure where you're going with this."

"There are three dishes I can make. Because a professional Michelin restaurant chef taught me." Rue blinked, like it still wasn't clear. "I could feed you well. If you're still hungry, that is."

She gave him a wide-eyed look and slipped into speechlessness. Then she moved closer, and the blood in his veins thickened as she pushed onto the tips of her toes. Her heat warmed him, and her chin tilted up, and her mouth—

He turned his head away before her lips could touch his.

Which, his body immediately let him know, was a supremely fucked-up idea. *Go back. Kiss her. Lock the door. Pull her shirt up and her shorts down. Bend her over. You know what to do next. She does, too.*

Rue took a step back, looking confused, maybe hurt by the rejection.

Eli's body revolted. He was so hard, he could feel his erection pulsate against the zipper of his jeans, bent at a painful angle. When she made to leave, he stopped her with a hand on her shoulder and spun her around. "Wait."

She lifted her chin. Her eyes held a hint of challenge.

"I live nearby," he said. A gambit. "You could come over. Retrieve your property."

"My property?"

"You left something in that hotel room."

He watched her scan her memories, and her eyes widened when she stumbled upon the answer. "You could have thrown them away."

"The thought never occurred to me."

"They're not your size, you know."

"They definitely worked when I used them." He was being deliberately crude, maybe to remind himself of what lay underneath this distance between them. Maybe to remind *her.*

"You can't have Kline, so you stole my underwear."

"Oh, Rue. I *can* have Kline." Her eyes narrowed, and he continued, "I just wanted a keepsake. If you don't want them back, you can leave them with me—it's a good home. But come over anyway. For fun."

That last *n* lingered between them. A long matrix of calculations played out on her beautiful face. He let her think it through, waiting breathlessly for the outcome. His heart skipped a beat when she said, "Okay. I'll come over."

Fuck.

Fuck.

He needed to calm down. He couldn't be this worked up, just because of a handful of words.

"Cool. I have one condition, though," he said.

"A condition?" She'd clearly never considered the possibility, and maybe he wanted to fuck her more than ever when she looked confused. It was the asshole in him, the one who got off on being one step ahead and in charge, the one who wanted to lock her in his room and keep her there for months.

"If I take you to my place, you're not running out on me."

Her arms crossed on her chest. "Are you planning on holding me hostage?"

"That seems like a lot of needless work. And a felony." He let go of her shoulder. It didn't seem prudent to keep touching her.

"I'm going to leave when I want to leave," she said calmly.

"I'm not asking you to marry me and have my triplets, Rue." He kept his tone casual. Anything resembling earnestness or emotional intimacy would have spooked her. "You don't have to stay any longer than you like. If you want to leave because it's too much, or you're bored, or because the sex is not what you expected and simply doesn't do it for you, by all means, go. But don't run out like you did last time. It scared the shit out of me. I'm asking you to communicate."

"I just . . ." She didn't continue, but he didn't need her to.

"I know." Something softened inside him at her lost expression. "It was intense for me, too." He had no illusion that he could

174

fuck her out of his system. If he was honest with himself, he'd known this was going to be something else from the very first night.

She was something else. Utterly unique. Unpredictable. Deliciously complicated.

Rue pointed at the water. "I have to go help out."

"And I have to do my best to sink Alec in a kiddie pool."

"A worthwhile endeavor." Her mouth curled. "I'll come find you when I'm done."

"Will you?" *Or will you chicken out again?*

"Yes."

Her expression was impenetrable, but there was something in her tone—something Eli recognized in himself. *Am I holding you hostage the same way you hold me? Tell me, Rue. Just between you and me.*

Because this time, he was sure she would come.

18

OUR CURRENCY

RUE

I drove behind Eli's hybrid, tailing him down the tree-lined streets of Allandale, through the soft glow of the bistro lights. He lived in a charming two-story single-family home, a mid-century construction with reddish bricks and a wide lawn that had me instinctively thinking of his ex-fiancée. Were we going to have sex in a bed he'd bought during a relationship-straining trip to IKEA? Was what had broken them up a disagreement over the Ekoln soap dispenser?

Irrelevant. None of my business. But I'd never been to a man's place. Maybe by accident in college, with some guy I wouldn't have recognized the following day if he'd sat next to me in Chemistry 201. This was Eli Killgore, though. Breaking my streaks. Ruining my plans. Making me want to do terrible, disloyal things.

"Still want to do this?" he asked, waiting for me at the door when I got out of the car. His voice had burrowed among the sulci of my brain and was now prominently featured in my dreams. A few dirty ones, which I could easily brush off, and lots of unsettling, preposterous scenarios. He'd stand behind and ask to observe my X-ray diffraction, or explain what a leveraged buyout was with Nyota nodding by his side. Whenever I reached out to touch him, he'd say, *Let's revisit this tomorrow.*

It was finally *tomorrow.* "Yes."

Instead of unlocking the door, he bent down and kissed me hard, a hand closed around my waist, the other palm pressing me against the wall. It was sudden, and instantly good, and the very opposite of the kind of restraint he'd shown back at the hotel, in Kline's echoey hallways, an hour earlier at the rink. He wanted me to feel trapped. To know exactly how hard he was and how quickly. To be aware of his strength, deep inside my bones.

"Jesus, you feel good." He trailed open-mouthed kisses down my throat. His fingers slid up to cup my breast, and his eyes followed suit. I'd never felt more beautiful than when he looked at me. Like I was the final prototype of someone's entire fantasy life.

"We should go in." My words labored against his lips.

"In a minute." His fingers skimmed between my flesh and the waist of my jeans. I sucked in the night air. "It's been a few long fucking weeks, Rue."

"I know."

With a predatory grin, he nipped at my throat. Chased that with a lick. Squeezed my ass in a way that could only be described as indecent. It felt like centuries before I heard the jingle of his keys, felt the push of his hand guiding me inside, watched the lights from the street disappear as Eli closed the door behind us, and—

I was assaulted. By a three-hundred-pound grizzly bear. It

bellowed at me as its paws slammed into my torso with the force of a dinosaur-extinguishing meteor, sending me careening back into Eli's solid front.

"Tiny, down." His voice was warm but authoritative. The bear—dog, a *giant* dog—trotted back, wagging its tail. It stared at me with something that couldn't anatomically be a smile, but fundamentally *felt* like one.

I plastered myself against Eli's chest. One of his arms snaked around my torso, holding me close. "Is it . . . hungry?" I asked, eyeing the mutt suspiciously. He must have been crossbred with a horse. His fur contained thirty different types of brown, and his tongue rolled out of his mouth like an ancient scroll.

"Always." With one hand still closed around my hip, he bent to give the dog several energetic pets, causing him to helicopter his tail and bark in bliss.

Maybe coming here had been a mistake.

"Are you allergic to dogs?" he asked, noticing my discomfort.

I shook my head, eyes never letting go of the mammoth. Was his name *Tiny*? What in the actual fuck?

"You're not *scared* of them, are you?"

I wasn't. Or maybe I was. I hadn't had sufficient dog exposure to be sure. "I'm not a pet person."

"I see. You hate animals." He sounded amused.

"I don't. I just like to maintain a respectful distance." Bruce ruthlessly ignored me, which suited me just fine. But Tiny circled me happily, eager for the cuddles and praise he was sure I'd provide any moment now.

"Well, he sure likes *you*."

As lush as his fur looked, I had no intention of reaching out. I'd read somewhere that dogs could tell good people apart from the bad ones. I didn't care to know the verdict. "Do you, um, need to walk him?"

"Not this late. We have a big yard and he has free access. He wants a midnight snack, though. Are you going to freak out if I let you go?"

My nails, I realized, were digging in his forearm. "Sorry." I released him, and he untangled himself with a smile that looked almost affectionate before he disappeared into the kitchen, followed by the beast. I heard puttering, cupboards opening and closing, and soft, patient murmurs. I caught myself smiling at the sound, and wasn't sure why. What did I care if Eli had a dog, or quail, or a raft of otters? When he returned, wiping freshly washed hands on his jeans, I immediately asked, "Where is your bedroom?"

"Not so fast." I cocked my head, and he smiled. "I want a story. Before we go upstairs."

Ah, yes. Our currency. "An ugly one that proves how terrible a person I am?"

"Doesn't matter. As long as it's true." He paused. "As long as it's just for me."

"They all are." I'd told him things I'd never admitted out loud to another soul. It was the same for him, I knew without having to ask. And I had the perfect story. "When I was eleven, Tisha and Nyota—her younger sister—started pestering their parents to get a puppy. It involved PowerPoints, Post-its left all around the house. They even got character letters from their teachers. Tisha liked cats better, but if they were going to get a pet, an alliance was necessary, and Nyota was younger. Less willing to compromise, you know? Anyway, they ended up adopting Elvis, a Chihuahua mix. He was . . . loud, and small. He pretended I didn't exist, and I returned the favor." I swallowed. "I was maniacally jealous of that dog. Because he got to stay with Tisha and her family every second of every day. He was fed, taken care of, doted on. While I had to go back home and deal with . . ." *My unpredictable mother, my little brother, who was getting more and more aggressive, the empty kitchen and the stench of mold. The certainty that if that was my life, I had to have done something to deserve it.* "I had to deal with a lot. So I looked at Elvis and was *so* resentful and thought, 'Why not me?' over and over, until it felt like—like a *cancer*, metastasizing in every interaction I had with Tisha. It took me a long time to wean myself off the habit. Maybe I never fully succeeded."

I waited for my cheeks to burn and for the shame to pour over me, like it always did. But it was difficult to blame myself when Eli offered no recrimination or disgust. He just accepted it openly, this story that I'd carried in my marrow for over a decade, like it was as natural a part of me as my lips or my arm.

So I said, "Your turn."

He nodded. Took a deep breath. "Last Friday I was out of town. I got drunk off vodka with some colleagues, went back to the hotel, and pulled up your contact. I typed a long, long text describing every single thing I've imagined doing to you. I left out nothing. And it wasn't a list, Rue. It was filthy, and indefensible, and exceptionally detailed. A fucking instruction manual. I have the faintest memory of writing it, and thankfully I fell asleep before I hit send, because when my alarm went off the following morning, it was there in the text box."

At first I felt shortchanged, and almost called him out for cheating—this wasn't our kind of story, cruel and bare and flustering. But that wasn't for me to decide, was it? Maybe for Eli, confessing to his loss of control was all those things.

"Do you want to know the last thing I'd written?" he asked.

I nodded, heart pounding in anticipation.

"How badly I wanted to fuck you into compliance." He shook his head, exhaling a rueful laugh, and gestured with his chin toward the staircase. "Still wanna do this?"

I didn't bother answering, but started the climb upstairs. When I turned to check if he was following, I caught his eyes glued to my ass. His smile was unrepentant, as though looking at my body was a sacrosanct right he planned to take advantage of as long as it was granted.

His bedroom was what I'd have expected from an adult man who hadn't planned on visitors: simply furnished, mostly neat, with an unmade king bed and the occasional item of clothing draped across a piece of furniture. The windows were street facing, and he brushed past me to pull the curtains. When he turned, I'd already toed off my shoes and taken off my shirt.

"Stop," he ordered.

I glanced down at my shorts. "Want me to leave these on?"

"Nah." He came closer. "Let me do it."

"Hardly efficient." Nor sexy. I was wearing my grocery-shopping clothes.

"Come on, Rue. You have to know I'm going to treat tonight like the second chance I never thought I'd get." Every catch of the zipper was loud in the quiet room. His large hands opened the front like he was unwrapping a present. Then, eyes fixed to me, he slid his hand inside.

The tip of his index finger tapped against the cotton of my panties. Brushed softly. "Nice."

Wet, he meant. I'd felt the dampness between my thighs, and now he knew it, too. "You can't be surprised."

"I don't need to be surprised to enjoy it." My shorts came off.

"You don't really need me to say it, do you? That your body is the most perfect thing I've ever seen?"

I cocked my head, observing him observe me, greedy and acquisitive. His eyes lingered on my breasts, belly, hips, thighs, all too *something* to be anywhere near perfect. But I loved my body, even in its flaws. I loved the things it could do on the ice and off, the pleasure it was capable of, the way it looked in the dresses I enjoyed buying. I loved that it had kept going through my first eighteen years, despite the adversities it had faced. And I loved that Eli liked it as much as I did. "I'm glad you think so. Feel free to use it as you like."

His throat jerked. "You have no damn idea what you're saying, Rue." He touched me like he was revisiting a yearly vacation spot, familiar and yet eternally yearned for. My lace bralette did not match my panties, but he didn't care. He cupped his palm around my left breast, his thumb finding my already hard nipple to brush against it, and I let my eyes drift closed as I arched into him. "You like it, don't you?" He did it again, and my breath hitched. When he pinched my nipple, I had to swallow a moan. "You know what I'd love to do to you?"

"What?"

He opened his mouth, then stopped himself. Laughed, wistful. "You'd be scared shitless if I told you."

"I would not."

He shook his head. "It's stuff that requires trust. Communication." His hand fell to his side, and I felt the loss like a stab. "Time."

"We don't have that."

"I know." His smile was not happy. He undid my braid, took a step back to look at me some more, and seemed even more pleased with that view. "Three times."

I frowned, confused.

"Let me make you come three times before you leave."

I tried to remember if I'd come that many times with someone else before. Or by myself. "That might be too ambitious."

"Might be." He shrugged, and I liked how he didn't act as though he knew my body better than I did. His self-assurance was never loud, always quietly, steadily present. "Still, let me try." He buried his head in my neck. Inhaled. "You smell so good. Every day since the last time, I thought about kissing your sweet cunt. May I?"

He was good at being in charge. Giving soft directions, concise instructions, precise commands. He wanted me on the bed, on my knees, my thighs on each side of his head, and got me there with little effort. He was still wearing his clothes, and I was bare atop his face. I felt him lick up into me, a long swipe that started from my clit and stopped behind my opening, and the burst of pleasure was so unexpected, I fell forward, catching myself on my palms to avoid collapsing into his hip.

"Too much?" Eli asked, still kissing and sucking and biting. I had to choke back a moan. He'd gone down on me last time, too, but he hadn't been immediately, magically good. It had taken him a while to find my spots and the right rhythm. Now that he knew the basics, he was a real threat, and reveled in it.

"Not too much." I began unbuttoning Eli's jeans, caressing his cock through his underwear as he continued to lick me. When he nipped at my folds, I slid it out of his boxer briefs. He was big in a way I wasn't used to and wouldn't have expected to enjoy, but I knew that already. When his hands squeezed my tits and he pushed his tongue inside me, I took him in my mouth as deep as I could, which was only about halfway.

We both groaned loudly, the sounds vibrating through our flesh. I tried, *really* tried to keep up with the way his tongue parted me and his fingers moved with increased purpose toward my opening. I tried to focus, pressing wet, clumsy kisses up the length of his cock, using my tongue to tease the ridge around the head. But the position was unusual and more intimate than I was used to, and the spreading heat made concentrating on anything but the pleasure rising up my spine next to impossible. I knew how to give as much as I got, but with Eli's hands gripping my ass and his thumb suddenly pressing against my hole, it was difficult to center myself, and—

"You're not good at this, are you?" He spoke against the inside of my thigh, sounding charmed as he chased the words with a sucking kiss.

"That's rude and—*ah*—hurtful."

"Hurtful? This?" He licked into me again, and my thighs trembled uncontrollably. He was *fantastic* at that, like he'd mapped every sound of pleasure to the anatomy of my cunt. Or maybe it was his sheer enthusiasm. Either way, I was on the verge of something. "Are you in pain, Rue?"

"No. When you said that I'm not—" He exhaled against my clit. I shuddered, forehead dropping to his muscular thigh.

"Poor girl." His fingers gripped my hips, bruising tight. "You seem to have issues focusing."

"It's . . ."

His fingers pinched my nipples. "Good?"

"Distracting." The word sounded slurred.

"It's okay. I'm going to come just from this." I hazily wondered what *this* meant, but after a beat he added, "From eating you out, that is." There was something about the way he said it, something admiring and eager, that had me contracting around the first phalanx of his finger when it slid inside me. "You can clean me up once I'm done. With your mouth."

The pleasure broke me apart like an earthquake. It was, without doubt, the most sudden orgasm of my life, something that started from a place deep in my brain as much as from the stimulation of my nerve endings. I found myself gasping against the jeans covering his thigh, swallowing embarrassing noises down my throat. His cock twitched next to me, precome beading from the tip, and once the first aftershocks had calmed I tried to take him in my mouth again, to *show* him how grateful I was for the pleasure he was giving me, but it was impossible to concentrate. Giving and taking were hard to combine, and from the curve of his cheek as he smiled against my thigh, he didn't mind.

It *amused* him, my lack of control.

"Eli, I *can't*—"

"You're okay, love," he soothed. "You're going to be fine. Don't you like this? Don't you like to come?"

I whimpered. His hands, large and strong and absolutely filthy, closed around the cheeks of my ass and spread me open. There was a hint of aggression in his touch, an ever-increasing directiveness, and I wondered if he was punishing me for depriving us both of this for weeks, or if he was just that impatient. Then he sucked my clit between his lips, and I stopped wondering anything at all, teetering on the edge of a second, stronger orgasm.

"God," he gasped. "You really are the sweetest fucking thing."

In that moment, I wanted him in my mouth more than I wanted to come. And when I moaned around his cock I thought that maybe he felt the same. His breath hitched, his hips arched in a way that had him nearly sliding inside my throat, and when he let out a deep groan, I wasn't sure what I felt first: the pleasure racking through me once again, or his come flooding my mouth.

We remained there, still, making sounds that belonged to wild creatures for long moments, our descent slow and laborious. And then Eli untangled us, kissed me deeply and gratefully, and laid me down on the bed, one arm around my waist. I felt like a transcendent being made of sensation and heat and the imprints of Eli's fingers on my skin.

"That was two," I said, small aftershocks coursing through me. I'd felt this way last time, too. Wrung out. Empty. Like my body was his puppet, something he could mold and shape at will.

Intense, he'd said, but the word seemed all wrong. This was frightening. Dangerous. I needed a moment to regain my bearings and was thankful when he withdrew his arm to cover his eyes. I wouldn't have been able to take any more closeness.

"Give me a second," he panted. "I can give you another. Or die trying."

I laughed, feeling sparkly on the inside. With my cheek pressed against the pillow, I observed this man who could make my body sing like never before. The exhaustion from the sex, the past weeks at work, the stress of being alive and for the most part alone began setting in. *One minute,* I thought. *One minute, and I'll get up. Make a big obnoxious scene about saying goodbye, since it's so important to him, and leave this bed once and for all. As far as last times go, this was a good one.*

I watched Eli's broad chest rise and fall to the rhythm of his labored breath. I watched him lick his lips absentmindedly and curve them into a hint of a smile at the taste. I watched him be unmistakably, unapologetically pleased with himself—and then, when my eyelids fluttered closed and the sounds from the streets muted in my ears, I watched him no more.

19

YOU KNOW WHERE THE CLOROX WIPES ARE, RIGHT?

RUE

It was the soft pitter-patter of the rain against the windows that woke me up, and the muted swish of a car riding past the house that finally convinced me to open my eyes. There was no disorientation. I immediately knew where I was, and that the digital clock blinking at me from the nightstand in lime green was Eli's.

It was ten forty-five in the morning.

The curtains were still drawn. Eli was nowhere to be found. I couldn't remember the last time I'd slept so deeply, so uninterruptedly, or so late. Maybe it was the bed—mortuary slab–solid, just the way I liked. The sex, perhaps. I had no clue, nor did I plan to investigate the matter further. As furtively as I was capable of, I gathered the breadcrumb trail of clothes we'd scattered around the bed, and slipped into the en suite.

It was the same gentle mix of cleanliness and chaos as Eli's bedroom. I peed, rinsed my mouth with some pilfered Listerine, and snuck down the stairs, stopping when I heard noises coming from the kitchen.

Shit.

I'd promised Eli I'd tell him before leaving. Back when I thought *leaving* would happen in the middle of the night. I was going to have to walk-of-shame this. Embarrassing, but not as embarrassing as Eli knowing how bad I was at sixty-nining.

I headed for the kitchen, ready to keep my goodbyes quick and honest. *Thank you for last night, Eli. I enjoyed it. I always enjoy it. It's starting to feel cruel, the combination of who you are and what you can do to me. Let's never meet again, okay?* But when I took a deep breath and made myself step inside, Eli looked different.

Like a tinier, prettier version of himself. Ferocious brown curls falling onto slight shoulders, eerily light blue eyes, and that half-warm, half-cutthroat grin. A few inches shorter than me. A girl. Briefly slack-jawed, until her surprise morphed into a smile. "Well, well, well. Look who got laid last night."

I lifted an eyebrow.

The girl instantly blushed. "Sorry! I didn't mean *you*, I would never—I meant my brother! Hi, I'm Maya Killgore."

The sister. Did she live here? "Rue. Siebert."

"So lovely to meet you. I promise I don't usually comment on random people's recent sexual history, just . . ."

"Your brother's?"

"Precisely." She finger-gunned me. "He never tells me shit, so I have to resort to ruthless investigative methods. Is he trying to wife you?"

"To . . . what?" I needed caffeine.

"Are you guys dating, or are you just using his body?"

"Um. The latter." A beat. "It's more of a reciprocally beneficial agreement."

"Nice. Good on you guys." She seemed sincerely happy. "Where did you meet?"

"I work for a company here in Austin. Harkness recently attempted to acquire us." And had not succeeded yet. It felt good to remind myself. Softened my guilt, too.

"Holy shit, you work for Kline? You know Florence?"

The shame at hearing Florence mentioned in Eli's house was so intense, I had to take a breath before saying, "Yes."

"What's she like? I picture her as a giant tentacled monster."

Why did *she* know about Florence? "She's a five-three redhead. Untentacled. Not particularly monstrous looking." To trim the conversation before it could grow its own appendages, I added, "She is a close friend of mine."

Maya's eyes went saucer wide, but a second later her pleasant smile was restored. "Would you like some coffee?"

"No, thank you. I was just going home. Is Eli . . . ?"

"He'll be back soon. I can text him, too."

"No need." I'd asked after him. I wasn't sneaking out. I'd text him once I got back to my place and make up a nonexistent Saturday morning engagement. *I man the arugula booth at the farmers' market. I AquaGym. Did I mention I'm a mother of four? They're waiting for breakfast.* "Thank you, I'll just—"

The front door—against which I'd nearly engaged in public sex the previous night—opened. The first to come in was the giant dog, who looked even larger and even happier in the daylight. He chose violence, and shook several gallons of rainwater all over the wooden floor, sparing no surface. The second, of course, was Eli. He pulled back the hood of a dark green windbreaker, and when his eyes found me, he said, "I was wondering if you'd still be here." He was smiling. Half-pleased, half-challenging, half-all-knowing.

Something hot and cold ran through me. "I—"

"*Rude*," Maya interrupted. "Are you trying to get rid of her?"

"If only you knew, Maya," he drawled. He draped his jacket over a high-backed chair, gaze never leaving me.

"Knew what?" Maya petted Tiny, who this morning was supremely uninterested in me. *Good boy.*

"Rue was a figure skater with Alec," Eli informed her instead of answering.

"For real? He's the *best.*"

I nodded. "He is."

"Do you still skate?"

"Not competitively."

"What about for fun?"

"I do."

"At Dave's rink?"

"For the most part."

"Wait." Those Eli eyes of hers narrowed. "Rue Siebert. I know you! Didn't you get a synchro scholarship for some place in Wisconsin?"

"Michigan. Adrian College."

"Oh my god. I remember you! We only overlapped for a few months but you were *so good.*"

"I wasn't that—"

"At mentoring, I mean. You taught me how to do a backward crossover, remember?" I didn't, but she continued anyway, grinning. "I sucked. Four other people tried, and I could *not* figure it out. Come on, you have to remember—I'm the girl who burst out crying in the middle of the rink. You brought me to a bench, sat next to me, and neither of us said anything for, like, half an hour. Once I calmed down you asked me if I was ready to start again and then I got the crossover on the first try! It must have been in the spring of—"

A car honked right outside. I jolted, and Maya rolled her eyes. "That'll be Jade." She picked up her backpack and an oversized, over-stickered water bottle. "It was so nice to see you again, Rue! I'm going to spend the day at the library, so you two should feel free to have morning sex on the table." She glanced at Eli from over her shoulder. "You know where the Clorox wipes are, right?" She was gone before he could reply, leaving us alone, looking at each other with something that felt a lot like understanding.

He knew that I was going to sneak out.

I knew that he knew.

And *he* knew that, too.

I lifted my chin with a hint of a challenge, and his lips widened into a grin, as though I was following a script he'd written in his head for me.

"Were you going to leave me a note?" he asked affably. "Or just text later?"

I kept my spine straight. "The latter."

"Less time consuming." He nodded, entertained, and opened a cupboard. Kibble tinkled into the dog's metal bowl, and Tiny, who'd begun circling me looking for the kind of affection that other people seemed to give effortlessly to pets, instantly lost interest in me. On the table above him, I noticed a developed chess board.

"Is that your game?"

Eli nodded. "Against Maya."

"You play a lot?"

"A fair bit. We're not Nolan Sawyer level, or anything—"

"Mallory Greenleaf level, you mean?"

He just smiled. "Do you really not remember my sister?"

"I . . ." I did, actually, if only because of the way she'd sobbed silently next to me. It had felt heartbreaking and relatable, and I'd wished there was something I could say. But I was going through the exact same, and I knew that no words existed that would have helped. "Is it okay that she saw me?" I asked.

"Who?"

"Your sister."

"Why wouldn't it be?"

"Maybe you don't want to share your hookups with your younger sister, who might very well be a minor." She didn't look it, but the older I got, the more every age under twenty-five blended together.

"She's almost twenty-two. Or thirteen, I'm never sure."

"You're the elder?"

He nodded. "Is Vincent older?"

"He's three years younger. And it's just us."

"I figured, since the cabin's split in two."

"Yeah." I didn't want to talk about him. "Your sister seems . . ."

"Nice?"

Actually, what I'd been thinking was that Maya and Eli looked comfortable together, and I felt irrationally betrayed by that. When we first met, I'd gotten the impression that their relationship was as fraught as mine was with Vince. "Does she live here?"

"Yup."

"Of her own free will? Or are you kidnapping *her*, too?"

"Believe it or not, she *asked* to move in." He seemed incredulous, too. "I offered to pay for an apartment near campus, but she wanted to live with her closest surviving blood relative. To keep an eye on her set of spare kidneys, probably."

I smiled, and so did he. Like amusing me was a rewarding micro-hobby of his.

"Is this the home where you grew up?"

"Nope. I grew up in South Austin. Riverside. The bank took that home about a decade ago, though. What about you?"

We never owned a home for the bank to take, my sleep-woolly brain almost responded. "I lived in Salado."

His eyebrow rose. "And you commuted every day to Dave's rink?"

"Yes."

He cocked his head. "How did you end up skating, anyway?"

"Tisha's mom used to be an ice dancer. She thought I looked promising, found Alec." I didn't elaborate on the rest. How liberating it had been, pushing through the cold of the ice, being away from my family. How grueling practice had become as the stakes had risen. How impossible it had been to consider quitting with the prospect of waived tuition fees dangling in front of my eyes. Instead, I changed the topic. "Do you bring home lots of women?"

"I believe you were a first." He shrugged. "Although my ex-fiancée used to live here."

"The chef."

"Yup."

I tilted my head and watched him lean against the counter, enjoying the way he filled a room. How concrete his presence felt. "How does that happen?"

"What?"

"How do you go from wanting to marry someone to . . . not?"

"Surprisingly quickly. With limited drama, too." No cheating, then. What else, though? Had they fallen out of love? Had she moved away for her fancy chef job? Had she broken his heart? "Have you ever been in a relationship?" he asked.

"By relationship, you mean . . . ?"

"A mutually agreed-upon, medium- or long-term romantic engagement. Dating, if you prefer." He smiled the same grin I'd felt between my legs last night. What we'd done should have helped me metabolize him, but I was no closer to finding him uninteresting than I'd ever been. The opposite, if anything.

A silver coin refusing to oxidize, that's what he was. A compulsive tingle hooked right in my belly.

"It's none of my business," he continued, "but I'd still love it if you told me."

"No. You're the first person I've been with more than once."

His lip curled. "Sex is that good, huh?"

It's because with you I never have to worry about being too odd, too unlikable, too out of tune. You never make me feel anything other than just right. But the sex *was* the best I'd ever had, so I simply said, "Yes."

My soft honesty seemed to disarm him. His face fell, and his eyes darkened. "Come here," he beckoned, just a flick of his fingers, and even though it meant betraying Florence, who'd given me the world, I did go. Let him pull me closer, into his chest.

"I believe," he murmured against my ear, "I owe you something."

"You can keep my underwear."

"Not that."

"What, then?"

"We said three times."

A buzzing, warm static filled the air between us. "It doesn't matter. It's not . . ." *It's uncountable. You, and the things we do, the things you give me, the things you make me feel, they're impossible to quantify. They are good in a way that goes beyond orgasms, and I can't really keep track, or tick off checkboxes. It's confusing.* You *are* confusing. "It's fine."

"Is it?" He filled the space between us. His mouth tasted of toothpaste and rainy mornings, his kiss at once shallow and intense, eager yet lingering. Not a *we're about to fuck* kiss. Not a *we just fucked* kiss. Those were the extent of my experiences so far, so I wasn't certain how to categorize this one.

Goodbye. Maybe it was a goodbye kiss.

He slowly pulled back. "You *can't* go out like this, Rue."

"What do you mean?"

"You're filthy. You need a shower, don't you?"

"I'll have one later."

"Later?" His nose curled in distaste, and I frowned.

"Is that a problem?"

"I was about to take one."

I wasn't sure how to respond. *How hygienic of you. My fondest congratulations. I hope it's everything you wish for.* "Okay. I'm going to—"

"Join me." His fingers braided with mine. "You have to shower at some point, don't you? Might as well make it fun." There was no way this was a good idea, and he must have seen it in my face, because he asked, "Why not?"

Because of Florence. Because you're a bad person, doing bad things. Because you're wrong, and against everything I stand for, and people could be hurt if they were to find out. Problem was, I didn't want to say no. I also didn't want to say yes, but it didn't matter.

Judging by Eli's smile, nodding seemed to suffice.

20

BIG FUCKING DEAL

ELI

He was enthralled.

Obsessed.

In love.

Not with Rue, who would slit his throat with a skate blade before becoming the recipient of any romantic affection from one of Harkness's partners. But Rue's body—Eli was fucking *enchanted*. Her solemn, dark blue eyes that stared at him with hesitance. The deadpan way she said the damnedest things, tripping him up every time. The smell of sex and *her* on his sheets earlier this morning, when he'd had to tear himself out of bed. He'd woken up raging hard, and she'd slept on, soundless, with a hand under her cheek and the other lightly fisted in front of her face, so deliciously at his disposal. Right there, ready to be plucked.

She unhinged him. There was something uniquely *good* about being in her presence, and he could see himself doing things that ranged from embarrassing to reckless to illegal, just for five more minutes with her.

Naked, ideally.

"Not too hot?" he asked, licking water from where it pooled inside her collarbone. He tried to play it cool, but he hadn't expected that she'd say yes to staying longer than she absolutely needed in order to get off. He'd spent half the night on edge, staring at the rise and fall of her chest under the sheet he'd laid on her, at the huddled, inconspicuous way she slept, convinced that she'd disappear if he dared to blink. But the morning light had come, and he'd found her next to him. He'd returned from walking Tiny, and her car had been parked in his driveway.

He was going to keep her. For himself. As long as he could.

"No. Not too hot." She tipped her head back, letting the jet of the shower hit her hair and forehead. He followed the rivulets down the long line of her throat, studying her body in the brightness of the skylight. Eli recognized traces of her rigorous training regimens—muscular arms, rounded quads, strong core. But the cut tone had relaxed to something full and supple. Eli had found her stunning from the very start, but she was irresistible now that he knew that just like Eli's, hers was the imperfect, well-used body of a former athlete. A body that knew ice. A mix of strength and softness that had his head spinning.

"You're staring."

"Yeah." He smiled. He was going to look at her until he died or until his eyes wore off, whichever came first. "Does it bother you?"

"No."

She turned to give him her back, hanging her head low to let the jet hit the back of her neck, and the shower stall wasn't so large that she could do that without her slippery skin brushing against his. After a long look and countless fantasies directed at the dimples just above her ass, he decided that this was an invitation and hugged her from behind, pressing her into his own body.

He'd showered with women before, but couldn't remember ever *bathing* one. And yet, Rue let him squeeze bodywash that was going to make her smell like him on his palm, let him nestle his erection against her lower back, and let him use his hands on every wet inch of her body.

Every. Single. One.

"I am actually able to do—*oh*—this on my own," she said, biting into her lower lip in a way that made him certain that a just god did exist after all. "But I appreciate the service—" Her voice dissolved into a hitched breath, then a low moan, and Eli pinched her nipples to hear more of that, and then rolled them against his palms, and stopped himself from whispering in her ear that he'd give her everything, *anything*, if only she'd let him come over to her place and do this for her seven days a week for the rest of his natural life. "I'm not sure whether this is making me excited or sleepy," she murmured, arching into his touch, her body a combination of vibrating stretch and intense relaxation.

"I can give you both," he said after a kiss to her cheekbone. "Let me give you both." She exhaled when his fingers finally began circling her clit, panted and gasped, open-mouthed, throwing back her head into the crease of his neck. "Good girl," he whispered as she shuddered against him, and then, in her ear: "Take it."

Her orgasm came almost immediately, and it was all Eli could do not to push Rue into the wall and bend her to her waist and get himself off between her thighs. He imagined himself begging to be let inside, *just the tip*, and the adolescence of it was at once amusing and mortifying. He exhaled silent laughter in the ball of her shoulder while she still shook with pleasure.

When her heart slowed, she noticed how hard he was. Or maybe she'd known before, and finally took pity. She turned in his arms, impossibly beautiful, lips glistening, cheeks fairy-tale red, and Eli had to close his eyes and stumble back into the tiles when her hand closed around his cock.

She stroked him firmly and slowly, as though the orgasm he'd given her had deprived her of the ability to function at a reasonable rate. It was torturous, but even when he began bucking his hips into her fist, swearing softly against her damp hair, tightening his grip around her hips, she never sped up enough to push him over the edge. "Fuck, Rue," he said, and then a frustrated, "you can't fucking—" And finally, humiliatingly, he begged, "Please." He bit into her neck, and she didn't shake her head or smile or say anything, she didn't give in to what he was asking, but her eyes met his squarely, lovely and blue and calm, and that did it for him.

When he came it was so violent, he couldn't remember ever feeling anything approaching the good of it, not even while fucking someone, not even as a teenager. The pleasure cracked him at the seams, left him gasping soundlessly, speechless, as though his body was too busy experiencing the magnitude of it to produce even the most inarticulate of noises.

So you like her mouth, and she has phenomenal tits, and gives a spectacular hand job, he told himself, heaving his way back to normalcy, knees weak. *So you feel like smiling whenever she's around and want to know what's in her head.* The way she still gripped him, his semen seeping out of her closed fist, was the closest to a religious experience he'd come in a while. *Big fucking deal,* he forced himself to think, but it left a sour taste in his throat, the same he experienced when lying to himself. Eli watched her watch him, her serene face always so at odds with the chaos she provoked inside of him, and when he couldn't take her silence anymore, he wrapped both hands around her cheeks and asked, "You still tired?" His voice was hoarse. He wasn't surprised.

She nodded.

"Okay. This is what's going to happen—now we sleep, in my bed. Together. And when we wake up, we do this again. And we stop bullshitting ourselves and each other about whether this is the last time, whether we're going to stop doing this, whether we have any control over how much we want this."

To her credit, she hesitated for only a couple of seconds. When she nodded at him again, earnest, a wave of relief crashed into him. "No, Rue. You say it. Say that this is not the last time. Promise me."

That took her longer. But she did manage to make her way around the words, and when he heard a soft "I don't want this to be the last time," he picked her up, toweled her off, and carried her to bed.

21

WOULD YOU LIKE TO DO THAT WITH ME?

ELI

Eli wasn't one for naps.

It had been a problem back in college, his near pathological inability to fall asleep during the day, especially when pregame rest had been mandatory; now that he'd escaped the NCAA exploitation machine, it only meant that any sleep he didn't get at night couldn't be made up for.

Rue had no such issues. She was breathing evenly a minute after he'd settled her on the bed. He sat on the edge of the mattress and stared for a long time, feeling creepy and teenage-ish and helpless to stop, feeling euphoric and smitten. He couldn't remember ever experiencing anything like this, which meant that he should tread carefully, that she could be dangerous.

He pushed a strand of damp hair behind her ear and made his way downstairs.

Forty-five minutes later a summer thunderstorm was in full swing, and Rue padded into the kitchen wearing yesterday's clothes and *not* the T-shirt he'd left out for her on the bed, folded on top of a pair of Maya's sweats.

He'd never been less surprised.

Her gaze skittered to Tiny, napping blissfully on one of his many beds, then flitted to the bowls of whipped cream and fruit on the counter, then landed on the pan near the stove. "What are you doing?"

"Fulfilling the promise I used to lure you here."

"You have done that." She looked sleepy and beautiful and confused. He had to physically restrain himself to avoid pulling her into him.

"The other promise. I said I'd cook for you, remember?"

"You don't have to."

Do not hug her. Do not kiss the tip of her nose. Do not run your hand up and down her back. You don't have to stick your fingers in her hair, and you most definitely do not need to fucking smell her throat. It'll just send her running faster than a reminder that you still own Kline's loan. "Come on, Rue." He gave her a chiding look. "I can't just fuck you nonstop without feeling like more of an asshole than I actually am. I'm going to have to feed you, just to keep you alive and responsive. No offense, but I'm not into the alternative."

She glanced away and then lowered her eyes, which was interesting. Atypical. Then said, "I'm weird about food." He kept his face straight. Made no movement. She was skittish, and he didn't want to spook her. He watched her swallow, twice, and offered no reaction when she added, "I struggle with non-sit-down meals. And with time constraints." She held his eyes. "I'd rather not eat than eat in a hurry or standing up."

"That's not weird." It did, however, make his chest icy and heavy. What she'd said about Alec feeding her. Tisha's picture. The obvious fact that she was a food engineer who focused on addressing food insecurity. He wasn't going to connect dots until she asked him to, but he reserved the right to nurse the cold, aimless anger that began churning at the bottom of his stomach.

"Not a huge fan of eating on the go, either." He opened a drawer and casually took out two place mats. "Glasses and plates are in that cupboard. Make yourself useful, Dr. Siebert." Her face betrayed nothing, but there was a trace of relief in her shoulders.

"Is this French toast?" she asked once they sat at the table.

He poured coffee in her cup. "Yes."

"And this is the fancy dish your fancy chef ex taught you to make?" She sounded skeptical.

"Never said that the dish had to be fancy. And I recommend you try it before you say one more word you *will* regret."

Her eyes narrowed, but she poured syrup on her toast, covered it with some of the fresh cream and the mix of berries, brought a bite to her lips with the air of someone who was doing him a big favor, and after chewing for a handful of seconds covered her mouth with her hand and said, "Holy shit."

He gave her his most *told you so* look.

"What the hell?" She seemed affronted. "How?"

"Secret recipe."

"It's *French toast.*"

"As you now know, not all French toast is created equal."

"You're not going to tell me what's in it?"

"Maybe later." He took a sip of his coffee. "If you behave."

She took more slow, leisurely bites, eating in a precise, methodical way that reminded him of the morning spent in her lab, and he watched her with a sense of accomplishment that couldn't possibly be justified.

What the *fuck* was she doing to him?

"I have a request," she said, dabbing a napkin to her mouth.

"I told you, it's a secret."

"Not that."

"What, then? A story?"

"It doesn't have to be. You don't have to . . . I don't need the terrible parts, if you don't want to share them. I just want to know about your ex-fiancée."

Ah. "What, precisely?"

She scouted for the perfect question, then settled on: "Who broke the engagement?"

"She did."

A pause. "Why?"

"Because I didn't love her the way she wanted to be loved."

Rue tilted her head. "What does that mean?"

By now it had been long enough that when he thought about McKenzie, the only feelings left were affection and gratitude. Their last conversation, though . . .

You are a successful adult man, and yet you put more effort into some harebrained vendetta you're chasing with your codependent friends than into being actually happy. You will choose your stupid revenge plan over me anytime, and we both know it.

You want *to be in love with me. You* want *to wake up in the morning and think of me. You* want *to want me, but you just don't.*

You can't fix it, because this is not about what you do—*it's about what you* feel. *The kind of love I'm looking for, not everyone has the capacity for it, Eli.*

McKenzie's words may no longer be the sharp knife they'd

been three years earlier, but the sting remained. "Not enough." His tongue roamed the inside of his cheek. "She meant that I didn't love her enough."

"Was she right?"

A beat, and then he forced himself to nod. *That* was what hurt the most.

"Are you two still friends?"

"Friendly. She wanted a clean break, but I hear from her more now that she's found someone else and is . . . happier than she'd ever been with me, for sure."

"Are you jealous of him?"

"I . . . maybe. A little. McKenzie was—is—fantastic. I couldn't give her what she needed, and I'm glad she's getting it from someone else. But I can't help being . . ." He made a resigned gesture. "Envious might be more accurate."

Rue stared at the heavy rain, pondering the matter like it was a complex set of assays to be performed. "*Couldn't* you? Give her what she needed, that is. Or did you just not want to?"

It was such a loaded, deceptively barbed question, Eli almost wondered if she'd ever spoken with McKenzie. But Rue was guileless. And curious. "I don't know. I hope it's not the former."

She nodded. "I might be like that, too."

"Like what?"

"Incapable of loving people the way they deserve."

"Really? What about Florence? Don't you love *her*?"

She glanced away. "I thought I did. I *know* I do, but maybe not enough, if I'm betraying her by being here with you." She took a long, calming breath, then looked at him again.

"What about romantic love?" Eli's heart pounded, and he wasn't sure why. "You think you could manage that?" he asked her.

Asked *them.*

"Maybe. Or maybe some people are too broken. Maybe . . . maybe things have happened in their lives, in their past, that have damaged them so bad, they're never going to get happy endings with the loves of their lives." She pulled up her knees and wrapped her arms around them. "Maybe some people are meant to be tragedies."

A knife in his fucking stomach, that's what Rue was. And a mirror he couldn't bear to look into. "So, is this my chance for a Q and A?" he asked, wanting to change the subject.

"What would you like to ask?"

He considered gently introducing the topic, but Rue was a fan of plain speaking. "Why don't you want penetrative sex?"

"Because I don't like it very much."

"Any reason in particular?"

"No. No traumatic story or medical issues, at least." She shrugged. "It's not that I actively dislike it. I just can't really come like that."

"Ah."

"I wouldn't mind it if that's all there was—there are other things that won't make me come and I'm happy to do. Obviously." She held his eyes, unflinching, and every single *delicious* thing she'd done for him was suddenly there, in the forefront of his mind. "But in my experience, penetrative sex usually leads to two outcomes, and neither is good."

"What outcomes?"

"A lot of men see penis-in-vagina sex as the end goal and forget everything else. Skip foreplay, move straight to the fucking, get their own, completely forget about their partner—which is *not* what I'm looking for. And that's the best scenario."

"The *best*?"

She sighed. "It's better than them deciding that they absolutely need to get me off during the sex, which almost always ends up with them dragging it out to the point of pain. I can't come from that, which means that we're at a very unpleasant impasse that forces me to *fake* an orgasm just to get it over with." She looked so genuinely offended, he couldn't hold in his laughter. He liked this about her: the way she went after her own pleasure, demanded her due. He liked *her*, period, even more now that the pieces were starting to form a defined picture in his eyes.

Ask me for anything, he thought, *anything at all, and watch me give it to you. Whoever came before me, they had no idea. I'm up for the challenge.*

"Why?" she said. "Would you like to do it?"

"Are you asking me if I want to actually fuck you?"

She nodded.

He held back a smile. "You can answer that on your own."

"Fair enough." She forked another neat piece of her French toast, balanced it with a perfect amount of berries and cream, chewed it for longer than it took Eli to scarf down a sandwich on his lunch break. Then asked, without hiding her amusement, "Are you anticipating curing me with your magic cock?"

That was *exactly* what he'd been hoping, of course. The idea of her coming with his dick inside her was intoxicating all on its own, but the idea of being the first to make her come like that was stuff he would get off to well into his old age. A permanent place in her sexual history. Something that would make her remember him. It was a fantasy, an inappropriate one at that, but Eli tried to avoid punishing himself too much for thoughts that remained contained in his own head. Self-loathing, he'd found, only got him so far.

"There's nothing you need to be cured of," he said, fully believing it. "But you might like it. With me."

"Right. Because of the aforementioned magic cock." She was teasing him, like she had that first night, before she'd known that she was supposed to hate him. He loved every minute of this.

"Because earlier you told me that you've never been with someone more than once. I have, and I can tell you that knowing your partner for more than two hours goes a long way when it comes to having great sex." He didn't mention that he wasn't so sure anymore. That she had redefined the concept of sexual compatibility for him. "I'd like to try, if you're up for it. If you come, good. If not, I'll still enjoy myself, and I can get you off half a dozen different ways before. And afterward."

She bit into her lower lip, mulling. "You won't get offended if I don't like it?"

"You like it when I put my fingers in you, don't you?" So discordant, the clinical way they were discussing the science of fucking and how transportive it felt when they were actually doing it. At least, how *he* felt. *She* was never going to allow him to get close to her in any nonphysical way.

"It's different," she reflected. "Your cock is much larger. And you know how to use your hands."

He should have recorded the sound bite. "I know how to use other things, too." He tried to say it as matter-of-factly as possible. Didn't succeed.

"I'm sure you think so." Her mouth twitched in a small smile. So did his. "What if I say no?"

"We continue on as we started. With no complaints from me." And a whole lot of gratitude.

She nodded. "I'm open to trying. But if I find it boring and yawn in the middle of it, don't take it personally."

"Noted."

"And I will *not* fake an orgasm for you."

He bit the inside of this cheek. "Likewise."

They stared at each other from across the table, condensation rolling down the half-full orange juice glasses, amusement vibrating between them. They were both aware of the improbability of the conversation they'd just had, over breakfast no less. They were both having fun. "I also have a question."

He nodded at her to go ahead.

"The kink stuff."

He leaned back in his chair and studied her closely. "What's your question?"

"I think you can answer that on your own," she parroted back at him, and he shook his head, giving up on not grinning.

"Do you want to know what I'm into?"

She nodded.

"Are you going to get scared if I tell you?"

"No. People can have all sorts of desires *and* avoid imposing them on others without their consent. I trust you."

That was dizzying. And definitely pornographic. Rue Siebert, *trusting* him. He could do a lot with that knowledge. Play around with the possibility. Maybe, if the stars aligned, act on it. "I enjoy . . . calling the shots."

She was silent for a beat. "I think I already knew that." He wasn't surprised, not after their conversation in one of Kline's labs. "You're good at stopping yourself, but sometimes I can tell that you'd rather be . . ."

He waited for her to finish. When she didn't, he said, "In charge?"

She nodded again, and he smiled at her reassuringly.

"Is it something you need? To enjoy sex?"

"No. Some of the best sex I've had incorporated no elements of that." *With you,* he didn't add.

"Was your fiancée into it?"

"She was. We were very well matched in that sense."

"Do you have a . . . sex dungeon?"

"I live in Texas, Rue. I don't even have a basement."

She hid her smile in her knees, then asked, "Did you hurt her? During sex?"

He shook his head. "It wasn't something either of us was interested in. It's more about control."

"*You* taking control?"

"It would be more appropriate to say that she surrendered hers, within the context of sex. These kinds of relationships require trust. Boundaries. Lots of false starts and abrupt stops as we figured it out. Some trial and error."

"So, if there was no pain . . . ?"

"I'd tie her up. Blindfold her. Hold her down. Tell her what to do. Do you know what orgasm denial is?"

"I speak English." Her look was faintly offended, and he huffed out a laugh.

God, what he wouldn't give to pin her down on this table. Show her *exactly* what he meant. "There you go, then."

"You know," she mused, "a guy I met on the app spanked me, once."

He let out a silent laugh. "Look at you. A professional kinkster."

"I know, right?"

"What did you think of it?"

She seemed unimpressed. "It was mostly ridiculous."

Eli wanted to lean forward. He wanted to smooth out the vertical lines between her brows and tell her that he was right there, and she didn't need to think about some asshole who was probably shitty in bed and couldn't get her off, because he *had* her, he was willing to *learn* her, he was *consumed* by her. But he didn't, because it would have sent her running. And the question she wanted to ask was swelling between them, stretching the silence to the limits of its comfort.

He didn't need her to say it. But fuck, he wanted her to. "Come on, Rue. Don't chicken out now." He watched her swallow. Her lips remained sealed, so he clucked his tongue. "It's not like you."

She seemed to agree, because she met his eyes squarely. "Would you like to do that with me?"

Under the table, his hand and his cock twitched at once. He thought about pulling her into his lap. Locking her in this house and throwing away the key. About the things he could do to her. Discovering her limits. Figuring out what she liked. Having her at his mercy. Making her enjoy it. She had no fucking idea how much fun they could have, just the two of them. "If you wanted to try, yes. Some of it."

"Like what?"

"Nothing that would push too hard, too quickly. Just you, letting me be in charge. And we'd talk everything over." His blood thudded loudly in his veins. In anticipation. Or worry that she might change her mind. "You could stay for the day. We could . . . experiment."

She blinked. "I should go home."

"Why?" He tried for an easy grin. Not too eager. "It's not like you have any pets."

She rolled her eyes, but she was amused. "I do have plants to water."

"The cactus you bought at the grocery store last week will be fine."

She chewed on her lower lip. He studied her long, graceful fingers drumming against the table, remembered how they'd felt wrapped around him. "Won't Maya be back?"

"Not until tonight. And I overheard her tell her friend Jade that I'm an incel. I'd love to show her that I do have *some* game."

She laughed softly, and Eli knew that he had her.

22

GOOD GIRL

RUE

When we returned upstairs, I had three messages on my phone.

Nyota, emailing the contact information for a real estate lawyer licensed in Texas and Indiana. **Good news is, he came highly recommended. Sad news: his hourly rate might reflect that.**

Tisha, informing me that she was going to Kline for a couple of hours to finish up something for "the anthropomorphized period cramp" (Matt), asking whether I wanted to join her. **We could take a joint dump on his desk on our way out. LMK.**

And Florence, who'd snapped a progress picture of a shawl she'd been knitting for me in beautiful shades of red—my favorite color.

"Everything okay?" Eli asked from behind me, and my first instinct was to hide my phone—which made me hate myself. Kline, my friends, my work—they were the part of my life I was *proud* of.

It was what I was doing with Eli that needed to be concealed.

"I have a story," I said, still facing away from him. I felt pressure against my eyes, but I wasn't worried. I'd stopped crying when I was a child.

"Go ahead."

"I owe everything to Florence. My job. My scientific freedom. My financial stability. The fucking shawl that she's knitting. And in return I'm here, in the bedroom of someone who's been making her life impossible, having *meals* with him, because . . ."

Silence. "Why? Why *are* you here, Rue?"

My chest felt heavy. I turned around. "Because I'm selfish, and careless. Because I want to be."

He nodded. Seemed to look around for a tale that could match mine. "I last spoke to my mother a few weeks before she died. My final words to her were that I hoped she wouldn't be as shitty a mother to my sister as she'd been to me."

We stood there, sodden with the weird catharsis that came from acknowledging the kinds of flaws and regrets and mistakes that lived in our bones.

He never ran, no matter how shameful. Neither did I.

"Okay, then," I said, taking a step closer. "Let's start."

Eli took off his shirt. He was handsome in a rugged, interesting way, but what I liked about him was the story his body told. The broadness of his shoulders, the product of a childhood spent honing his body. Strong, long arms. A few scars here and there, where he must have taken hits and kept going. "Did you play defense?"

He smiled. "How did you know?"

"Lucky guess. Do we need a safe word, or something?"

"Why don't we just . . . communicate, for now? I tell you what

I'd like you to do, what *I* would like to do, and you can tell me no, or ask me to stop. Does that sound good?"

"It sounds better than screaming 'broccoli' because you're pulling my hair too hard."

He laughed. "That's the spirit. Are you okay with me holding you down?" He stepped closer and gently pulled my hands from the back pockets of my jean shorts. Then he closed one hand around both my wrists with surprising ease, trapping them on my lower back. "Like this."

Heat bloomed in my stomach. Blood rushed to my cheeks, but I nodded.

"If you change your mind, just ask me to let go."

"I won't."

He scanned my face. "I'm serious. If you don't like something I'm doing, you'll tell me immediately."

"I'm down for whatever."

"Really? For whatever?"

I nodded.

"So I can press you into the mattress right now and fuck your ass without lube?" I froze. A *now who's up for anything?* eyebrow rose on his forehead, and I had to stop myself from fidgeting in his grip. "Thought so," he said softly. "Take off your clothes and lie face up on the bed, Rue. And if something bothers you, *anything*, tell me."

I was naked in just a few moments, aware of Eli's eyes trailing my every move. Stopped in front of the bed. "You can," I said over my shoulder. "But I've never done it, so maybe not *without* lube."

He stood completely still, but something behind his eyes

stuttered, as if his brain was short-circuiting. By the time I lay down, he looked calm. His fingers traced the valley between my breasts, then played my rib cage like a piano. He was still wearing the gray sweatpants he'd put on for breakfast, the outline of his erection straining against the soft material.

"Would you like me to do something about that?" I asked. Wasn't that the point? For me to service him in some way? The idea had me pressing my legs together in anticipation.

But he shook his head. "How about we start slow? Just relax."

"So what do I do?"

He chuckled. "But of course."

"What?"

"You always need something to do."

Did I? Yes. Ever since I was a child, having a goal was the best way to avoid thinking about whatever misery I was going through. How did *he* know, though?

"Because I'm the same way," he whispered, leaning in for a kiss on my cheek. It felt menacingly intimate. "Why don't we say that your job is *not* coming, since you speak English so well?" His hand shifted to my abdomen, then pressed lightly, his weight on my flesh delicious.

"I can't come? Ever?"

"Not until I tell you. It doesn't matter how close you are, you wait for my permission. Okay?"

"Doesn't sound too hard. *Not* having orgasms with a man is something in which I have plenty of experience."

He muttered something that sounded a lot like *mouthy*, and then bent down to kiss me in the way I'd become accustomed to, at once restrained and absolutely filthy.

So new for me, recognizing someone's kiss fingerprint. Being familiar with Eli's fresh, woodsy scent. "This is a recurring dream of mine," he said against one of my nipples before biting it softly.

I sighed in pleasure. "What is?"

"You. Naked. Doing as you're told." His thumb pressed against my lower lip. "I've always liked being in charge, but with you it's something else altogether. Because you're so slippery, maybe. It's a powerful fantasy, having the right to order you to stay put." He sounded like he was working through a math problem. When our eyes met, his smile was self-effacing. "Let's get started, shall we?"

He did what he always did: kiss my breasts, trace the edge of my hip bone, inhale the skin of my throat. It turned me on, but I couldn't see the destination, and it made me restless.

Which amused him. "Relax." He examined the white shadow of my appendectomy scar.

"But what should I—"

"I just told you." His hand slid between my thighs. Teased them apart. "Relax."

"Don't you—" Air rushed out of my lungs when he parted me with his thumb. His breath hitched, too.

"You're always soaked when I first touch you, Rue." His thumb moved unhurriedly from my entrance to my clit, and then down again. I arched into his touch, heat radiating through my nerve endings. "I like to think that it's my doing."

"It's *my* doing," I bit back. Laughter rose from deep in his chest, making me even wetter.

"I might like your tits even more than your lips. And I *definitely* like your honesty even more than your tits. Believe me, that's saying something."

I'd expected him to go down on me, because he seemed to truly enjoy it, and because if the game was to push me to the edge as quickly as possible, it would have been the cost-effective way. But he took his time: he rubbed me leisurely, lightly, just the tip of his fingers over my cunt, and little by little I melted into his touch. I closed my eyes, lay back, and it could have been three or twenty minutes later when I noticed how close I was.

Trembling.

Gripping the sheets.

Chewing on my lower lip and arching into every stroke.

The climb had been so gradual I'd barely noticed, and when I looked at Eli with a disbelieving expression, he smiled, almost sweetly, and eased the tip of his middle finger inside me. "You're already right there, aren't you? Clenching around my finger."

"*Because you*—" I groaned. His calm was destabilizing. I was more worked up than I could remember being, and he was unaffected.

"You know I'm not going to let you come for a long, *long* while, don't you?"

I squeezed my muscles around his thick finger and reveled in his sharp exhale. His cock was still hard, impossibly larger. "What about y-you?"

"Me?" He took his hand away, and I bit back a whimper. I watched him stroke himself from above his sweats, then take his cock out for a few more pumps. "I can come whenever and wherever I choose, Rue. Now. Later. Now *and* later. Isn't that fun?"

I closed my eyes, trying to push his entertained tone out of my head, asking my body to wind down. This felt like a joke, a joke I wasn't in on. All I wanted was—

"Let's try again, okay?" His voice was soft and patient, and I instantly felt more at ease. But the way his palm spread my thighs was feral, and his mouth on my cunt reminded me that *he* was in control.

It was agony. Or the best thing I'd ever felt. After what felt like hours, I still couldn't make up my mind. All I knew was that Eli spared no quarter, and brought me up and up and up with his mouth and his fingers and sometimes with his deep, filthy voice, and then, when I felt like I was going to explode from the tension dilating inside me, he stepped away and left me bereft. Once, I almost came, and he punished me with a soft bite at the edge of my cunt that had me shivering, ready to promise him *anything* for one more second of contact. I was willing to get myself off with my own fingers. To hump his leg. To be his fucking servant—and then he decided that I was fidgeting too much, and did what he'd promised: he restrained me, both my wrists in his hand, and pinned my arms to my stomach. Opening my legs wider, arching into his mouth and his touch, were the only possible ways to prolong contact with him. And that's what I did, holding back my pleas until I had no choice but to beg.

"*Please.*"

"Please, what? What do you need, Rue?"

"I can't. Please, please, *please*, make me come. Or let me make myself come. *Please.*"

He clucked his tongue against my clit, not quite hard enough. I was going to die. "I thought you were an expert. I thought it was easy for you, not coming."

"You have to—*please*. You have to."

"Is this too much, Rue? Would you like me to just finish you off?" He kissed my belly button, jarringly chaste after the places his mouth had been for the past hour. "Broccoli, Rue?"

I let out hysterical laughter. "No. *Not* broccoli," I panted, not sure where the answer came from. Sheer stubbornness. That underlying suspicion that this was doing as much for him as it was for me. There was power that came from giving him something he so clearly wanted. I was miserable and soaring like never before. "I can take it."

"Are you sure?" His long finger arched inside me. He really did know how to use his hands. Bastard. "You're really tight right now. Are you sure you can give me a few more minutes?"

I wasn't, but I nodded vehemently. Overcompensating.

"I've wanted to do this to you since I saw you at that hotel bar. I went home afterward and lay in this bed and thought about how *serious* you were, how self-possessed and solemn, and I imagined how nicely you'd come apart." He bit softly at the top of my pelvic bone. "I'm fifteen again, Rue. You wouldn't believe it, how much I jerk off, thinking of you."

I was unglued. *He* was ungluing me. "How much longer?"

"You've done so well, baby. It's your first time, and you've made me so happy." He rewarded me with another open-mouthed kiss, and pride burst inside me at his words. "Can you give me five more minutes? Five more, and then I'll let you come."

His tone was patronizing. Insulting, really, but it wound me up even harder, cramming more pleasure inside me. "Okay."

"That's my girl. And then you can come however many times you want."

Just once was going to be enough. It was going to rip me apart and wreck me forever. "Okay."

"But I'm not going to make it easy." I opened my eyes and met his. Dread mixed with the heat in my belly. *I hate you,* I thought, loving every second, every touch, every fragment of this. "One last sprint, Rue. Five more minutes, but I get to . . ."

He didn't say what, but his tongue licked up my slit again—this time with purpose.

I gasped and arched almost completely off the bed.

"Don't come," he reminded me, and I nodded blindly, kept nodding as he told me to remember my promise. "Be good, Rue," he repeated, but the flat of his tongue was pressing against my clit and I couldn't—just *couldn't*.

My legs began shaking, then my arms, and the tingling pressure in my abdomen exploded into shock waves that crashed through my body.

I couldn't help it, so I screamed, sure that this was the most severe, unyielding pleasure anyone had ever felt at once. Too big for my body and too intense for this world. I was grateful for Eli's hands holding me, keeping me tethered to *something* as my vision narrowed, as everything but the splendor of it receded.

Then, once every sensation in the galaxy had cycled through my body, I fell limply on the bed and realized what I'd done.

"Shit." I sat up. Eli's grip must have loosened, because I could easily free my hands. It hadn't been five minutes. It hadn't been *one* minute. "I'm sorry."

He shook his head, watching my still-trembling body with a transfixed expression.

"I—shit. I know I wasn't supposed to—I'm *sorry*—"

"Stop apologizing," he ordered distractedly. Instead he moved on top of me, blanketing my body, one arm on each side of my head. He stared at me like I was a beautiful, exotic flower that had the power to kill him with a pollen drop.

"I didn't mean to—"

"You are *so fucking hot*." He leaned down and kissed me, almost violently. "You don't understand what you do to me. Because *I* don't understand what you do to me."

"It wasn't five minutes. I . . ."

He exhaled against my cheek. "Rue, don't you get it? It's the whole damn point, to see you lose it. Why do you think I do this? To see you go wild." He was hard, grinding against my belly through his sweats. His muscles trembled with impatience, and his breath was all over the place. He seemed as far gone as I'd felt just a minute earlier.

"Are you going to—I don't know, punish me? Spank me?"

He laughed. "I'd rather fuck you." His muscles flexed as he lifted himself up. I felt the mattress shift, then heard rustling noises as a drawer slid open. When I could see his face again, he was holding a condom in his hand. "Okay?" he asked.

We'd discussed this. Was I really up to it?

Yes. Yes, because I had no doubt that Eli would stop if I needed him to.

I nodded.

"Good girl." He kissed me again, firmly this time.

"Because I'm letting you do it?" I asked against his lips.

"No. Because you thought about it before saying yes."

He rolled the condom on, his cock almost obscene covered in latex, and then slathered it in lube. I doubted he'd need it, but appreciated the consideration. It had been a couple of years for me, and when he laid on top of me, I almost expected it would be like my first time, a pinching discomfort requiring some adjustment.

Something large and blunt prodded against my opening, and as he pushed in, I felt an impression of intense fullness. Then, abruptly, with his cock no more than one or two inches inside me, Eli halted. His arms caged my shoulders, and he muttered something that resembled *unbelievable*, and then something like *thank fuck we're doing this with a condom*. His forehead sank into the pillow, right next to my head.

"Goddamn," he muttered.

"You okay?" I asked. My hand traveled up and down the divot of his spine, brushing the planes of muscles on either side. They twitched under sweaty skin.

"Fuuuck." The word was muffled by the pillow. "Give me a second. Be a good girl and don't move."

I didn't move. But he felt so large and foreign inside me, I needed to test the stretch and the limits of him, find out where he ended and I began. So I clenched around him, and that was all it took.

"*Fuck*, sweetheart, you *can't*—"

One of his hands slammed down between our bodies, and when I glanced down, I realized that only the tip of his cock was inside me—and that he was cupping the base in a mix of desperation and self-defense. In vain. Eli was already shuddering, eyes screwed shut and face twisted with pleasure as he made unrestrained noises and came inside me.

And came, and came, and *came*.

He was in the throes of something that seemed to transcend pleasure, and I watched every moment of it, spellbound, until every last drop of sensation was milked from him. And when it was finally over, when Eli managed to collect himself and open his eyes, I couldn't untangle what I found on his face.

"Fuck," he said, shifting up, hands cupping my face, and he looked—for some reason he looked absolutely *ruined*. Devastated.

I wasn't sure what possessed me to do it, but he looked like he needed it, and I turned my head and pressed a soft, reassuring kiss into his shaky palm.

It seemed to ignite something in Eli, because his mouth found mine with a kiss. And then another. And then even more, so many that I lost count. After a few minutes he softened and slipped out of me, and murmured something against my lips about not wanting the condom to leak, but managed to get rid of it with little fuss. Then he dragged me onto his chest, locked his arms around me, and kept on kissing me, kissing me, kissing me. Like he didn't know that the sex was over, like he wanted to prolong it. And I didn't mind. Not for now. Not for a while.

I had no idea how long we stayed like that. I only knew that the kiss became many, all languid and never-ending, and that the light in the room grew dimmer and the shadows longer, and that we would have continued—if only the doorbell hadn't rung.

23

A WONDERFUL LAY

ELI

At first he shut the sound out, wrapped his arms tighter around Rue, and went on kissing her.

He'd just had the most intense orgasm of his life, his body was still processing the past hours, and he was fully immersed in the out-of-body experience of Rue *not* running away from him after he'd fucked her. Or come as close to fucking her as he'd been able to get before losing it.

He *was* smitten, and not inclined to fight it.

But the doorbell rang again, and the shrill noise turned into a nagging feeling that sank into his pleasure-addled brain like a brick.

"Shit," he muttered against her lips, then pulled her even closer. She was pliant and glowing and happy, and he'd had no intention of moving except to feed her or fuck her again. "*Shit.*"

"What?"

"My friends. They're here. We had plans."

She gave him a sleepy, wheel-spinning look. "Are you happy about that?"

"God, no."

She smiled, and his heart leaped in his rib cage. He could do even better. He could make her fucking *laugh*, with some practice and lots of luck. "Could you pretend not to be home?"

"They have a set of keys."

"I see."

"And they'd have seen my car outside."

"True." She nuzzled under his chin, just as reluctant to move away. "Looks like you're going to have to interact with them."

He groaned in her hair, unable to let go of her, this woman who despised herself for wanting him. Had he ever felt this way before? He must have. Just couldn't remember.

"Should I sneak out of the window?" He gave her a puzzled look, so she continued, "I have no issue with walk-of-shaming out, but maybe *you* do?"

"Please, don't tie my sheets in a rope." He extricated himself from her, and the skin of her shoulder immediately rose in tiny goose bumps. He traced them with his thumb and forced himself to say, "Just come down when you're ready."

"Okay."

He got up and watched her close her eyes and stretch sinuously on the sheets, fisting his hands to his sides to prevent himself from getting back into bed. He washed up haphazardly, put on a worn flannel and a pair of jeans, and by the time he was downstairs, Minami and Sul were already on the couch, cuddling Tiny as though he were the baby they were not so secretly trying for and taking advantage of Eli's HBO subscription.

He leaned against the doorjamb and tried for an irritated look, but Minami wouldn't have it.

"Well, well, well. Look who's finally up, bright eyed and bushy tailed. How was your napper, champ?" Minami grinned. Then frowned. "Since when do *you* nap?"

"Since never. I have someone over."

Her eyebrow shot up. Even Sul, Mr. Mountain of Impassivity, stared wide-eyed. "In the middle of the afternoon? Or from last night?"

"What do you think?"

She pursed her lips, twice. No sound came out, twice. Sighed. "Sul, could you whistle suggestively for me? I've been practicing, but it's so *hard*."

Sul obeyed—quite skillfully—like the whipped lovesick idiot he was.

"Thank you, babe. So we interrupted you, Eli?"

"Yup."

"Sad." A pained nod. "But whose fault is it for not canceling today's dinner in advance?"

He gave her the finger just as Hark let himself inside. "Hey." His hair was coated in tiny droplets of rain. "Did your sister finally get a new car? High time."

"Nope."

"Then whose Kia is in your driveway?"

"Eli has *someone* over," Minami singsonged. "He'd forgotten that he was supposed to make us risotto."

Hark's eyes were outraged as he held out two bottles. "Does this Verdicchio I extensively researched and bought to pair with it mean nothing to you?"

"Less than."

"Fuck off," he said mildly, glancing at Sul and Minami. "I'm going back to my place and ordering pizza."

"Leave the Verdicchio," Eli ordered.

"As I already mentioned, you can fuck right off."

"It's okay. I'm leaving."

They all turned toward the new voice. Rue was coming down the stairs, one hand on the banister as she stood on the landing.

Eli's heart thudded. His brain couldn't compute.

After their shower, her dark hair had dried in wilder curls than he was used to. Barefoot, heavy-lidded, and with no makeup and a blue-tinted mark that Eli had definitely sucked on her throat while coming inside her, she was absolutely breathtaking. Lush and full and so *deeply* fucked and fuckable.

You're not. You're not leaving. You're staying till I've had my fill, and a little past that.

But her eyes were guarded, and the silence tense. It occurred to Eli that he'd never told her that his friends would be from Harkness. And they had not expected the woman upstairs to be Rue.

Minami was the first to recover, shooting to her feet with a wide smile. "Rue! It's lovely to meet again."

Rue descended the stairs. "Nice to see you, too."

Minami leaned forward to hug her—a bit of absurd comedy, considering that Rue was nearly a foot taller, and clearly unsure as to what was happening. He watched her stiffly reciprocate, debating between being amused and going to her rescue, but Minami kept the matter brief. "Don't leave—let's all have dinner together! It's always the four of us. I'm bored to tears with these three."

Eli's muttered "wow" came at the same time as Hark's snorted "harsh" and Sul's stoic "we're married, but okay." Minami's smile held a *let's be friends* invite, but Rue seemed uneasy and replied, "I'm not sure it would be appropriate."

The atmosphere thickened. Suddenly, the room wasn't populated by Eli's friends and the woman he was seeing, but by Florence's protégé and those who sought to take over Kline. Rue against the world, out of place and alone and uncomfortable.

She often looked exactly like that, and as long as Eli had any say in it, she was never going to be made to feel that way on his watch. "If anyone's leaving, it's them," he said firmly. His eyes held Rue's, until Hark added gruffly, "Thank you, asshole. Rue, we should all have dinner together. It's obvious that Eli wants you here. He's the birthday boy, after all."

"It's your birthday?" Rue's eyes widened. "It *is* your birthday," she said, maybe recalling his driver's license. "I . . . Happy birthday, Eli."

His heart skipped a beat, then thumped loudly in his chest. If they'd been alone, maybe he'd have told her, *Thank you, Rue. You gave me the best birthday I've had in a decade.* Or maybe not.

"Eli doesn't like people to acknowledge his birthday in any way," Minami warned. "We may gather to celebrate it, but we may not admit to why we're gathered."

"And it doesn't have to be weird," Hark added gruffly. "Our counsel would advise us not to talk about anything Kline related, anyway." Rue remained quiet, so he added, "Besides, I parked behind your Kia, and you're going to need some crazy maneuvers to get out. Are you good at that stuff?"

She winced. "Absolutely not."

"Then you really need to stay. You can't make me move my car; it's raining and Eli fixed the cracks in the driveway by himself. It's quicksand out there."

Minami laughed. Sul smiled, and so did Hark, this time sincerely. Rue just looked at Eli, as if asking for guidance. "Stay," he said in a low but audible tone, and after a long pause she nodded.

"Okay. Thank you for having me."

Relief rammed hard into him. "Let me go make this fucking risotto you dickheads ruined my Saturday for."

"Gotta love a warm welcome," Minami said, before chatting Rue up. Eli couldn't hear what they were saying, but he trusted Minami to be decent. Unlike Hark, who followed him into the kitchen with a deep scowl.

"I'm assuming you're here to put the Verdicchio in the fridge?"

"Wrong. Try again." Hark set the bottles on the table. "What the fuck are you doing, Eli?"

He crossed his arms. "What does it look like I'm doing?"

"It looks like if you stared at that girl any longer you'd have jizz coming out of your eyeballs."

"Woman. And: classy."

"*And* it looks like you're doing Florence Kline's friend. *And* it looks like you brought her into the house you share with your *very* young sister."

"Maya's in her twenties. *She* has people spending the night all the time." Hark's scowl deepened. "Dude, what *is* your deal?"

"How long has it been with Rue?"

"On and off, a few weeks."

"Jesus, Eli. Aren't there *other* women?"

"Sure, but I don't want them."

"What about the racquetball girl?"

He frowned. "Who?"

"The one we met when—"

"Stop right there. I don't want Racquetball Girl, or any other girl, because they're not Rue."

"Oh, come off it. What's the real reason?"

"This *is* the real reason. I like her. She's a wonderful lay and she smells amazing and I love having her around. Do you want to read my fucking diary?"

"No, I want *you* to remember that things are heating up, and we're closer than ever. Have you considered the possibility that Florence might be using her to find out shit from us?"

Eli did, right then, for all of a second. "She isn't."

"How can you be so sure? Because you have discovered the heights and the depths of sweet star-crossed love with her?"

"Because she never brings up Kline. Because *I* have been pursuing *her*. And because she's not the kind of person who'd do that."

"And you know her *so* well. All of what, two hours?"

"I know her well enough."

"Goddammit, Eli. How serious is—" He interrupted himself, and when Eli followed his gaze, he saw Rue in the doorway.

He wondered how much she'd overheard, but her face was inscrutable as she asked, "Do you need any help with the cooking, Eli?" She ignored Hark, who, to his credit, managed to look contrite. He brushed past Rue with a murmured "excuse me," and Eli was just glad to be alone with her again.

It was fundamentally fucked up, this feeling that his friends of over a decade were intruding on his life with Rue—a woman who would pour a Class 8 chemical down his nostrils for Florence Kline. Or even just recreationally. And yet, here he was.

Smiling at her.

His heart skipped when she smiled back faintly.

"Are you trying to steal my secret recipe, or do you just feel weird being with Harkness people in the other room?" he asked.

"The latter. I . . . I'm not very good with people I don't know."

"Ah." Eli readjusted his mental image of Rue. She'd always been self-assured with him, at ease ever since the first night. He'd noticed that she seemed to be more reserved with others, but he'd chalked it up to a slightly aloof personality, not social anxiety.

"Is this recipe secret, too?" she asked.

"It's not." His chest felt tight. "Come here, I'll teach you."

She padded to the stove but deviated when she noticed a bowl of fruit. She picked up an apple, holding it in a pensive way that pulled a fond smile from Eli. "Are you thinking about the microbial coating?"

She nodded. "I finished collecting data yesterday."

She seemed excited, and he felt inexplicably pleased. Would congratulating her sound patronizing? "It's a fantastic project."

She smiled, and he felt like he'd won the lottery. "Thank you."

"What will you do next?"

"I'm not sure yet. Once I have the patent, I'll have to decide if I want to license it or market it myself."

Something about the phrasing gave him pause. "Won't *Kline* own the tech?"

"No. I will. Florence and I had an agreement from the start."

Eli's hand tightened around the handle of a knife. "Did she— are you—" *Get a grip, asshole. Use your words.* "Do you have a written contract for that?"

"Of course." She gave him a puzzled look and put the apple back. "Why? Were you hoping to steal my intellectual property together with the rest of Kline?"

There was a bite in her words, but he was too swept by relief to mind. "Something like that." He needed to change the topic. "Do you cook?"

"Not well, but I like to have proper meals. Food is what I splurge on."

She said it like it was a luxury. "I'm glad you're staying."

"Why?"

"I like to feed you well." There was a pang of regret in his chest. McKenzie had tried to teach him as much as she could, but Eli had been too busy building a business. What a waste. Rue could have marveled at his kitchen prowess for weeks on end. "You can grate the cheese. Try not to shave your fingers—Minami's in one of her vegetarian phases."

They worked as well in his kitchen as they had in her lab, except that this time Eli took the lead and was surprised by how studiously Rue applied herself, treating garlic and olive oil like they were highly volatile substances. Cooking with McKenzie had been a lot of fun—McKenzie, who was bright and sunny and made everything turn into banter and kisses flavored with whatever ingredients they'd been using. Rue was nothing like that. She was intense and focused. A real fortress. She spoke little, always relevant questions and the occasional deadpan joke that had Eli biting his cheek to avoid laughing. She rarely volunteered information, and never started sentences with *I*.

And yet. There were shy smiles, and the rapt way she stared at his hands, and when he stood behind her to stir, she leaned back against his chest, just a little, just enough to make his brain and his heart and his dick pound in ways he wasn't ready to analyze.

What would it be like to be in a relationship with her? Long, comfortable silences. Incessant honesty. Peaks and valleys. So easy to imagine some poor, hapless guy hanging from her every word. Making a full-time job out of teasing her. He'd put her at the center of his universe, and feel on top of the world when she eventually returned the favor.

Just the thought made him feel jealous, and angry, and a little sad.

"Is it ready yet?" Minami asked, popping by the kitchen. "Sul's starving. I saw him lustily eyeing Tiny and had to distract him with saltines."

"In three minutes. Thanks for saving my dog."

"I consider myself more Tiny's friend. You're incidental."

"Of course." He kissed Minami on the forehead on his way to the fridge, and she took the chance to whisper in his ear, "It's called an undercut."

He gave her a puzzled look.

"You've been staring at Rue's hair like you wanted to know."

Rue couldn't possibly have heard, but when he was back at the stove, she eyed him strangely. "What?" he asked.

She shook her head. "Nothing."

Rue liked the risotto, which had Eli trying to play it cool even as he was ready to take a victory lap around the block and invest in some fireworks. Dinner went without incident, and the conversation didn't touch sensitive topics; it flowed mostly among Harkness people, but Minami, and even Hark, made an effort to include Rue. She *was* shy, he realized, but he wasn't sure whether the others were able to recognize this in her. Perhaps Tiny did, because he put his chin on her knee and gazed up at her with an adoring expression that seemed like a parody of Eli's.

He was absolutely charmed by her inability to interact with his dog. He pictured her waking up in the morning, making her way outside to walk Tiny, politely but assertively asking him not to eat other dogs' shit. When she lifted a hand, as though considering a tentative pat on Tiny's head, Eli almost held his breath. She gave up after a few moments of nervous hovering, and Tiny looked absolutely crestfallen.

Me, too, buddy, Eli thought. *Me, too.*

Maya returned while Hark was in the middle of a scathing recount of the art house movie he'd watched the night before. She first gasped, then smiled, then roasted them. "Oh my god—is this a *party*?"

"It's a *dinner,*" Minami said while hugging Maya. "Which is what passes for a party among people in their thirties."

"Must be hard, being so millennial." The last word was clearly an insult. She hugged Sul, made heart eyes at Rue, but stopped short of Hark. "Hey, Conor," she teased. Her cheekbones were flushed pink. From the night chill, Eli hoped.

Except it was June. In Texas.

"Hi, Maya." Hark nodded, pointedly looking elsewhere. He was always nice enough to pretend not to notice Eli's sister's crush, but did a miserable job of it.

"There's leftover risotto in the kitchen," Eli said. When his sister left, Hark's eyes followed her. Then he poured himself another glass of wine and downed it in a single gulp.

"You know there is this thing called sipping? It's not tequila," Minami pointed out. She and Sul hadn't been drinking much.

"Isn't it? Who's to say?"

"Its molecular structure, for one."

"Electron pairs are overrated," Eli interjected.

"They are not. And that's why *I* finished my PhD in chemical engineering and you two did not."

Eli and Hark exchanged a look, mumbled "savage" and "low blow," and then stopped in the middle of shaking their heads. Because Rue glanced between them, then focused on Eli and asked, "You were in a chemical engineering PhD?"

Fuck.

The table fell silent. Eli considered damage control possibilities, but Hark beat him to it. "We sure were."

Rue turned to him. "Where?"

"Same as you." He leaned back in his chair. "UT."

"You both were in grad school. In the engineering department at UT Austin," Rue repeated, confused.

"Correct."

"When?"

"A few years before you, I'd guess. Your boyfriend came in the year after mine. Same mentor, though."

"Hark," Eli warned, but Rue talked over him.

"And why didn't you finish?"

"What an interesting question." The twist of Hark's mouth was bitter. "We were asked to leave."

"Hark." This time, the warning came from Minami, who was usually better than Eli at getting him to behave. Problem was, she could not order Rue to stop asking questions.

"Why? What happened?"

"Oh, it was so long ago, I can barely remember. But maybe your *friend*—"

"*Hark*." Eli rose to his feet, palms on the table. Rue looked puzzled and out of sorts, and he didn't like it. She wasn't going to be ambushed with a piece of knowledge that would hurt her—not on Eli's fucking watch. "Enough."

"My friend?" Rue asked, at a loss.

This time, Hark tipped his glass at her, drained what was left of his wine, and then lifted his hands in surrender. His smile was once again charming. Directed at Eli. "I know, I know—I'm an asshole. But what the fuck is left in life if I can't be an asshole when I'm drunk?"

Eli rolled his eyes. "How about decency?"

"Eh. Overrated."

Eli and Minami exchanged a long, conversation-containing look, punctuated by Minami clapping once and getting to her feet. "Since Rue might be too polite to ask Hark to go drown himself in a claw-foot bathtub, how about we just call it a night?"

"Sounds good even to me," Hark muttered.

"Fantastic. You're clearly not sober, so we'll just drop you off on our way home. You can pick up your car tomorrow, when you slink back here to beg for Eli's forgiveness for the way you acted in the presence of his friend."

"I should leave, too," Rue said. Eli hated how small her voice sounded, or the idea of her going anywhere. But her posture was tense, and it was obvious that she didn't want him to protest.

He held out his hand. "Give me your keys." He glared at Hark. "I'll move your car out of whatever mess this jackass made."

When Eli came back from the rain, Minami was talking with Rue in hushed tones. ". . . just drunk," he heard her murmur. "He gets weird. Honestly, the Verdicchio should have been CBD infused. Hey, if you ever want to get coffee, my corporate email is just my first name. I check it, like, every twenty minutes. It's a problem." He sighed, went into the kitchen, and returned with a Tupperware of leftovers.

"For me?" Hark asked. His smile was sheepish, but Eli wasn't going to let him off the hook just yet.

"Nope. *You* can eat shit." He deposited the container in Rue's hands, then murmured, only for her: "Drive carefully, okay?" He leaned in and pressed a kiss on her soft lips, one that she may not have expected, but still returned. "And if you want to . . ." He had no idea how to finish that sentence. *Talk? Fuck? Play Uno? All of the above?*

She nodded, but Eli wasn't sure she understood what he meant, or how to explain it without sending her running.

"Okay, we're going," Minami said. "Byeee, thank you for dinner!"

Eli sighed and watched them trickle outside, desperate for one last glimpse of Rue's face, but he caught none.

24

I DON'T DISLIKE HIM

RUE

And you're assuming they were referring to Florence, because . . . ?"

I watched Tisha's forehead crinkle on FaceTime and nodded. It was the same question I'd asked myself a handful of times since yesterday.

Or one hundred.

"Because I have exactly two friends. And if it's not Florence . . . is there something you want to tell me?"

"Good point," she conceded.

I scratched my temple. I'd slept poorly and fitfully, my brain an agitated mess of Conor Harkness's taunting voice, white wine filling my glass, and the way Eli had rested his chin over my head as he stirred the boiling water. At some point early in the morning, right before falling asleep, I decided that I needed some distance from Eli. To help my body process what he could do to me.

"I looked them up," I told Tisha. "As much as I could. Most of the hits regarding those four—"

"Eli and his Harkness friends?"

"Correct. Most hits are about their recent finance work, but with some digging—"

"Define 'some'?"

"A couple hours of exploration of digital archives. Tisha, I can place three of them—Minami, Hark, and Eli, at UT ten years ago. In the chemical engineering department."

"What about the other one?"

"Sul. Still at UT, but in chemistry." I pressed my lips together. "I'm not the best at reading interpersonal dynamics—"

"Understatement. Please continue."

"—but I think that the original friend nucleus was Minami, Hark, and Eli. Sul became part of the group when he married her."

"I can see that."

I was glad Tisha thought so, because I wouldn't have bet a string of used dental floss on my own analytical skills. "They did overlap with Florence at UT. Minami got her PhD from Cornell eleven years ago, with a dissertation on biofuels, so she must have been a postdoc there. Hark's mentor was Dr. Rajapaksha."

"Who?"

"Some guy who retired before our times, even though he was still young. And I found an old page about Eli. It misspelled his last name—only one *l*—and that's why it took me a while. His mentor was also Dr. Rajapaksha. And in his first year Eli won some kind of early-career grant for his work. Guess what on?"

Tisha's forehead wrinkled even more. "Please, tell me it's not biofuels."

I couldn't do that, so I said nothing.

"Okay." Tisha blew out some air. "Could they have been at UT when Florence was, and involved in her area of work, and *not* have crossed paths with her? Would that be possible?"

I worried my lower lip. "I don't think that there were any faculty I wasn't aware of back in grad school. But one of my thesis committee members called me Rhea throughout my defense, and I doubt he'd recognize me if we met at the supermarket."

"But what if you launched a hostile takeover of his lemonade stand?"

"I . . ." That's where the tangle of my thoughts became unteasable. "In that case, I cannot imagine that he wouldn't at least do *some* research on me." Tisha nodded, and I continued, "It's possible that that's exactly what Florence did. Maybe she had no memories of them until she researched them."

"And forgot to update us."

"Or maybe she simply hasn't had the time or energy to look them up."

"Only one way to find out."

I nodded. "My performance evaluation meeting is tomorrow. I'll ask then."

"Good plan. Except, how are you going to bring up the fact that you were sharing a meal with those people?" I winced. "I guess you could just tell her the truth. 'Florence, my monthly dose of shitty orgasms is currently being provided by Eli Killgore— nothing personal.'"

I glanced at the pepper plant on my windowsill.

"Oh, wow." Tisha whistled. "Not shitty, then."

Not shitty. More like magnificent, and nuclear, and probably sex redefining. At least for me.

"What's he like?" Tisha asked. "Eli, I mean." I massaged my

temples, trying to stave off the mortification, and she quickly followed up with "It's not—Rue, I'm not trying to be accusatory. If despite *my* advice and *your* common sense you're still seeing this guy, I'll support you through your questionable choices because I love you and because you've done the same for me. The least you can do is share the filthy deets."

"Right. He's good. Very good." *It's the whole damn point, to see you lose it.* "He's a little . . ."

"What?"

"Bossy."

Tisha's eyebrows rose. "In a bad way?"

"No." I wasn't sure I was ready to get into the weeds of it, yet. Not that Tisha wouldn't cheer me into buying my own set of flogs.

"Okay. What else? What's *he* like as a person?"

"I don't know him as a person."

"You've spent *some* time with him. You must have talked about something. What did you find out?"

Nothing, I nearly said, but the word was swallowed by an avalanche. *College athlete. Sister, friends, dog—they all love him. Honest, but never cruel. Not put off by how awkward I am, my silences. Formerly engaged. May be destined for tragedy, just like me. Easy to talk to. Almost a pro scientist. Would have been good at it, too. Has some horrific stories—almost as horrific as mine. Teases me, but never like he's laughing at me. Kind. Funny. That undercurrent of unease that seems to permeate most of my social interactions—it's just not there with him. Great cook. Great to cook with. Effortless.* "That I don't dislike him." Not at all.

"Hmm. He *is* cute in that 'I play rugby on Sundays' kind of way."

"Hockey. He plays hockey."

"Sure. He's also a finance bro. Did you talk about cryptocurrency?"

"No. We talked about . . ." *We tell each other the kinds of stories that we couldn't tell anyone else, because they'd make people uncomfortable, or sad, or feel like they need to laugh politely, minimize, comfort. We share horrible things that we have done, that have been done to us, and then wait and see if the other is going to be so appalled that they'll finally leave—but somehow that never happens. We don't make small talk. We cut through the flesh and show the stories that live in our skeletons.* "Cooking. He likes to cook."

"Wow, that's convenient." Tisha's eyes seemed to pierce through me. "And, just to reiterate . . . this is still just sex?"

I nodded without letting myself think about it too hard, but there must have been something in the air, because on Monday morning I received a text from Alec.

> Tonight we're closing early for maintenance of the HVAC system. The rink will be empty, and Maya and Eli Killgore will come over to skate. I figured I'd ask if you wanted to join.

> And in case you're wondering: yes, Dave is trying to set you and Eli up. He seemed to believe you two hit it off when you exchanged one and a half words at the fundraiser. But don't worry, Eli's a good guy. He'll leave you alone.

Alec had been so kind to me, it was next to impossible to be annoyed at him, which only left room for amusement. I was heading to see Florence, so I made a mental note to decline later. Spending non-naked time with Eli didn't seem wise.

"Hey, stranger. Why do I feel like I haven't seen very much of you lately?"

I smiled and took my customary seat in Florence's office, cross-legged in my favorite chair. Quarterly performance evaluations were never something for which I bothered working up anxiety. Florence was supportive, and I was good at my job.

"Just busy finishing up the provisional patent."

Florence took off her reading glasses. "It's in the lawyers' hands?"

"Yup."

"They might be waiting for my approval on that—I've been swamped, but I'll get it done tonight."

"Perfect." I attempted a small smile, and Florence cocked her head.

"You look tired. Is everything okay?"

"No. I've been sleeping poorly."

"You don't have to stay," Florence told me reassuringly. "These things are just formalities. Go get some rest—you remain my best employee. Want a raise?"

"Always."

"I'll talk to accounting."

I chuckled, unfolded my legs, and made myself ask, "The Harkness situation. Is it solved?"

My question seemed to surprise her. "What do you mean?"

"The investors to buy back the loan, did they come through?"

"Not yet. Close, though."

"What's the holdup?"

"Usual bureaucratic shit." She shrugged. "No need to worry."

"And then they'll be out of our hair?"

"I hope so."

"Did you . . ." I swallowed. "Did you know that the Harkness founders are chemical engineers? At UT. Grad students in the department when you still taught there."

Florence was briefly motionless. Then she picked up a pen, clicked it twice, and put it down again. "Are you sure?"

I nodded. "I looked them up online." Not false, but not the whole truth. I wish I could have said that Eli was forcing me to hide things from Florence, but I needed to take accountability. It was my own inability to stay away from him that had turned me into a liar. "Is it possible that you crossed paths? Briefly, maybe? They were working on biofuels, too."

More stillness. Another shrug, stiff this time. "No. Categorically, no. I would remember if we had."

Why are you denying this so vehemently? Why does it feel like you're hiding something?

"Rue, is this . . . Has Eli Killgore contacted you? Put strange ideas in your head?"

I shook my head. *Who's hiding something now, Rue?*

"Listen, I can tell that you're nervous about Harkness. And I appreciate that you worry about me. But there is absolutely *no* need to research these people." She leaned closer, so close that her green eyes shone. Her cold hand took mine. "I know that this whole legal business is unsettling, and maybe it's making you second-guess things you know. But the truth is, when I was at UT, I worked so hard on my tech, in off-campus labs, that I barely showed up in the department. And if I've crossed paths with Harkness before . . . well, that explains why they're targeting Kline so aggressively. Maybe they've been keeping their eyes on us all these years, waiting to pounce. But them knowing *me* doesn't mean that I knew *them*, and honestly, they're dicks. I don't care to know where they're from, or what their story is. I just want them gone from my life."

It made sense. So much sense, all my questions were answered. So much sense, I turned my palm and squeezed hers. "I get it," I said, feeling a million pounds lighter than when I'd entered this office. "And you're right."

Florence's lips stretched into a reassuring smile. "Stop worrying, okay? I've got it all under control."

I nodded. Stood, almost lightheaded from relief. Made it to the door.

"Rue," Florence called. I looked at her from over my shoulder. "It's getting long again."

"What is?"

Florence pointed to the left side of her own head. "Your undercut. Might be time to trim it again."

"Yeah. I think you're right."

"Where does time go?"

I had no answer. So I smiled my goodbyes, and went back to my office, putting the matter out of my head—until that night, when I got into my car and heard a weird sound.

25

DOES IT REALLY *NOT* SOUND
LIKE A FANTASTIC IDEA?

RUE

The voices of Dave, Alec, and the HVAC maintenance guy came from the hallway on the right, so I took a left turn and headed for the hockey rink. I'd expected to find Eli; I did *not* expect him to be alone.

My day had taken a shitty turn when the real estate lawyer recommended by Nyota told me that he wasn't taking on new clients. The rink, though, soothed me. It smelled like childhood, and aching muscles, and the bored stares of skaters' parents during Saturday morning practice. I walked to the bench, taking in the circles Eli drew on the ice, his ever-messy hair, the pockets of sweat darkening his long-sleeved gray shirt. The echo of the stick hitting the puck.

He was in no way unique. Most hockey players skated this way—forceful, rhythmic strides, a seamless combination of strength and grace, swift turns and powerful stops. I'd never been particularly drawn to them, but Eli was my never-ending exception. Eyes on him, I went to stand next to a pair of beat-up sneakers and waited for him to notice me. Less than five minutes later he glided to me—breath labored, grin wide.

It was a punch in the stomach, how happy he was to see me. How happy *I* was to see him.

"Alec invited me," I said when he stopped at the glass boards.

He took his gloves off and wiped his brow with his forearm. "I'm sure Dave's doodling our wedding invitations on an HVAC user manual."

I smiled. His scent was as familiar to me as the ice's, the way they blended confusing to my senses. "He said your sister would be here, too."

He shook his head. "Homework. Or whatever the hell they call it in college."

I nodded. Made myself go straight to the point. "You left something in my car."

He examined me for a long moment. Cheeks red and curls wild, chest still rising and falling a beat too quickly—I'd never wanted to touch him more than in this very moment. And then his lips curved. "Hi, Rue. Nice to see you on this lovely summer night."

I rocked on my feet. "Hi. And likewise. You left—"

"Yup, I heard you the first time." He held out his hand over the guards, palm facing up in invitation. "Come skate with me."

What? "I don't . . ."

"I know you can skate, Rue. I've seen you do it with my own two eyes."

"When . . . ?" A thought occurred to me. "You watched my old competitions. Online."

He nodded. "You weren't kidding about 'Pump Up the Jam.'"

I exhaled a laugh, wondering if I should feel stalked. But hadn't I researched *him*, too? "No, I wasn't. I told you, no sense of humor."

"Sure. Come on in. Let's skate together." He noticed my hesitation. "You're already here. It'll be fun."

"I don't have my—"

"There's a roomful of equipment over there." He pointed past my shoulders, and I actually tried to picture it—the two of us, skating together. Being close. Keeping track of each other on the ice. *Okay,* I said in my head. *Yes. Let's do it. I want to do it.*

In fact, I wanted to do it so bad, I really shouldn't. "I don't think it's a good idea, Eli."

His smile froze. "It doesn't have to be a *date*. You already turned me down for that. But there is an empty rink, and you can pirouette around to your heart's content. Or whatever it is that you people do."

He made it sound simple. But skating could be so . . . intimate. Even more than sex. And if Eli and I were to go beyond sex, then my betrayal of Florence would run too deep for comfort. There had to be some limits. I had to set some limits. "I didn't come here for that."

He exhaled a self-deprecating laugh and skated away. He grabbed the puck, came back, and a moment later he was on the bench, changing into his shoes.

"Are you leaving?" I asked.

"Yup." Sweat beads trickled down his temple. He'd clearly been at it for a while. "So you can skate on your own."

"But that's not why I came."

"Right. True. We only meet for two reasons—to fuck, and to return things that we leave in each other's cars." He flashed me a smile, and his face was so unbearably familiar and attractive, and I had to stop myself from reaching out. "What did I forget?"

I dug into my pockets and held out the keys I'd found under my seat. He stared at them with a frown, then said, "They're not mine."

I frowned, too. "They have to be."

"And yet." He went back to his shoes. "Who else has been in your car?"

Tisha. But I knew what her keys looked like.

"Sorry you made the trip for nothing," he said. "I'd love to believe that you planted the keys as an excuse to see me—"

"I didn't—"

"—but that would be too much wishful thinking, even for me. Sure you don't want to skate?"

I nodded. My eyes lingered as he tied his shoelaces. "Do you always train alone?"

"This is not really training. Just playing around a bit." He stood, hoisting the laces of his skates over his shoulder. "I don't like crowds, that's all. When the rink is available, I take advantage."

"Do none of your friends skate?"

"Some of my former teammates have gone pro. None in the area—Austin's no hockey hot spot."

"What about the Harkness people?"

"Hark, yes, decently. I took Minami once, and she spent one hour on her butt. Sul didn't even put on skates." He smiled like they were beloved memories, and began heading out. I hurried behind him, feeling like an ugly duckling trying to catch up with an uninterested swan.

"What's the story there?" I asked, unwilling to let the conversation end.

"What do you mean?"

"Hark and Minami, they're weird with each other."

"Good catch."

"Obvious, if *I* picked up on it."

He gave me a fond look, like my oddities were something he treasured. "Just your run-of-the-mill love triangle."

"Like in *The Hunger Games*?"

He halted. "You read *The Hunger Games*?"

"Tisha wanted me to, but I'm not really the fiction type." Made-up stories confused me. I preferred dwelling in facts. "I watched the movie, though. I enjoyed it."

"Look at you." He resumed walking, delighted. "Hark and Minami dated for a couple of years. She broke it off. Hark never got over it. She married Sul."

"Fascinating."

"Is it?" He gave me a pained look.

"Not as much as *The Hunger Games*, but yes. Sul seems . . . quiet."

"He talks even less than you do."

"I talk."

"Hmm. Sure. Then my damn sister developed a very age-inappropriate crush on Hark, and the triangle became a square. I might just hate all of them."

"You are clearly the real victim of the situation."

"So glad that came across."

"Are Maya and Hark . . . ?"

"No. God, *no*."

"Well, as far as you know," I added, just to annoy him. His glare had me laughing. "I've definitely had sex with guys ten or fifteen years my senior. And look how well-adjusted I turned out."

He snorted at my deadpan delivery. I was a mess. He knew it.

I didn't mind. "As much as I wish all this *wellness* for my sister . . . *not* with Hark." He gave me another half-hearted glare. "What about you and Tisha?"

"What about us?"

"Is it just the two of you?"

For me, yes. I'd had two college roommates, who'd not been fans of my "stuck-up, superior, bitchy airs" in the first semester, but had slowly realized that I was just stumped by social situations. They'd taken me under their wing, brought me to parties, come to cheer for me at skating competitions. We were still in touch, but life was busy, and they both had families. "Tisha has several other friends, whom she constantly introduces me to." I shrugged. "Most people don't like me very much."

We stepped outside, into the oppressive heat of the dimly lit, deserted parking lot. Our cars were the farthest from the entrance— and the closest to each other.

"I'm not surprised," Eli said.

My eyebrow rose. "You're not surprised that people don't like me?"

"You never try to be anything but what you are." We stopped by his vehicle. "I think people are puzzled, and intimidated, and generally unsure of what to do with you."

"*You* are not unsure."

"No. Then again, I like you very much." Another blinding grin that had my heart somersaulting. Then his expression sobered, folding into something that looked like sorrow. "You're a wild ride, Rue. I've never met anyone like you, and never will again."

Something swelled at the base of my throat. "That's okay. You'll meet plenty of better people."

"Will I?" His Adam's apple rolled. He opened the back seat and threw in his equipment. When he turned back to me, his cocky smile had reappeared. "Have a great rest of your night. Like you said, you're not here to hang out, and this is not a date. The keys are not mine, so unless you want me to fuck you in my car, I'll see you—"

"Yes," I said.

Very quickly.

It was not premeditated. The possibility hadn't even occurred to me. But now that it was on the table, I wasn't going to be embarrassed at how eager I sounded.

I just wasn't ready to say goodbye.

Eli looked surprised. And incredulous. And angry. And amused. And once he'd cycled through another handful of emotions, he said, "Part of me wants to feel offended. That you won't skate with me for five minutes, but are okay with being fucked in the middle of a parking lot."

"And the other part?"

Eyes fixed on mine, he opened the passenger door. "Get inside."

I'd done it a few times in college—sex in cars, frat bathrooms, once in a locker room. Stupid, when discovery was always possible, and I'd grown tired of it early on, because nothing felt good enough to offset the anxiety of being caught.

But Eli *did* feel good enough. Eli was dragging me over the center console, arranging me to kneel on his lap, and the only things standing between us and something very embarrassing were air and darkness.

Foolish and irresponsible. But as always, things went from zero to incendiary, and stopping seemed impossible. "Did you wear these soft pants because you wanted to get fucked?" he asked when his hands slid into my leggings.

"I wore them because they're comfortable—*oh*." His thumb found my clit.

"Sensible. Pragmatic." The tip of his finger prodded against my entrance. "That's my type, apparently. Maybe once you're out of my life I'll just jerk off to budgeting plans."

He was still sweaty, and maybe I should have found it gross, but he smelled divine, and I licked the salt off a spot at the base of his neck. And that was it, because by now he knew me. My body, my sounds, my pleasure. It was the only possible explanation, the only reason I was convulsing in his arms in less than five minutes, while Eli exhaled soft laughs against my mouth and whispered filthy little things into my ear, feeling my body clutching hotly around his fingers. "You're really good, aren't you? You're fucking perfect."

It wasn't a question, but I nodded. "Do you have a condom?"

He bit my jaw. "We don't have to—"

"I want to. I liked it." I'd been thinking about what had happened in his bed for two days. At work. At night. At every hour. "I liked how much you liked it," I added.

"Yeah?"

"Yeah."

"You liked that I wasn't even able to put it in you before I came?"

I nodded. His fingers were still inside me, and I clenched around them.

"You like that I feel like a teen around you, don't you?"

I nodded again, eager. He groaned. "Well, sadly I don't have a condom, so—" He froze. "Hang on. Maybe in the glove compartment, from last year."

I was the one who checked, the one who found it, the one who eagerly unbuttoned Eli's pants while he tore it open with his teeth. He angled me so that I wouldn't get banged up against the steering wheel, and gathered my ass in his hands in the dirtiest of ways, and then he was pressing upward. Inside.

I braced myself. He was big, and hard, but he pushed in gently, with shallow, relentless strokes. "You okay?"

I took a deep breath. Nodded.

"Very good." He nuzzled against my cheek. "Take the rest, then."

He used his palm to spread my thighs apart, as though we could never be close enough. When his pelvis came into full contact with mine, and his cock slid as deep as I could take him, right to the hilt, I let out a low, guttural groan. "Fuck, yeah. You really are an amazing fuck, aren't you?"

I sighed, trying to adjust.

"Put your arms around my shoulders." He kissed my mouth, and I realized that we hadn't done that yet. He was fully inside me when his lips first found mine, and god, it felt good. "When you said you weren't into this, I had these lofty, deluded dreams of showing you the pleasure of a slow, thorough fuck. In a bed, possibly. But I highly doubt it's going to happen anytime soon, and I'm not even sure I care anymore . . ."

I liked this: his big body moving in mine, the stretch of him, the way he rocked into me. I liked that he seemed to be less in control than I was, the power of it. I fundamentally trusted him not to hurt me, and he seemed to trust me just as much. His undoing was electrifying, and never frightening.

I'd just come, and still felt the echoes of that pleasure reverberating through me, fueled by the way Eli seemed utterly lost. A lot of men had complimented my breasts, ass, face, and I'd welcomed the idea of being just a body. I'd purposefully sought out partners who'd be willing to see me as little as I wanted to be seen. But I loved the way Eli looked at me like I was something special, something more. Like I could easily exhaust the entire spectrum of his needs. Like he couldn't imagine looking anywhere else, ever.

"I know you don't like to—but if—" He wasn't fully coherent, but I understood when his hand slid between us and his thumb began to describe nice, slow circles on my clit. "The good news, for you," he said hoarsely, "is that I'm unreasonably fucking crazy about you, and this isn't going to last too long." His rueful tone made me loop my arms more tightly around his neck.

"Don't hurry on my behalf," I said. It wasn't painful, or boring. The hot pressure was pleasant, as was his tight grip on my hips as his cock pushed in and out of me. The way his thrusts would become choppy and erratic before he'd remember himself and suddenly stop, as if to draw out the experience. Not in an attempt to get *me* off, but for himself. And the knowledge of how much he was enjoying this, with the dragging movement of his thumb, had warmth spreading inside me, a new kind of tension building up, and—

Eli bit into my shoulder, and it was over. His movements stuttered inside me a few times while he slurred into my throat a litany of praise that ranged from sweet to incredibly dirty. "Fucking unbelievable," he rasped at the end, his laughter a breathless puff against my cheek.

I felt a tinge of disappointment. It had been good, very good, and it felt too soon for it to be over—

"Rue, I'm going to tell you something you don't want to hear," Eli said. His thumb resumed its movements on my clit. A shiver of pleasure rose up my spine. "It was always going to end this way." His cock was softening inside me, a pleasant stretch that was little more than a counterpoint to the strumming of his fingers. "Even if we hadn't matched on that damn app, we'd have met in this rink, or at Kline, or walking down the street. And I'd have seen you, talked with you for about five minutes, and you would have looked at me all serious and curious and uncompromising, and I would have known that I needed to do this with you more than anything else in the whole damn world."

My orgasm came fast and beautifully. Eli's hands roamed greedily all over me as he pressed soft kisses to the base of my throat. And then, after a while, he said, "I want to drive you home."

I was boneless, still trying to get my brain to restart. "My car is here."

"I'll pick you up tomorrow morning and drive you back here." He leaned back. His expression was earnest. At least I thought so—my eyes were watery, like I'd been crying. Except I never cried. Maybe my eyeballs were sweating. Summer in Texas, not too improbable. "Let me make you dinner." He traced my mouth with his thumb.

"That would be nice," I said.

"Come to my place. Let me take care of you. Let me teach you how to pet dogs. Exposure therapy, sweetheart."

I let out a small laugh, but I was scared. That he was asking. That I wanted to say yes. "I don't know if it's a good idea."

"Really?" He kissed my cheek, open-mouthed. "You moving in. You, quitting your job so we can do this twenty times a day. Me, retiring to service you full-time. Us, fucking around for the rest of our lives. Does it really *not* sound like a fantastic idea?"

My heart jolted. *Yes,* it said. *Yes.* I just wanted to be with him. Was it so bad? Florence didn't have to know. No one did. Just the two of us.

"Don't say no, Rue," he murmured. A low, heartfelt appeal. "Don't do this to us."

I didn't let myself think about it. "Okay."

His smile could have powered the entire city. "Okay."

"Okay," I repeated, and we were both laughing silently in each other's mouths, and then kissing, and I thought that maybe, if perfect moments existed, this could be one of them.

I disengaged from him, hiked over the console, fumbled my leggings back up my hips. I let out something that sounded disturbingly like a giggle, but my body was still buzzing, thanking me for the best twenty minutes of its life. And Eli was still looking at me like I contained the entire universe.

I leaned against the headrest while he cleaned himself up, and then began putting back all the papers that had fallen out of the glove compartment. "I'm sorry," I said. "Next time you have to show your registration you're going to have a real hard time . . ."

I stopped when my eyes fell on a familiar name.

Kline.

It was an oddly formatted stack of papers, covered in plastic. Eli muttered something about tossing the condom and folded out of the car, but I kept on reading.

RULE 202 PROCEEDINGS IN AID OF INVESTIGATION OF CLAIMS AGAINST KLINE INC.
Oral deposition of Florence Carolina Kline.

I turned the page. **APPEARANCES**, the new header read. **FOR HARKNESS LP, ELI KILLGORE.** I turned another, and another, and then more, until the text resembled something like a movie script. A list of Qs and As.

Q. Very well. And, Dr. Kline, when did you first meet the founders of Harkness?

A. I don't see why this matters.

Q. Could you please answer anyway?
A. I'm not sure I remember. I probably met them all at different times, anyway.

Q. As far as you can recall?
A. I guess I first met Dr. Oka when she interviewed to become a postdoc in my lab, about twelve years ago. It would have been a phone call, because at the time she lived in Ithaca, and then we met in person when she moved to work with me. I believe I met Conor Harkness around the same time, when he enrolled in the PhD program at UT.

Q. You taught at UT at the time?
A. Correct.

Q. And Eli Killgore?
A. He was the last to arrive, so I must have met him . . .

Q. About a year later?
A. Yes, that sounds correct.

Q. Is it correct to say that you served as a mentor to all three of them?
A. Yes, it is.

"Rue?"

I looked up from the file. Eli was back inside the car.

"What is this?" I asked him.

His eyes fell on the papers in my hands. On the page to which they were open. "Fuck, Rue."

"It was in your glove compartment."

"Shit." He sighed and ran a hand down his face. "Shit."

"Eli, what is this?"

"It's a deposition."

"When was Florence *deposed*?" I asked—then realized I could find out on my own. I checked the date on the front page and gasped. About two weeks ago. "Journal club. The day you were at Kline, and I . . ." I shook my head, incapable of making sense of anything. "Who—who gave you the right to depose her?"

He massaged his eyes. "State court. There were irregularities in the documents she turned over, and we asked for an oral—"

"It says here that she knew you, before. Ten years ago. Is it true?"

He hesitated. "Rue." His tone was gentle. "It's a legal deposition. She was under oath."

"But she told me . . ." I shook my head, feeling as though the planet were spinning too fast for me. "Today she told me that . . ."

Eli's expression softened. *Pity,* I thought. That's what it was. "Let's discuss this at home. I didn't want you to find out this way. This is a very complicated—"

"No. No, I—Florence lied to me." My eyes burned, and my chest was on fire. "And you—why didn't you . . . Why did *no one* . . ." I shook my head and opened the door of the car.

Eli's hand closed around my wrist. "Rue, wait—"

"No. I—*no.*" I freed my hand and wiped my cheek. My palm was fully dry. "I don't want to—I'm *sick* of this. Do *not* follow me, or I swear to god—"

"Rue, let me—"

I got out of the car and let my fury swallow me.

26

TAKE STOCK OF YOUR
SHITTY, SOLITARY LIFE

RUE

On Tuesday morning I called in, saying that I didn't feel well and I'd work from home.

Tisha texted me at 9:00 a.m. (**You okay? Also, did I lose Diego's house keys in your car?**) and I replied, Yes, and yes.

Florence texted me at noon (**Hope you feel better soon**), and I did not reply at all.

She was my friend, and I wasn't going to write her off for lying to me. After all, I was a liar, too. I'd lied to Florence about Eli for weeks, even after she'd given me multiple opportunities to come clean, and I'd felt like shit every time. I'd had my reasons, and it was entirely possible that Florence had hers.

But I needed to understand *what* exactly she'd lied about. And it was obvious that both she and Eli had withheld the truth from me, and that neither of them could be trusted on this matter. It left me with limited options.

I decided not to bring Tisha into this until I had a complete picture, which meant that it would have to live exclusively in my head for a while. I had breakfast, lunch, and dinner. Wrote what felt like thousands of work emails. Worked on my patent's paperwork. Noticed that some of my seedlings had germinated, and transplanted them into the hydroponic system, taking care to submerge the fragile roots with nutrients.

Then, around 7:00 p.m., there was a knock at the door. *The super*, I thought, checking on my AC vents like I'd asked. But a last-minute instinct prodded me to look through the peephole.

My brother was pacing outside my door, a stack of papers rolled up in his hand.

I closed my eyes, took a deep breath, and stepped back as quietly as possible, ready to pretend not to be home.

"*Goddammit*, Rue, open the door. I know you're in there."

I covered my mouth and sank into a chair.

It was okay. The security chain was on. He was going to leave soon.

"Your new doorman told me you're home."

Shit. A new doorman. Had I known about him? No. I remembered no notices.

"We can make this as easy or as hard as you want, Rue, but I *am* going to be here until you agree to do this."

I pushed the heels of my hands into my eyes, determined to stay quiet. But when Vince spoke again, his tone was much softer. Suddenly I was ten again, and he was seven. We hadn't seen Mom in days. He'd been crying for hours, and all I wanted was to make him feel better.

"Rue, please. You know I love you and I don't want to be doing this. But you're being unreasonable. The money from this sale would be life-changing for me. The Indiana Realtor called yesterday—they have a buyer who'll take the cabin as is, in cash. I get it that you want to know more about Dad, but how does *that* come before my financial security? You have your fancy job, but I didn't get to go to college. I didn't get *tons* of things."

I wasn't softhearted, but the least hardened spot in my heart belonged to my brother. It had taken me years and lots of therapy to stop myself from bailing him out every time he put himself in some shitty situation. I wasn't going to start again, but the feeling that I owed him an explanation remained.

So I said through the door, "I've been looking for a lawyer who can help us figure this out. I don't want to leave you in the lurch. My plan is to buy your half, but we'll need to work out—"

"I *knew* you were in there." Vince's voice harshened. "Open up!"

"No." I took a step back from the door and tried to sound stern. "I'm not going to let you in my apartment when you are being aggressive—"

"I'll fucking give you aggressive—" The door shook within its frame. I leaped back.

What the hell—?

Another heavy thud. Vince was kicking my door.

"Vince." My heart pounded. "You need to *stop*."

"Not until you let me *in*." He punctuated the words with another heavy blow.

Fuck.

I took a deep breath, trying to get my bearings. My door was sturdy, and he was unlikely to get in. But it wasn't *me* that I worried about: if he continued, one of the neighbors would call the police. I *should* call the police, but as fucked up as it sounded, I was never going to do it. Vince had once stolen a box of Oreos from H-E-B just for my birthday, back when he was barely able to read and write. It had been the sweetest thing anyone had ever done for me.

No police. No Tisha, who despised Vince and would probably show up with a kitchen knife and stab him. No other options.

A real "take stock of your shitty, solitary life" kind of moment.

The door groaned under another blow. A drop of sweat ran down my spine as my alternatives narrowed, then shrank to a single one.

My phone was on the couch. I picked it up and tapped on an unsaved number. Waited two, three rings. And when the person on the other side of the line picked up, I didn't wait for them to talk before whispering, "I'm sorry to do this, but I really need your help."

27

BELIEVE ME, I'VE TRIED

ELI

The scene wasn't as bleak as he'd expected.

Vincent, who looked as sullen as the last time they'd met, was taking a rest from his breaking and entering efforts and sat on the hallway floor, head tipped back against the wall. When he heard footsteps against the linoleum, he glanced lazily in Eli's direction, then did a double take.

Eli had been ready to go nuts on him, but the berserker rage he'd felt during Rue's call extinguished almost instantly. What a sad, miserable asshole her brother was. Not even worth a couple of educational slaps.

"Go home," Eli ordered, bored. Rue wasn't going to open her door until Vince left, which meant that he stood between Eli and where Eli wanted to be.

"What are *you* doing here?"

"*I* was invited. What are *you* doing here?"

"Are you seeing my sister?"

"Yes." Not even a lie. He'd *seen* Rue several times. Had fully expected not to *see* her for a while after last night, but now, thanks to her asshole brother, he was about to *see* her again. "You need to drop this. You know that, right?" Vince was Rue's brother, and Eli was going to keep his own temper in check out of respect for her. But he had his limits, which was why he stepped closer and lowered his voice. "You can't act this way around her, okay? Because she's going to get sad. And if she gets sad, then I'm going to get mad. And there *will* be consequences."

Vince scrambled to his feet. Perfect punching height for Eli, but once again—not what Rue wanted. "If you don't stop interfering—"

"Here's the deal." He dropped his voice further, angling his back so that if Rue was watching, she wouldn't be able to read his lips. "Your sister obviously cares about you. She called *me* here because literally anyone else, from the doorman to her neighbors to the fucking mailman, would not hesitate to call the authorities. But here's what she doesn't know." He leaned forward. "I have an entire team of lawyers at my disposal who can make your life very, very hard. Which means that I can ruin you without getting you arrested *or* beating you to a pulp. I wouldn't even need to make her sad." He straightened, pleased at the narrowing in Vincent's eyes.

"I just want to talk to her," he bit out.

"Then schedule a fucking meeting."

"We have a buyer right *now*. She's being selfish."

"Good. She should put herself first. Now, will you get the fuck out of this building, or do I have to make a couple of calls?" He took his phone out of his jeans and dangled it until Vincent shook his head and stalked away, stopping to kick the banister on the landing like the childish fool he so clearly was. Once he was gone for good, Eli knocked softly.

"It's me."

A few beats and the door opened. Rue stood in the middle, half in the shadows, looking like a paler, less substantial version of herself. She didn't quite meet his eyes, and Eli was tempted to make a detour for the parking lot to rough Vincent up.

"I wasn't sure who to call—"

"No need to explain. Can I come in?"

Her eyes widened, like the thought hadn't occurred to her. "You don't have to stay."

"I know."

She tensed. "I didn't call you here because . . . I don't think that just because we had sex you should be at my—"

"I am, though. At your disposal." He smiled at her, small but reassuring. If she needed to tell herself that this was just fucking, she was welcome to do so. He refused to play the game any longer. *I'm not going to follow the rules, Rue. I'm not going to behave. I'm not going to pretend this is enough.* "I'll stay for twenty minutes, just in case Vincent's waiting for me to drive off."

Her head bent low, and there was a slight tremor to the hands she stuffed in her pants. But it wasn't until they entered the living room that he could fully see her expression. Ever-armored Rue Siebert looked forlorn, and ten years younger, and a hundred times more fragile. The sight of how much she hurt hit him with violence. He wrapped his hand around her forearm, pulled her closer, and it was more for himself than for her. "Hey. It's okay."

They'd hugged dozens of times by now, always within the

constraints of sex. This embrace was different: It had no direction and existed only to provide comfort. It was warm and eviscerating and dangerous. More forbidden than anything they'd done so far.

And then he felt it: the small shivers running through her back, her forehead pressing between his pecs, a choked sound she swallowed. She was crying.

Eli's heart sank.

"It's okay, baby." He kissed the crown of her hair and held her as tight and as long as she allowed. "It'll be okay." Minutes later, when she slid two hands on his chest and pushed him away, he had to clench his fists to avoid drawing her back into his arms. And that was when his vision broadened from its Rue-induced tunnel and shifted to his surroundings.

The apartment was *magnificent.* Or, what she'd done with it. The place wasn't large, and the layout was nothing special, but Rue hadn't lied about having plants. In fact, the entire room was lush, every surface covered in green. Cacti, flowers, a few ornamental pots. But Rue's favorite cultivation method was clearly hydroponics. There were towers, and shelves, and a couple of kits she may have built on her own. Most of what she grew was produce: Eli spotted basil, tomatoes, mini cucumbers, peppers, lettuce, and that was just at first glance.

Her house was a beautiful, honest-to-god garden.

He puffed out a laugh, thinking about the raised bed he'd bought two years ago to grow herbs for the kitchen, the one he'd never gotten around to putting together. In fact, it was still packed in the garage. Had been there for so long, Maya had given it a name.

Fucking Herbert.

He glanced back at Rue, wanting to say something, but it wasn't the right time to compliment her agricultural skills. She'd walked to the couch and collapsed herself in front of it, on the floor, back pressed against the cushions, knees to her chin. Like her brother, in the hallway earlier.

Eli sighed and sat next to her, allowing his arm to brush against hers.

"I don't usually cry," she said, wiping her eyes with the back of her hand.

"I figured."

"How?"

"Just a hunch." She hadn't cried last night, and that fucking deposition had given her plenty of reason. "Your general *vibe*, as Maya would say."

She smiled through her sniffles. "It's because he's my brother."

"I know."

"He's younger. My brain is wired to constantly feel that I have to take care of him."

"I know."

"He's being a total asshole. I'm being a complete pushover. This could escalate to a really dangerous level. I need to figure out a solution to this. It's just . . ."

"Believe me, I *know*."

His sincerity made her finally look up from her knees. "It's embarrassing," she admitted.

"What is?"

"Maya's . . . great. The first night we met, you said you two used to not get along, but clearly you worked through your issues. Meanwhile, I'd get a restraining order for my brother if I weren't a fucking wimp."

He nodded. "Maya *is* great, and we now have a good relationship that I wouldn't change for anything. But . . ." He swallowed. "Want a story?"

"Depends. Is it terrible?"

His laugh was low. "It's the most terrible of all of them, Rue." It wasn't an exaggeration. Her nod was solemn.

"I don't even know where to start. How about—Maya is great now, but when she was fifteen, she slashed the tires of my car because I told her she couldn't go to a midnight screening of some shitty horror movie on a school night." He winced at the memory. "And when I grounded her to punish her, she slashed the new set, too."

Rue's eyes widened. And then deviated from their routine: she asked a *question*. "Who gave you the right to tell your sister what she could and couldn't do?"

"Are you siding with *her*?"

"No." She sniffled. "Maybe?"

He chuckled. "I got custody of her when she was eleven. The court gave me the right. Literally."

"And your parents?"

"They died one year apart from each other. Unrelated. My mom first, acute leukemia. Then Dad—car accident."

"How old were you?"

"Twenty-five."

"And you were her only remaining relative?"

"There are some scattered uncles and second cousins, but none here in Austin, and none she knew well. I was an adult and her brother. There was no question in anyone's mind that I should be the one taking care of her—not even in mine."

"If someone asked me to take care of an eleven-year-old, I wouldn't know where to start," she mused.

"Same here. Maya was a toddler when I moved out for college. I didn't get along with my parents, so I rarely went back home and hardly saw her."

"Is that why the last thing you told your mom . . . ?"

"About being a shitty mother?" He sighed. "My dad was the kind of disciplinarian who'd ground you for days for a perceived eye roll, and I was . . . a shithead. His approach did *not* work for me. Constant fights, ultimatums, threats—them trying to get me to be less wild. Me being ever more wild, out of spite. All that teenage shit. And my mom, she deferred to him in everything, so." He shrugged. "If I could talk to them now, adult to adult, maybe we'd get over that stuff. But I moved to Minnesota to play hockey. Took all sorts of part-time jobs. I'd go back home once a year for a couple of days, tops. Then grad school started, and you know how busy it gets. I was in the same city as my family. I *could* have visited more, but home was a place where I'd been miserable for three-quarters of my life, and there was so much baggage on both our ends. The last time I saw my mom was on my birthday. They invited me over for dinner. The conversation devolved into the usual recriminations. A few weeks later my mother died." He'd had a decade to work through the kinks of these regrets, and they were still tangled in his head. Always would be. As it was, he couldn't stand his fucking birthday. "Then my dad, fourteen months later. And I was my sister's guardian."

Rue's eyes held neither pity nor condemnation. "Was Maya . . ." She shook her head. "Were *you* okay?"

Had anyone ever asked him that before? Everyone's focus had been on Maya, rightfully so. Eli's heart thudded, and he covered it with a laugh. "I was definitely *not* okay. I was freaking the fuck out. I didn't know Maya at all. I had no money, I'd just been kicked out of my doctoral program, and my parents' mortgage still needed to be paid. And Maya . . . initially, she was just mourning. Later, the grief turned into anger, and she had to take it out on someone. The two available options were me and herself, and she spared neither." He swallowed. "I don't think she would deny that she was kind of an asshole. Then again, I was *severely* underqualified."

Rue laughed, bubbly and wet, and even in the midst of recounting his worst story, he couldn't believe how rare and lovely it sounded. *I like you when you laugh. I like you when you're serious. I like you all the damn time.*

"Did it get better?"

"Not for years. Before she left for college, it was slammed doors and screaming matches and acting out. In hindsight, I can't imagine how devastating it must have been, to have a brother who's fundamentally a stranger tell you what you should do. When she left for college, she was done with me. I was half-convinced I'd never see her again. By then Harkness was doing well and I could afford to send her to school wherever she wanted. You know where she picked?"

"East Coast?"

"Scotland. She went all the way to fucking *Scotland*, just to get away from me."

She tried to hide her smile. "I hear it's very beautiful."

"I wouldn't know. I was never invited to visit."

Rue snorted a laugh. He had to force himself to stop staring. "She did come back, though."

"She did. And she was different. She was an adult, and I didn't have to be an authority figure anymore. She'd lived abroad for years, and I could trust her to take care of herself." He massaged the back of his neck. "She used to complain about my despotic tendencies, but I was terrified. She was wild and unpredictable and fragile, and ordering her around was the only thing I could do to keep her out of harm's way. I began understanding my parents and what they'd gone through with me, except that they were dead and it was too late, and that degree of mindfuckery is just . . ." He shook his head. "She'll always resent me a little, and maybe I'll always resent her. But the pain of it has dulled. I truly enjoy watching her doing her shit. She's way smarter than I was at her age. She's resilient. She's determined. She's kind. *And*, the whole experience gave me something very important."

"What?"

"A total lack of interest in having children."

Rue laughed again, and had he ever yielded more power than right at this moment? Had anything felt better than making her smile when she'd been crying only moments ago? It was fucking intoxicating. Screw science or finance—*this* could be his craft. He could spend the next few years learning the nooks and crannies of her moods, studying her temperament, cataloging her disposition in all its little idiosyncrasies, and once he'd accrued an adequate body of research, it would be his mission and his pleasure: make Rue Siebert happy.

Way more satisfying than his current job description.

"*I* didn't even need to be my brother's guardian to reach that conclusion," she murmured.

"Bragging's not cool, Rue." He smiled at her amused look, and glanced at the clock hanging on top of a plant rack. It had been twenty minutes. More.

"Thank you. For coming."

"Thank *you* for calling me. I'm a simple guy who used to channel his aggression into hockey and now has a boring corporate job. I need to get my kicks somewhere. And . . ." *I was thinking about you anyway. I want you to reach out to me when you need something*—anything. *I want more. If I came clean about that, how would you react?*

She nodded like she understood the unsaid. Seemed on the verge of opening up and admitting to something that Eli really, really wanted to hear. Then, at the last moment, defaulted to their usual: she rolled over and wedged herself between his open legs. Her eyelashes were dark half-moons as she glanced down, assessing his body with all the thoroughness of a merciless examiner. Heat surged inside him, the exhilaration and sheer pride that always came from being the object of her attention. Then she took his face in both of her palms and leaned forward.

She tasted like dried tears. Eli deepened the kiss on instinct, but instantly came to his senses. "Rue." He wrapped his hands around both her wrists. "I didn't come for this."

"And I didn't call you for this." She gave him a solid, even look. "Can we do it anyway?"

He scanned her face. "If you ask, I'm never going to tell you no. You know that, right?"

"I had my suspicions."

The kiss resumed, slow, calm, salty, and Eli was able to keep himself in check for about two minutes. Then, it was over. He pressed her into him, pushed into her, ran his mouth down her throat, and when her fingers raked through his hair, he asked, "Here? Or in bed?"

She walked a step ahead and led him down the hallway. Her fingers, wrapped loosely around his, felt as explosive as any other sexual act they'd ever engaged in—positively perverse, given how little real intimacy she usually afforded them. Being escorted inside Rue's bedroom was like the first time a girl had guided his hand under her shirt: forbidden, terrifying, life rearranging. He wondered if she'd had any other man in her room. Decided it was unlikely. Tried to get his heart not to pound out of his chest.

She was messy in her private space. Surfaces not covered by plants were draped in discarded clothes, unopened mail, empty mugs. It made her room even smaller and cozier, her unmade queen bed narrower. She didn't bother apologizing for the clutter, and Eli *loved* that.

He tried to imagine what sharing a living space with her might be: a constant fight to keep her chaos from encroaching on his part of the room. Tripping over the straps of a discarded bra on his way to the bathroom. Memorizing her unsmiling face in the soft morning light. Dreaming of her at night without being afraid to wake, happy in the knowledge that if he reached out, his hand would meet her soft skin. Soaking in that unacceptable feeling that permeated his cells whenever she was nearby. She sat on the edge of the mattress, looked up at him with the intent expression she reserved for talk of nanopolymers, and he couldn't survive one more second without his head between her legs.

It was becoming easier and easier, getting her off. Like a well-trained musician, he knew exactly how to play her. Satisfaction hit him hard as he dragged her underwear to the side and made her sigh, and shiver, and come over and over, with his mouth and his tongue and his fingers. When she pushed his head away because it was too intense, he saw it in her eyes: she hadn't thought she was capable of this pleasure. When they were together, she sometimes doubted that her body was really hers.

"Whenever you want to feel like this," he murmured at the inside of her thigh, "call *me*. Use *me*." Her heels dug into his back like little fists. "I think about doing it every second of every day anyway."

She collapsed back on the mattress, one arm thrown over her eyes. Eli wiped his mouth with the back of his hand, unbuttoned his too-tight jeans to give his dick some respite, and then moved up to force her to look him in the eyes some more. She didn't seem inclined to, and he waited patiently, a knight seeking an audience with his beautiful, iron-willed queen.

"I should have condoms. Somewhere in the medicine cabinet in my bathroom." Her voice was still raspy from the cries. "I don't think they're expired yet, but . . ." She arched off the bed in a deep, lazy stretch, and when she stayed like that, a perfect bow of elongated muscles, Eli hooked a finger in the hem of her shirt and pulled it up. He stared at her full breasts, mesmerized, willing himself to be patient.

"We don't have to."

"I know."

"We can do anything that you—"

"I know."

Her arm moved, and her peaceful eyes were on him. His heart was louder than he could remember. "So I *did* cure you with the unique prowess of my magic cock."

"You have healed me. My appendix scar has disappeared. I'm not allergic to pollen anymore."

He huffed. "They weren't my best performances." He wasn't embarrassed, per se. He'd enjoyed fucking her too much to attach anything but highly positive feelings to the act.

"It's a turn-on, to see you like that." She bit into her lower lip. "You're not the only one who enjoys giving pleasure to others."

His vocal cords felt paralyzed, so he went to the bathroom.

When he caught his reflection, what he found in his eyes was terrifying. He'd told himself to be careful with her, over and over. To keep his guard up. He'd failed, miserably.

You're fucked. Completely, irrevocably fucked.

Rue had taken her remaining clothes off. She gave him a small smile and took care of him, undressing him slowly, methodically, and Eli was transported to another reality—one in which at the end of a stressful workday, Rue was the thing he'd been looking forward to since morning. In which he'd spent his meetings deconstructing the scent of her skin. Time was stale from nine to six. The subject of every email contained her tranquil eyes.

"Why are you looking at me like that?" she murmured, kneeling in front of him to rid him of his jeans. A spectacular image he was going to treasure in his old age.

"Like what?"

She shrugged.

"Like I want to fuck you?" *Like I want you?* "I can't make it stop, Rue." *Believe me, I've tried.*

She stood, and he buried his head in her shoulder, laughing at his own idiocy.

"You'll have to put it on," she instructed, handing him the condom.

"Want me to teach you how?"

She shrugged. Her breasts bounced—a masterpiece of gravity. "It's not a skill I have particular interest in acquiring."

Fuck, he *liked* her. "No, you wouldn't."

He wasn't certain how they ended up with him lying back against the headboard and Rue on top, her hands balancing on his shoulders, slowly sliding him inside her, inch by torturous inch. He wanted to tell her that she was killing him. Wanted to order her to get the fuck on with it and let him just *be inside her*. But he let her take her time, and eventually he was as deep as he wanted, and she was taking all that he had to offer, and that was simply overwhelming. Once again, he was grateful for the condom dulling the sensation, or it would have been all over, right now.

"How does it feel?" he asked. He didn't have the tightest reins on his control.

"It feels . . ." She moved experimentally. He bit back a groan. "Full. Nice." She pressed a kiss to his shoulders. "You know what I like best?"

"My preternaturally medicinal cock?"

She laughed. He nearly choked on his breath. "Sure. But also, when we do this, you practically *vibrate*." Her fingertip traced the taut curve of his triceps, nail lightly scraping. "Every single muscle in your body is tense, and I can feel how much you want to move, and yet you're not, and it makes me . . ." She tilted her hips at a perfectly disastrous angle, and he had to grip her hips and force her to be still and take a deep, shuddering breath before his third time fucking her turned out to be even more lackluster than the first two.

"Jesus Christ, Rue."

She nipped at his earlobe, and he couldn't help himself anymore, so he closed his fingers around her waist and began moving her, up and down. For a second he lost himself to the feeling of it, the tight squeeze of her muscles, the taste of her tits in his mouth, the soft yield of her ass under his fingers. He hooked his arms under hers and was moments away from chasing his orgasm, but when he looked at her face, she was staring down at him, interested but detached, and everything inside him screamed, *Fuck, no.*

Not this time.

"Rue." He let out a breathless laugh. "If only you knew how fucking good this feels to me."

"That's nice." She bent down to kiss his cheek. "I want you to feel good."

He groaned. "Okay, new plan." He guided her off him. "I'm going to turn you around."

"Around?"

"Yeah. That way I should be able to . . ." He arranged her to face the wall, then guided her until her palms were on the headboard. He pushed back inside without giving her time to adjust. Her gasp matched his grunt. "I can control my thrusts better. And I can touch you more easily." He pressed an open-mouthed kiss against the valley behind her ear. "And even if you don't come, at least you can . . ."

He circled the heel of his hand against her clit first, then his fingers. He pushed in and out of her, shallow thrusts that had her ass grinding against his groin. "How are you—"

"Good," she exhaled. "I like it."

"Yeah?" He touched her some more. "Is it working for you?"

She nodded, and he felt her breath speed up. "You just—you really know where to touch me. And it's not even . . ." She whimpered at another stroke of his thumb, and when she contracted against him, he felt his balls tighten and the pressure at the base of his spine tingle. "I think maybe I could . . ." She exhaled again, but he knew what she was about to say.

"Yeah," he breathed in her ear. "Maybe you could."

Every thought of his own pleasure was forgotten. He surged against Rue, as deep as he could go, and once he bottomed out, he kept his strokes shallow and began moving his fingers on her. "Like this?"

She nodded eagerly, almost violently, and Eli felt like this was what he'd been put on this earth for—get Rue off, right here, in this very moment. "Oh, sweetheart. Why does it feel like you're going to come, huh? Why do you feel so wet and soft and—"

Abruptly, she seized around him. Her entire body clenched, the sound of her winded breath stopped, and even though all Eli wanted was to fuck her into the mattress, he pushed in to the hilt and let her ride her orgasm until she collapsed in his arms.

"You just came around my cock," he rasped out. His words sounded shocked—just as shocked as he felt.

She nodded, lost for words.

"Rue." He kissed her temple. Her cheekbone. The line of her jaw. He held her to himself with shaking hands. "I'd like it if you said it."

Her voice trembled. "I just came around your cock."

"Okay. Okay. I need to—I'll finish, okay? Let's see how long it takes me to . . ."

He pushed in, then out again, then in.

And that, apparently, was how long it took.

28

IN ANOTHER TIMELINE

RUE

My eyes fluttered open to the uncharacteristically loud rumble of a faraway motorcycle, and stayed that way when I noticed Eli's head next to mine on the pillow.

The moon must have been near full, because despite the darkness and the late hour, I could see him clearly. The perfect emperor nose. The curls, at once flattened and wild. The slight part of his lips and the regular breaths, matching the surge and fall of his shoulders.

We'd fallen asleep facing each other, sweat still cooling on our bodies, eyes searching as we willed our hearts to slow down. Neither of us had moved in the intervening hours. Eli's hand still grazed my lower back, forearm draped over my waist, an unfamiliar but pleasant weight.

I remained still in the bluish quiet of the night, pretending to be a photograph of myself, emptying my mind of everything but the faint scent of petrichor seeping in through a window. A few minutes later, Eli's eyes blinked open, too. "Hey. What time is it?"

He was the kind of insufferable person who slept quietly and woke gracefully. No disorientation from an unknown bed, or the hours of daylight he'd lost. Just that peaceful expression, and his hand resuming where it had stopped before our unplanned nap: drawing scribbles into my skin.

"Eleven." I glanced at the clock. "Eleven fifteen, actually. Don't you need to go home and walk your dog?"

I was genuinely curious, but halfway through I realized that my words could have been construed as an attempt to kick him out. Eli, though, just smiled, like he often did when I was my odd, socially awkward self.

He smiled like I *delighted* him.

"Tiny's with Maya." He propped himself up on the mattress. My eyes caught on his strong biceps. "But yes, I should leave if—"

"Wait." I reached out. Wrapped a hand around his forearm. "Can you wait?"

"Wait?"

"Could you stay a bit longer?"

His brow furrowed with worry. "I'll stay for as long as you—"

"I didn't mean to imply that you should leave. Just—you told me your worst story. Before you go, I want to tell you mine."

"Rue, you don't owe me—"

"I know. I want to. But this one, it's not like the others. I don't think you'll be able to look past it. So I'll just tell you. And then . . . then you can leave."

His eyes softened. "You were able to look past mine."

"It's different. Mine is bad. Mine is my fault. Mine is . . . I'll just tell you." I pulled the sheets up to my chest. "I don't talk about this stuff to anyone. My brother. The way we grew up. Tisha knows some of it, because she was there, and Florence . . . it's not something you say over dinner."

"Rue."

"So I'll tell *you*. And if you decide to . . . I guess you and I were never meant to be part of each other's lives. Being with you was a betrayal from the very start. I just couldn't stay away."

His expression was inscrutable.

"And if you can't bear to look at me after all these things I'm about to tell you, you'll just leave, and everything will be as it should. It'll be like I screamed them from the edge of a cliff." Cathartic, but ultimately meaningless. Lost in the ether. Nothing would change, except for this one moment in time, in the quiet of our bed. "Okay?"

Eli briefly cupped my cheek, then immediately let go, as if aware that I couldn't have borne a prolonged touch. His eyes, his tone, everything about him felt distant and enigmatic. "Go ahead," he said, and I was thankful for it.

I started before I could change my mind. "My dad left when I was six. Vince was a little more than three. I don't remember life before, so I assume things were mostly fine. After he was gone, though, we were poor. Not always. It depended on a lot of things. Whether Mom had a job. What kind of job. Whether something broke in the house and we needed to replace it. Healthcare expenses. That kind of stuff. When I was thirteen, for instance, our landlord decided that she was going to sell our apartment, and between moving to a new place and the increase in rent . . . it wasn't a good time."

I felt naked in an uncomfortable, intolerable way. I spotted one of the oversized T-shirts I slept in, quickly pulled it over my head, and then sat up, cross-legged, to continue. "My mom—she had her own issues. Mental health, I'm sure. Some addiction. As I understand it, her parents were part of one of those ultraconservative churches, and when she decided she didn't want to stick around, they withdrew any sort of financial and emotional support. She had us when she was very young, and . . . What I'm trying to say is, she's not the villain of this story. Or maybe she is, but she was a victim first.

"We didn't have lots of material shit growing up, and that wasn't fun. But the worst part was, by far, being hungry." I glanced down at my hands and took a moment to collect myself before resuming. *I'm saying it. I'm doing it. It's out there.* "A lot of people think that food insecurity means constant, systematic starvation, and sometimes it plays out like that, but for me . . . I wasn't hungry all the time. I wasn't always malnourished. I wasn't deprived of food for days on end. But sometimes, when I was hungry, there just wouldn't be anything to eat in the house, or money to buy it. Sometimes that would go on for two, three days in a row. Sometimes it was more than that. Holidays were the worst. In the summer I couldn't get free lunches at school, which meant no guaranteed meals, and that sucked. I remember my stomach cramping so hard I thought I would die, and . . ." I covered my mouth with the back of my hand. Exhaled slowly. "I say 'I,' but it was the two of us—me and Vince. Whatever hunger I felt, he did, too. And Mom . . . I'm not sure how to explain this, but she completely checked out. I don't think she realized, or even cared that there was no food in the house. By the time I was ten, I'd learned that I shouldn't go to her when I was hungry, because she'd just smile and lie to me that she'd go shopping soon. And by the time Vince was seven, he'd learned that if he was hungry, *I* was his best bet."

Eli's eyes shone with understanding, but I wasn't done. For someone who never, *ever* talked about this, it was disconcerting how many words I had.

"Again, this wasn't all the time. We'd go entire weeks with casseroles for dinner and milk in the fridge and cereal in the cupboard. But then Mom would quit, or lose her job, or break up with a boyfriend, and there would be stretches of nothing, where Vince and I had to ration stale crackers. And because it was all so fucking unpredictable, it was hard to enjoy the good times. They could end any second, so we were constantly on the edges of our seats.

"I developed certain . . . strategies. I'd steal a few dollars as an emergency fund. Sometimes from Mom's purse. Other times from other places. I was a very opportunistic thief." I let out a laugh. "Vince and I got into the habit of eating as quickly as possible. We were afraid to be discovered, or that Mom would come and ask where we'd gotten the food from, or that she'd take it from us. Eating at home was a constant source of anxiety. And naturally, everything we ate was very cheap and poor quality. We didn't have fresh vegetables at our disposal. The little money we had, we'd use to buy stuff that would keep. I'd go to Tisha's house and there were these big bowls overflowing with fruit, and it seemed like being in a Disney movie. Princess stuff, you know? The apotheosis of luxury."

There, I'd learned that food was more than just calories and nutrition. Food was what brought the Fuli family together every night, what the parents of figure skaters made for their kids after a hard practice, what people talked about when they came back from weekends spent in quaint coastal bed-and-breakfasts. Food was collagen, the connective tissue of our society, and if I hadn't grown up with enough of it, well. Clearly, it had to mean that I wasn't tethered enough to anyone, and never could be.

"You said that you left for college and never came back, and, Eli, I did the same. Alec and the figure skating program—I owe him *everything*. Thanks to him I got my tuition waived. I jumped on a plane, left for the dorms on the earliest possible move-in date, and didn't come back for two years. I just couldn't. I was on the college meal plan, which meant I could eat plenty, but I still had so much anxiety around food. It was triggered by the weirdest shit—having to eat in a rush, small portions, the cafeterias being closed for Thanksgiving. It was irrational, but—"

"It wasn't," he interrupted gently.

I glanced away. "Either way, I wasn't functioning. So I looked around. A campus therapist helped me find coping strategies, but . . . I was healing, and I just couldn't force myself to go back home." I swallowed. "You went back for Maya, Eli. But I . . . I was eighteen, and Vince was fifteen, and I left him. I left him alone with Mom for *years*." The burning pressure behind my eyes threatened to overflow, and I had no wish to fight it. Instead, I remembered a summer night, when I was thirteen. A sleepover at Tisha's. The following day Mrs. Fuli had sent me home with leftovers— pasta with chicken, a side of grilled zucchini, and a fruit salad, all fresh and delicious. When I'd returned home, Mom was gone and Vince was sitting on the couch, listening to the news on a TV that had only three channels. His eyes had widened in sheer joy at the sight of the Tupperware containers in my hands, and watching his delight as he worked his way through the food had made me happier than I'd been in a long, long time.

Being able to keep Vince fed, *that* had been happiness. And when I couldn't, that's when I'd begun to resent him, and the unfairness of what was being asked of me.

"I did go back, eventually. And Vince . . . he said he forgave me.

But things soured anyway. He grew up and made choices that I simply can't . . . We've been on and off through the years. His current behavior is completely unacceptable, but I hope you can see why me calling the police on him is not really a—"

Two things happened simultaneously: my voice broke, and Eli dragged me into his lap, between his thighs, his arms bands of steel around me. Tears slid down my cheeks, and I hated it a little, this weakness of mine, this inability to deal with my past and with my infinite guilt. But it was nice, having told someone. Taking this stinging pain inside me and putting it outside my body for a little.

"You did what you could." His hand caressed my hair, my back. "You did enough."

"Did I?" I pulled back and wiped my cheeks. "Because look at us." He stared in confusion, his palm warm around my nape. "My story and yours had the same beginnings. Our siblings. The ice. Engineering. But the ending . . . You and Maya found each other, while Vince and I—it's like one of those Finish the Picture worksheets. Except that yours became a beautiful painting and mine is a fucking—"

"Rue, no." He shook his head energetically, like I shouldn't even contemplate the idea. "Maya *wanted* to be found. Mending that relationship went both ways. This," he said, angling his head toward the entrance of my apartment, "is *not* on you. Please, tell me you understand that."

Maybe I did, at least rationally. But I wasn't able to feel it in my stomach. I let out a soft, viscous laugh. "Do you think that maybe there's another version of us, somewhere in another timeline? Where we're not just a messed-up lump of scar tissue, and we're whole enough to be capable of loving others the way they want to be loved?"

He stared at me for an endless moment, and a silly thought nestled into my mind. *If I were able to love someone, I would choose you. In that timeline, I would want it to be you.*

But then he said, "No, Rue."

"Well, that's depressing."

"That's not it." He swallowed. Held my eyes with determination. "I just don't think that we need another timeline to be able to do that."

It knocked me wordless. My heart stopped so abruptly, I was afraid it wasn't going to start anymore. "I'm done. You can leave now, if you want to," I said evenly. I couldn't believe he'd want otherwise—in my experience, staying was the exception, and leaving, the rule. I hated the thought of him being gone, but maybe it was for the best, to untangle us from this intimacy we'd sunk into.

"Can I?"

I nodded. "I promise I'm fine. I don't need you to keep hugging me, or—"

"I'm not hugging you."

"Yes, you—"

"No, here's what's happening." He shifted us around until we were lying down, not unlike the way we'd fallen asleep earlier. Except that he was definitely *hugging* me, pulling me into his chest and holding me there. Whenever I breathed in, his clean scent filled my lungs. "I'm waiting for you to calm down. Once you're not upset anymore, we can fool around again. Then I'll go home. Okay?"

"Okay," I said. It sounded like a good, not overdramatic plan. And despite the night's events, I was, above all, not overdramatic.

"Perfect. Just close your eyes and relax, okay? The sooner you relax, the sooner we can do something fun."

"Like what?"

"We could fuck again—that worked well. Or maybe you can suck me off. I'll think about it."

I took a deep breath and willed myself to calm down. It was going to be good, moving back to the sex. Something I was familiar with. Something I could control.

But I relaxed a little too much, and ended up falling into an exhausted, dreamless sleep in under a minute. We did not fuck, and I did not suck him off, and he did not go home.

Instead, Eli's arms stayed around me for the rest of the night.

29

EVEN IF YOU DON'T

RUE

Eli woke up at dawn, cursed softly, and gently disentangled from me.

I didn't pretend to be dead to the world, but made the semi-conscious choice to keep my eyes closed and drift back to sleep. The last thing I remembered was his weight dipping the edge of the mattress. He lingered, perhaps looking at me. Then he pushed a strand of hair behind my ear and leaned forward to gently kiss my forehead. Tired, comfortable, maybe even a little happy, I dozed off once again, lulled by the rustle of Eli pulling his clothes back on.

I didn't wake up until several hours later, when I stumbled into the kitchen and pawed around for a mug and the coffee maker, then stopped in my tracks when I spotted the note, written on my latest unopened IRA envelope.

He'd circled my middle name on the address box (Chastity, the bane of my already plenty-baned existence), and placed three exclamation points on its right, which made my eyes roll and my lips curve. Underneath, he'd written:

Call me if you need me.

And then, right below, scribbled more hastily, as though he'd decided to add something when he was already halfway out of the door:

Call me even if you don't.

My heart thumped, and I allowed myself to think about the previous night. I waited for the shame to catch up and crash into me, a wave of pure mortification, but it never came. I'd told Eli my worst story. And he didn't seem to care.

A magnetic pen that read KLINE in blue letters and usually resided on my fridge sat next to the envelope, reminding me of what I'd have to do today.

I called in to work again, this time to take a day off. I got dressed for the record heat, grabbed my car keys, and headed out.

30

I GUESS THIS *IS* REVENGE

ELI

When Anton's head peeped in the doorway to announce, "Someone's here to see Hark," Eli nodded without bothering to lift his eyes from the financial statement he was studying—until Minami, who sat right next to him on the stupid exercise ball she insisted on using in lieu of a chair, asked, "Is it a visibly pregnant woman holding a homemade DNA test kit?"

"I . . ." Anton shifted on his feet. "This feels like a problematic question."

"I am a problematic person. Is it?"

"Um, no?"

"Okay. Just asking, because you're making a really weird face."

"What face?"

"Like you're expecting trouble."

"Yes. Well, no. But this woman came in, asked to talk with

Hark, and when I pointed out that she didn't have an appointment, she told me her name and said, 'He'll want to see me.' Which seemed weird and kinda . . . movie-like?"

"*Very* movie-like," Minami agreed with an intrigued bounce on the ball.

Eli felt a prickle of unease at the base of his neck. "What's the woman's name, Anton?"

"It's . . ." He squinted at the Post-it in his hand. "Rue Siebert. Her ID checked out."

Eli and Minami exchanged a long, teeming look.

"Tell her that Hark will be right out," Eli instructed.

"But Hark's on his way back from Seattle—"

"I am aware." He held Anton's eyes. "Tell her anyway."

Minami waited for them to be alone before asking, "Why is she looking for Hark and not *you*?"

There was a single logical answer. "She wants to ask him about Florence."

"What?"

"He indirectly mentioned Florence at dinner the other night. Rue wants to know more, and she thinks he'll tell her."

"But why wouldn't she ask *you*?"

Why, indeed.

He'd been expecting her to dig into the matter, ever since she'd found the file in his car. Last night he'd been tempted to bring up the deposition and tell Rue the whole sordid story, but there had been no room for that between them. Still, he thought they'd made some progress when it came to trusting each other.

And the fact that she'd rather get answers from Hark . . . Eli did not like that.

"Maybe you should wait till Hark's back," Minami said. "So the burden of breaking her pretty little Florence-loving heart won't fall on you."

"If her heart has to be broken, I'd rather it be me. That way I can help her pick up the pieces."

"Then go ahead and tell her. If it's not one of us, it'll be Florence—and as we can all attest, she's a remarkable liar. She could turn Rue against you, and then you'd lose her."

"Lose her?" He snorted. "Do you think I have her now?"

She scanned his face. "I think you want her."

"Yeah. I also want world peace and for my dog to live forever."

"Come on, Eli. I've seen you with Mac. I've seen you with lots of truly amazing girls."

"Women."

"Oh my fucking—we've been joined at the hip for the past ten years, Eli."

He shook his head and turned off his monitor, not bothering to hide his amusement. "Are you breaking up with me?"

"I've never seen you like this, Eli."

He stopped mid-action. Resumed. "Like what?"

"When she's around, and even when she isn't, you're distracted and you moon and you—have you told her how you feel?"

Jesus. "Minami, she is . . . *very* hurt, and *very* emotionally un-available. I don't think she's ready for that kind of conversation." *But last night,* a hopeful voice whispered in his head. He'd inched closer to discussing feelings with her than ever before, and she hadn't kicked him out of her apartment. "If I'm not careful—if I don't pace this just right, she's going to run. I need to take it slowly."

Minami looked at him with something that could have been pity. "You don't look like you want to take it slowly."

He rose, mostly to avoid screaming *I fucking know I don't* at one of his closest friends, whose advice and care he valued. "Any more pearls of wisdom, Dr. Phil?"

"Just be careful. That's all."

He took off his glasses and headed down the sleek hallway, nodding at two junior analysts and an intern. When he strode into the lobby, Rue sat on one of the leather couches, hands in her lap, legs neatly folded at a ninety-degree angle. Her posture was impeccable, unfidgety and calm as ever within the chaos of the world around her. It reminded him of the first time he'd seen her, at that hotel bar. He had a couple of seconds to observe her before she noticed him, and used them to the very last drop, drinking her in like she was the end of a century-long drought.

Her eyes widened in surprise when she noticed him. He could sense it between them like a physical object, the awareness of this ever-deepening connection between them. But Rue instantly lowered her gaze, as if to sweep it—sweep *him*—away.

Have you told her how you feel?

Out of the blue, Eli felt *anger*. Abrupt, intense, bottomless anger, equally directed at Rue and himself. Her presence in his life and in his head was uninvited. The power she held over him, he had never meant to yield it. Which meant that she must have taken it without his permission. Robbed him of it. And after everything that had happened between them last night, she'd chosen to go not to him, but to *Hark*. *That* was the degree of trust that she afforded him.

"Follow me," he ordered without hiding the edge in his tone.

She rose slowly, but Eli didn't check whether she was keeping up. He led her to his office, noted with relief that Minami was gone, and closed the door.

All he could feel was resentment.

He wanted her so much. *So. Fucking. Much.* Every time he saw her, fucked her, smelled her, he wanted a bit more. He wanted to make her twelve-course lunches, hold her down, build her a research lab. He wanted *everything*, including things that made no sense, things that should not go together.

And Rue could clearly see his fury. "Eli," she said. Not scared, or distant. Just compassionate as her cool fingers wrapped around his cheek. Like she actually cared. She rose as tall as she could and pressed a featherlight kiss to the base of his jaw.

It was a brief, beautiful moment of hope, and it twisted Eli's heart until he couldn't bear it.

"No," he said. He forced her to retreat, and when the backs of her thighs hit the conference table, he spun her around.

They were both immediately, inexplicably winded.

He barely waited for Rue's palms to find the table. He spread her legs with his foot, tore at the opening of her pants, and pulled them just low enough for what he had in mind. He unbuckled his belt, loud in the quiet room, and slid his cock out of his slacks, pulling her underwear to the side. He teetered, pressed against the wet lips of her cunt, nearly breaching her hot entrance, ready to push inside and show her that she was his—

He was out of his fucking mind.

In the hallway, mere feet and a single unlocked door away from them, someone was discussing weekend plans. Eli's thumb grazed Rue's clit.

She shuddered. "Do it. *Please.*"

He shook with restraint, his vision blurry with want. Rue bucked back, and he had to grip her hip to avoid sinking inside her.

Fuck.

He wrapped his arms around her stomach, hugging her to himself as tightly as he could. He would have taken any excuse to let her go, but she was mellow in his arms, and when he buried a pained groan in her throat, she wrapped her hands around his forearm and held on to him as firmly as he held her.

Eli's rage dissolved into soul-deep resignation. He had no right to resent her for being the best and worst thing to ever happen to him. And if his heart wasn't going to survive her, then so be it.

He extricated himself from her slowly, not meeting her eyes as he readjusted her clothes, then his. When he was done, she leaned back against the table, a fine tremor in her hands, and met his gaze head-on.

In the hallway, people laughed and said their goodbyes.

"Eli."

The things I want from you, Rue—you have no idea, and maybe never will.

"I'm sorry."

He almost laughed. "For what?"

"For wanting to ask Hark instead of you. It's just . . ." Her voice was low. "He was the safest option."

His eyes narrowed, and she gave him one of her *what don't you get?* stares.

So *this* was falling for someone. A ruthless expansion of the senses. The meticulous, unintentional cataloging of a person's head tilt, the shape their hand made around a wineglass, the little tells in their gaze.

"If you think you can trust him more than you can trust me—"

"It's *because* I don't trust him." Her lips trembled. "Whatever Hark tells me about Florence, I can choose not to believe. With you . . . once you tell me, I'm not going to be able to walk away from it."

Eli was going to have to hurt her, and he hated *that* even more than anything Florence had done.

He nodded and crossed his arms again, fingers drumming against his biceps. "We were Florence's grad students."

Rue nodded. "It was in the deposition."

"Minami was her postdoc. Hark and I didn't originally come to UT to work with her, but she took us on when our mentor left unexpectedly. It was not a passing acquaintance. If she says she doesn't remember us, it's a deliberate lie."

"And then Florence left you, too? And now you're looking for revenge?"

God, he fucking wished. "Then she stole our work."

Only a single, slow blink betrayed Rue's surprise. "Not the fermentation tech. That was her idea."

"The fermentation tech was *Minami's* idea. Florence's idea, the one she'd gotten millions of dollars to test, dead-ended in year one of the grant. Florence had to pivot. Hark and I needed a new lab, and no one else had the funds, the expertise, or frankly the will to take us on. Florence was barely older than us, had never had graduate mentees, but she was obviously a talented engineer. We had to choose between working with her and leaving the program. It was a no-brainer."

"And then?"

"For two years, we worked that sometimes shitty, sometimes rewarding grad student life. You know what that's like. A lot to be done, but the process we'd isolated was promising. Then we had a breakthrough."

"Was Florence an active member of the research group?"

"Short answer, yes." He thought about it. Tried to collect his opinions in shapes that were as fair as they could be. *The things I do for you, Rue.* "I might be biased, so you'll have to compare and contrast with Florence's recollection. Mine is that, intellectually, Minami was very much leading the project. Florence was a great sounding board, but was busy. We never stopped asking her for advice, but over time we transitioned to mostly reporting our progress. Her grants covered stipends and materials. She also rented off-campus lab space. Which *did* seem odd, but she said that renting pre-equipped labs was less expensive than buying new equipment, and the funding institute had recommended it. Fair enough, we thought. We were done with classes and didn't need to be on campus. You know what grad school's like after comps—no formal oversight. We ended up mostly isolated from the rest of the department. Our codependency origin story," he added dryly. He had no clue whether Rue believed him—his fathomless, enigmatic girl.

"And when the tech was ready?"

"We had a breakthrough two years in, before the summer. By this point we were off-site students, virtually no contact with anyone at UT. We got a month off for the summer. Hark and I backpacked in Europe. Minami had just met Sul. We came back, and it all went to shit.

"At first we just couldn't get in touch with Florence. She wouldn't reply to emails, answer phone calls. We were worried about her, so we went to our department head. That's when we discovered that Florence had quit, and there was an ongoing dispute between her and the university regarding the rightful owner of the tech. Bayh-Dole Act of 1980 and that shit. Meanwhile, the three of us are glancing at each other, wondering what the fuck is going on."

"What did Florence say when you next saw her?" Rue asked.

"You were there."

"What do you mean?"

"The next time I saw Florence was at Kline, last month. Florence refused to meet us, or to otherwise acknowledge our existence, for the past decade. There was no closure for us, which made it even harder to move on. Once, Minami waited by her apartment, hoping to confront her. She went on her own, figuring Hark and I might come across as intimidating."

"And?"

"Florence called the police on her."

There was a slight flinch that a less devoted observer of Rue might have missed. Once upon a time, Eli might have found some degree of happiness in telling her the truth, because it would have meant taking something away from Florence. All he could think about now was what he was taking away from Rue herself.

"For whatever it's worth, and after ruminating over the matter for years, I don't believe Florence planned to cut us out from the start," he said. "Hark disagrees."

"Why do you believe that?"

He shrugged. "Contextual clues. Wishful thinking? She was openly unhappy at UT. The biofuel tech could be brought to market and get her out, but Florence needed to *own* the patent. And the only way she could keep it was by proving that she hadn't developed the tech with federal funds. Unfortunately, our stipends were on record, paid with federal grant money."

"Ah."

"She had to minimize our involvement. We were an . . . endurable sacrifice."

"Why didn't you report her?"

"We did. But even just a decade ago, things were different—and we hadn't been seen around in *years*. There was little proof of our involvement. For all UT knew, we'd been playing pinball for twenty-four months. It was our word against hers, and a grad student's word was worth very little. *Then* the case became highly publicized." Rue couldn't have missed the cable news pieces, the op-eds, the way public attention had been suddenly riveted by the very uninteresting topic of patent law. "Charming young female researcher tries to change the world with environmentally friendly fuels, does the work on her own time and dime, and UT wants to take ownership away from her. David taking on Goliath. A PR nightmare for UT, and they wanted it swept under the rug. *It* including the three of us, and the fuss we were kicking up, because them fucking over one person sounded bad, but them fucking over *four*? Even worse. Hark and I were asked to leave the program. Minami's contract wasn't renewed. We had no money. We saw two lawyers, and they both told us that we didn't have a case. And then my father died, and that shit seemed like the least of our problems."

Rue briefly closed her eyes. "Is *this*"—she made a vague, all-encompassing gesture toward Harkness's headquarters—"revenge for what Florence did?"

Had Harkness begun as a means to hurt Florence as much as she'd hurt them? Undoubtedly. But it had morphed into something else altogether. Eli *liked* his current job. Private equity was a shit-show that left destruction in its wake, and he felt proud of the priorities they'd set for themselves. They cared about their portfolio. They focused on the long-term health of companies. They made *some* difference.

"*This* is the only way we had to take back what was ours. Hark's father is made of money, but he refused to support Hark in any endeavor that wasn't finance related, and this . . . We had the starting capital. It was the only way we could get the tech back. I'm not going to lie, Rue. Things are not looking great for us, and Florence is withholding key documents and making our lives impossible every step of the way, but I still hope we can get the tech back. It's been years, and we haven't spent every breathing second resenting Florence. But we kept an eye on Kline. And when the loan went up for sale . . ." He shook his head at his own idiocy. So many words just to say, "Yeah. I guess this *is* revenge."

"And what is it that you want . . ." She seemed temporarily lost for words. "What's your happy ending?"

What a loaded question. "Kline is not doing well. The tech should have been brought to international markets years ago. The company expanded too quickly, is unfocused and—we have reason to suspect—insolvent. Florence has surrounded herself with yes-men instead of competent advisers. In the ideal scenario, Florence's loan defaults. We take control of Kline, appoint a board with actual expertise. No employment shrinkage, no reduction of wages. Better science."

"And you own the patent?"

"And we own the patent."

Rue glanced away with a frown. For the first time since the conversation had begun, he knew for certain how she felt.

Sad.

"Thanks for being honest, Eli. I really appreciate it, but . . . I have to go now." She walked past him, but then stopped and retreated for a short moment, just enough to rise on her toes and press a kiss to his lips.

Eli let her go, but when her hand was on the doorknob he said, "Rue."

"Yes?"

He stared into her wide, unclouded eyes. Said, "Nothing," instead of the truth: anything. *Everything.*

He thought he caught a split second of hesitation, but it must have been a trick of the light. Still, he stood in front of the closed door for longer than he cared to admit, hoping that she would come back.

31

DIFFICULT CHOICES

RUE

Minami was waiting for me on a bench in the ground-floor lobby, a cross-legged figure leisurely sipping from a water bottle. She didn't call me over, but I sat next to her anyway.

"He told you about Florence?"

I nodded.

"Just wanted to make sure. Otherwise, I would have."

I studied her pretty, relaxed face. The steel underneath her calm demeanor. "You and Eli are very close, aren't you?"

"Oh, yeah. I get fed up with Sul and Hark all the time, but Eli's my rock, as cheesy as it sounds. Did he tell you that it was his idea? The final breakthrough for the tech. We were stuck for *ages*, and then he figured out the last step. And he was so proud." She smiled. "He was the kid, you know? The youngest. Hark was broody and worldly, but Eli was pure sunshine. Kind and fun and a total flirt. It has dulled over the years, because of everything that happened with his family, but you can still see that spark, right?"

I could. I did. And I wasn't sure what someone with that kind of spark was doing with someone like *me*.

"I adored him from the start," Minami continued. "But, Rue, it doesn't really matter. I didn't want you to know because of Eli. I wanted you to know because of *you*." She stood. Looked down at me with a grave expression. "You and your friend should watch your backs with Florence. Neither of you deserves to go through what I did."

When I pulled in to Kline's parking lot, the sun baked high in the sky, and Florence was already outside, sitting on one of the benches on the side of the building. There was little doubt that she was waiting for someone.

"Hi, Rue," she said, when I walked to her. Her hair was a fiery, bright orange in the midday light, a stark contrast to her melancholic smile. "Eli emailed me."

I frowned. "He did?"

"He told me he gave you his version of what happened. Said I might want to give you mine." She laughed softly, and there was some fondness for Eli in it, as though she liked him despite herself. "You know what he wrote to me?"

I shook my head.

"That when it all went down, ten years ago, what hurt him the most was not being able to understand the actions of someone he trusted. He'd never wish this on you, and thought I should give you an explanation." She pressed her lips together. "He didn't ask for an explanation for himself. Didn't insult me. Wasn't even passive aggressive. All three of them—Minami, Hark, Eli—have refused to talk to me ever since the loan was bought. Not a single communication happened without lawyers standing around. And here Eli Killgore is. Breaking the streak. For you."

Florence's words lingered in the air. My heart felt at once laden and wrung through a strainer. "And?" I asked. I could not bring myself to take a seat next to her.

"I'm not sure what he told you."

It sounded enough like an admission that I had to brace myself. "Just give me your story, then."

"Okay. I . . ." Florence ran a hand through her hair and sighed heavily. "You have to understand, Rue. The world is not black and white. There are shades of gray. There are difficult choices that people have to make sometimes. The UT job . . . the UT job was *really* bad. I realized that despite my grants and my output, they weren't going to offer me tenure. It had happened before, to people more qualified than me. There were a couple of lawsuits and several investigations going on, all started by women in the department who'd been treated unfairly. Fucking terrible. And that's when . . ." She shrugged. "Brock was a big part of it. Which should have been a red flag, but at the time our marriage wasn't quite the dumpster fire it later became, and we were actively working on saving it. We were trying to have a baby, if you can believe it. We were brainstorming ways for me to get out of academia altogether, considering a move, maybe. Talked about it for *months*. In the end, pivoting to industry made the most sense. I was thinking of just getting a research staff job, but—Rue, will you sit?" She squinted, covering her eyes with her hand. "The sun is right behind you."

I didn't move. My feet were rooted to the ground. "But?"

"Well, it was Brock who brought it up. He said, 'What about all the biofuel stuff you've been working on? Can't you start your own company centered around that?' And I . . ." She paused for a long, long while. "I began looking into how I could make it happen."

My heart dropped into my stomach. "And you didn't give the others any of the credit."

"Come on." She laughed. "Hark and Eli were never going to get *credit*. They were grad students, for fuck's sake. No grad student gets credit for the kind of ideas they help refine. Their contributions were grunt work. Was I supposed to share the patent with two men, just because they'd run a couple of assays for me? Please. I knew they'd be fine."

Eli hadn't been, though. Nor Hark, I suspected. "What about Minami?"

"See, that's . . ." Florence nodded slowly. "That really *does* hurt, in hindsight. I feel horrible for not including her in the patent. But I didn't have any other choice. You know how *hard* it is, for women in our field. I was in a terrible situation, and—"

"Minami is a woman, too, and a more junior academic," I interrupted harshly. I highly doubted Minami's career had been as privileged as Florence's. "And that's not—Florence, having it hard doesn't give us a pass to cheat other people out of their work, especially not to screw over *people who have it harder.*"

"I know. And I felt horrible—why do you think I spent the following years knee deep in mentorship programs, trying to uplift junior scientists? I was trying to *atone* for that."

"The only correct way to atone is to *give Minami credit.*"

"Rue, if I hadn't done what needed to be done, you know who would have owned the patent? Not me. Not Minami. Not Eli or Hark. *UT* would have owned it."

"So what?" I blinked in confusion. "So it was okay to sacrifice everyone as long as *you* got it? It was Minami's idea."

"Only partially! I helped Minami refine it. I lent her my expertise. If it hadn't been for me, it wouldn't have moved past the most preliminary stages."

"That's not what Eli thinks."

"Then he's *lying*. Do you really believe *him* over me?"

You did *lie to me*, I wanted to say. Why *did you lie to me?* But the answer was obvious. And even if everything Florence was saying was true, even if her contribution was superior to everyone else's, did that make what she'd done forgivable?

I studied her face, truly seeing it for the first time. Florence stared back, and then began laughing. "You know what this feels like?"

I remained silent.

"Like Eli and I are fighting over you." She was still chuckling, but I could not see the humor. And my heart did hurt for Eli, but . . .

"The person on whose behalf I feel the most outrage, right now, is Minami."

"Rue. I . . . I just hope you'll be able to see my point of view. I hope that you realize that I had to make some very difficult choices, and forgive me."

"It's not *my* forgiveness you need," I said.

She called after me, but I strode to my car without hesitation.

32

LET'S TRY TO MAKE IT RIGHT

RUE

And you're *really* sure that she admitted to it?" Tisha asked for what had to be the fourth time. I'd already replied to the first three, but still didn't blame her. *I* could scarcely believe it, and had gotten it straight from the source.

"I am."

"And it's not some kind of . . . I don't know, a stroke. Or, I don't know how common folies à deux are these days, but maybe Florence and Eli are both in the throes of one? Maybe it's not quite the way Eli painted it? A misunderstanding, in which Florence is not nearly as gaslight-gatekeep-girlbossy as he's trying to make her out. Or the Harkness people could be biased and exaggerating their contribution to the tech. I mean, are you *really* sure that she—"

"Admitted to it?" Diego shouted from Tisha's kitchenette. Then he came to lean against the doorjamb—a bare-chested, bespectacled, body-built nerd who couldn't have been more Tisha's type.

Tisha had supposedly been working from home, but her short kimono clearly broadcast that they had been in the middle of something when I barged in. Diego had taken my uninvited appearance like a champ. "Rue, could you please tell Tisha whether you're *really* sure that Florence admitted to it?"

"I'd rather not."

"Let us know if you change your mind."

"Never."

"Understood."

I hadn't liked a Tisha boyfriend this much in years, and hoped he'd stick around. Even Bruce seemed to be a fan, rubbing himself against Diego's calves while shooting me his repertoire of skeptical glances.

"Okay, you two can stop being chummy and cahootsy against me."

Diego and I exchanged one last cahootsy look before he disappeared into the bedroom. It was an immense relief, being with Tisha. Sharing the burden of today's discovery. The last few hours had upended the last few years of my life, but Tisha was here, unchanged. Still standing as everything else crumbled down.

"If Florence admitted to doing that shit—and yes, I know she *has*—well . . ." Tisha shrugged. "Listen, I love her. You love her. She did so much for us, and we're probably going to keep on loving her, even if she fucked up. At least we'll try. But this is not a small thing. This is someone's *livelihood*. This is someone's hopes and dreams and entire career. We have to do something."

"I know. But what?"

She scratched her temple. "What if it was your patent that Florence had stolen? What would you want Minami to do?"

My mouth was dry. "I would want her to help me make it right.

Even after ten years. Even if she wasn't the one responsible to begin with, I would want her to be on my side."

"Okay." Tisha nodded. "Then let's try to make it right."

"We have no evidence. If UT swept it under the rug years ago—"

"Reporting it won't do anything." Tisha bit into her lower lip.
"I'm not sure what else, though. We might not be the best people
to figure this out."

An idea hit me. "No, we aren't." I let out a breathless laugh.
"But you know who is?"

33

SAD, BEAUTIFUL FORTRESS GIRL

RUE

The sun was already setting, but I worried that he might still be at the office, and that not finding him might force me to reconsider what I was about to do. Thankfully, I spotted Eli as soon as I pulled up to his street.

He was unlocking his front door, but he turned around when he heard my car approach. In the dusk, his eyes widened. Then softened. I got out quickly, without bothering to collect myself, and marched to him with an outstretched hand.

Eli stared at my open palm for a long while. "What is it?"

"Take it."

He plucked out the USB. "What's on it?"

"You know what."

His expression traveled from confused, to understanding, to shocked. "No." He shook his head and tried to return it. "Rue, I didn't tell you so that you—"

"I know. But she took it from you. From Minami. From Hark."

"Rue."

"And we agree that she shouldn't have."

"We?"

"Tisha and I."

He stared at the USB pinched between his fingers, silent.

"If Kline is breaking the terms of the loan contract, then Harkness has the right to know. I'm not giving you any secrets. These are just . . ."

"The documents she should have handed over weeks ago?"

At least, I hoped so. I had access to Florence's office and computer—and a healthy ignorance of financial records. But that's what Nyota was for.

After a brief hesitation, Eli slid the USB in his pocket. "Thank you, Rue."

"You're welcome." I took a deep breath. "Can I . . ."

He tilted his head.

I swallowed. "The last few days have been . . . difficult. For me. If tonight . . . if I asked you to take me in and let me stay with you, and not mention a single word about Florence, or Kline, would you—"

He opened the door before I could finish the sentence—an unequivocal invitation—and a wordless conversation passed between our locked gazes.

Can I trust you, Eli?

Always.

My heart leaped in my throat. I stepped inside—and was assaulted once again.

"Down, Tiny," Eli drawled, not bothering to hide his delight at the way his dog's paws rested on my midriff. "I'm not letting her leave anytime soon. You'll get to snuggle later." Tiny licked my chin, and I flinched.

"I don't really snuggle."

"Color me shocked." He took off his glasses and set them next to a stack of unopened mail. Not Harkness's Eli anymore, but mine.

Mine.

It was half-ridiculous and all pathetic to think of him in those terms, but relief flooded me anyway. "Is it a vanity thing?" I asked.

"What?" He grabbed something from a shelf, and Tiny circled us and jumped up and down, clearly in the middle of a galvanic episode. Were all dogs this shamelessly *happy*? Science should study their blood. Come up with good drugs.

"The glasses. You only wear them at work. Are you trying to come across less like a former hockey player and more like a nerd?"

"I only wear them at work because, according to my ophthalmologist, I have the eyesight of a man in his eighth decade and need glasses for reading and staring at computer screens."

"Ah."

"But thank you for telling me that I look like a dense jock."

"I didn't—"

"Shh. I know. Let's go." He unspooled some kind of flat rope. It was . . .

Oh *no*. "Where?"

He hooked the rope to Tiny's collar. "To walk my dog."

I took a step back, and he followed. Gently pried my hand from my side and slid the leash around my wrist. "Eli, I shouldn't be in charge of—"

"If you stay, you're going to have to earn your keep."

I shook my head. "I'm not really a—"

"Pet person?" He looked at me like nothing I could have said would surprise him. Like he knew not just the contours, but also the shaded, buried parts of me. At the very least, he knew that they existed. "Let's go." His voice was kind but adamant, and I had no choice.

I followed Tiny's indiscernible interests all over the sidewalk, feeling his leash tug determinedly at my fingers. Several neighbors were out, walking their own dogs, and they stopped often to exchange pleasantries (with Eli) and vigorous butt-sniffings (Tiny).

"Not what I had in mind when I came over," I muttered, pulled in the direction of Tiny's whims. Eli seemed unfazed, and never made a move to take the leash from me, not even when Tiny freed himself to chase a squirrel, forcing me to run after him in what had to be a *Looney Tunes*–worthy display.

"Don't worry, I *will* fuck you later," Eli murmured once I was back at his side, nodding at an elderly lady who was walking a poodle that looked eerily like her. I glanced at Tiny, then Eli. There was a resemblance there, too—the messy, curly brown hair. Was this a *thing*? "But since *you* came to *me*, I figured we could do things my way."

"We always do things your way."

"Do we?"

We didn't, and I knew it. Since the very start, I'd been the one setting boundaries, making requests, building fences. Probably because, since the very start, I'd sensed he'd be willing to push past them. His role had been well defined: respect my wishes, follow my lead.

But after the last few days, it was obvious that he wanted a hazy, undefined *more*. Which was hazily, undefinedly terrifying.

"Don't worry, Rue. I'm not going to ask you for anything

scandalous, like to skate with me." He glanced at me in tender amusement, as if I were a child who still believed in leprechauns at the end of the rainbow. "This is not a date, or anything as gross and morally perverted as that."

And yet, it felt just as disturbing. Back at his house, he took a couple of minutes to send the files to his team, and then sat me on a stool while he prepared something with couscous and stir-fry and spicy, mouthwatering scents.

"Is this the last of your signature dishes?"

"Yup. I'm going to have to learn a few more if I want to keep luring you here."

Do you? Are you sure you want me around? "Where is Maya?"

"Camping."

"Doesn't she have summer classes?"

He shook his head. "On break. Left early this morning."

I'd come here because I couldn't stand to be alone with my thoughts, but with the darkening sky, the rhythmic chopping sounds, the veggies sizzling in the pan, my mind drifted back to Florence. What she'd done. The way she rationalized her actions, as though a valid justification for her behavior existed. There had to have been a point, in my years of knowing her, in which she had expressed some kind of belief that hinted at her capacity for something like this. And I'd missed it.

"Relax." Eli's voice startled me. His large hands wrapped around my shoulders, thumbs digging firmly into the knots between my scapulae.

"I am relaxed."

"Sure."

"I am."

"Rue." Something light and warm nuzzled the crown of my

head. His nose, maybe. "If you're here to avoid thinking about it, then do so."

"I'm sorry. I know I'm not good company. I should be more . . ."

"More?"

"Engaging. Chatty. Sociable. Charming."

He circled my stool to catch my eyes, and I fought the impulse to guide his hands back to me. "Should you?"

I shrugged, and he went back to the stove and tossed the veggies in one smooth move. My social inadequacies were old news by now, but what if Eli didn't understand the full extent of it? What if he thought he knew me, but—

"You're enough, Rue. And if you aren't . . . I just don't mind." I stared at his back as he worked, watching his muscles play under the cotton. "I said it before, but I *do* like you. You're funny, even though you like to pretend you're not. You're loyal—to the wrong people, sometimes, but that's still a quality that I deeply appreciate, even more so after what happened ten years ago. You have a strong sense of what is wrong and what is right. You're deliberate, and you'd rather shut up than lie—even to yourself." He began plating the food. In his perfect profile, I saw a twitch of a smile. "And as we've already agreed upon, you're a fantastic lay who smells amazing."

It was my cue to laugh at his joke and dismiss the rest, but my heart was beating hard in my throat. "I'm not sure what to say."

"You could return the compliment."

"I should praise your sense of justice and morality?"

"Not *that* one."

"Ah." I nodded. "I guess you're an okay lay, too," I said flatly, and my heart galloped when he laughed from someplace deep in his chest. "You don't resent me?"

"Why should I?"

"If it hadn't been for what was stolen from you, I wouldn't have this career."

"You would still have *a* career." He carried both plates to the table and waited for me to join him.

"Sure, I'd be working somewhere else. But my project was funded with something that was taken from you."

"No, I don't resent you for that. It looks like *you* are resenting yourself, though. And we agreed that tonight wasn't about that." Eyes still on me, Eli scooped up a forkful of food and began eating. "Did Vincent come back?"

I blinked at the abrupt change of topic. "No. I've been calling real estate lawyers, but it's summer. A few are on vacation, a few are not affordable, some are not taking on new clients. I want to buy him out, and I have some money set aside. I'd been saving it for the down payment on a house. Or for when my car frees itself of its mortal coil. Or in case I need a new kidney."

"Those three things have vastly different costs, Rue."

"Have fun on *The Price Is Right*, Finance Guy."

He smiled. "Eat up. Your food's getting cold."

I'd assumed we would transition to sex after dinner and loading the dishwasher, but Wednesday night hockey was, to my shock and awe, something that existed. When Eli twined his fingers with mine, led me to the couch, and turned on the TV, I was uncertain how to react, but didn't protest.

His arms, wrapped around me, felt equally alien and mundane. In the uncertainty of the night, I let myself be led down the path of least resistance and sank into his body. He was warm. He smelled good. Outside of sex, I'd never touched someone for such a prolonged time, but contact with him was soothing. "Watching team sports" ranked somewhere below "tweezing spines out of a cactus" on my list of enjoyable activities, but this was, somehow, good.

Really good.

When Eli muttered, "That's some bullshit," either thirty seconds or forty minutes later, I blinked in confusion. I'd been *that* relaxed.

"What happened?"

"That penalty shot the ref called."

"Ah."

"The player with the puck jumps sideways to avoid a hit, barely gets clipped, and the defender gets called for a trip. Come the fuck on." He waved his hand, charmingly aggravated. "Refs have been shit all season," he muttered. His eyes flitted to me before moving back to the TV. Then did a double take. "What's that face? If you think it was a legitimate penalty, I swear to god, I will cast you out to the mercy of the elements."

"The temperature is really nice tonight. And I have no opinion. I don't know the rules at all."

He smiled. "Don't worry, I'm *not* going to teach you."

I gave him a puzzled look.

"You grew up around rinks. You'd have learned everything there is to know about hockey by now if you were interested. You don't need me imposing my shitty hobbies on you."

A dense, heavy weight suddenly pressed against my sternum. Burned behind my eyes. "No?"

"Nah. Just tell me I'm right and the ref's a shithead."

I swallowed the lump in my throat. "You're right and the ref's a shithead."

"You're a natural."

We exchanged a smile. The primal, gravitational force tugging me toward Eli was not new, but this was different. A new hum, buried deep, hidden below the frequency of civilization, and it was so much—so, *so* much—I couldn't bear it.

"Eli," I said.

"Yes?"

I thought I'd be rid of you by now. I thought I'd sweat you out. But it's like you've stolen a little piece of me. And I'm afraid that when this is over, I'll go back to my life, and my shape will have changed—just a little, but enough that I'll no longer fit into my lonely, angular hole.

"I don't know," I said, as sincere as I could be.

"No?" He sat back, assessing me calmly. I couldn't shake the needling sensation that he understood something fundamental, something nuclear about us that *I* could not yet accept. "I think you *do* know, but I might be mistaken." His half smile was conciliatory. "Am I mistaken, Rue?"

My chest constricted. I was stripped. Uncomfortably seen. "I think," I said, moving my hand up the inseam of his pants, "that we've been talking too much, and that's not like us."

His breath was a sharp intake when I cupped him through the fly of his pants. He was instantly hard. "Yeah? What's like us?"

He didn't help me, not even by shifting a single inch, but it took me very little to free his cock. By the time he was in my hand, hot and huge, I felt less fragile. "This." I knelt between his knees, put my mouth on him, and it felt like the world made sense again.

It was new—not giving a blow job, but giving one to someone whose body I'd become familiar with. Eli had become muscle knowledge, the wheres and hows of his pleasure seeped into me of their own free will.

"It's almost fucked up, how much I like my cock in your mouth," he said, and then he swore, shuddered, swore again. After a few valiant seconds of resisting me, he combed both hands in my hair and began thrusting, moving my head in the exact rhythm he wanted. I craved this—to be just a mouth and body again. To be *used* by him meant that I could not be *observed*, a second of precious respite from what was growing between us.

He was gentle, because he was Eli, but he was also rapidly losing control. He groaned. His grip tightened, his thighs tensed, and he was right on the verge—until he stopped me. "Nice try," he half laughed, half panted. The accusation heated my cheeks. "Not working, though." He took my chin between his fingers and forced me into a slow, deep kiss before carrying me upstairs.

There was usually, at some point of us being together like this, a moment in which the floor tilted and we tipped over—the momentum so fast and hard, we forgot ourselves and tumbled into bed. But this time it was *slow*, excruciatingly so, and it was Eli who paced us. He lingered on every inch of skin he uncovered, marked it with his hands and eyes, celebrated all progress with kisses and grazing teeth. It felt like revenge—like he wanted me to pay for trying to make him lose control.

"Hurry up." I tugged impatiently at his clothes, but he ignored me and took his time, even when I begged. "Why are you being like this?"

"Because I can," he said, and I had no choice but to settle into his touch, trembling with pleasure under his slow, thorough hands.

He'd changed the sheets. It was a weird thing to register, but I couldn't help it. The new ones were a deep blue and smelled like fabric softener. I couldn't understand why he left me to retrieve his belt, but my heart raced as he moved my wrists above my head, tied it around them, and then tethered me to the bed. He was slow, giving me every chance to stop him.

"Good?" he asked, voice low. The request was simple: *I'm going to be in charge. Okay?*

I nodded eagerly. The makeshift cuff was loose enough that I could have freed myself, but I had no intention of doing so, not when it anchored me to the here and now.

"Okay, then."

The last time we'd done this, he'd teased me within an inch of my life, and I expected more of that. Instead I felt the wet tip of his cock across my thighs, my belly, pushing against my entrance. He groaned with something that sounded like bliss, then stopped himself.

"Shit. I'm going to get a condom in a second, I swear."

He rubbed against me for a few more seconds that turned into minutes, and then, with some choked profanities, opened his nightstand drawer.

A moment later he pushed inside me.

I felt it down to my toes, how thick he was, the burn of the stretch. Gasped in shock at how sudden it had been, how incredibly *good*. Pleasure used to be something I had to work on, something to climb toward, but this was instantly, aggressively enjoyable in a way I couldn't comprehend.

And Eli knew it. "Come on, baby." He sounded amused, if breathless. "I'm not even all in yet." He kissed me on the lips, something featherlight that immediately turned filthy and deep. Then he rocked a few more times and suddenly he *was* all in, and we were panting in each other's mouths, uncoordinated and frozen in time.

Eli white-knuckled the dark sheets. I tugged at the belt, finding that being restrained heightened my pleasure. When he rocked upward inside me, the lick of heat that ran through me almost frightened me. "Oh my god." He did it again, and I moaned. Loudly. "Why does this feel so *good*?"

"It's the way I'm aligned." He ground again. The base of his cock rubbed against me, making me shiver. "I can stimulate your clit without touching it. I think that's the trick of it with you."

He knows my body, I thought. *Like I know his.* "It's nice. I—oh god." He moved again, and I felt myself clench against him. "I like it," I exhaled.

His groan melted into a soft laugh. "I know, Rue. I can feel it."

I was on the verge of coming in minutes—the pressure, the delicious drag in all the right spots, his chest brushing against my nipples. Heat climbed inside me, and I closed my eyes and arched my back to better push against it. *A little longer,* I thought. It felt so punishingly good, I wanted it to last. But Eli was talking into my ear, telling me how criminally beautiful I was, a danger to his peace of mind, that sometimes he wished he'd not checked his phone when I'd first messaged him; he wished he'd flung it to the other side of the room and spared himself. The low rumble of his voice and his shallow movements—I was going to come apart, any second I was going to—

Eli stilled.

Underneath him, I was as tense as an unplucked guitar string, the pleasure at once extraordinarily close and immensely out of reach.

"Good?" he asked against my ear.

I nodded. My cunt throbbed, swollen around his cock.

"Look at me, Rue."

I tilted my hips into him, trying to get the friction I needed.

"Open your eyes, and look. At. Me."

My eyelids fluttered. Eli's face was right above mine, beautiful and familiar. Sweat dripped from his temples, dampening his dark hair. I watched his hard expression, still dazed and overstimulated by having him inside me.

"Good girl." He rewarded me by surging upward. My thighs twitched, and I let out a long moan. "Doing what she's told. And you know what good girls get? I think you do know."

Blood pounded in my ears.

"I'm glad you're enjoying this. After all, that's the point of fucking."

I didn't follow, but he bent my knee with his palm, and I nodded anyway. My prize was another roll of his hips that had his pubic bone right against my clit. I almost went over the edge. Not quite, though, and the noise slipping out of me was pure, mortifying frustration.

"Which is exactly what we're doing. Just fucking, right?" he asked, nipping at my throat.

"I—oh god. Eli, *please*."

"Please, what?" He shifted so that both his hands twined with mine, and suddenly we were even closer. The fresh scent of his sweat flooded my nostrils. He was strong, heavy, and I never wanted him to stop. "Ask for what you want, sweetheart."

"I want you to move. Please, *move*."

He did move, but instead of grinding he pushed in, then out, and *that* was the difference between excellent sex and the cruelest of disappointments. "Like this?"

"*Eli.*"

"No?"

"You know it's not. Just—*please*." I could barely recognize this bumbling mess he'd made me into. And I never wanted him to stop.

"You want me to make you come, don't you?"

I nodded vehemently.

"Of course you do." He kissed me softly on the mouth. I was pinned underneath him, completely at his mercy while he moved inside me in the obscenest of ways, and yet his kiss was disarmingly sweet. "I'm going to make you come however many times you want, however many *ways* you want. But you have to do something for me first." He spoke in a calm, determined tone, but his muscles strained, and he wasn't any less ready to finish than me.

"Do what?"

"I want you to look me in the eye, and tell me that this is just fucking."

I froze. "What?"

"You heard me." His voice was kind. Another kiss pressed against my cheek. "Tell me that all we're doing is fucking, and I'll make you come." He balanced on his elbows and made a couple of shallow, experimental thrusts. His face contorted with pleasure, and he stopped. "That's it."

"Eli."

"Come on." He looked down at me, patiently. "Just say it."

"Why?"

"Why not?"

I wasn't sure. I squeezed my internal muscles around him, hoping he'd start *moving* again. Eli looked overwhelmed, and very tempted for a moment, but he recovered after biting the pillow and groaning against it. "Once again, nice try," he exhaled.

"I just want you to—"

"Stop? Because these are your options. I stop right now. Or I continue, after you say what you need to say."

I glanced up at him in confusion, but he was inscrutable. The idea of my body losing contact with his was repulsive. My skin would feel so cold without his heat.

"What's the problem, Rue?" His fingers tangled with mine, palms flush against each other. He sounded almost . . . The more I hesitated, the more tenderly he looked at me. His voice dropped to a low murmur. "It can't be that difficult a choice, can it?"

It couldn't. It wasn't. But he'd wound me up, and without him inside me, above me, I was never going to come down. I couldn't think properly, to the point that the only possible response was the honest one.

"I don't want to say it," I rasped. "I don't want to."

"Ah." He sounded utterly unsurprised. "Do I stop, then?"

I shook my head.

"Let's introduce another option, then. You explain to me *why*." His lips curved in a kind smile. Whatever this game was, he was winning it. I could tell even without understanding the rules. "You explain to me why you don't want to say it, and I'll spend the rest of the night fucking you. I'm going to devote the rest of my natural life to making you come so hard, we'll both lose our minds."

"Why are you doing this?"

He laughed silently before kissing me again, and this time it was slow and bottomless, thorough like only Eli could be. I arched into him, trembling. But then the kiss died, and no response came. Instead, Eli leaned his forehead against mine.

"Rue. My sad, beautiful fortress girl."

His voice was so fully, tragically heartbreaking, I could no longer keep my eyes open. *I hate you,* I thought, just as a single tear rolled out of my eye and streaked my temple. *Like I've never hated anyone before.*

He had given me three options to choose from. One was unbearable. One felt wrong on a visceral level. The remaining . . . the remaining would require me to explain something I myself didn't understand.

I forced my eyes open, found Eli's, and chose the fourth.

"It's not just fucking," I said. In the quiet of the room, my voice was like shattered glass. "But I—I don't know why, and I *don't*—"

The kiss that silenced me was nuclear. For long seconds we were both feral, suspended in time, interrupted—just Eli and me, breathing each other in, trying to be as close as we could. "Don't worry, sweetheart," he said into my ear. "You'll figure it out. I'll help you, okay?"

When he began moving again inside me, my body lit up with the force of an atomic explosion. And less than half a minute later, I came so hard my vision went black.

34

UNTRODDEN TERRITORY

RUE

I woke up at the crack of dawn, curled into Eli's chest. The sex had lasted for hours, but I couldn't recall when precisely it had ended or having made the conscious decision to stay over. It mattered very little: after what I'd admitted to last night, I no longer required mental gymnastics to justify sleeping at his place.

I gently freed myself and pulled up my shorts, staring at him. He was on his side, bare chested and only half-covered by the sheet, his hair a beautiful, chaotic nightmare. I thought about running a hand through it, and the impulse was so hard to resist, I had to force myself to turn away.

My phone informed me that it was early—early enough that the sky wasn't fully bright yet—but I had a lab booked for the morning, and couldn't show up smelling like sex and Eli. With one last lingering glance and the overpowering feeling that I should stay, I made my way down the stairs.

As soon as I was no longer around Eli, an insidious sense of dread began spreading through me. My stomach ached. My bones were heavy. Something dense solidified in my chest, and the farther I got from the bedroom, the heavier it became.

It was not just sex, what he and I were doing. He knew it, and so did I. And now . . . what *now*? What did people do, once they acknowledged that they had something—*someone*—to lose? What was expected of me? What if Eli decided that *he* didn't want *me*?

It was untrodden territory, and I felt scared and nauseated.

Calm down, I told myself, taking a deep breath. *Get yourself home. Take a damn shower.*

Tiny sleepily escorted me to the front door. He stared up at me with small, hopeful eyes, and before slipping out, I found myself reaching out. It took me about three attempts, but I managed to clumsily pat him on the head—and shockingly, I didn't screw it up. His tail swung in delight, and I smiled. Maybe there was hope for me, after all.

I didn't notice the sunrise until I was in my car. I hadn't seen one in months, maybe years, and the golden light beckoned me home and bathed the street in a warm, gentle glow. My eyes burned, as though unable to contain the emotions of the past few days. There had been plenty, many of them confusing, and I had to hit my sternum with my balled-up fist before starting the car.

I was about five minutes from home when my phone rang.

New York City was only one hour ahead, but Nyota was the kind of "work hard, play hard" person whose early mornings were likely to be spent at the office—or staggering home from the club. Still, I couldn't remember the last time I'd received a call from her at such an odd hour.

"Is Tisha okay?" I asked when she picked up.

"I hope so. She better not be dead, because I have zero time to go scatter her ashes at some meaningful but hard-to-reach location. If there's a mountain to climb or a boat to rent, you're going to have to take care of it."

"Sure."

"Nice. Consider this a legally binding agreement, because I *will* hold you to it." She sounded exceedingly satisfied. "Were you able to give those statements to Harkness?"

"Yes. It's nice of you to check on it at"—I glanced at the dashboard clock—"six forty-two a.m."

"Yeah, that's not what this call is about. What's that noise? Are you driving?"

"Yes."

"Okay, well . . ." A pause. Nyota sighed, and alarm tingled in my belly. "I think you should pull over. I have something very important to tell you, and it's pretty fucking atrocious."

35

CAN'T HAVE BOTH

ELI

Eli was so fucking giddy, even his own damn dog found him irritating.

"I know, I *know*. Not ideal," he told Tiny during their morning walk, when he kept glancing back with a forlorn expression, as if wondering where his new favorite human had gone. "She'll come over again soon."

He was certainly going to try to lure her back tonight. And maybe it wasn't going to be too hard—because she'd as good as acknowledged that she *wanted* to be with him. He knew it, and Rue knew it, too. Together, they were different. Unlike anything before—or after, he suspected. And last night she'd finally given them a fighting chance.

"Just trust me," he told Tiny when the lovelorn puppy eyes wouldn't stop. "And stop pining. It's undignified."

His morning was full of off-site meetings, and he glided

through all of them. "Eli! Why do you look so much *better* than usual?" Anton asked him when he strode through Harkness's lobby. Eli considered firing him on the spot at the implied insult, but the paperwork would have delayed his reunion with his one true love: texting Rue.

Which was delayed anyway, when Hark impatiently gestured him inside from the glass window of a conference room. "Do you ever pick up your damn phone?" he asked before Eli had even closed the door.

"Not during meetings, no."

"What about when the meetings end?"

"Depends on how annoying the caller is. Are you conducting a survey pertaining to habits around electronic devices, or is there something you need to tell me?"

"It's about Kline," Minami said. Eli glanced at her and Sul for the first time. Noticed their serious expressions.

The tension in the room finally cut through his good mood. "What happened?"

"The documents your girlfriend gave us," Hark said. A minute earlier, the words would have made him smile. Hark's tone, though, gave him pause. "The lawyers went through them."

"Already?"

"Not that time consuming. She sent precisely what we needed."

Yup, that was his girl. "And?"

Hark's mouth twisted into a smile. "Florence's fucked, Eli. She's underwater on her ratios, the audited financials might as well have been written in crayon on a diner menu, and she's got fifteen material contingencies under the couch cushions. But you know what's fucking brilliant?"

Eli shook his head.

"The insolvency clause. If Kline is unable to meet its financial obligations or pay off its debts, the lender will be able to convert the debt into equity—or claim ownership."

"We knew about that already."

"But we didn't know how bad off Kline was. And that it's never going to be solvent by the end of the second quarter."

"That's June thirtieth," Eli said unnecessarily. Everyone at the table already knew.

"Less than a week, Eli." Hark grinned. "We got it. We really got it."

"There's more," Minami interrupted, sounding incongruously cautious. Eli's scalp tingled in alarm.

"What?"

"So." She nibbled at the inside of her cheek. "Florence knows she's in deep shit. She might even know that Rue gave us the books—I don't know. But she's aware that her only choice is to pay back the loan before the quarter ends."

"Doesn't matter," Hark interrupted. "There's no way she can gather enough funds—"

"There isn't," Minami agreed, still looking at Eli. "That's true. But that won't stop her from trying, and since she's exhausted most of her avenues, the only way for her to generate cash is by selling company assets."

Eli pulled out a chair and sat—next to Hark, across from her. "She can't sell the biofuel tech. It's the collateral for the loan. So if that's what you're worried about—"

"That's not what worries Minami," Sul said, and the tingle sharpened. The energy in the room was just off. Beside him, Hark was buzzing with excitement. The others looked, at the very least, preoccupied. "There are other assets Florence is shopping around."

"Such as?"

"Tech from side projects. Such as Rue's microbial-coating patent."

"She can't. I already asked Rue about that—she has a written agreement with Florence that she will retain ownership of whatever tech . . ." he trailed off. Minami's and Sul's looks were pointed in a way he couldn't misconstrue. "No. There's no way."

Minami just nodded.

"She has a *contract*."

"That was never ratified by the board."

Eli pinched the bridge of his nose. "Fuck." He thought about Rue last night, the last time they'd had sex. Her slow, graceful movement against him. Her breathless laugh as he listed everything he loved about her in toe-curling detail. The serene, trusting way she'd fallen asleep in his arms.

He felt queasy.

"The contract isn't worth the paper it's printed on," Sul said. "Florence can sell the patent, and she will. She has a buyer."

The room fell into a tense silence. Eli leaned forward. "Is Rue aware?"

"I doubt it. She clearly did not have the foresight to consult a lawyer or wonder about Florence's character. Not very smart," Hark drawled. Eli's head swung around, ready to fuck off ten years of friendship, but when their eyes met, Hark looked self-effacing. "Once again, she reminds me of these three assholes I know."

"How do *we* know about the buyer?"

"Sheer luck, that's how," Hark said. "The buyer is NovaTech. And Hector Scotsville's brother is CTO there. I met with Hector this morning to go over some agri-tech shit, and he told me about this fun coincidence, since we're connected with Kline."

"Fuck."

"Florence has been shopping around Kline's techs and compounds for the past few weeks. According to Hector, the microbial coating was off the table until *very* recently."

"Florence may know that Rue gave us the books," Minami said. "Could it be a punishment of sorts?"

"It's possible." Eli ran a hand through his hair. "And they did have a . . . confrontation. It might have convinced Florence to go ahead and sell. But who the fuck buys a patent that's not even registered yet? Why does NovaTech even want it?"

"They're a packaging solutions company," Sul said.

"Getting rid of the competition, then."

Hark patted him on the back. "Gold star."

Eli shook his head. This day. This *fucking* day. It had started so well. Humbling, how bad it had become all of a sudden. "Nova-Tech is going to buy Rue's work of *years*, and then they'll trash it so they can keep on selling their packaging. All because Florence lied to Rue with a contract that was never legally binding."

"Good recap. Infinitely shitty of Florence, but legal. Seems to be her sweet spot," Hark said. "She's not going to raise enough funds to buy back the loan, not even if she finds a buyer for every single piece of tech at Kline's disposal. But the deadline's coming up, and it'll be fun to lie low and watch her put up the saddest lemonade stand—"

"We're not going to do that," Eli said.

Hark blinked. "Not going to . . . ?"

"We're not going to lie low. We're not going to let her sell Rue's patent. Once it's sold, it's gone. Even if we later get control of Kline, we won't be able to reverse the deal."

Sul stared at him thoughtfully. Minami and Hark, though, just exuded a combination of puzzled and pitying. "I don't think it's within our power to stop her," she said gently.

Eli stood to pace. "What if we lay out our cards? Tell Florence we have the books. We know she's in breach. We could try to negotiate with her—offer her more time if she doesn't sell Rue's patent, for example."

"Hang on a minute." Hark bolted to his feet, too. "Are you having a massive stroke you forgot to tell us about?"

Eli just stared at him.

"Because it sounds like you're saying that we should give up our strategic advantage, an advantage that could put Kline in our hands in a matter of *weeks*, to stop the sale of Rue Siebert's patent. Rue's a very nice lady, no doubt, but also someone we've known for about five fucking minutes, and I'm glad that sleeping with her is working out well for you—"

"Hark," Minami admonished.

"—but I'm not sure that just because *you* are gone for her, she's someone *we* should consider when making decisions that will affect plans that were years in the making."

"We're not doing it because I'm *gone* for her," Eli gritted out. "We're doing it because it's *right*."

"How is this our goddamn business?" Hark took a step closer. Eli did the same. "We owe Rue Siebert nothing. *You* owe Rue Siebert nothing. You can't tell me that you're willing to jeopardize something that sent us to hell and back, for *her*. Does she even give a shit about you?"

"It's not the damn point. What Florence is about to do to her is exactly what she did to us a decade ago."

"And so what? For fuck's—if you want Rue so bad, marry her. Make her have your babies. Buy her a house with thirty rooms and a private lab where she can fiddle around and develop twenty more techs. But you can't buy *her* love with *our* dreams." Hark had been loud, but his voice dropped back to a menacing tone. "You can't have both, Eli. You either get Kline, or Rue's patent. Which one is it?"

36

THE MOST TRAGIC STORY

RUE

Perhaps it should have been irritating, the way Tisha's questions to Nyota piled on top of each other, the sharp replies, the sisterly bickering. Instead, I found the familiarity of it reassuring, anchoring in a way nothing else had managed to be since this morning's call.

"I'm just saying that I don't understand how a contract that has been *signed* by both parties can be *not* valid—"

"And *I* am just saying that since *I* acknowledge my lack of expertise on the matter and don't come telling you that pipettes should be shoved up your ass, *you* could face the reality that you did not go to law school and extend me the same courtesy—"

"Ooooh, but of course, if you're such a legal hotshot, why did you *only now* realize that Florence's contract wasn't binding?"

"Because, and this is going to *shock* you, I am a professional bankruptcy lawyer whose primary source of income comes from charging rich people obscene amounts of money for very small amounts of my time, and not from looking over my shitty sister's shitty childhood friend's shitty contract. I will allow a few seconds for your mind to be blown."

"Listen here, *you* shitty—"

"I had forgotten all about the contract and made room in my brain for, I don't know, *stuff I need to know to win court trials or something*—until Rue told me what Florence did to Harkness. That's when I got suspicious—"

"Was it my fault?" I asked softly. My office plummeted into silence.

Both sisters turned to me—Tisha, worried, and Nyota, uncharacteristically willing to forsake the usual roasting in favor of some heartfelt sympathy. "No," she said firmly through FaceTime. "Well, yes. But you were a young academic, which often translates to 'appallingly uneducated in anything that has real-life implications.' You probably still are, to be honest. Uneducated, that is. Not young. You're both decrepit—"

"Why are you taking this so well?" Tisha interrupted her, frowning at me. "Not that I expected histrionics or tears, but this is an exceptional amount of resilience, even for you."

I made myself shrug. Saying *Because she did the same to Eli and Minami* felt too depressing.

"If it's any consolation, since Florence knew she didn't have the right to give you ownership of the tech, you could still sue her for whatever the company makes on the sale," Nyota said quietly.

But I didn't care about money, at least as much as it was possible to not care after having grown up without it. Even as a child I'd known that the reason I was unhappy, hungry, lonely, was not the lack of *money*. Money was the middleman, the broker between my miserable life and decent food, clothes, opportunities. Opportunities that would let me leave home and become someone else.

My project, though, had *meant* something. I'd cradled it and nurtured it, believing that it could make a difference for someone out there. But the contract wasn't valid, because I'd trusted the wrong person.

Stupid. Just *stupid*.

Was this how Eli had felt all those years ago? This soul-crushing combination of shame, resentment, and resignation? "Is there any way—any legal way—for me to make this right?"

"Maybe?" Nyota rolled her lips. "Probably not, but I'm not the best person to advise you. I'm happy to help however I can, but I'm not a patent lawyer. I can ask my friend Liam—he's way more knowledgeable—but he just had a baby and is on paternity leave." She scratched her head, pensive. "I guess you *could* confront Florence, in the hope that it was an honest mistake. Maybe she truly genuinely forgot the final step in the contract, and she might be willing to rectify. But it's also possible that by confronting her, you'd be *alerting* her that the patent is hers, which she could use to her own advantage. We should think this through very carefully, because a misstep could . . . Rue? Where are you . . . Tish, where the hell is your weirdo friend going?"

Nyota's and Tisha's voices drifted out of earshot as I stepped out of my office and stalked down the hallway. I was rarely impulsive, but there was nothing well planned about the way I strode across Kline, or about the side of my fist as I knocked on Florence's door.

"Not now," Florence called from inside.

I opened the door anyway. And when I noticed the man sitting across from her, in the chair *I* had claimed years ago, my heart sank.

"Rue," Florence was saying, "I'm in a meeting. Could you please—"

"What are you doing here?" I asked. *Not* to Florence.

Eli's smile didn't reach his eyes. "So lovely to see you, Dr. Siebert. I'm excellent, thanks for asking. You?"

"What are you doing here?" I repeated.

"Just chatting with an old friend."

My eyes flitted to Florence, who looked as collected as always—with the exception of her right hand. It was fisted around a pencil so tightly, I wondered if it was already snapped in two. "Eli, what are you doing—"

"Here? No need to concern yourself, since I'm leaving." He stood. His smile to Florence was soulless, the opposite of the ones I'd been receiving from him in the last few days. "You should walk me out, Rue."

"I need to speak with Florence."

"Of course. After we catch up." He cupped my elbow. "I'm sure Florence will be here all day, at your service."

She frowned at both of us. As far as social situations went, this one was undecipherable. "I don't understand what's happening," I murmured.

This time, Eli's smile was more his kind, warm and teasing. Just for me. "Don't worry," he said gently. Then, turning to Florence: "Let me know before tonight." He pushed me out of the office with a hand between my shoulder blades, and before I could ask more questions, he'd taken my hand and was guiding me into an empty conference room. Inside, he didn't let go. His fingers skimmed up my wrist and closed around my upper arm. He stared at me, gulping me in, and my chest heated with a terrible weight.

"Rue," he said urgently, "I need to know why you were going to meet Florence."

"Why?"

"Because I'm *asking* you."

"I . . ." I swallowed. Opened my mouth to tell him—and then a terrible tendril of distrust curled inside my belly. *He's with Harkness. They're about to own Kline. They're about to own your patent.* "Why do you want to know?"

His eyes narrowed and he leaned in. "Because I'm on your side. That a good enough reason?"

After a pause, I nodded. It was true. Eli *was* on my side. He had been, over and over, a *friend* to me. Even if thinking of that specific word in relation to him felt at once banal and earth shattering.

But hadn't Florence been my *friend*, too? I'd been wrong a lot recently. I clearly had a history of putting my trust in the wrong people.

"My project," I said. "The microbial coating."

"Florence owns the patent."

I blinked at him. "How do you know?" He held my eyes and didn't reply, so I continued, "I . . . maybe she meant to have the board ratify the contract and forgot. It might have been an oversight. I'll talk to her and—"

"Come on, Rue." His fingers squeezed my arm gently, as if to coax me awake. "You know it wasn't."

I swallowed. "It's my only choice, Eli. I have to ask Florence to fix it and hope that she will."

"Listen to me carefully. Florence has been selling intellectual property to gather funds to buy back the loan. And she already has a buyer for your tech."

My blood pounded in my throat. It was over, then. "I . . . I need to speak to Nyota." I attempted to leave, but Eli didn't let go.

"No, you need to listen to me." His tone was serious, but gentle and reassuring. I felt myself panic anyway.

"I just—I have to do something."

"Not right now. Right now, you need to let it be."

"Let it be?" I blinked at him in disbelief.

"I'm working on this, Rue, and I promise that I'm going to fix this for you. I'm going to make sure you keep your patent. In exchange, I need *you* to promise me that you won't confront Florence yet and that you'll lie low for a couple of days. I'm in the middle of negotiations, and it's important that you trust me."

My panic grew. "I . . . are you seriously asking me to just wait and do nothing while she might sell my work?"

"Yes. Because there is nothing you can do."

"But there's something *you* can do?"

"That is correct."

I took a step back, and his grip slid to my elbow. "Eli, you know how much this tech means to me."

"I do. And you know how much the biofuel tech meant to me."

I recoiled. "Is this what's happening? You want me to go through what *you* went through? Some—some messed-up cycle of thievery?"

"That's not what I—" He ran a frustrated hand through his hair. "I'm going to take care of you. I'm here to help you."

But I felt dizzier than after a double toe loop. Things were happening too fast, and I couldn't keep up. All I could parse was the

fear that my work would be taken from me. "Harkness is the reason I'm in this situation to begin with," I pointed out.

Eli's face hardened. "*Florence* is the reason you're in this situation. Harkness may have precipitated it, but I'm not talking to you
on behalf of anyone but myself. You're the scientist I could never
be, and I respect you infinitely for this, but these kinds of deals are
what *I* know. Let me negotiate one for you. Let me take care
of you."

My brain scrambled to consider the possibilities. This was Eli.
I could trust him, right?

You trusted Florence.

"How—how do I know that you're not just saying this because
Harkness wants to own my patent, too?"

He seemed briefly on the brink of exasperation, but compassion flickered in his eyes. "I know how you feel. You're wondering
how the fuck you got yourself into this situation. Why you trusted
the kind of person who would do this to you. You're second-
guessing every single thing you've done in the last few years and
wondering if there is something wrong with you. You're angry,
because Florence was your friend, and you relied on her for more
than just a salary or lab space. I get it. Believe me, I have been
right fucking there." He looked at me like we were on the edge of
a cliff, and he was asking me to take his hand. "Rue, I need you to
acknowledge that I'm not her."

"Eli, I . . ." My throat choked up. I was confused. Overwhelmed.
And he must have known, because his voice became even more
gentle.

"Hey. You said it yourself—you and I, we're not just fucking."
His smile was hopeful. Encouraging. "I'm here for you. You can
trust me."

But could I? *Should* I trust anyone? Had there ever been a time in my life when trust had not ended in disappointment? And why should Eli be different? "Why would you . . . why would you even do this for me?"

He finally let go of my arm, and for a split second I wondered if he was, at last, fed up. Done with me. But it was less than a heartbeat, and then he was close again, hands cradling my face, thumbs swiping my cheeks, eyes tethered to mine. "Why do you think, Rue?"

I blinked at him, letting his question float through my head, unable to grasp the answer that was right in front of me. He watched me patiently, waiting for a response, *any* response. And when none came, I saw something fade behind his eyes.

He leaned in, tipping his forehead against mine, and the closeness was heaven. "Would you like a story, Rue?"

I instantly nodded. I needed something—*anything*—that would help me understand.

"Hark and Minami broke up over ten years ago, but he never got over her. Never. I simply could *not* understand why he wouldn't move on after she so clearly had. 'Could not be me,' I thought. I was *so* sure. And then, Rue, I met you. And you casually cracked my life into *before* and *after* you." His lips curved. For a moment he looked genuinely happy. "Out of all the people I've met, the things I've wanted, the places I've been, none has ever felt as necessary as you do. Because I love you. I love you in a way I didn't think I was capable of. I love you because you showed me how to fall in love. And I don't regret it, Rue. I wouldn't want it any other way. Even if you can never say it back. Even if you never think about me again after today. Even if you were right after all, and you're not capable of love."

He let go of me, and we were back to the cliff. Except that my hand had slipped from Eli's, and I was free-falling. Already broken, or soon to be.

"Isn't this the most tragic story you've ever heard?"

I couldn't find my words, but it didn't matter. He left the conference room with a single nod that felt like the deepest of farewells, and I stood still for a long, long time, trying to convince my body to remember how to breathe.

37

THE FRIENDS WE MADE ALONG THE WAY

ELI

Minami found him sitting on one of the swinging chairs on the back porch, the ones Maya had bought at a yard sale and restored the previous summer, when she'd been between undergrad and her master's and had wanted a relaxing craft project to free her mind. The sun was on the verge of setting, a blend of blue and gold and orange hues, and Eli thought it a fitting way to bookend this long, messy, poignant day in which so many things had come to a close.

"Isn't it too disgustingly hot to be outside?" Minami asked.

He tipped his bottle at her and smiled. "Beer's nice and cool."

"God, I'm jealous."

"Have one, too."

"Can't."

"Yeah, you can. They're in the fridge."

"No, Eli. I *can't*."

He frowned, confused. Then it dawned on him all at once, and his eyes bugged out of his face. "Holy shit."

"Yup."

"Are you really—"

"Yup, yup."

"When did you—shit. When you were sick, you weren't really—"

"Nope. Well, I *was* puking my heart out. Just not for the reason you thought."

He hadn't thought it possible, not after the last few hours, but happy laughter burst out of him. He stood, enveloping Minami in a bear hug. "Jesus. *Wow.*"

"We're so happy," she said against his T-shirt.

"I bet." He shook his head, amazed. "You're going to be fantastic parents. Obnoxious, too."

"I know. And you're going to be a great uncle who constantly spoils her and undermines our authority."

Her. Minami couldn't possibly know yet, but he liked the idea. "I would settle for no less." He drew back. Took in her smile and shining eyes. "We should celebrate. How about a cold beer?"

"Fuck off." She plopped on his chair, sighing in pleasure as she sank into the soft cushions.

"I think Maya has root beer somewhere."

"Oh. Do you have vanilla ice cream?"

"Maybe?"

"I would give my firstborn for a float."

"Nah." Eli waved her off. "Keep her."

Five minutes later he came back with the first float he'd made in over two decades. Minami accepted it with a smile, and as he pulled up another chair, she asked, "Guess how pissed Hark is?"

"About the baby?"

"Oh, he doesn't know about that yet."

"Planning to put off telling him until you're in labor in Harkness's gender-neutral restrooms?"

"Only if he walks in while she's crowning. Guess how pissed he is about the deal we made with Florence?"

Eli exhaled. "I'm assuming he's sharpening his kitchen knives."

"And you'd be correct."

He took the first sip of a fresh beer. Work was going to be shit for a while.

"Unfortunately, he's not showing it," Minami continued. "I wish he raged at me a bit. Or called me names. Told me I'm a traitor, that I took away his one motivation in life, that I deserve what Florence took from me. You know, the kind of over-the-top dramatic shit he always spouts when he becomes angry and his accent gets unintelligible."

"I'm familiar," he said dryly.

"But he's just sourpussing. Icily polite. Like when I told him Sul and I were going to get married? I was bracing for an explosion, and what I got was a four-hundred-dollar toaster."

"What the fuck?" Eli lifted his eyebrow. "Is it encrusted with diamonds?"

"No. It looks like the twenty-five-dollar toaster I had in grad school."

"Fuck capitalism, man." He snorted. "Don't worry, this time around it wasn't your doing. I'm the one who put Rue before Kline. It's me he's pissed at."

"I was the deciding vote, though. I sided with you." She sucked an impressive amount of sludge through her straw. "How did you know that I would, by the way?"

The thing was, he *hadn't*. Not before Hark had asked them to put the matter to a vote. What he *had* known was that Rue stood to lose something that meant the world to her, and he wasn't willing to accept that without a fight. "You know what I think?" he said.

"What?"

"That what nearly happened to Rue was so similar to what Florence did to us, I'm not sure he'd have allowed it, either. He tries to play the part of the asshole, but . . . I can't see him living with that."

"You think he counted on us to overrule him?"

Eli shrugged.

"Wow. He's such a shithead."

"I can't prove it."

"Such an *alleged* shithead."

Eli laughed, and a comfortable silence descended, filled by cicadas and slurping sounds. Until she asked quietly, "Do we have a deal?"

He nodded. "The lawyers are writing it up."

"Do tell."

"Florence won't be selling the patent, or any other company asset. The patent will be Rue's. In exchange, we'll forgive the loan, and get a sixty percent equity in Kline. The other investors keep thirty-five."

"And she gets . . . ?"

"Five percent. Which is five percent more than she deserves. We allow her to stay on as CEO. We get three of the five board seats and observer rights at board meetings. And, as a bonus, I threw in a little gift."

"Which is?"

"I'm not going to key her car."

"You're very generous."

"Am I?" He sighed, wondering at the empty ache in his chest, resisting the urge to massage his sternum, to think about Rue. He'd known what he needed from her for a while, but putting it into words had precipitated the feeling, amplified the way every single nerve in his body simply *wanted her*. "Maybe I'm just an idiot."

"No maybes there. How was it, talking to Florence face-to-face?"

Eli remembered her flushed face as he let her know that they had the books. Her bitterness and resignation as they ironed out the kinks of their deal. "I'd tried to imagine it, you know? How it would happen. What I'd say when I finally spoke to her again."

"Like, in the shower? When you have those forty-minute conversations with yourself?"

He gave her a baffled look. "How long are your showers?"

"A normal length, shut up."

"In my environmentally conscious, non-shower conversations, I was going to tell her how incredibly shitty my life had been after what she did. About my parents, and Maya. How I had to take two minimum-wage jobs literally three days after it all went down, and the absolute mortification of failing at the one thing I cared about. I was going to take every single moment of misery and anger and desperation the three of us had in the past ten years and throw them in her face and ask her . . ."

"*'Are you not entertained?'*"

He laughed. "Something like that. Hark and I talked about this several times, mostly drunk. He always said that he wanted to make her *pay*. Make her feel like a fool for what she'd done to us. And part of me gets it, but the bigger part just . . ."

"You just wanted her to understand the hurt she caused. Maybe get a nice apology."

"How did you know?"

"I just know *you*. A disgustingly unpetty person." She rolled her eyes theatrically. "I swear you need classes."

"I don't know about that. Because when I was there, with Florence . . . I just pitied her. More than a little." He looked at Minami's dark eyes. Her familiar, beloved round face. The expectant tilt of her chin. "She's alone in this mess she's made for herself. She has always been her own personal endgame. Played shady games, won shady prizes. If I hadn't been negotiating for Rue's patent, we could have kicked her out of Kline altogether. No five percent, no CEO. But I'm not even sure that matters, because everything she owns was built on top of lies, and she hasn't changed. We have, though. And we've stood by each other."

"Well, Hark is probably going to need a couple of weeks of cooling down before any more consensual by-standing occurs."

"Up to a month. But the point is, everything she has can be taken from her. While we have built something that—"

"Please don't say that the real equity in the biofuel tech was the friends we made along the way."

He set his beer on the small glass table and locked eyes with her. "Minami, I'm going to ask you to get off my porch and go fuck right off."

She let out a sound that Eli could only describe as a cackle. "Sul says I'm funny."

"Sul's more whipped than a bowl of mashed potatoes."

"Don't you whisk those?"

"Maybe?"

"McKenzie would know."

"She would."

"I'll text her. Also, he's only whipped because I'm funny."

"I've never once seen him laugh."

"And that's the reason he's in love with *me* and not with *you*. I make him laugh. In the privacy of our home."

Eli shook his head. Rue made him laugh, too. She made him eager to do unspeakable things for just one more minute with her. She made him crave that comfortable, expansive silence between them. Rue made him stop and think, and above all she made him *yearn* like he'd not thought himself capable of, and he wanted to spend the rest of his life cataloging the ways she shouldn't have been *right* for him, and yet still managed to be *perfect*.

Rue eviscerated him and made him anew. And if she didn't want the product of that . . .

Well. That was for him to accept.

"If you had asked me two weeks ago, I'd have told you that the only happy ending to our story was with Florence out of Kline. But now . . ." Minami's lips curved in a small smile, her profile as familiar to him as his sister's. "We control the board—and the tech. I think the way things turned out might be for the best."

"Yeah?"

"We started Harkness out of revenge, and we let spite fuel us. And don't get me wrong, I don't regret our multi-presidential-term revenge plot. But we have accomplished so much more and—"

"Gained friends along the way?"

She punched his arm. "We make really good money. We get to work with amazing scientists and help them develop amazing shit. And fine, yes, we have each other. Maybe it's not what we'd envisioned, but it's good." Her eyes gleamed suspiciously. "And now you have Rue."

Eli glanced at the sun sinking into the sycamore trees. "If Rue is ever ready or willing to be had."

"We all have shit to work through. It's just a matter of time."

He said nothing, letting himself feel the tight knot in his throat, the ache that came with not knowing when, *if* he'd see her again. He'd made his move, and her silent reaction had been loud and clear. Her shocked look when he'd told her that he loved her. Unfortunately, the gap between "not just fucking" and "wanting a relationship" was wider than the Sargasso Sea. "I don't know."

Minami reached out and closed her hand around his. "I'm sorry."

"Yeah. Me, too."

"I swear I'm not trying to be condescending—"

"What a promising start."

"—*but*, I know this whole being-madly-in-love thing is new for you, so I'm going to impart a piece of wisdom to you. Ready?"

"Go ahead."

"No one dies of a broken heart."

A soft laugh eased out of him. "Good to know, because it fucking hurts." He let out a deep breath. "There is something I want to do for her. But I'm not sure she'll accept it if it's from me."

Her look was concerned. "I think you've done enough, Eli. Shouldn't you keep just a *tiny* bit of dignity?" It was a joke, but Eli's reply was serious.

"I want her to be all right more than I want to keep my dignity."

"Christ." Minami gave him an aghast look. "On second thought, you *might* die from a broken heart." She drained what was left of her float and set her glass on the table. "Okay, hit me. What do you need this fatigued, overworked, pregnant woman to do for you?"

38

WE ALL HAVE OUR BAGGAGE

RUE

I delivered my notice letter to Florence in person, the day after Kline's lawyers sent me a board-ratified contract that gave me full ownership of my provisional patent. The day after discovering what Eli had given up in exchange.

I didn't owe Florence a confrontation. However, I remembered what Eli had said about closure. My confidence in my people-judging skills was at an all-time low, but if there was anyone I could trust, it was Eli. I knew that now, and I'd known before he'd made it possible for me to hold my new contract in my hands.

I'd fucked up. Big-time. But vulnerability had a time and a place, and a meeting with Florence Kline was less than ideal.

"Do you have anything lined up?" Florence asked me, staring at an undefined spot on my forehead from across her desk. She looked pale. Exhaustion had carved deep lines that bracketed her lips, darkened the circles around her eyes.

"Just interviews. Next week." I'd lined up four by reaching out to grad school acquaintances, my PhD adviser, a recruiter. I didn't love change, and switching jobs was never going to be easy for me, but it was unavoidable.

"Good." Florence nodded. "Do you need references?"

"I put down someone else."

An infinitesimal wince. "Right." She rubbed the heel of her palm on her temple. "Am I correct in assuming that Tisha will follow you?"

She was. "You'll have to ask her."

She sighed. "Rue. I had no other choice. You gave them the books and put me in the position of having to sell—"

I had no intention of listening to Florence's justifications, so I stood. "Thank you for everything," I said, meaning it. "I'll get back to work. Will you let HR know, or should I?"

"I'll take care of it." Her lips thinned. "For what it's worth, I *am* sorry, Rue. I cared about them, and I wouldn't have hurt them if it hadn't been absolutely necessary. And I care about you, whether you believe it or not."

"I believe it. You just care about yourself more, and that's your right. I'd rather not surround myself with someone who'll hurt me just to get ahead, and that's mine."

Her eyes hardened. "Then there will be no one left to surround yourself with, Rue."

I shrugged and walked out, thinking that she was wrong. Thinking about Eli.

I had lunch with Tisha, and by common agreement we didn't mention Florence once. We'd spent days dissecting every single red flag, every missed clue, every misstep, and we were exhausted. Two hours later, while finishing up a report for Matt, I received an

email from Kline's HR, letting me know that I was being terminated starting the following week.

*Because your position has been terminated, you are eligible
for a severance package that amounts to one month's worth
of salary for each year you worked.*

I sat back in my chair, staring at Tisha's calendar. For the first
time since finding out about what Florence had done, I allowed a
splinter of sadness to pierce through my anger. I'd lost a friend,
when I had very few to spare to begin with.

I care about you, too, Florence.

I left my desk at five o'clock. In the parking lot, while rummag-
ing through my bag for a pair of sunglasses, I heard someone call
my name. Minami was leaning against the bumper of a green
Volkswagen beetle, and my single, all-obscuring, fight-or-flight reaction to seeing her was: *Eli.*

Eli, Eli, *Eli.*

It was like a burst of fire through my veins, a jolting reminder
of what I'd been trying to come to terms with for the better part
of a week. My hands trembled, and I stuffed them in the back
pockets of my jeans.

"Hi!" Minami grinned. "How are you?"

It took a moment for me to calm down enough to say,
"Good. You?"

"Good! I'm not going to take up too much of your time, but I
wanted to give you this." She held out a document folded in a plastic case. I accepted, but must have looked confused, because she
explained, "It's a contract that details your payment plan for the
other half of your house. House? It was a house, right? I forget.

Anyway, we had our lawyers get in touch with your . . . brother? I once again forget."

My pulse fluttered in my throat. "What does it mean?"

"Well, nothing if you don't sign it. But our legal team worked as a mediator, found estimators, and made sure you could reach an agreement for a payment plan. Same thing you'd have gotten around to doing eventually."

"How?"

She shrugged, like real estate jurisprudence was as obscure as necromancy to her. "We have really good lawyers. And they're on the payroll anyway. We might as well make use of them. It'll save you time and money. And no, Eli didn't tell me the story behind all this. I'm not all up in your business."

"Did *he* ask you to do this?"

It was a stupid question, but Minami didn't point it out. "He didn't want to put you in an uncomfortable position, or make you think that you owe him something or feel pressured into . . . dating him? Going with him to sex clubs? Not sure what you guys have been up to."

I frowned, thinking that if Eli thought that I could be pressured into dating someone, perhaps he didn't know me. Minami laughed. "What?" I asked.

"Nothing. Just, he said something like, 'Not that she's the type who can be pressured into doing anything she doesn't want to,' and your face tells me he probably was right, and . . ." Minami laughed some more, and waved her hand.

"I know what you did," I said.

"What *I* did?"

"Harkness. The loan forgiveness. It was a trade for my patent, wasn't it? You let Florence stay on as CEO. You gave up your advantage so that I could keep my patent."

"Well, yes. But also . . ." Minami sighed. "We have the board. And we're free of this horrible thing that happened ten years ago. We did get closure, and maybe it wasn't the perfect circle we thought we'd be getting—more like a *very* squiggly line. We can all move on, and I don't mind that, not at all."

"Thank you, then." I looked down at the contract, which was probably the only closure I'd get with Vince. A messy, squiggly line indeed. But maybe I could move on. "And thank you for this."

"No problem. Just let the lawyers know if you're okay with it and they'll finalize it."

I nodded, and closed my eyes, thinking about Eli asking his lawyers to do this. On the phone after hours, sitting at the table in his kitchen with Tiny curled at his feet. Saying, *I have a . . . friend. Who might need help.* Eli worrying. Eli caring enough to—

"You okay?" Minami asked.

"Yeah. Is he . . . ?"

"Eli?" Minami hesitated. "Not at his best, but he'll be fine. I'm not telling you any of this to make you feel bad. I know what it's like when someone you care about is in love with you and you can't reciprocate the feeling. It's messy, and you feel guilty, and—"

"That's not it," I blurted out. It was so uncharacteristic, this unsanctioned exit of words from my mouth, that I almost couldn't recognize my voice. "That's not what it is," I added, outwardly calmer. The inside of me was burning with sudden, petrifying heat.

Minami's head tilted. "You don't feel guilty?"

I swallowed. "It's not that I don't . . . reciprocate."

"Oh." Minami looked around, befuddled. Stroked her flat stomach a few times. "Um. Do you want to talk about it?"

I could barely explain it to myself, the profound panic that had seized me when Eli had told me that he loved me. The immediate, soul-crushing certainty that if I let myself take what he was offering, I would undoubtedly disappoint him. And then, when he'd walked out of that conference room, the loss stabbing at my belly. I had majorly fucked up, and I knew that, but the hows and whys of atoning for it were something I was still in the process of analyzing. Meanwhile, the inside of me was tender and bruised like a pulled muscle. "Not really, no."

Minami laughed, relieved. "Okay. Well, then . . ." She shrugged and reached for the driver's door, but stopped mid-motion, as though a crucial piece of information had occurred to her. "I have no idea what is going on between you two. And I only know you very superficially, so I might be off the mark. But if what prompted you to break it off with Eli is *not* lack of interest, and what you're worried about is more somewhere in the realm of . . ." She gestured inchoately, like a very enthusiastic painter. "You not being good enough for him, or not being sure that what you can offer him is worthwhile, or just being afraid that navigating a relationship with him might be too complicated, you might want to give him a call. We all have our baggage, and Eli's not the type to hold anyone's against them. Although, on my end, it would be better if it didn't work out between you two."

I blinked. "It would?"

"I *love* the name Rue. Big *Hunger Games* fan here." She pointed at her abdomen. "If she's a girl, and she *is* a girl, I'm seriously considering it."

I glanced down at Minami's belly. Was she . . . ?

"But if you end up in Eli's life, it might just be too confusing, so . . ." Minami gave me a bright smile and got into her car, muttering, "Boy, am I *selfless*." I watched her leave, waving weakly as she drove past me, and allowed her words to ring in my ears long into the night.

39

MEAT TO BE, OR SOME SHIT

ELI

The first thing he thought when he stepped inside the faintly lit, empty rink was: *Fuck*.

Because the rink was, in fact, *not* empty. Which meant that the trip had been a waste.

He sighed and stopped in the hallway, hanging his skates on his shoulder and checking the text Dave had sent earlier that day.

> No practice today. Alec and I are out, but feel
> free to stop by the rink and let yourself in if
> you like.

Except that the lights under the ice were clearly on. The metallic scrape of blades against the ice was clearly audible. And then, once the hallway ended, he could clearly see her.

Her.

Gliding smoothly with the kind of ethereal elegance only people who'd lived half their lives on the ice could achieve. Circling the rink in a swooping loop. Coming to a fluid stop the second she spotted him and then just looking, eyes dark in the gentle light, soft curves turned into sharp angles by the vertical shadows, pitch-black clothes a dramatic contrast with her pale face.

Eli could recognize a setup when he saw one, just like he knew the value of a strategic retreat. And yet he closed the distance between them until all that separated them was a thin plexiglass barrier. And the million things he needed from her that she might never be willing to give.

"What is this?" he asked. He hadn't heard from her in over a week, and her silence following their last conversation had been answer enough. It wasn't her fault if she didn't want what *he* wanted—in fact, it was part of what he'd fallen for, the messiness, the unflinching honesty. But he did need some space to come to terms with what the rest of his life would look like.

"Rue," he asked again, a touch impatient. "What's going on?"

"Would you like to skate?"

His eyebrow rose, but her expression remained sphinxlike. "Did Dave put you up to this?"

"No. But I did ask him to text you."

"Why?"

"Please, Eli. Will you put those on"—she pointed at his skates—"and join me?" She looked calm, but it was the fastest he'd ever heard her speak.

"I thought we agreed that skating together is not what our relationship is about?"

"Please," she said softly. Because everything, *everything* about her was soft, even her hard shell, and instead of what his response should have been—*Rue, I'll do whatever you ask, but please take pity on me because I don't know if I can take more of this*—he peeled off his shoes and tied his skates, stepping into the rink without bothering to hide the tension in his muscles.

He was on the ice, his first home. Standing across from the woman he loved, whose response to him declaring his love to her had been—nothing. Nothing at all. As much as he wanted to hope that she'd lured him here to announce that she could possibly see a future in which she loved him back, it was more likely—

Oh, *shit*. He *knew* the reason she'd wanted him here. She was going to spend the next twenty minutes dutifully spelling out her gratitude toward him for helping her fix her patent situation.

If she offered him a thank-you blow job, he was going to wail like a fucking baby.

"You're welcome," he preempted.

Rue's glance was confused in the jagged silence.

"That's why we're here? So you can thank me for the patent."

She bit into her lower lip, and Eli would have drained his bank account to buy the right to pull it from her teeth with his thumb. "I suppose I should do that, yeah. Can we . . . ?" She gestured at the ice.

Sure. Why not. If they skated side by side, he wouldn't have to look at her while she told him how much she appreciated his helpful assistance.

"I should have texted you. I didn't mean to ambush you." They were already moving in unison. Like they were meant to be, or some shit. "But you wanted to skate together, and I . . . I thought you might appreciate a grand gesture."

"Yeah?" He shook his head. "Not sure you and I are grand gesture types, Rue."

"And yet you've done so many for me."

"Have I?"

"Over and over." She laughed, silent. "You pretty much stole all my options. I don't know how to do something that is even remotely like returning your most prized possession to you. You've set me up for failure."

This was nice. Lovely, even. But gratitude was the last thing Eli wanted from her. "I appreciate this, Rue. Really. But I didn't do this to hear how thankful you are—"

"Well, it's a lot. But since you already know, we can skip that part and move on to the next topic."

Thank fuck. "Which would be?"

"An apology." Her voice was limpid. She surprised him by flipping around and skating backward in front of him, as if eye contact with him was crucial for what she was about to say. "You asked me to trust you, and I treated you like you were the kind of person who'd screw me over, even when you've been nothing but truthful with me. My behavior never reflected that. So, I'm sorry, Eli."

The apology was, if possible, more depressing than the gratitude. "Rue, you had just found out about Florence. I think some temporary lack of faith in humankind is to be expected." He smiled reassuringly and stopped with a precise movement. So did she, just a handful of feet ahead. "If you don't mind, I'm going to head home—"

"I do."

He cocked his head. "Excuse me?"

"I do mind. I have more things to say." Eli felt a burst of warm, tentative hope, until she added, "What you did for me, with my brother."

He really needed to stop fooling himself. "That was the lawyers, but I'll happily pass along your thanks. Have a good—"

"Stop." Her fingers closed around the sleeve of his shirt, tugging at it. He felt her knuckles brush against his skin, her touch as electric as ever. "Please, Eli. Let me speak. Five minutes."

She sounded more vulnerable than ever, and was beautiful in a way that made his lungs struggle to hold on to air, and—what the hell. Maybe being near her was a sharp ache, but loving someone and saying no to them didn't seem to go well together. He could give her five minutes out of the rest of his life. He could give her *anything*. "Of course." He began skating again.

So did she, this time by his side. "I . . ." She was silent. Opened her mouth with a couple more false starts that were not like the Rue he knew at all. And then, when he was about to prod her, finally said, "Can I tell you a story?"

"You can tell me whatever you want, Rue."

She nodded. "I used to think that endings could be happy, or sad. That stories could be happy, or sad. That *people* could be happy, or sad. And I always figured that my ending, my story, me, would always fall in the latter."

He itched to take her in his arms, but let her continue.

"But then I met you. And you made me wonder, for the very first time, if there was a flaw in my reasoning. Maybe people can be happy *and* sad. Maybe stories are messy and complicated. Maybe endings don't always include solutions that tie everything together in a bow. But that doesn't mean that they have to be tragedies."

"I'm glad you think that." He really was. She may have robbed him of his peace of mind, but he still wanted her to have hers. One more fault to add to the humbling business of falling in love, he supposed. Distracting. Fucked up. Self-annihilating. Sweet and ex-cruciating at the same time.

"But you said that it was." Her expression was solemn and se-rious, so intensely *Rue*, he felt it right in his bones.

"I'm sorry, I'm not following."

"At Kline. In the conference room." Her throat bobbed. "You said that we were tragic."

Ah. They were rehashing and dissecting his failed love declara-tion. "I didn't mean to—"

"And I want you to know, we don't have to be. Because trage-dies have sad endings, and we don't have to have one. We don't even have to be over."

Eli's pace on the ice remained steady while the words pene-trated his frontal lobe. "We don't have to be over," he repeated slowly, reluctant to let his hope color her words with meanings that weren't there. "The last time we talked, Rue, I thought that maybe we'd never even started."

"And I'm sorry I made you believe that. I think . . ." She shook her head. Carried on skating with that unimpeachable posture and hard-earned grace. "You know, I think the sex is a big part of the problems between us."

"The sex?"

"Yeah."

He snorted out a laugh. "Rue, if there is *one* single thing that was never a problem between us, it was the sex."

"That's not what—it was good. And I'd love to have more of it." She bit into her lip. "But it overshadows other things I want to do with you. Talking. Listening. Just being around you. It's so new to me, to crave someone's presence. Wishing I could run something by you. Having meals with you—that you cook for me, preferably."

Blood roared hopefully in his ears. "So you're recruiting cheap kitchen labor," he murmured to mute it. She was giving him very little. He'd told her that he loved her, and she was admitting to enjoying his company.

Maybe Eli had no dignity, but he'd take it.

"I can actually cook satisfyingly well—"

With a push of his skates, Eli blocked her path and came face-to-face with her. Rue nearly crashed into him, her hands gripping his biceps for balance.

This close, he could count the spikes of her eyelashes. Watch her trembling lips as they pressed together.

"What do you want, Rue?" he asked.

"I'm trying to articulate it, but I'm not very good at it."

"No way. Really?"

Her pale cheeks flushed.

"Say what you want to say, and do it now," he ordered. "You have two minutes."

She wasted thirty seconds just glancing around the rink, searching for who the fuck knew what, and Eli's stomach began to grow heavy with dread that he'd once again read too much into too little. But she eventually took a deep breath, and when she spoke, her tone was solid and assured. "I thought I could never be happy. But with you, Eli . . . I have never felt the way I do with you. *Never*. And I think that's why it took me so long to put words to it."

His heart beat in his throat. "What words?"

"Safe," she said.

He forced himself to remain silent.

"And accepted."

More silence. Harder, this time.

"And enough."

That, he couldn't take. "Rue. You have never been anything but enough."

She glanced away. The back of her hand rose to wipe at her cheek.

"And something else. Something I didn't have the language for. It was growing between us, and I didn't know how to name it. Even when I could finally imagine life as something shared. Even when I trusted you. Even when my mind was always full of you. There had never been anyone like you, and for a long time I didn't have the word."

"What word?"

"Love."

The world stopped. Tipped over. Returned to its original state—but brighter. Sharper. Sweeter.

Perfect.

"If you still want me to love you, I really think I *can* love you back. Because I already do." Two tears streaked her cheekbones. "And if you don't, I guess I'll be loving you anyway. But if you were to give me another chance—"

"Jesus." He wanted to laugh. He wanted to spin her around. He wanted to ask her to marry him right now, before she could change her mind.

Her jaw worked. "Is that a no on that second chance?"

"God, you're so fucking . . ." He shook his head, and then caged hers between his hands, leaning closer. Breathing in her scent. "I love you, Rue. *You* are the only chance there is."

Her eyes shone bright. "Yeah?"

"Yeah." He felt a bone-deep, chest-warming amount of joy— like she'd taken a knife from his heart and placed it back in her drawer. She still had the power to destroy him. Always would, he suspected, hold him in the palm of her hand.

He hoped she'd be merciful.

"Does this mean that we're going to be dating?" she asked solemnly. Her mouth struggled to shape that last word. He couldn't help pressing his thumb against her full lower lip.

"It means that . . ." *That you're mine,* the uncivilized part of him screamed. *That I'm going to take you and hoard you.* "I'm going to be open with you, because I wasn't always, and that was a mistake. Okay?"

She nodded.

"It means that I'm not going into this thinking that there will be an ending. Do you get my meaning?"

She nodded again.

"And I'm going to—I'm going to want to see you every day. I'm going to learn more dishes and pack your lunch and write cute little notes on it. I'm going to ask you if you want to sleep at your place or mine and always assume that we're spending the night together. I'm going to think about you all the damn time. I'm going to assume I'm watering your plants when you're out of town. I'm going to hold your hand in public. I'm going to *kiss* you in public. I'm going to organize surprise parties for you with your friend. I'm going to send a hundred texts per day with stupid online shit I think you should see. Clingy as fuck, Rue. Can you do it? Can you live with me as your boyfriend?" The word seemed as reductive as *dating. For now,* he told himself. *For a short while.*

"I am really bad at replying to texts."

"I know."

"And I don't love surprise parties."

"I *know.*"

"But the rest . . ." She smiled against his thumb. "Yes, please."

He leaned into her ear. "I'm going to do the filthiest things to you."

Her breath hitched. "You do have a ridiculous sex drive."

"So do you."

"So do I."

He pulled back, and it was her turn to press a soft kiss against his thumb, even if her eyes were serious as she warned, "I'll never be easy to be around, Eli."

He knew that. He *loved* that. He wanted nothing more than to learn every inch of her, his complicated, mercurial dream girl.

He leaned in for a kiss. But before, he said, "I can imagine worse fates."

EPILOGUE

RUE

ONE YEAR LATER

My voice was muffled by the pillow, dampened by my own gritted teeth, but I hated how reedy and desperate it still sounded when I said, "I hate this."

"Really?" Eli remained motionless inside me, but the heel of his palm traced every knob of my spine, soothing my tremors. It made no difference, because his other hand was busy pinning my wrists to the mattress. "Because *I* am into it."

Of course he was.

He had come.

Twice.

Inside me, wherever struck his fancy.

I, however, had not. It had been hours, and I was a trembling, unsatisfied mess. He got like that, sometimes—pushy and overbearing and everywhere, and I just couldn't . . .

I groaned into the pillow.

"You're really not enjoying yourself?" he whispered, this time against my ear.

"I'm not," I lied.

"My poor girl." He clucked his tongue, and I was going to kill him. As soon as he let go of me. And let me come. "Why is that?"

Because.

"Is it too much, Rue?" He nuzzled the curve of my throat, and the movement made him surge deeper inside me. I was swollen and used, and it felt so good, I might cry. In fact, I was already tearing up. "Is it broccoli, baby?"

"No! *No.* It's just . . ."

"Just?"

I circled my ass against his groin, and his muted, amused grunt ended with him gripping my hip bone and holding me still. Asshole.

"Why are you grinding against me, sweetheart?" He kissed the ball of my shoulder. "We both know that you can't come in this position, anyway."

"Then why don't you just let me *move*?"

"Because *I* can come in this position. And I'm trying to save myself for you."

I whimpered—half plea, all frustration. "Please. I need you to—"

"I know *exactly* what you need." His mouth on my earlobe was, briefly, all teeth. "You don't have to tell me." He tsked. "Come on, Rue. I'm offended."

"Then why don't you—"

"Because I'm having fun. Want me to stop? Just say the words."

I could have. I could have told him to put an end to this. I'd done it before, when it had become too much, when I'd felt like I was going to squirm out of my own skin, and he'd stopped without asking questions. I let myself contemplate the possibility: Eli turning me around, making me come with his mouth, rocking me in his arms for long minutes, until I pushed him away or fell asleep, whatever came first.

But as much as I *hated* this, I *loved* it too much to give it up. And why would I ask him to stop when I had other ways of getting what I wanted? A bit dirty. Manipulative, maybe. But resourceful. I knew exactly what the words would do to him, and mumbled them into the pillow to my own advantage.

Eli stilled.

Leaned his forehead between my shoulder blades.

Asked, "What did you just say?"

This time I lifted my head. Enunciated clearly. "I love you."

It changed everything. I felt him shudder inside me. Tighten his grip around my hip bone. Take a deep, broken breath. Excitement bubbled within him—twelve months in, and the words hadn't worn down yet.

"Okay, you know what?"

I shook my head against the pillow, shivering.

"I think I'm done playing. I want to look at you. Let's just . . ." He let go of my wrists. Turned me around. It was a little dizzying, how quickly everything changed.

His eyes were locked with mine.

His kisses were deep.

His arms closed around my waist to scoop me up.

He was inside me again in a matter of seconds, relentlessly deep, but it felt completely different from before. This time, neither of us had anywhere to hide. This way, *this* way I really could—

"Hi," he told me with a smile that I couldn't physically return.

Instead, I solemnly replied, "Hi," and then he was moving inside me and whispering sweet things in my ear, about how perfect I was, how much he liked me, the sheer improbability of my beauty, and that he knew, he fucking *knew* what I'd done, but he was always going to let me get away with it, because he loved to hear it so much. And then his fingers found my clit, and it was all over. I was coming this time, and he was holding still and then groaning and falling apart with me. *Again.*

"What are you thinking?" he asked afterward, the sweat cooling on our skin, his heart a steady beat under my ear.

I felt my lips twist in a shadow of a smile. "That this was a really nice way to start our vacation."

My life might have changed, but I hadn't. Which wasn't a problem, because Eli seemed to be okay with the way I was—and that was that.

Whenever I'd imagined myself in a relationship, I'd envisioned an exhausting series of social niceties, facades to meticulously keep up, chitchat that I wasn't sure I'd be able to produce even under duress. Eli, unsurprisingly, required very little of that. He allowed my silences, and had long conversations with me when I wanted to. He gave me space, but pulled me into his life if I gravitated away. He made fun of me, especially when I made fun of *him*.

Being with him had meant other things, too, like an unconditional acceptance in his group of friends, a growing relationship with his sister, a *dog*. But I had thought people overwhelming before falling in love with one, and still found it hard to navigate many interpersonal situations. As Tisha had put it, *You don't have to enjoy all the social shit just because you enjoy being with Eli. He's so into you, I doubt he cares.* After that, it had all fallen into place.

(I had to admit, however, that Tiny had grown on me.)

(I was ready to die for that beast, and I was not prone to exaggeration.)

So, no, I hadn't changed. But my life sparked a little brighter—and that was that.

"The deck needs some work done," Eli told me on the porch of my cabin, while I leashed Tiny and let him lick my cheek like the pushover I'd become. The power of dogs was astounding. "I might be able to take care of it on my own."

I'd not expected to feel a deep sense of immediate connection with my father's cabin, and I'd been right. But I was a homeowner, and it felt nice, being in possession of something that someone had wanted me to have. I adored how secluded it felt here, the fresh air, the woodland scenery. Plus, I thought when the phone pinged with a text, we had cell reception.

"Tisha?" Eli asked. "More questions about your totally straightforward and reasonable forty-three-step instructions on how to take care of the children?"

My plants, he meant. "Nope." I showed him the notification, and he snorted.

"Oh, come on."

"What?"

"You need to uninstall that app."

"It's how we first met. It has a sentimental value."

"And you are so sentimental." He tugged me down the path that led to the hiking trails we'd planned to explore.

"Did you? Delete yours?"

"I deleted my profile after the first time you stayed over at my place."

I glanced at him, feeling that cozy warmth that was always there when he was around. "It's in bad taste and overdone."

"What is?"

"Bragging about how you knew before me."

He laughed and pulled me in for an embrace. "I don't think it's overdone. In fact, I'm not sure it's done enough."

Around us, everything was wild. The sun-dappled trees, the sound of little critters going about their lives, Tiny's enthusiastic explorations. "If we come back this winter," Eli told me an hour in, when we stopped for a break, "we might be able to skate on that pond." He crouched down to retie his shoelaces, and I glanced at the water, a small smile curving my lips.

This winter.

"Are you picturing the myriad ways in which we could die?" he asked from behind me.

"Yup." We could try, but would have to drill in the ice to check, first. We needed at least five inches to—

"Hey, Rue?"

"Yeah," I said distractedly.

"Since we're here."

"Yes?"

"I was wondering."

I turned around. He was still tying his shoes, head bent low.

"Would you like to get married?"

Eli looked up. Met my eyes. His words glided buoyantly around my head for a few seconds, devoid of any significance. And then their meaning clawed into me, and I was suddenly made of heat. "What did you say?"

"Marriage. Would you like to?"

I opened my mouth. Stayed like that.

"To me, that is. I should have specified."

I could feel my pulse in my fingertips. My body, my brain, I was all heartbeat. "I . . . is this how one proposes?" It was a genuine question.

"I'm not sure." Eli shrugged. "I've never done this before."

"Yes, you have. You were engaged."

"Was I?"

"I have met her. She is very kind. She made us dinner and—"

"Ah, *yes*. It's coming back to me. Well, that engagement came about when the two of us looked at each other and decided that getting married was a good next step. There was never a proposal."

"I see."

Would you like to get married?

He'd said that. Hadn't he?

"Shouldn't . . ." My cheeks heated. I was dizzy. "Shouldn't you be on your knees?"

He glanced down at himself. He was, in fact, on his knees. On one knee. Which I knew. I was just—flustered. That's it.

"And have a ring?" I added.

"Jesus, Rue." His smile was delighted. "For someone who lets me tie her up and slide plugs up her holes on a weekly basis, you're a *traditionalist*."

"That's not it." I took a deep breath. Tried to think about it calmly. "It doesn't seem like a good impulse decision to make. You can't just propose on a whim in the middle of a walk. You should probably think about it a lot more. Make sure it's what you really want."

He rolled his eyes, sighed, and pulled something out of his pocket. It was a—

I gasped.

"Better now?"

"When did you even—"

"Around eleven months and three weeks ago."

My eyes were going to roll out of my head. "This is unhinged."

"I know. But you asked." He grinned up at me, and my hands were trembling. The rest of my body, too. Was he really . . . ?

"Is it because you really like the cabin? And my patent?"

"Yes, Rue. I'm asking you to marry me because Texas is a community property state and I want to own half your stuff. You uncovered my long con. Are you going to pass out?"

"Maybe," I said in all seriousness.

"Then move away from that precipice, please."

I took a step forward, and then we were there. He'd asked the question. I'd heard and understood it. And all that was missing was my answer.

"It's fine, if you're not ready. This is not an ultimatum." His eyes and voice and smile were soft. He didn't sound nervous, or scared, and I thought that this man—he knew what was in my heart just as well as I did. "I've been feeling like asking for a while, so I did. But I can check back in a few months."

"Don't."

"No checking back?"

I shook my head. "Don't bother, there's no point. My mind is made up, and I won't change it."

It was a cheap trick, and someone else would have fallen for it. But Eli—Eli understood my words for what they were, and he smiled, took my hand, slid the ring on my finger. He didn't stand, and instead buried his face against my stomach, nuzzling into me.

I ran my hand through his hair, glanced at the trees, smelled the earth, and said, "I was so wrong."

"About what?" he asked against my shirt. It meant that he probably couldn't see my smile, and wasn't that too bad?

"About whether my story could ever be happy."

ACKNOWLEDGMENTS

Thao Le, my agent, and everyone else at SDLA. Sarah Blumenstock, my editor, as well as the rest of my Berkley Romance team (Liz Sellers, Kristin Cipolla and her cipollina, Tara O'Connor, Bridget O'Toole, Kim-Salina I), and everyone else in PRH's various departments who worked on getting this book into shape and putting it in the hands of readers. Lilith, for the perfect cover illustration. Katie Shepard, for the Finance Bro Markup. Margaret Wigging and, of course, Jen, for helping me make this mess a slightly less messy mess. My foreign publishers. Booksellers, librarians, and every reader who has ever picked up a copy of any of my books or clicked on one of my fan fictions. My author friends and my nonauthor friends. My family—including my cats, my deer, my racoons, my foxes, and my single possum. Love you, guys.

Justin Murphy of Out of the Attic Photography

ALI HAZELWOOD is the #1 *New York Times* bestselling author of *Love, Theoretically* and *The Love Hypothesis*, as well as a writer of peer-reviewed articles about brain science, in which no one makes out and the ever after is not always happy. Originally from Italy, she lived in Germany and Japan before moving to the US to pursue a PhD in neuroscience. When Ali is not at work, she can be found running, eating cake pops, or watching sci-fi movies with her three feline overlords (and her slightly less feline husband).

VISIT ALI HAZELWOOD ONLINE

AliHazelwood.com
AliHazelwood
AliHazelwood

LEARN MORE ABOUT THIS BOOK AND OTHER TITLES FROM *NEW YORK TIMES* BESTSELLING AUTHOR

ALI HAZELWOOD

SCAN ME
or visit
prh.com/alihazelwood